From Under Mountains

volume one

Created by

Claire Gibson • Sloane Leong • Marian Churchland

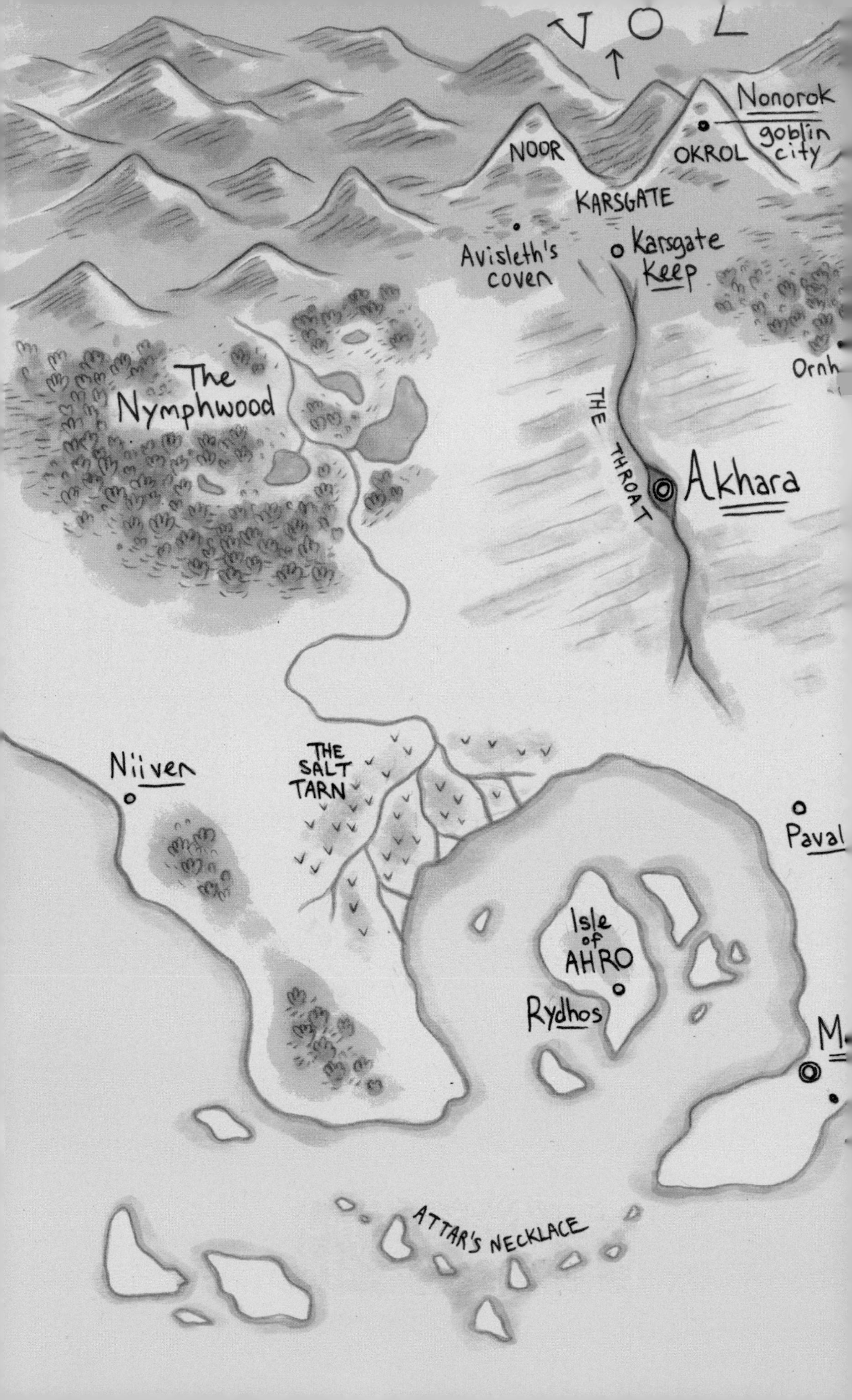

VOL
Nonorok
goblin city
NOOR
OKROL
KARSGATE
Avisleth's coven
Karsgate Keep
The Nymphwood
THE THROAT
Akhara
Ornh
Niiven
THE SALT TARN
Paval
Isle of AHRO
Rydhos
M
ATTAR'S NECKLACE

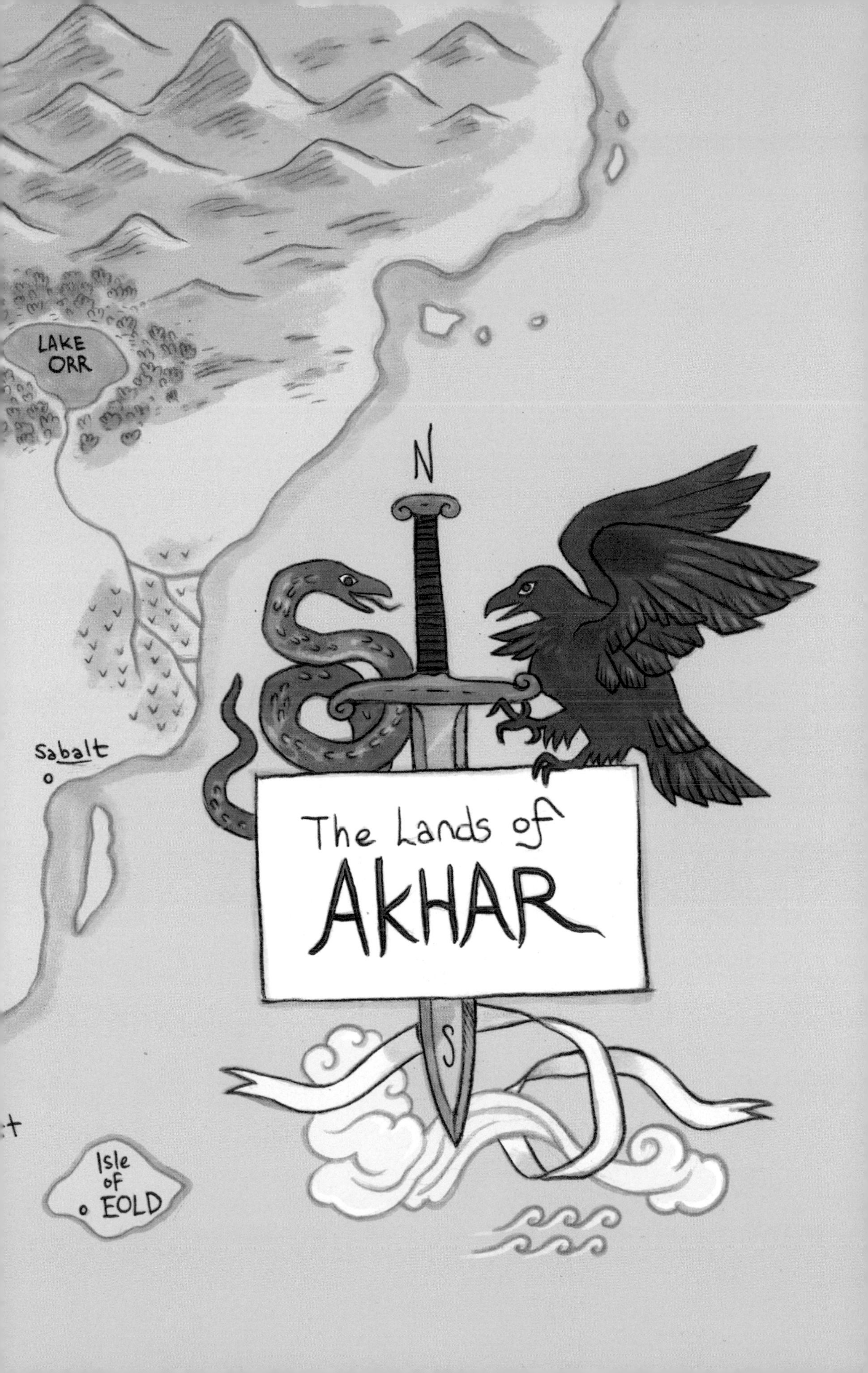
LAKE ORR
N
S
Sabalt
The Lands of
AKHAR
Isle of EOLD

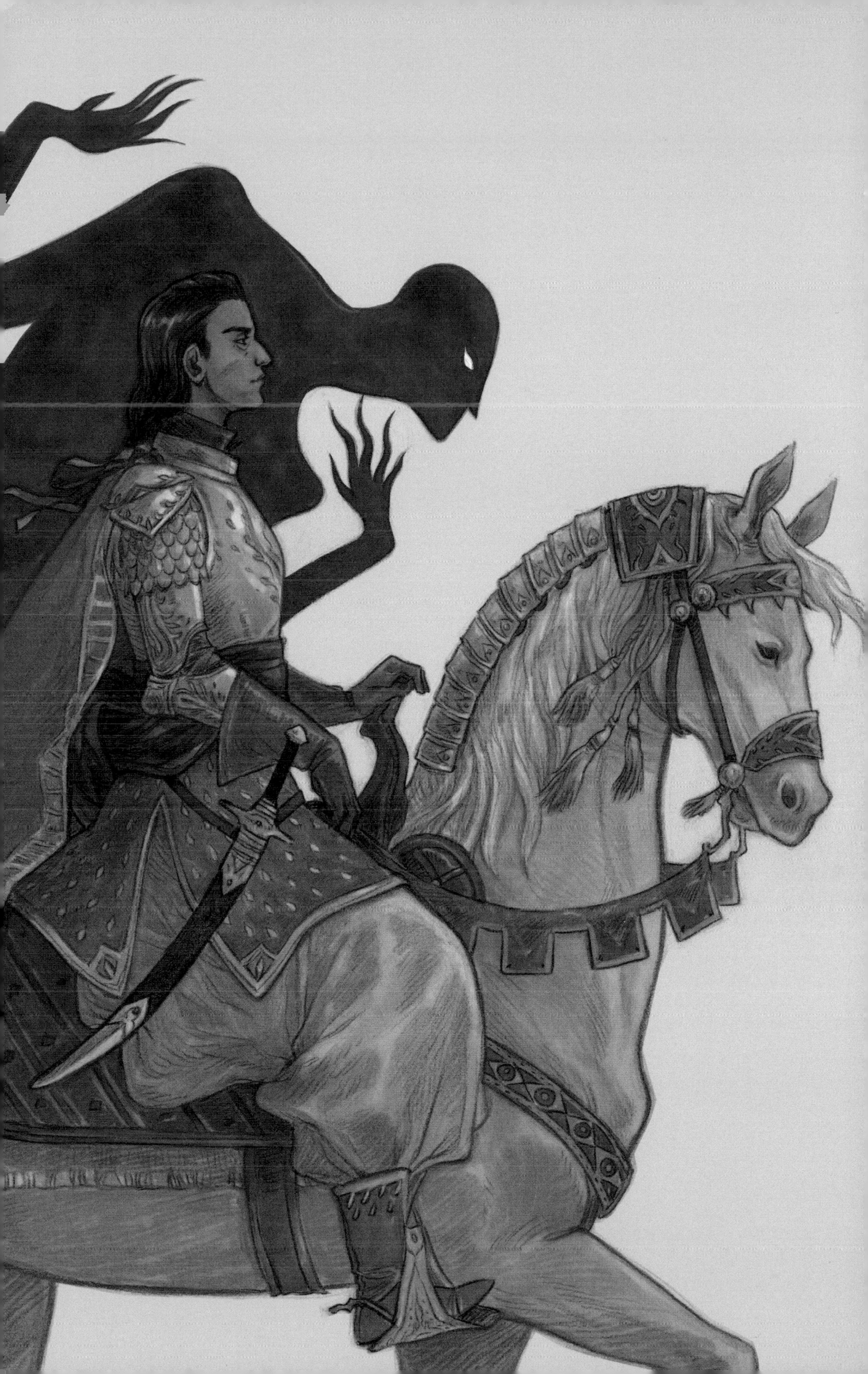

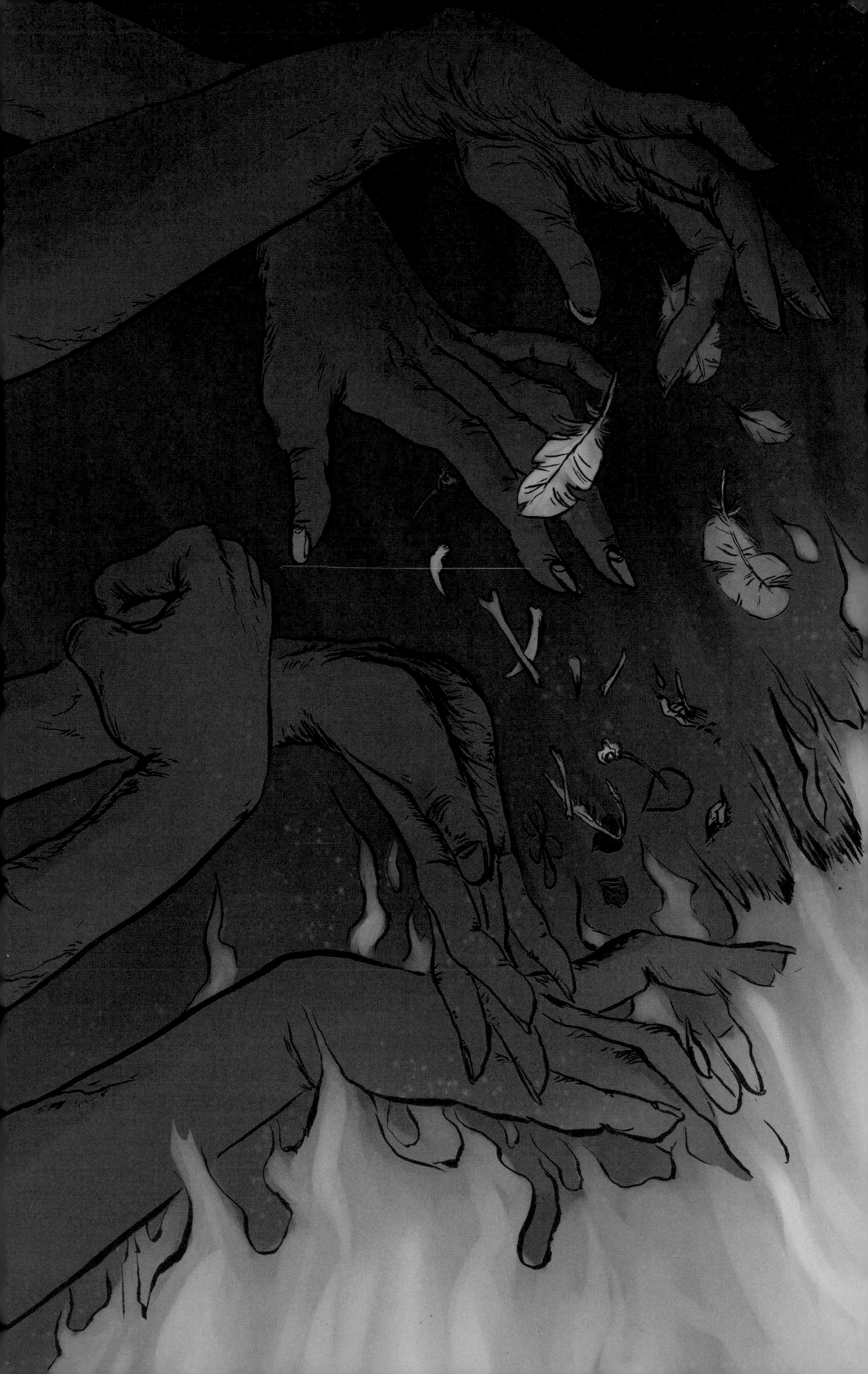

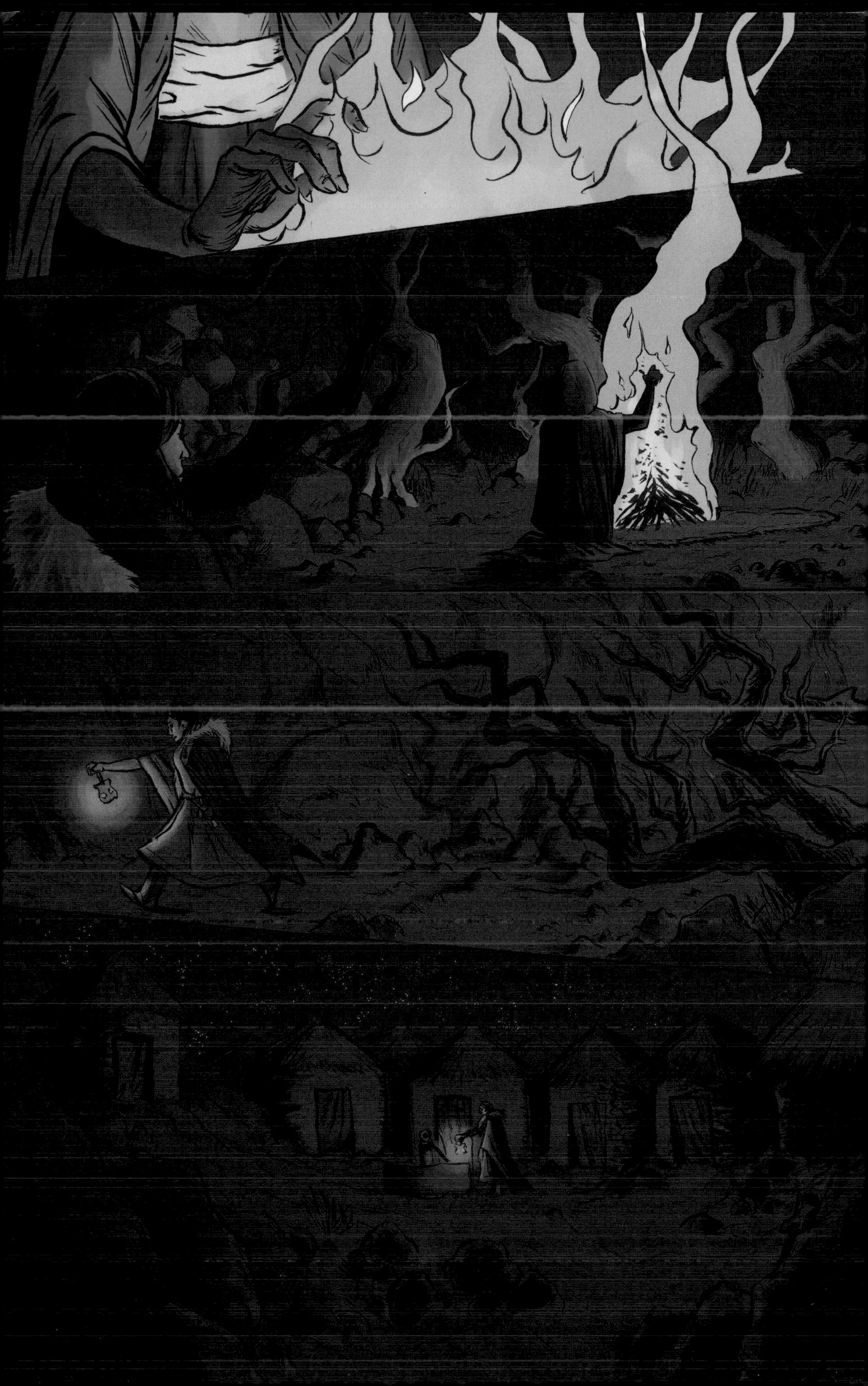

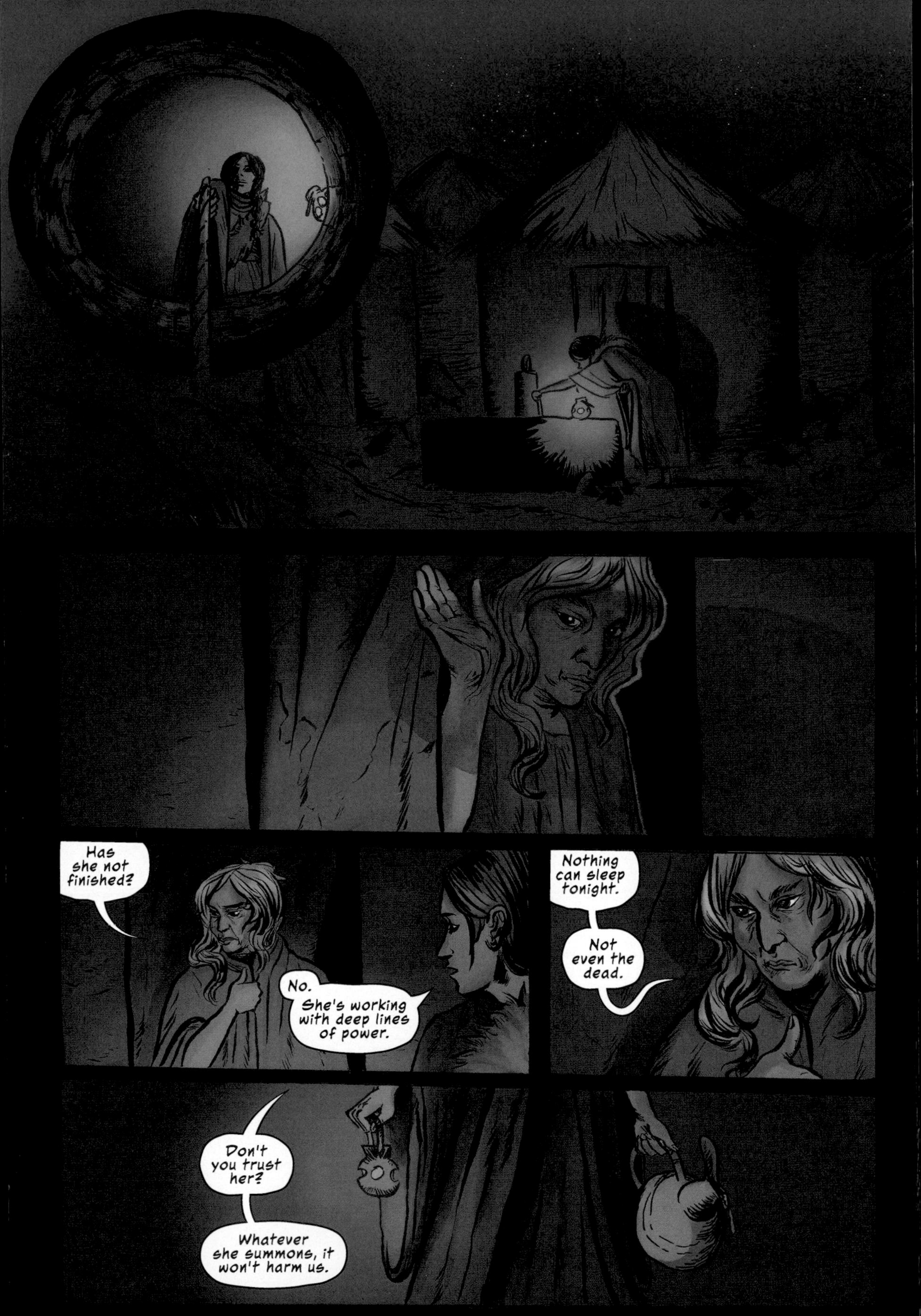
Has she not finished?
No. She's working with deep lines of power.
Nothing can sleep tonight.
Not even the dead.
Don't you trust her?
Whatever she summons, it won't harm us.

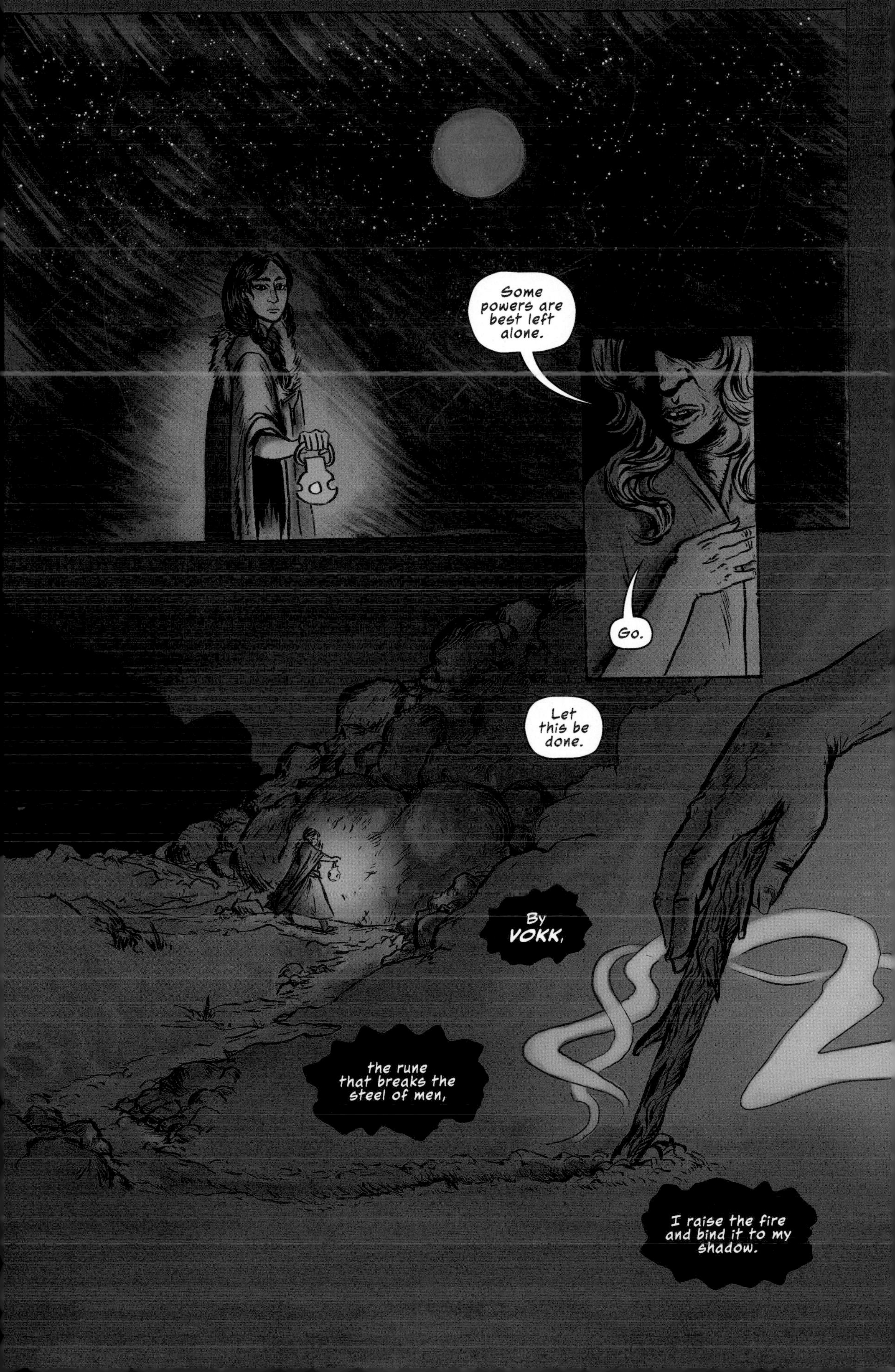
Some powers are best left alone.
Go.
Let this be done.
By VOKK,
the rune that breaks the steel of men,
I raise the fire and bind it to my shadow.

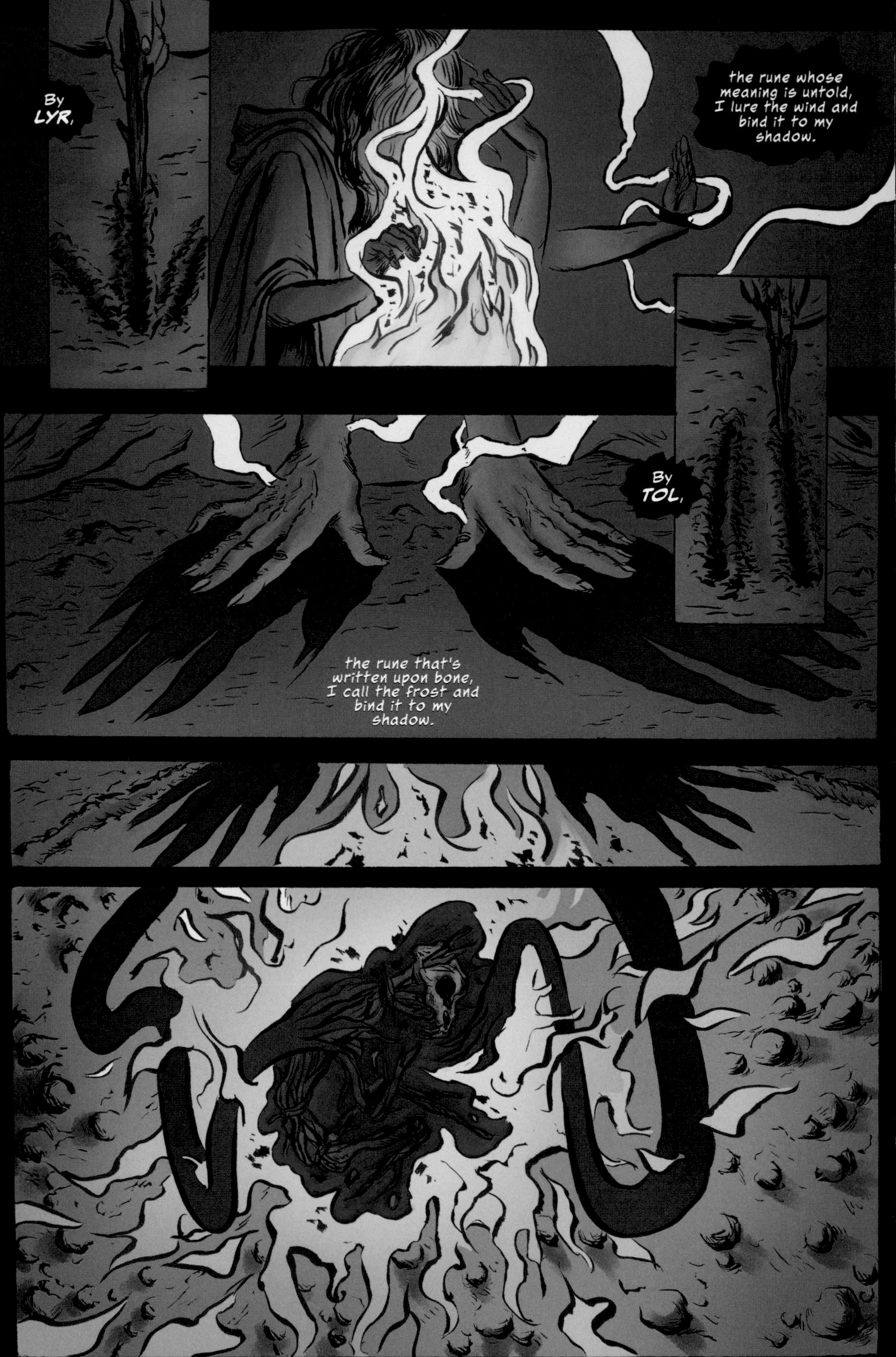
By LYR,
the rune whose meaning is untold, I lure the wind and bind it to my shadow.
By TOL,
the rune that's written upon bone, I call the frost and bind it to my shadow.

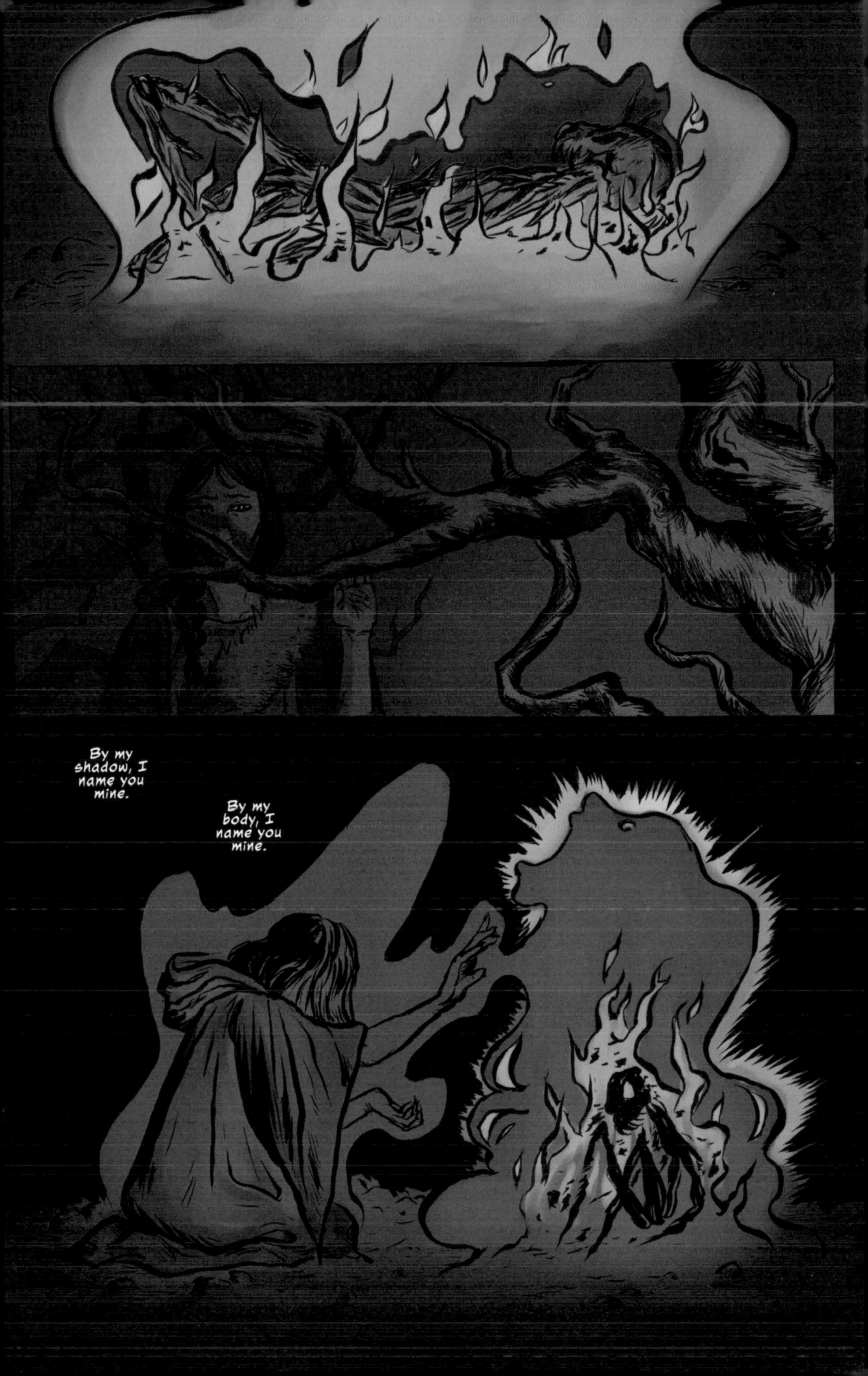
By my shadow, I name you mine.
By my body, I name you mine.

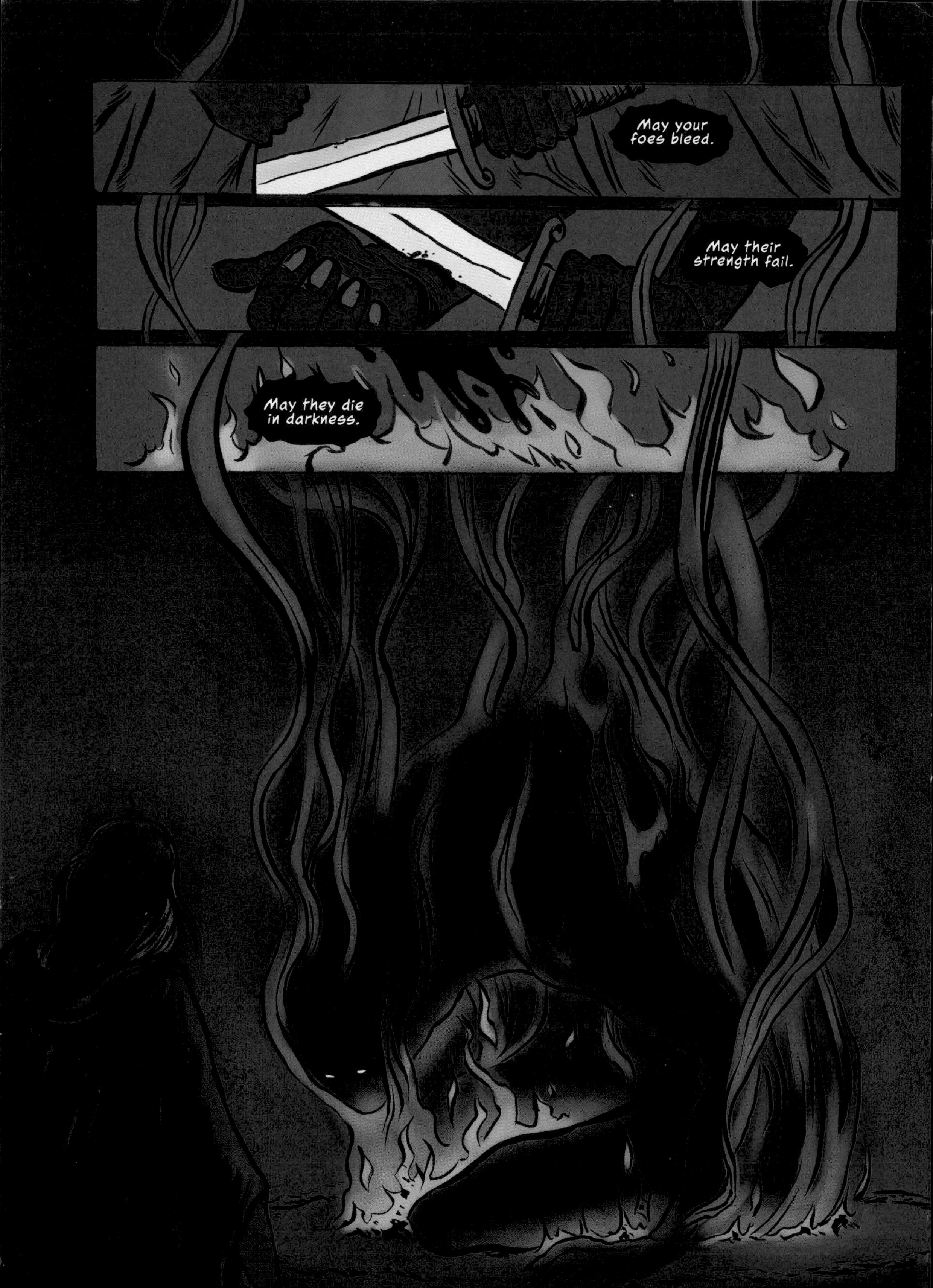
May your foes bleed.
May their strength fail.
May they die in darkness.

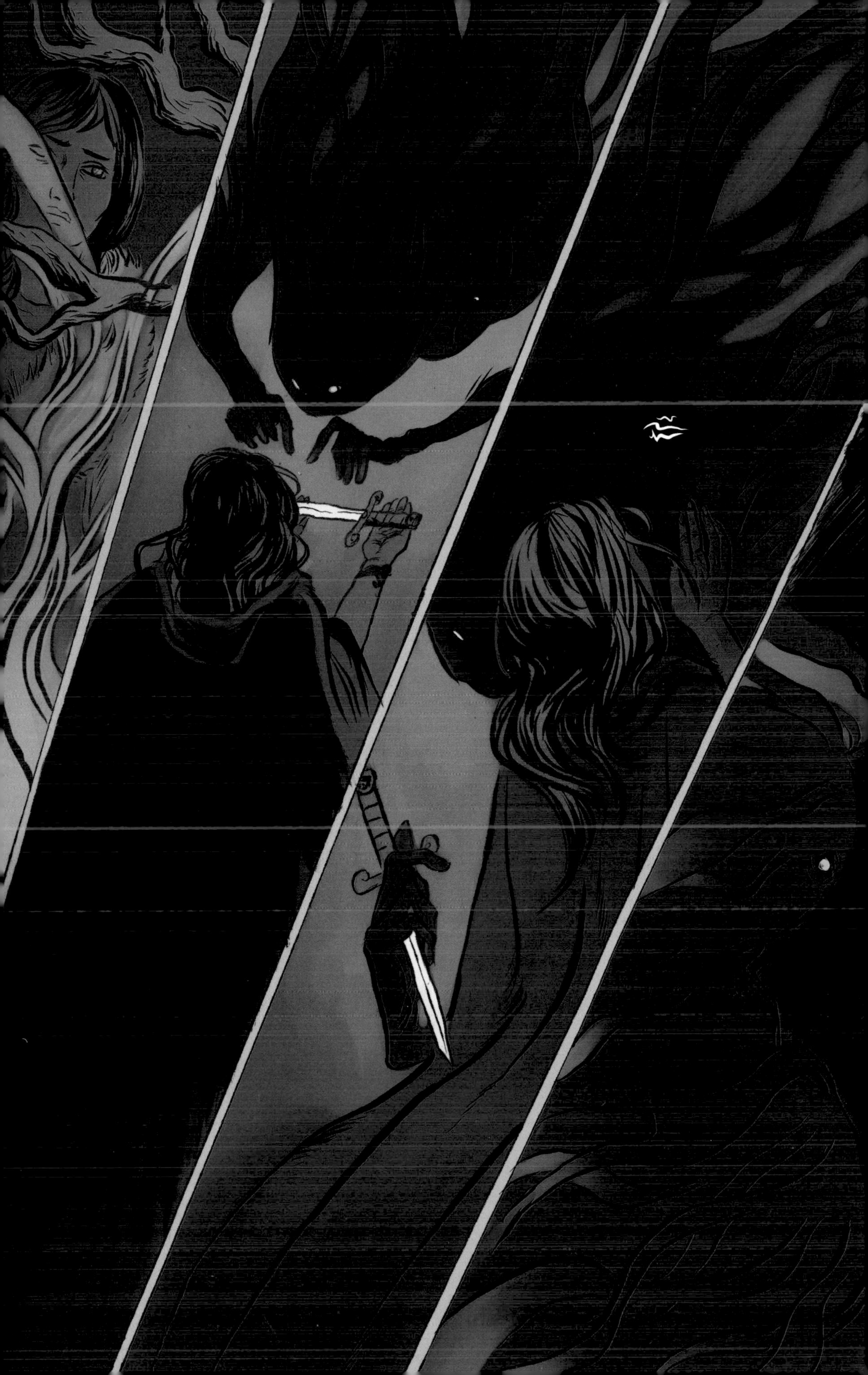

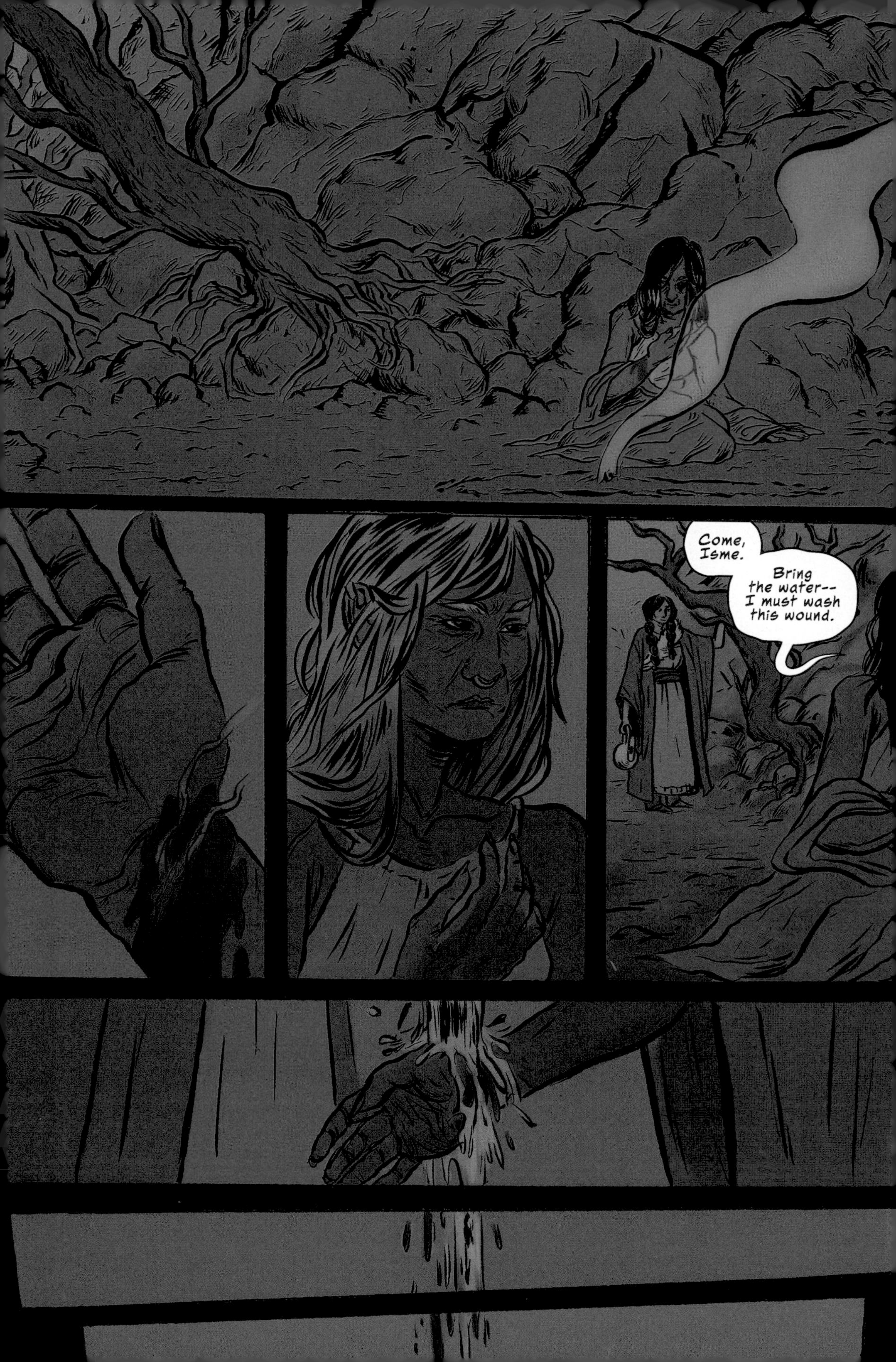
Come, Isme.
Bring the water-- I must wash this wound.

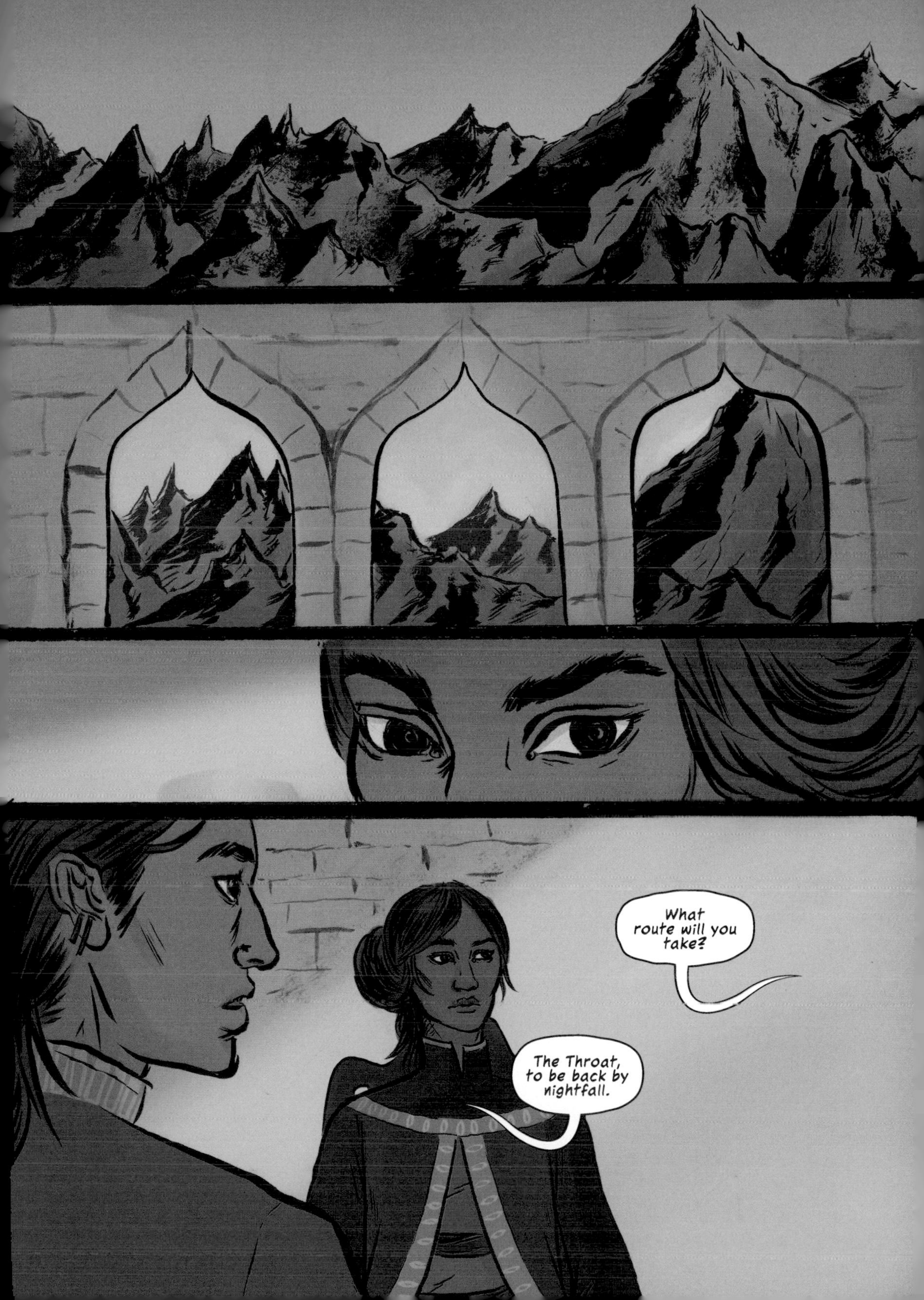
What route will you take?
The Throat, to be back by nightfall.

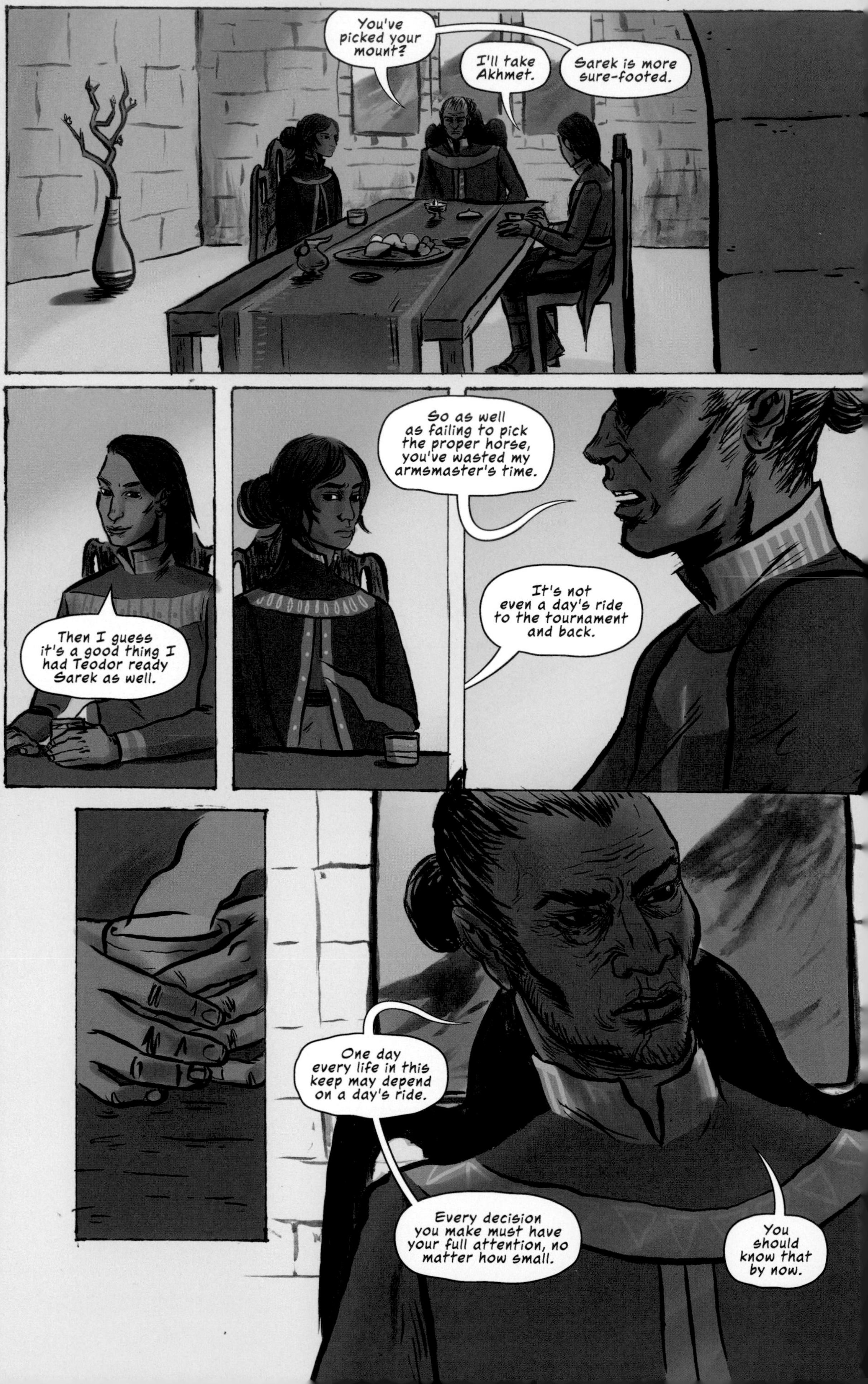
You've picked your mount?
I'll take Akhmet.
Sarek is more sure-footed.
Then I guess it's a good thing I had Teodor ready Sarek as well.
So as well as failing to pick the proper horse, you've wasted my armsmaster's time.
It's not even a day's ride to the tournament and back.
One day every life in this keep may depend on a day's ride.
Every decision you make must have your full attention, no matter how small.
You should know that by now.

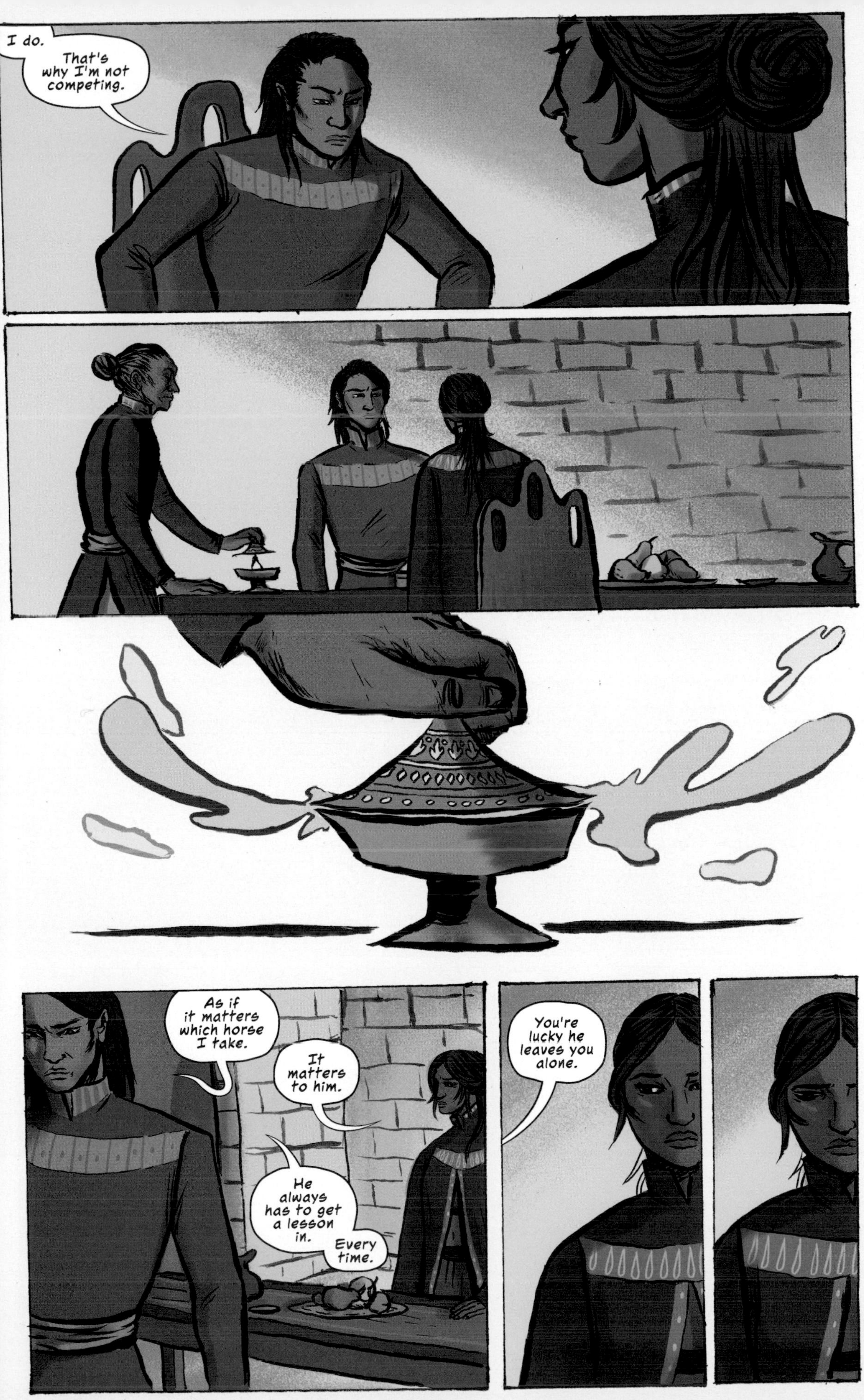
I do.
That's why I'm not competing.
As if it matters which horse I take.
It matters to him.
He always has to get a lesson in.
Every time.
You're lucky he leaves you alone.

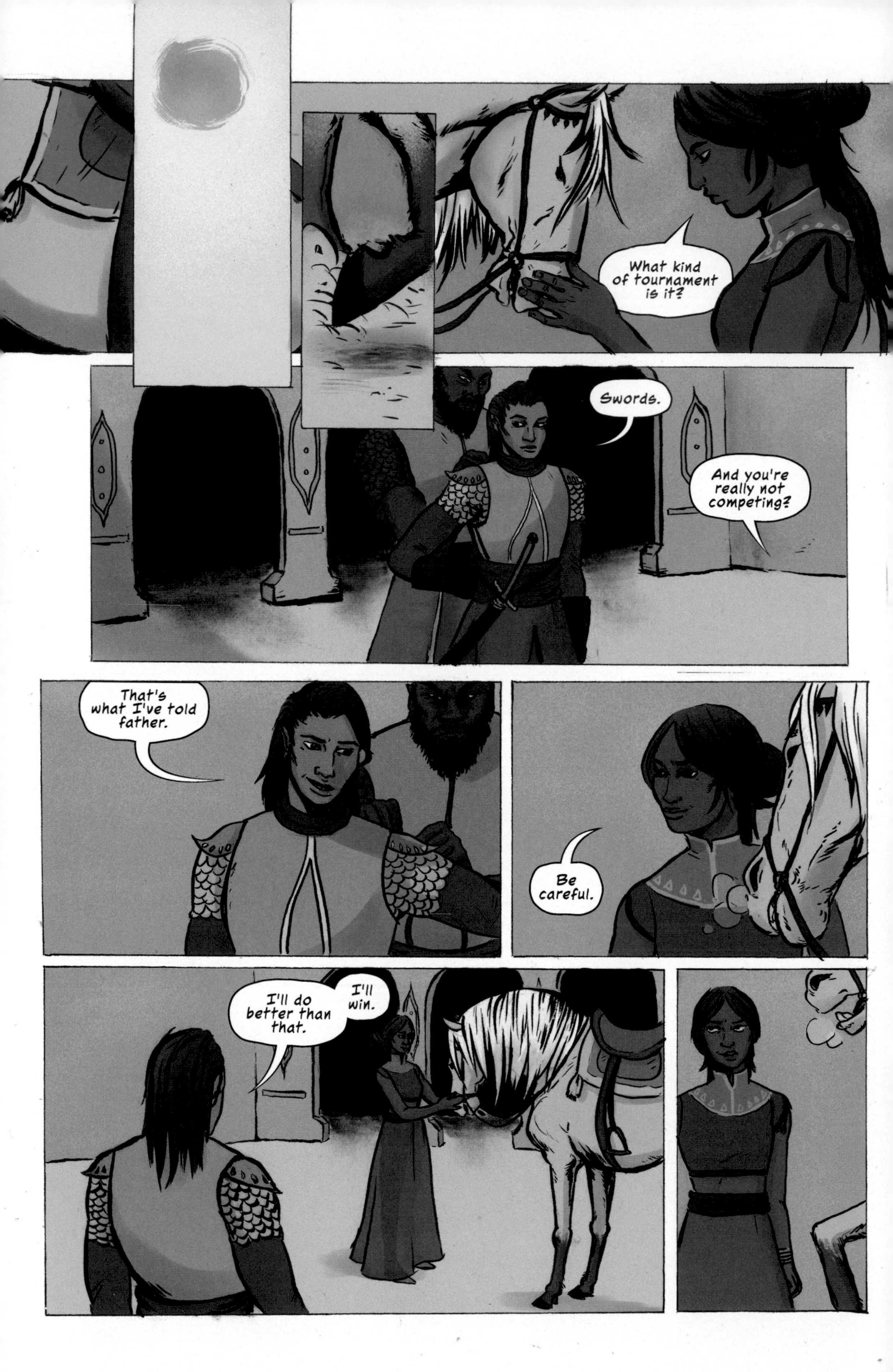
What kind of tournament is it?
Swords.
And you're really not competing?
That's what I've told father.
Be careful.
I'll do better than that.
I'll win.

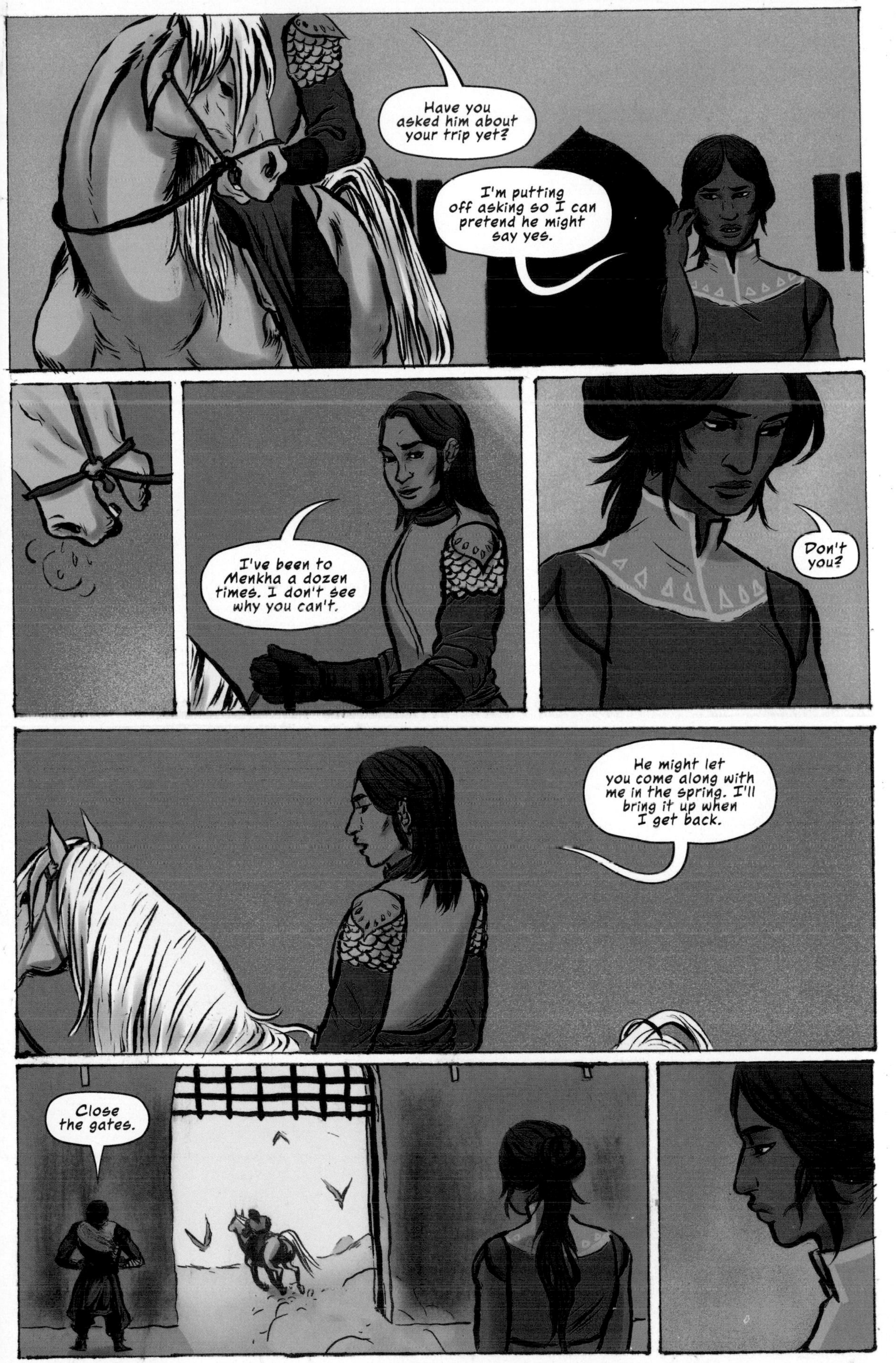
Have you asked him about your trip yet?
I'm putting off asking so I can pretend he might say yes.
I've been to Menkha a dozen times. I don't see why you can't.
Don't you?
He might let you come along with me in the spring. I'll bring it up when I get back.
Close the gates.

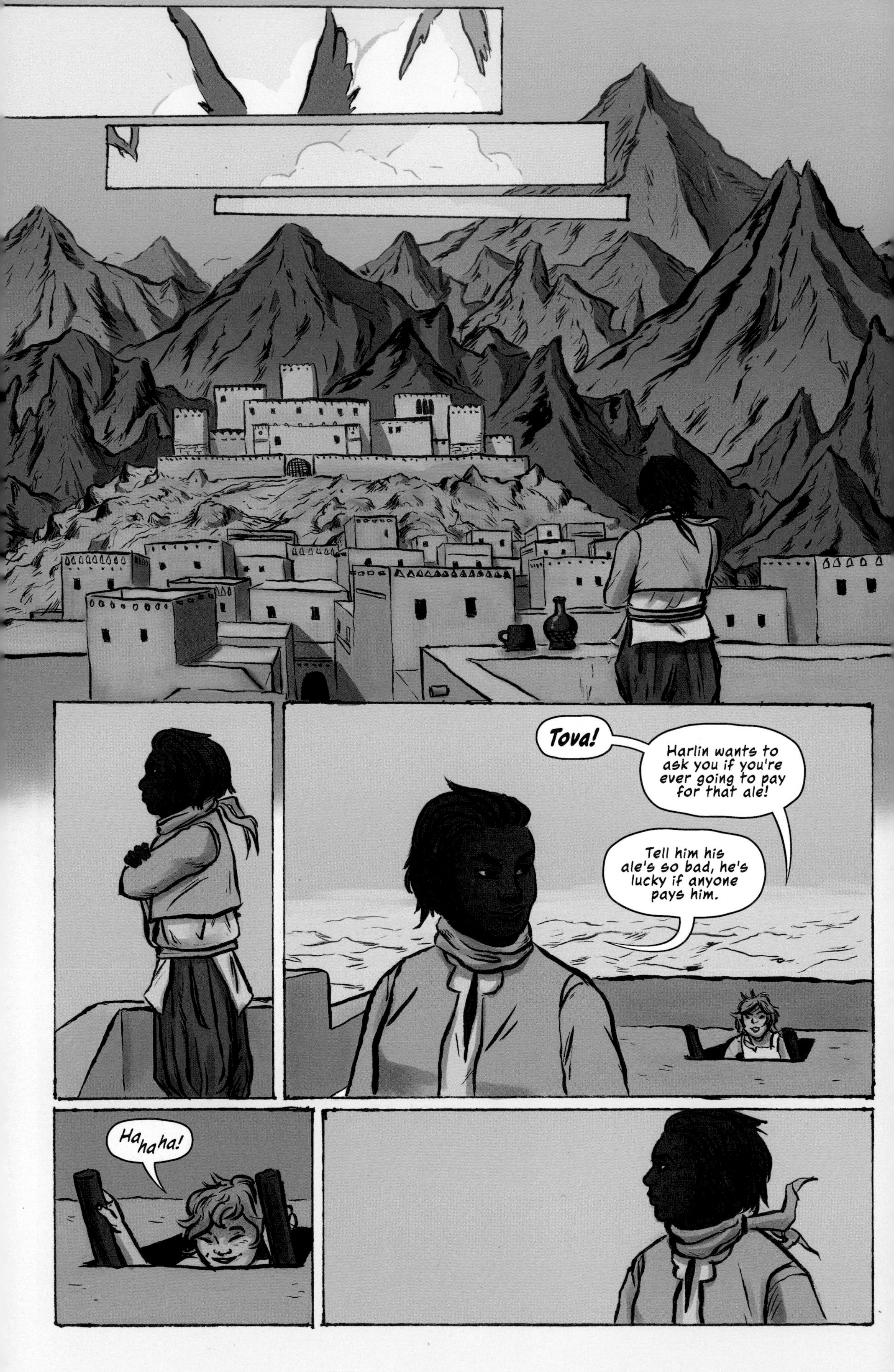
Tova!
Harlin wants to ask you if you're ever going to pay for that ale!
Tell him his ale's so bad, he's lucky if anyone pays him.
Hahahaha!

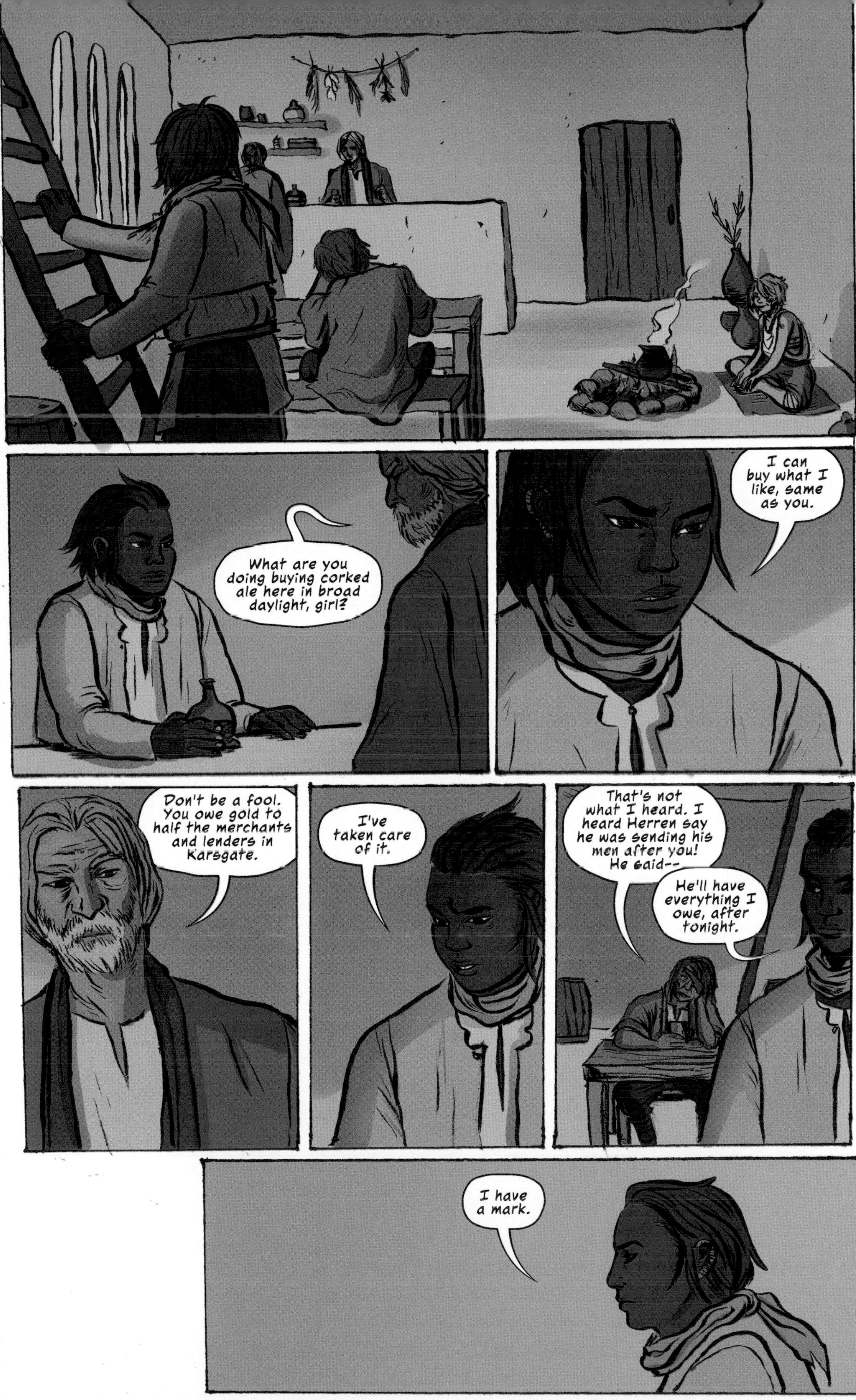
What are you doing buying corked ale here in broad daylight, girl?
I can buy what I like, same as you.
Don't be a fool. You owe gold to half the merchants and lenders in Karsgate.
I've taken care of it.
That's not what I heard. I heard Herren say he was sending his men after you! He said--
He'll have everything I owe, after tonight.
I have a mark.

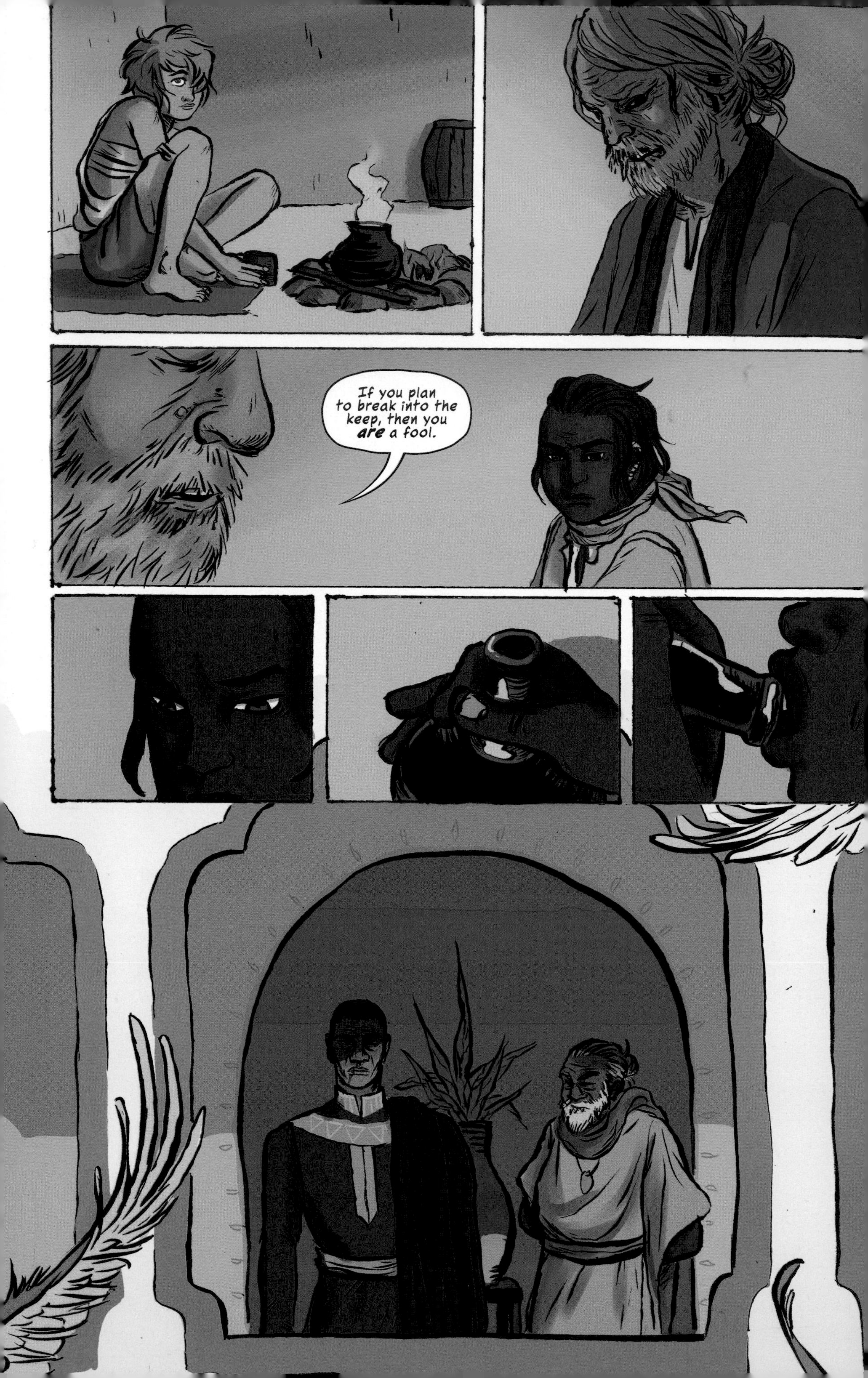
If you plan to break into the keep, then you **are** a fool.

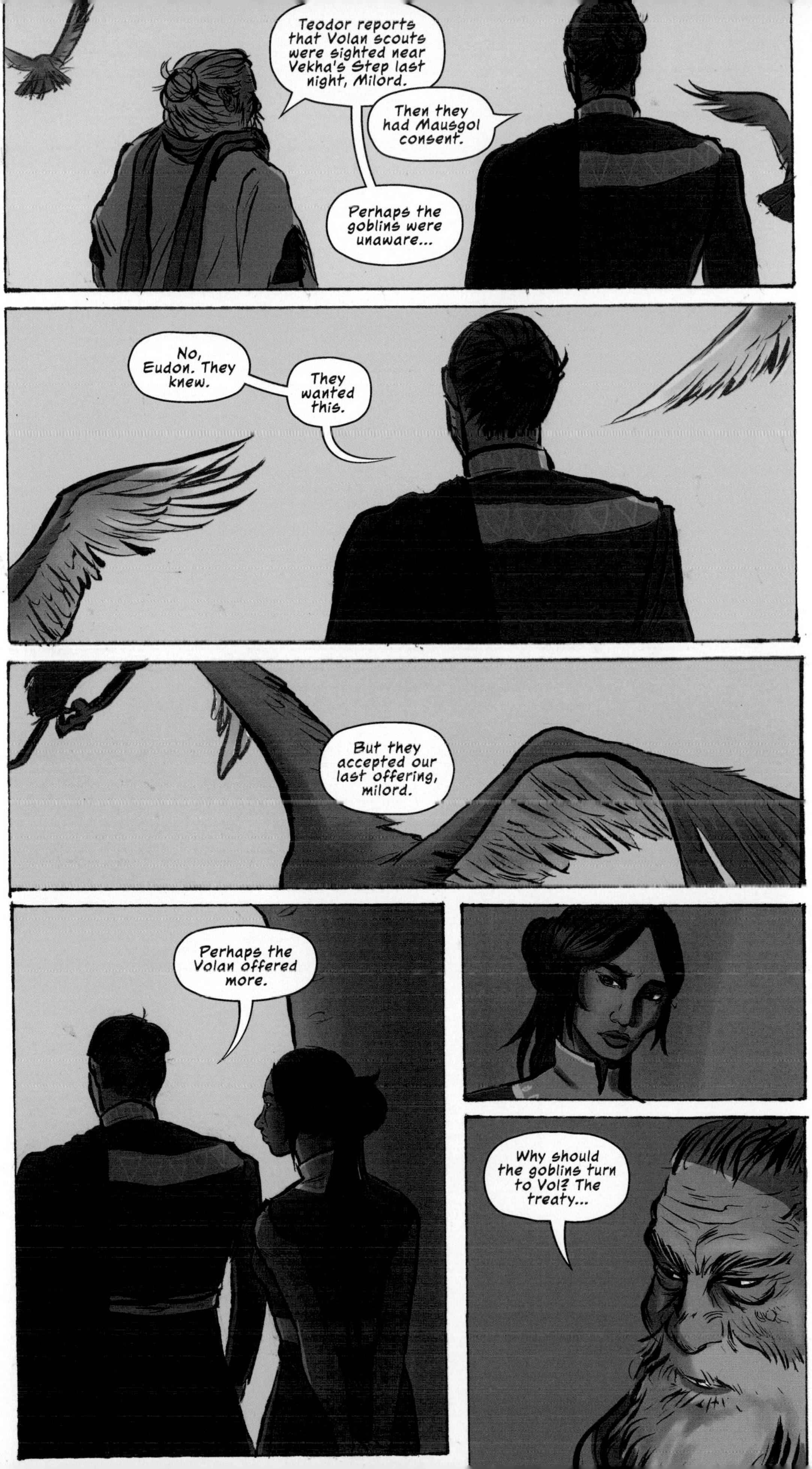
Teodor reports that Volan scouts were sighted near Vekha's Step last night, Milord.
Then they had Mausgol consent.
Perhaps the goblins were unaware...
No, Eudon. They knew.
They wanted this.
But they accepted our last offering, milord.
Perhaps the Volan offered more.
Why should the goblins turn to Vol? The treaty...

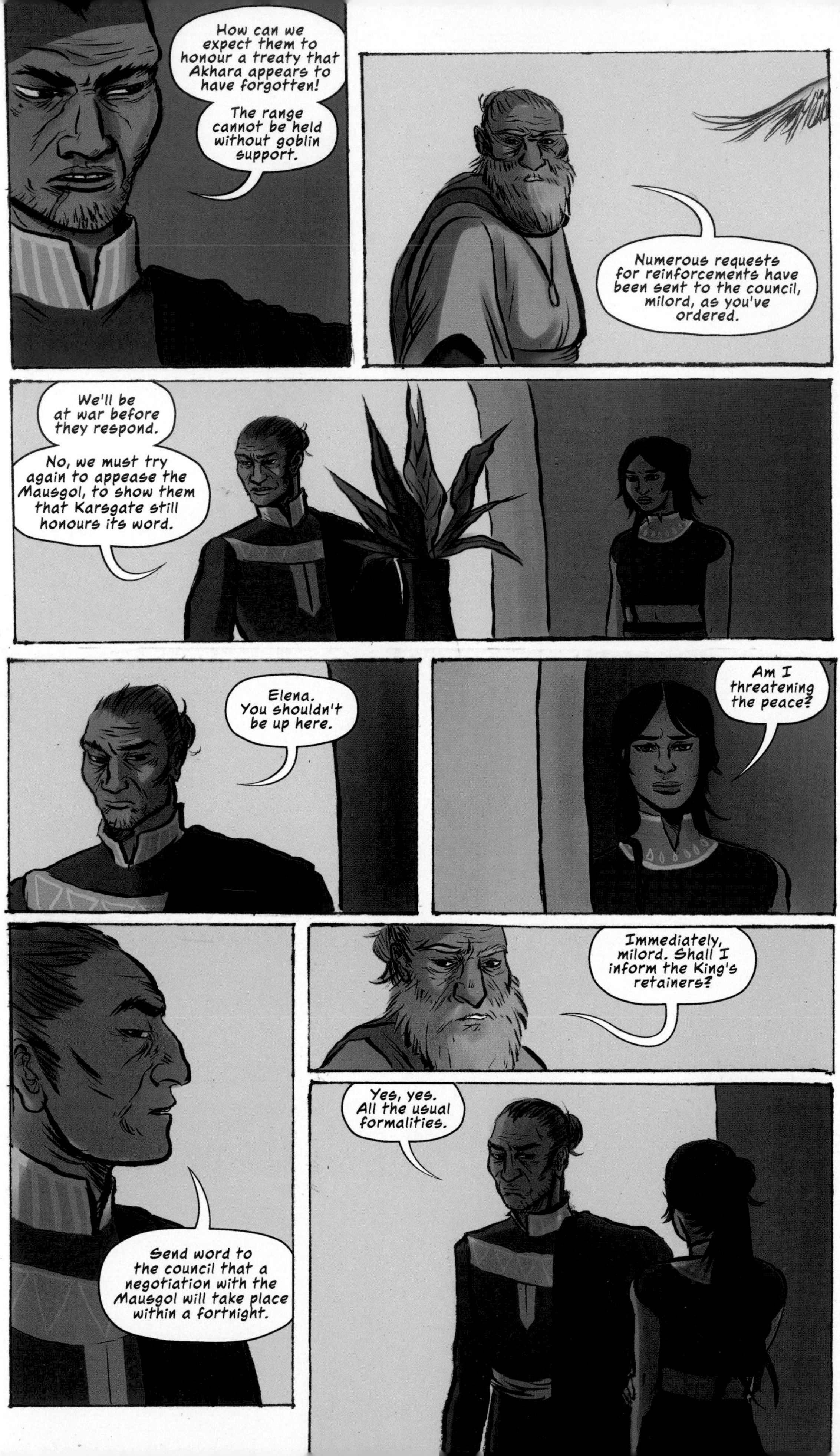
How can we expect them to honour a treaty that Akhara appears to have forgotten!
The range cannot be held without goblin support.
Numerous requests for reinforcements have been sent to the council, milord, as you've ordered.
We'll be at war before they respond.
No, we must try again to appease the Mausgol, to show them that Karsgate still honours its word.
Elena. You shouldn't be up here.
Am I threatening the peace?
Send word to the council that a negotiation with the Mausgol will take place within a fortnight.
Immediately, milord. Shall I inform the King's retainers?
Yes, yes. All the usual formalities.

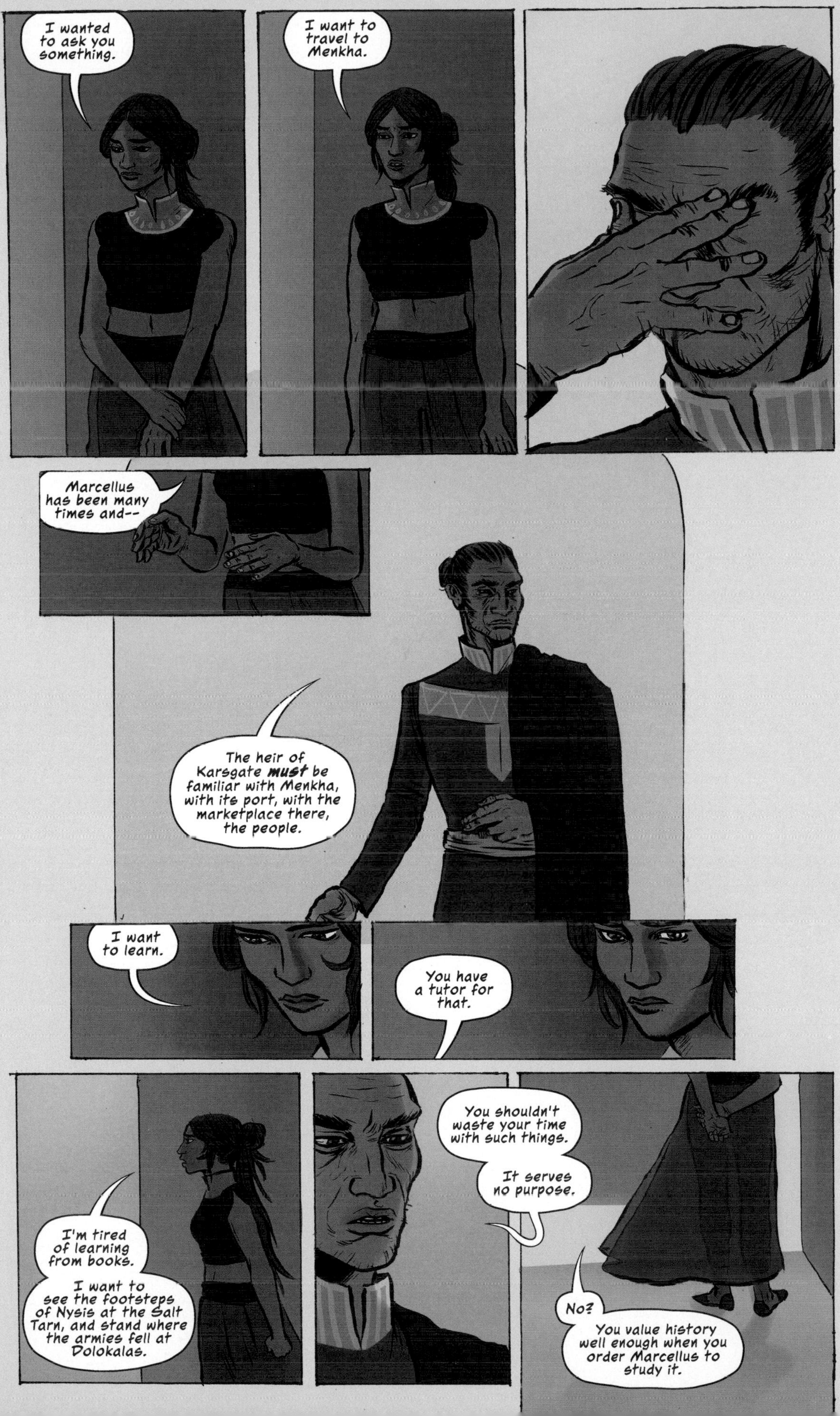
I wanted to ask you something.
I want to travel to Menkha.
Marcellus has been many times and--
The heir of Karsgate **must** be familiar with Menkha, with its port, with the marketplace there, the people.
I want to learn.
You have a tutor for that.
I'm tired of learning from books.
I want to see the footsteps of Nysis at the Salt Tarn, and stand where the armies fell at Dolokalas.
You shouldn't waste your time with such things.
It serves no purpose.
No?
You value history well enough when you order Marcellus to study it.

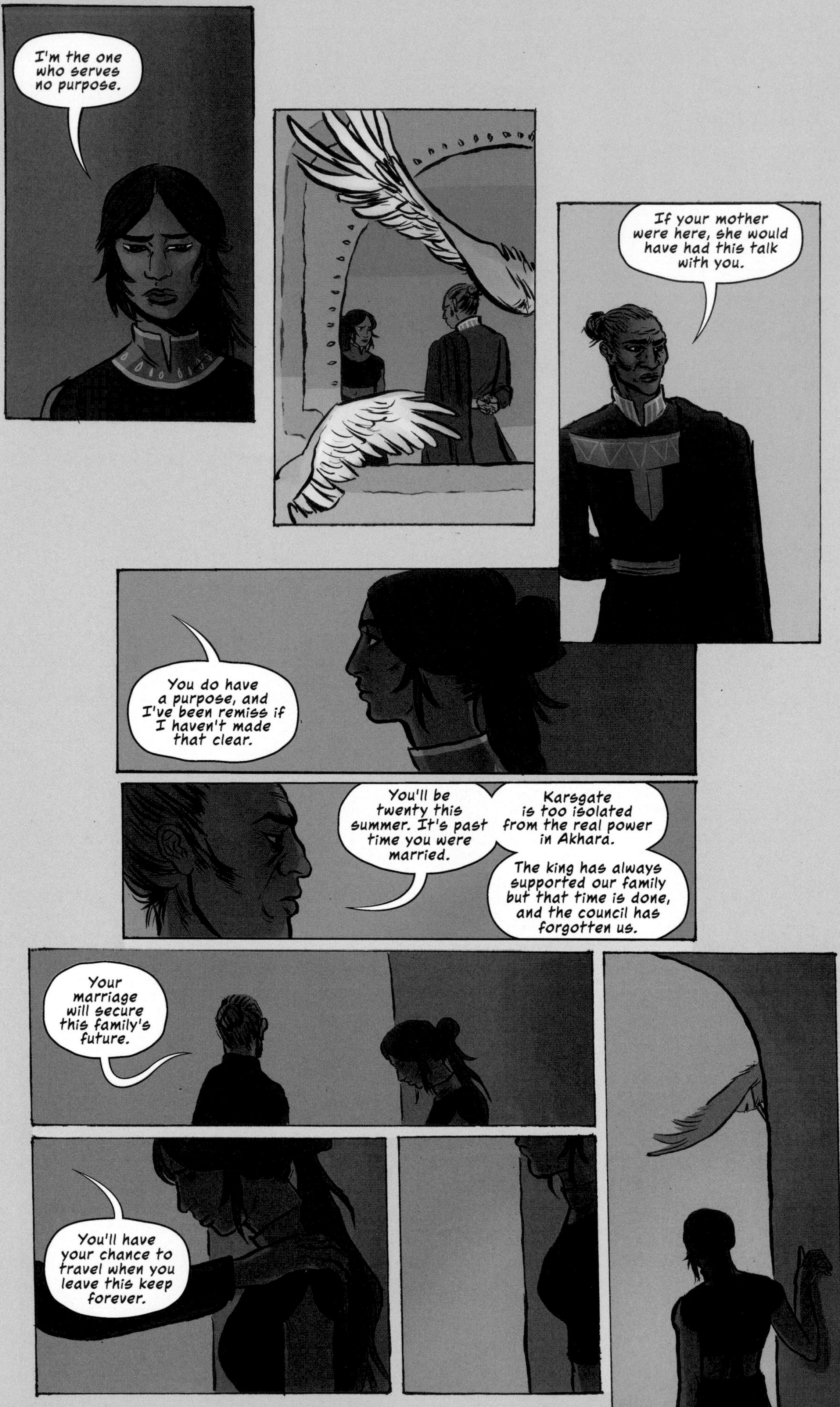
I'm the one who serves no purpose.
If your mother were here, she would have had this talk with you.
You do have a purpose, and I've been remiss if I haven't made that clear.
You'll be twenty this summer. It's past time you were married.
Karsgate is too isolated from the real power in Akhara.
The king has always supported our family but that time is done, and the council has forgotten us.
Your marriage will secure this family's future.
You'll have your chance to travel when you leave this keep forever.

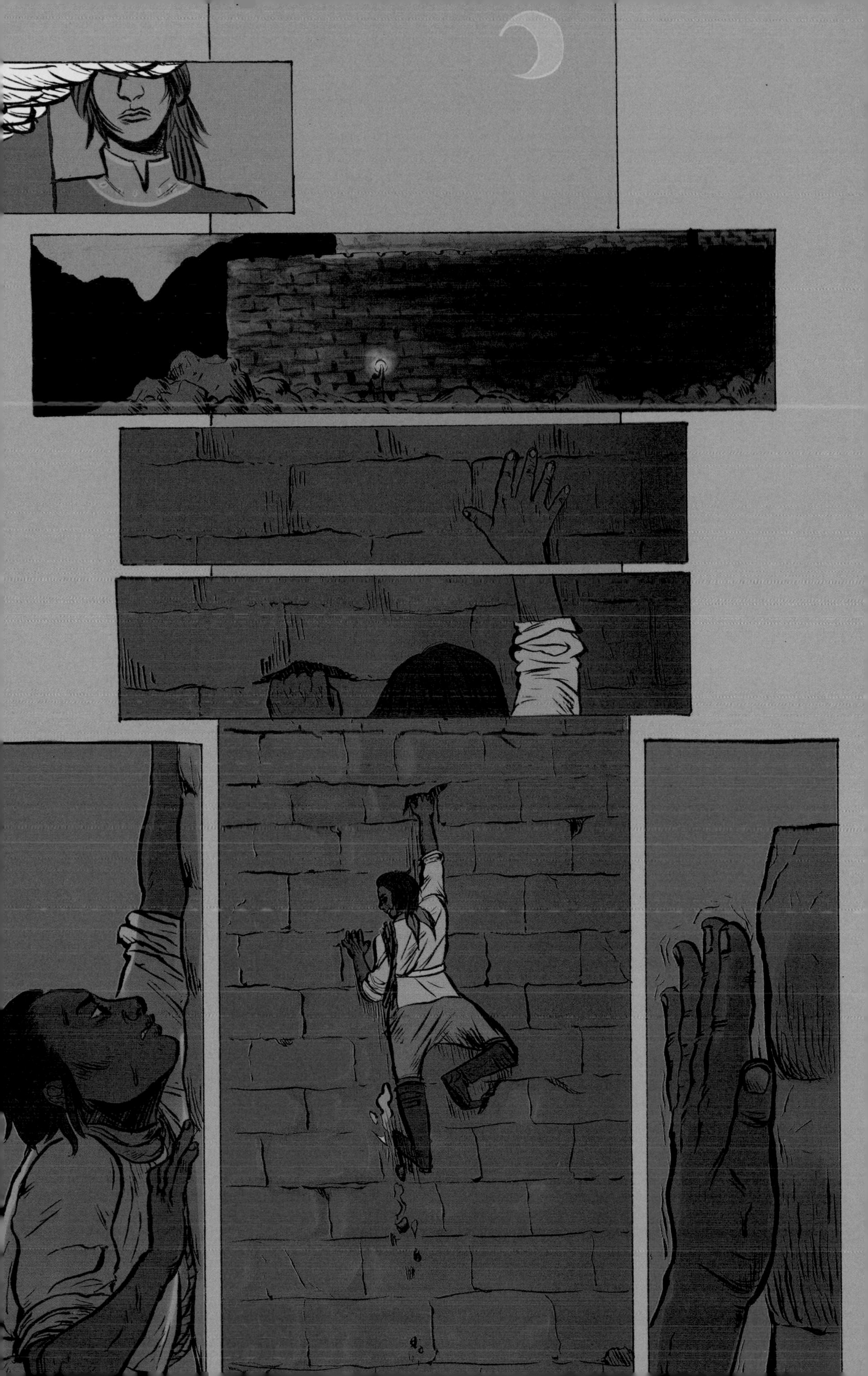

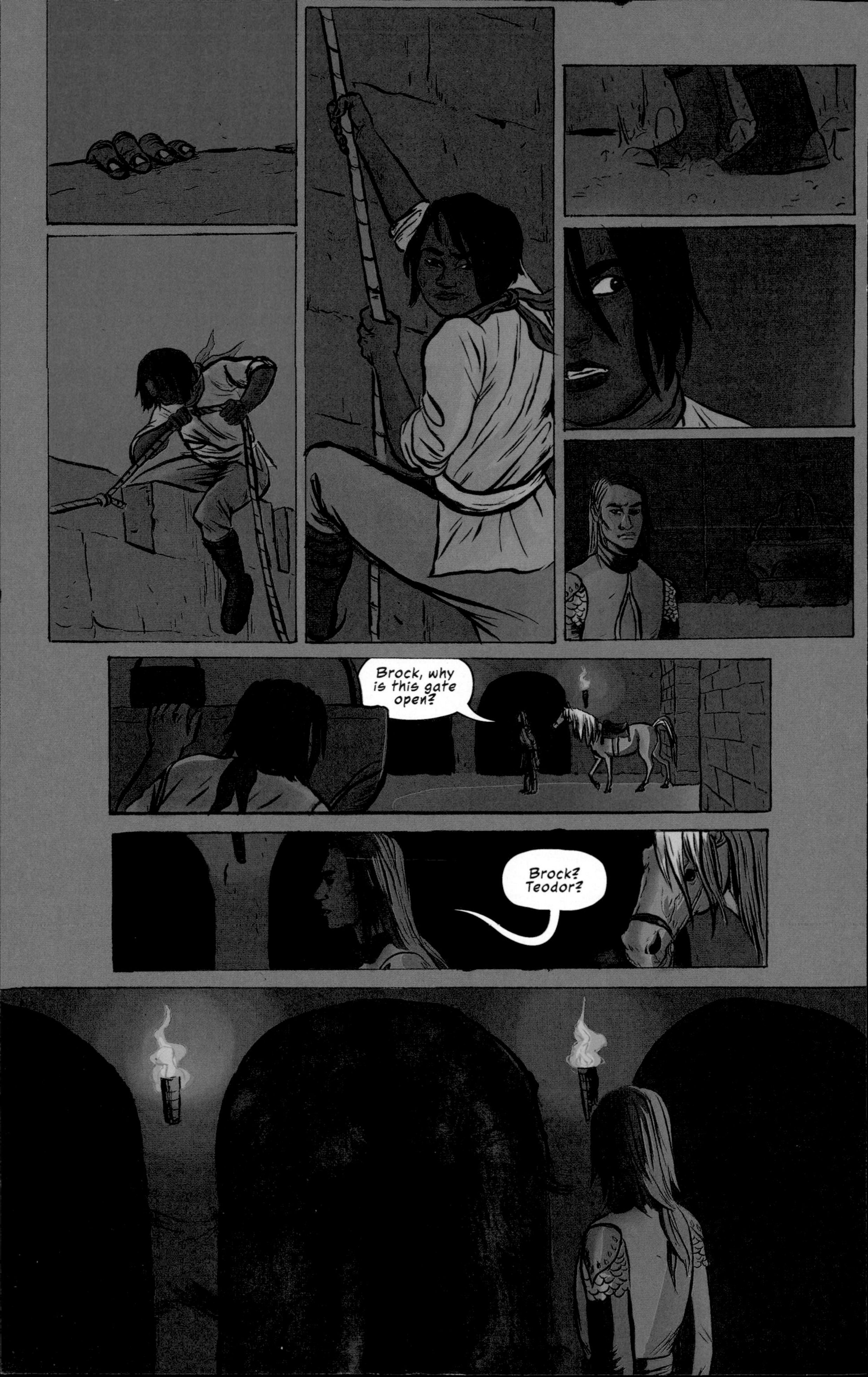
Brock, why is this gate open?
Brock? Teodor?

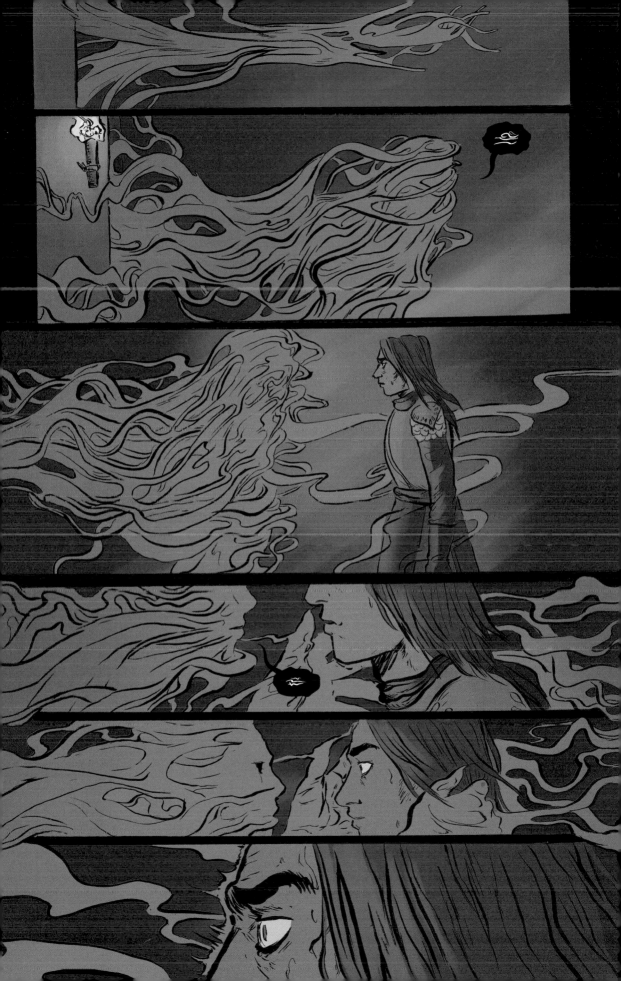

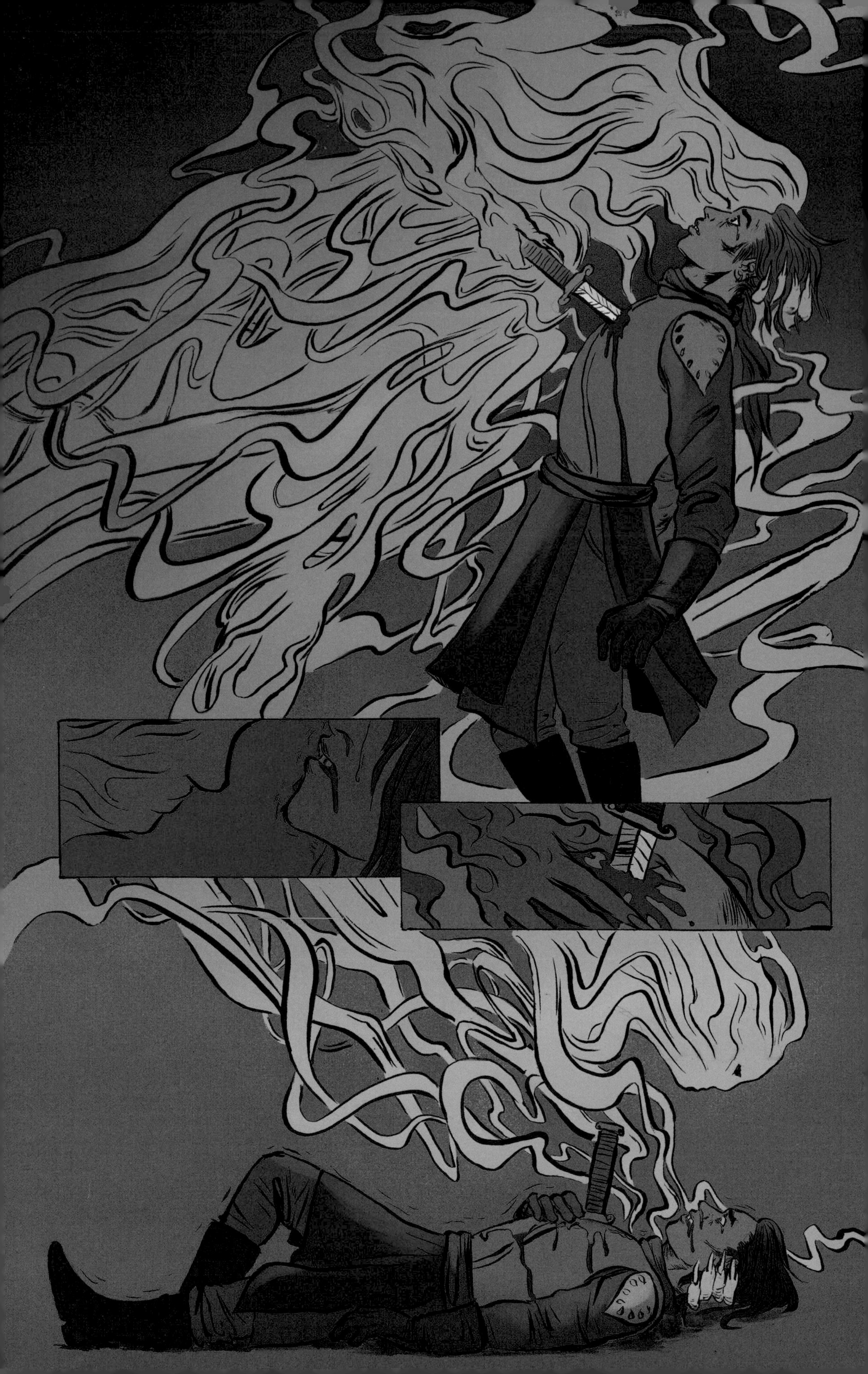

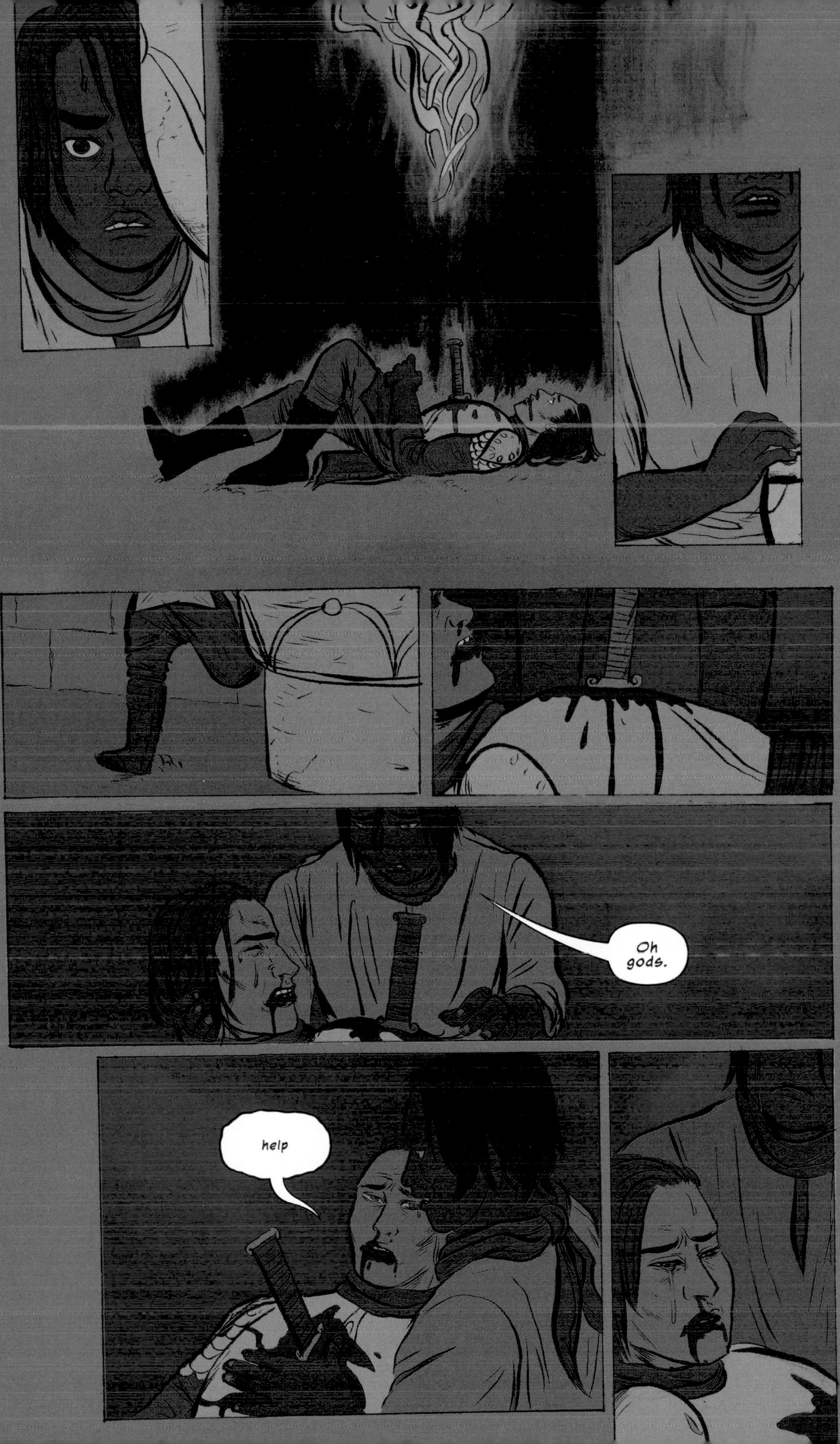
Oh gods.
help

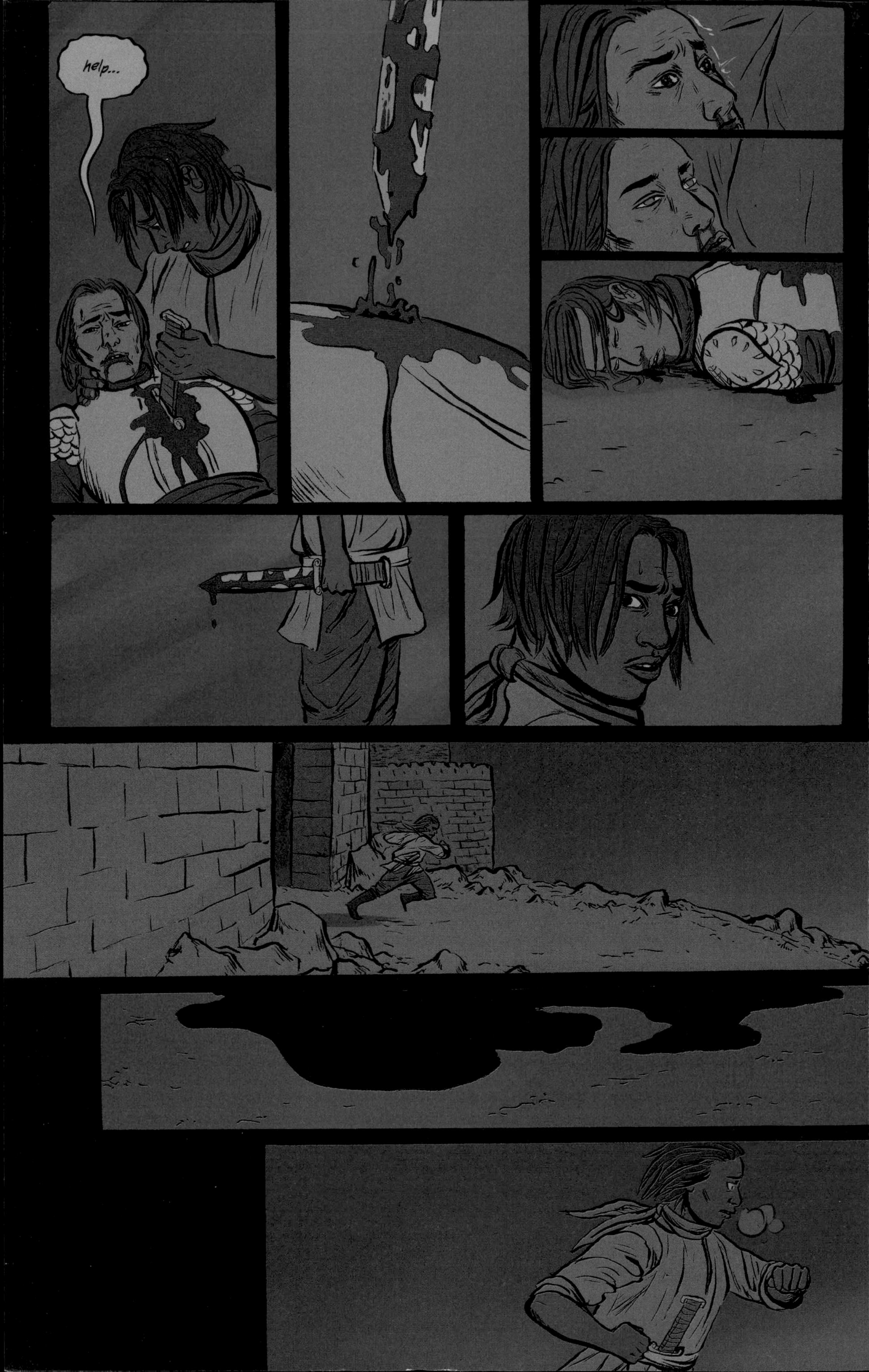
help...

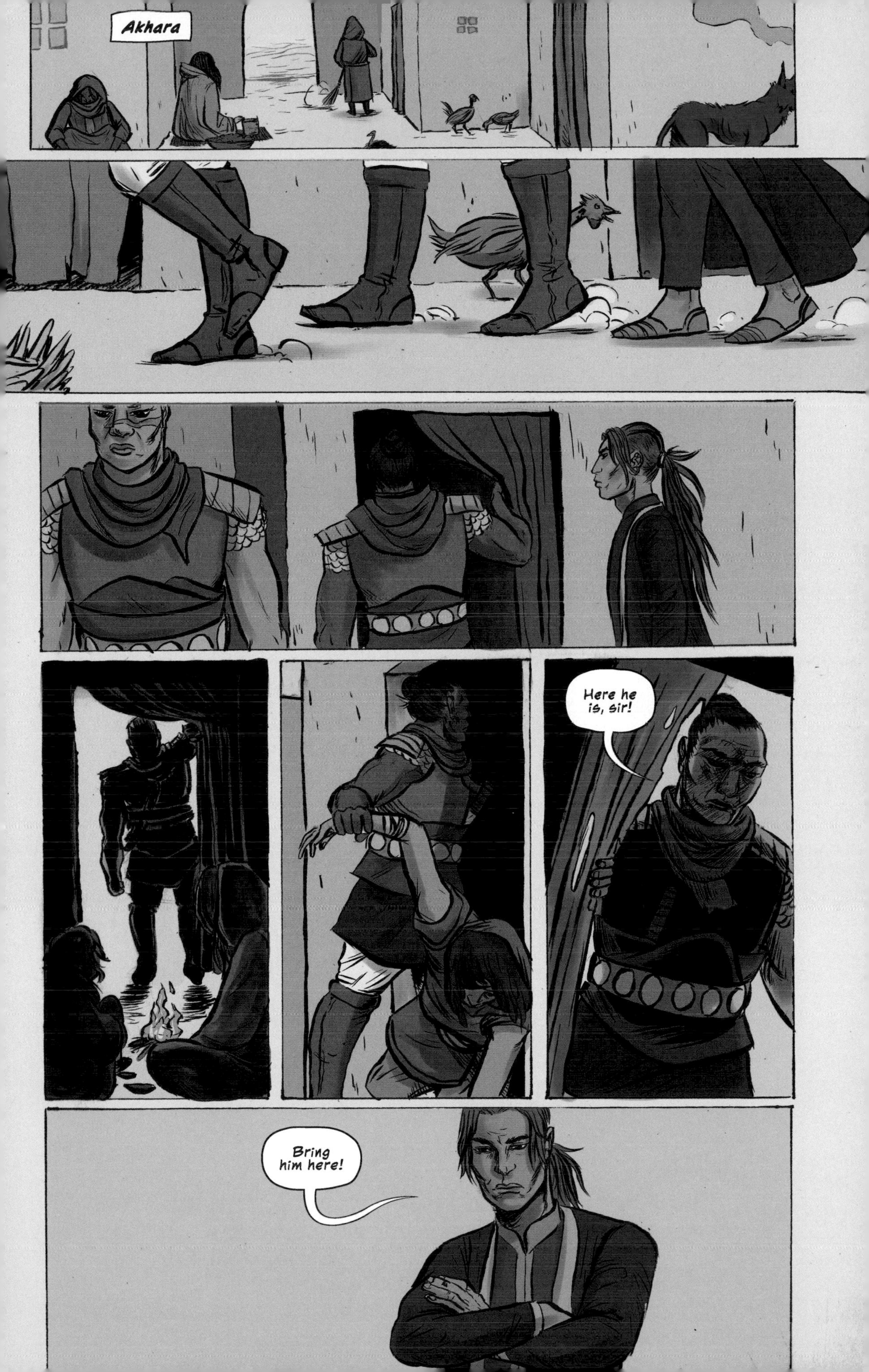
Akhara
Here he is, sir!
Bring him here!

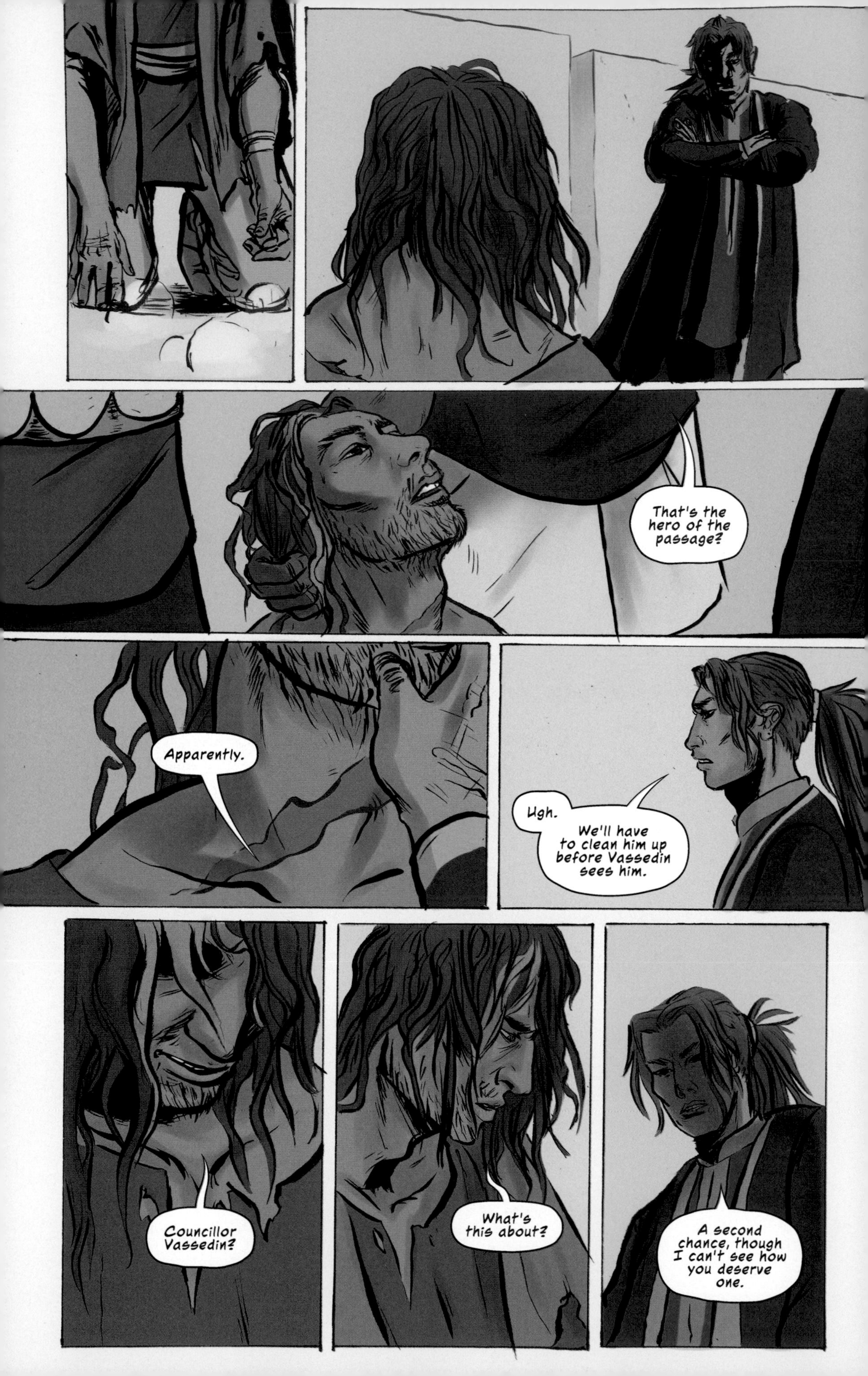
That's the hero of the passage?
Apparently.
Ugh.
We'll have to clean him up before Vassedin sees him.
Councillor Vassedin?
What's this about?
A second chance, though I can't see how you deserve one.

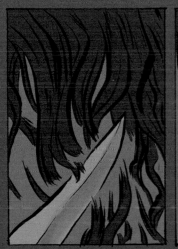

You wanted something?

Have some respect for the Councillor, you--

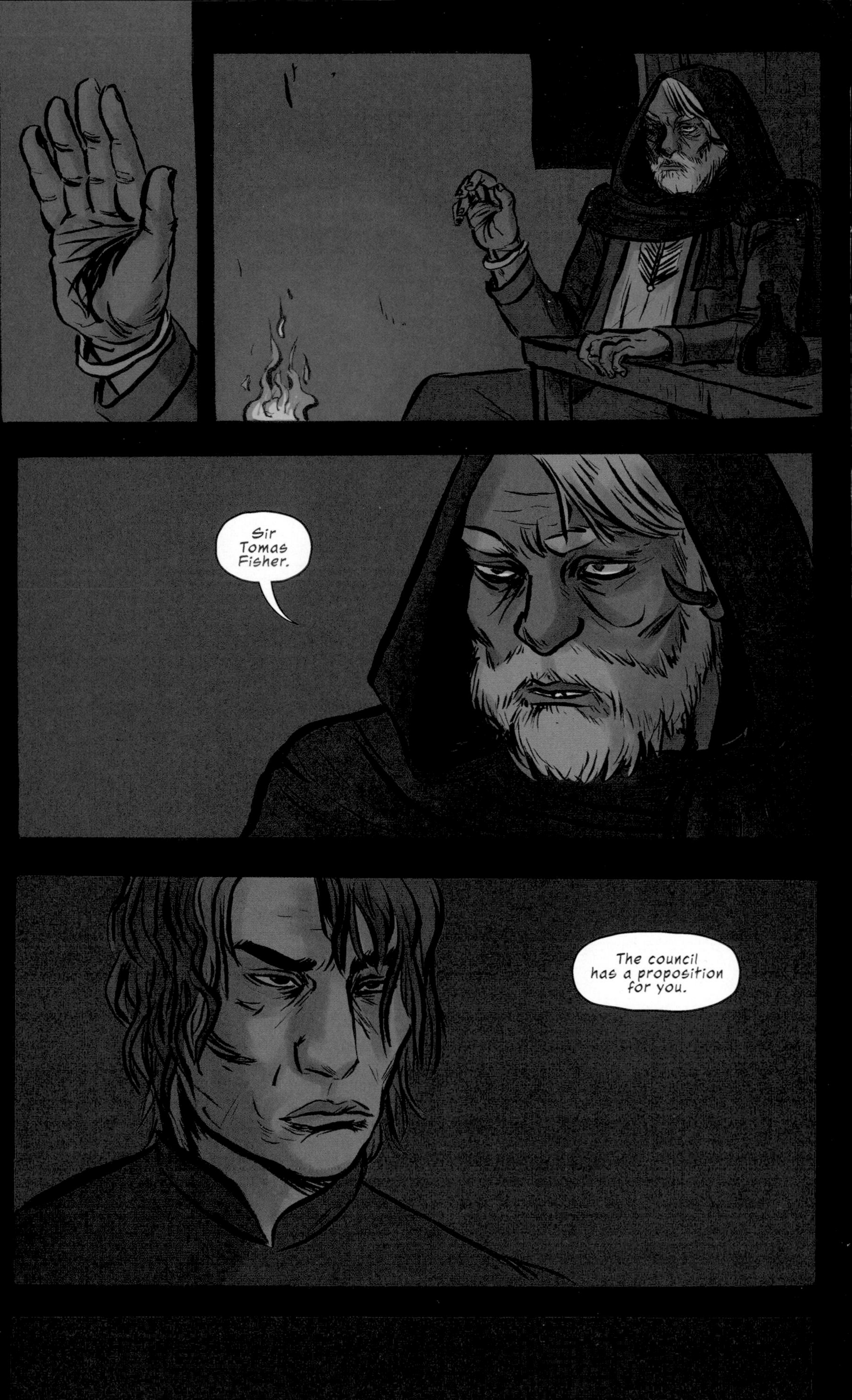
Sir Tomas Fisher.
The council has a proposition for you.

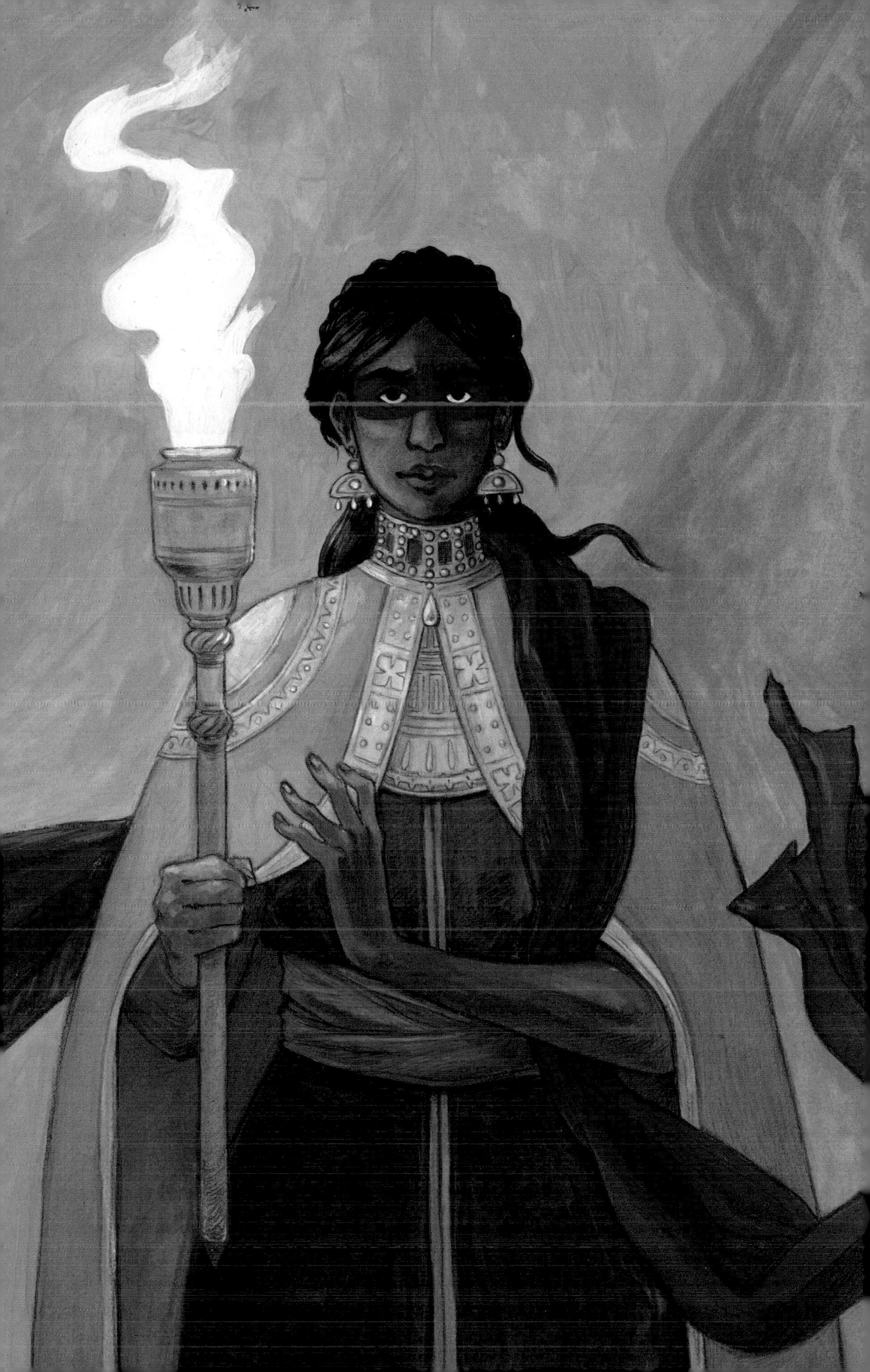

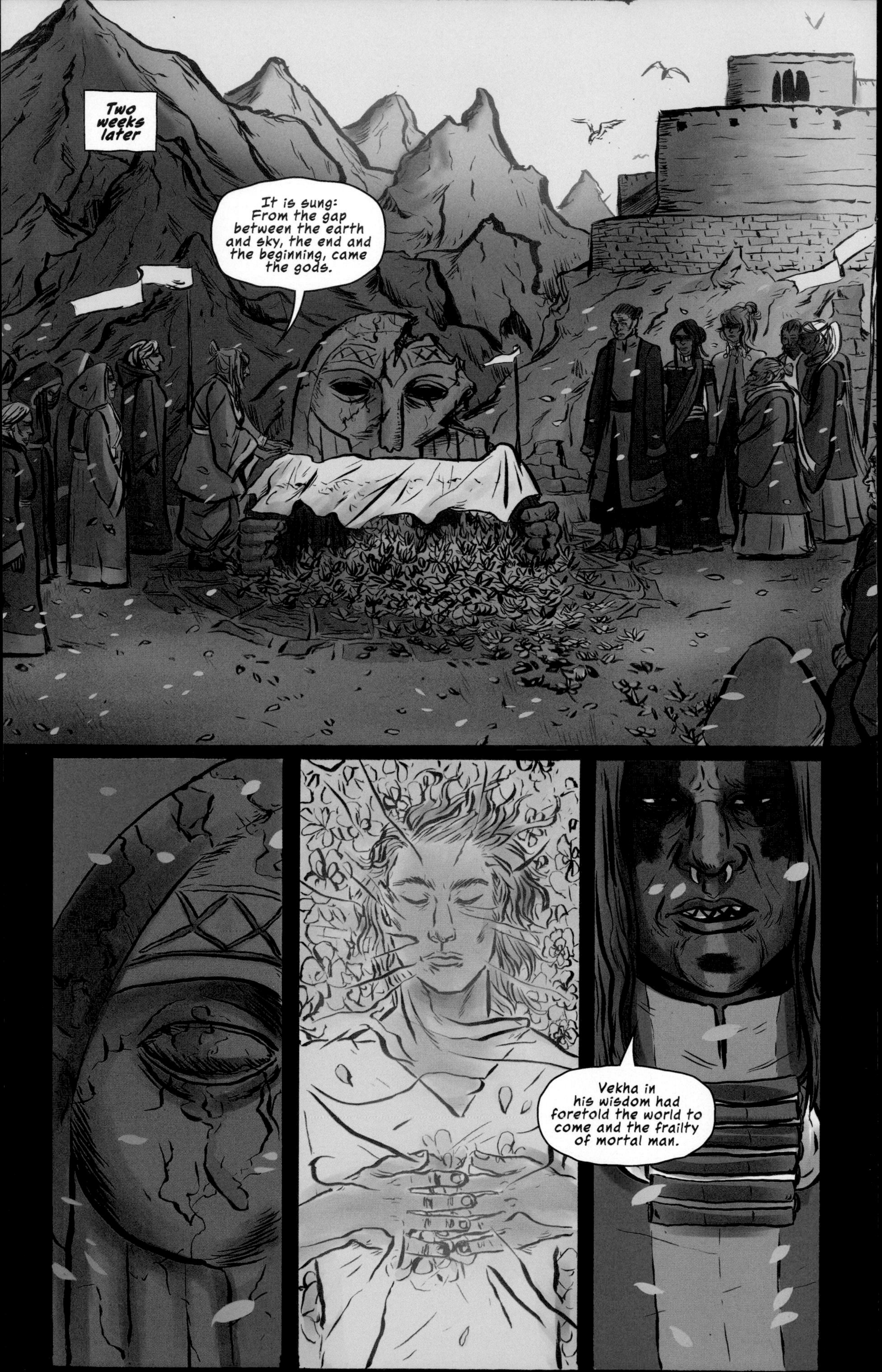
Two weeks later
It is sung: From the gap between the earth and sky, the end and the beginning, came the gods.
Vekha in his wisdom had foretold the world to come and the frailty of mortal man.

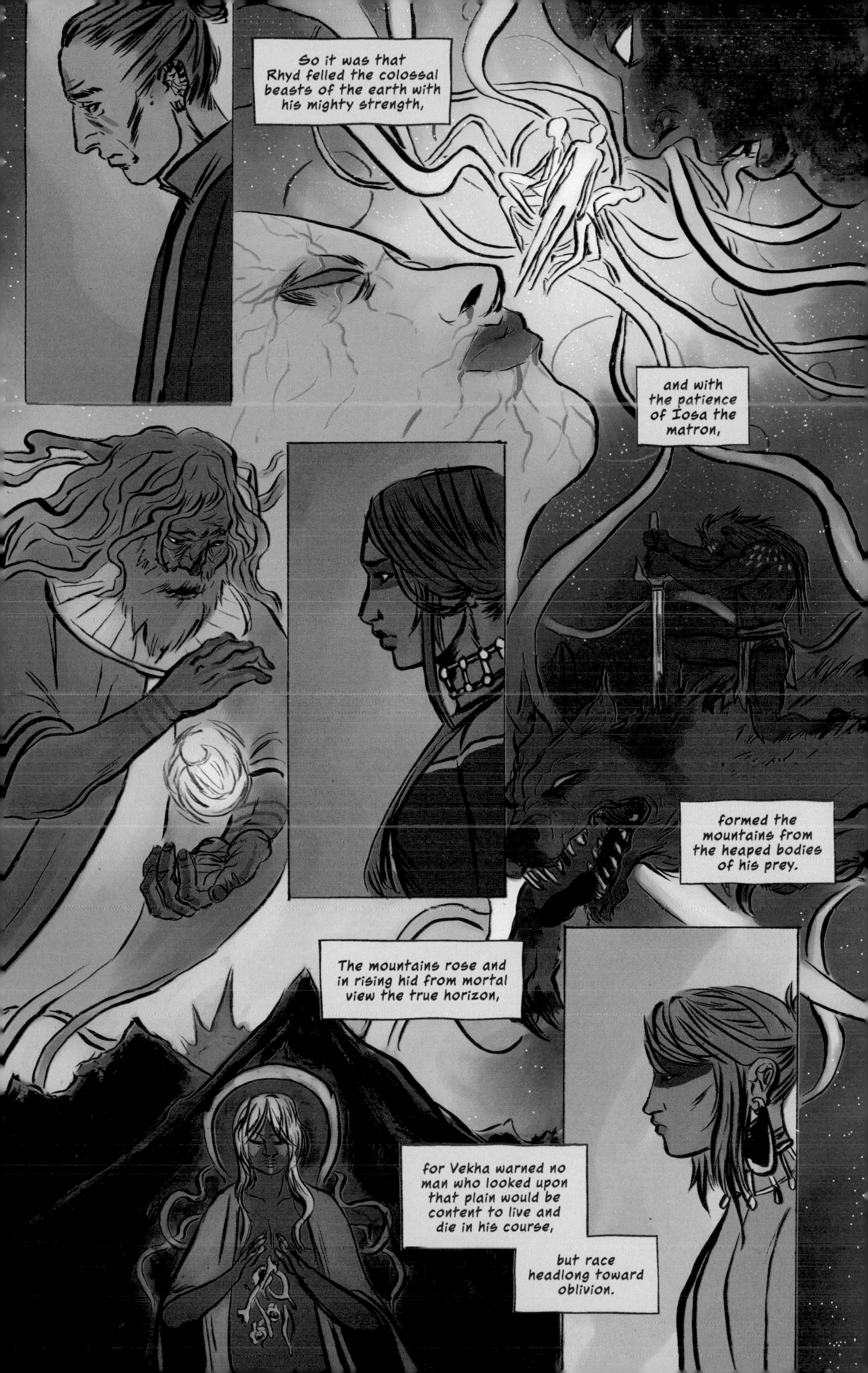
So it was that Rhyd felled the colossal beasts of the earth with his mighty strength,
and with the patience of Iosa the matron,
formed the mountains from the heaped bodies of his prey.
The mountains rose and in rising hid from mortal view the true horizon,
for Vekha warned no man who looked upon that plain would be content to live and die in his course,
but race headlong toward oblivion.

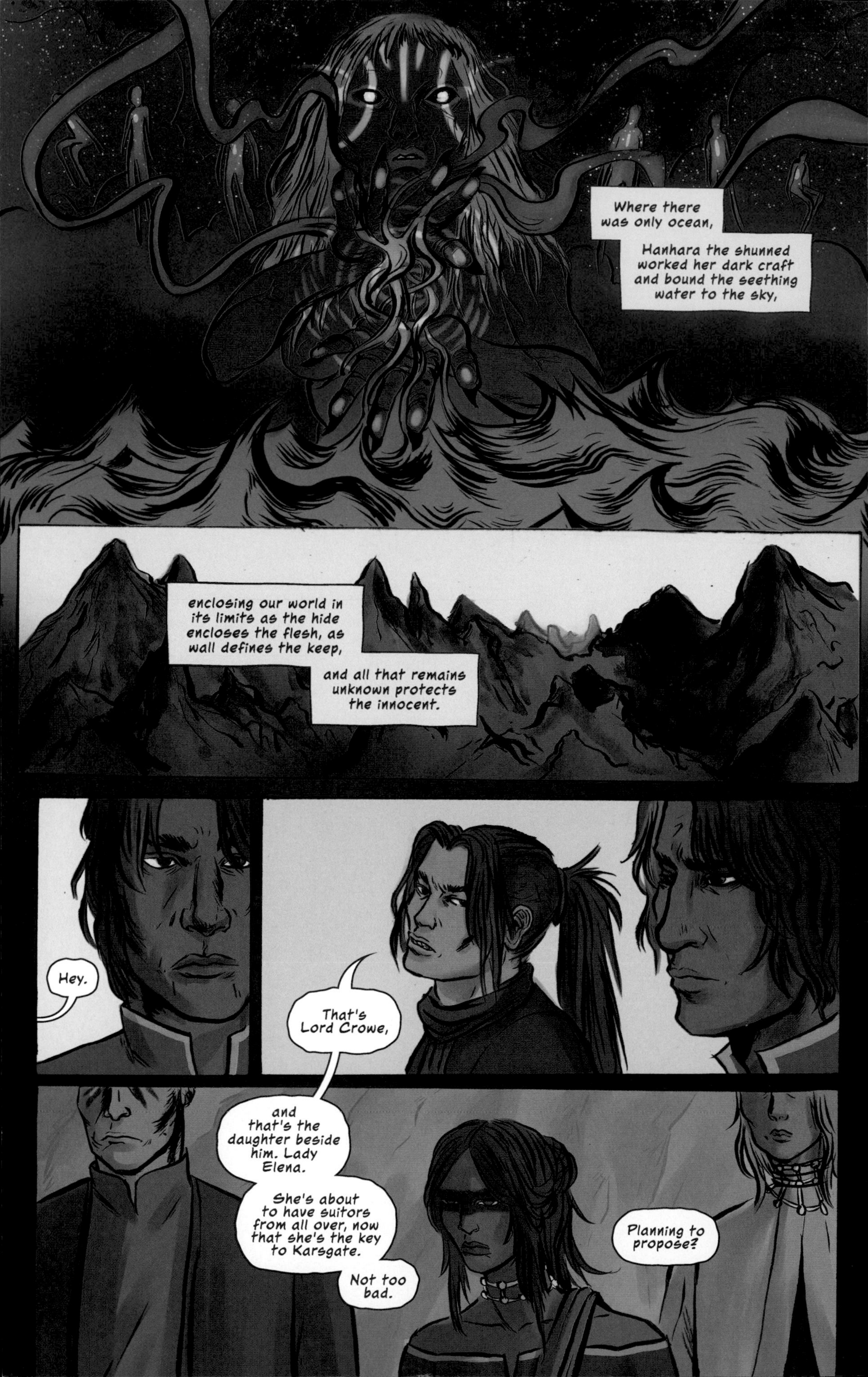

Where there was only ocean,
Hanhara the shunned worked her dark craft and bound the seething water to the sky,
enclosing our world in its limits as the hide encloses the flesh, as wall defines the keep,
and all that remains unknown protects the innocent.
Hey.
That's Lord Crowe,
and that's the daughter beside him. Lady Elena.
She's about to have suitors from all over, now that she's the key to Karsgate.
Not too bad.
Planning to propose?

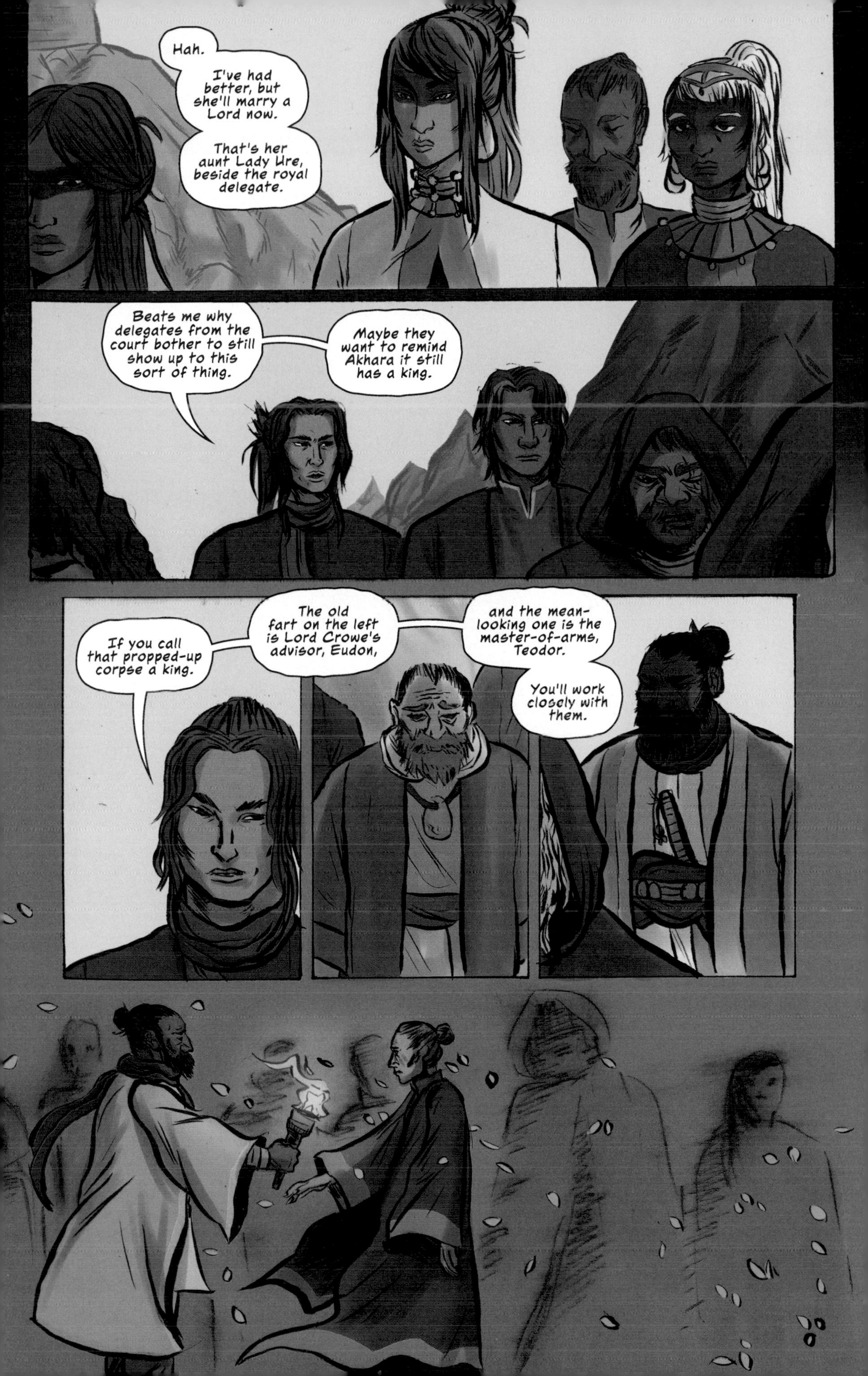
Hah.
I've had better, but she'll marry a Lord now.
That's her aunt Lady Ure, beside the royal delegate.
Beats me why delegates from the court bother to still show up to this sort of thing.
Maybe they want to remind Akhara it still has a king.
If you call that propped-up corpse a king.
The old fart on the left is Lord Crowe's advisor, Eudon,
and the mean-looking one is the master-of-arms, Teodor.
You'll work closely with them.

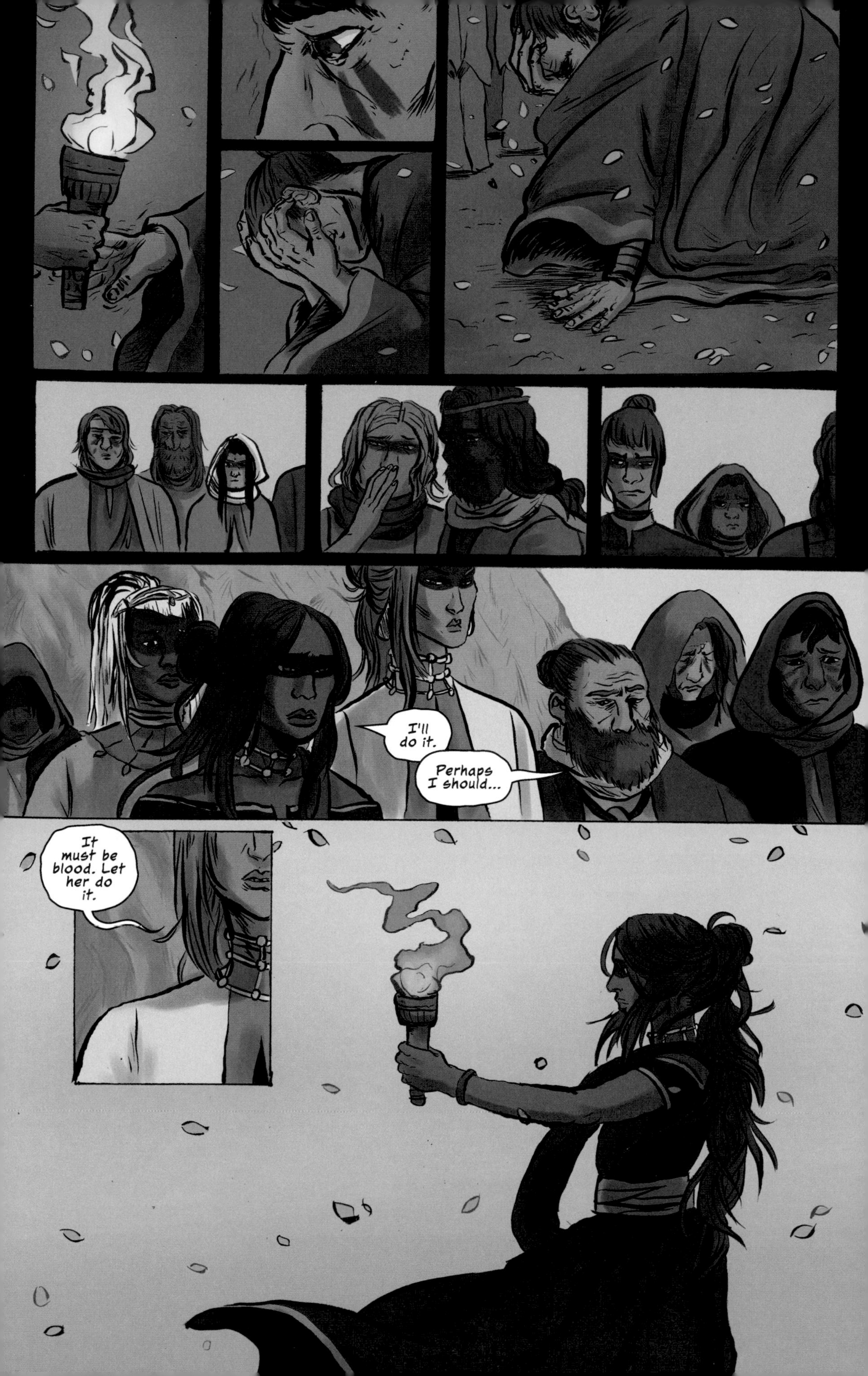
I'll do it.
Perhaps I should...
It must be blood. Let her do it.

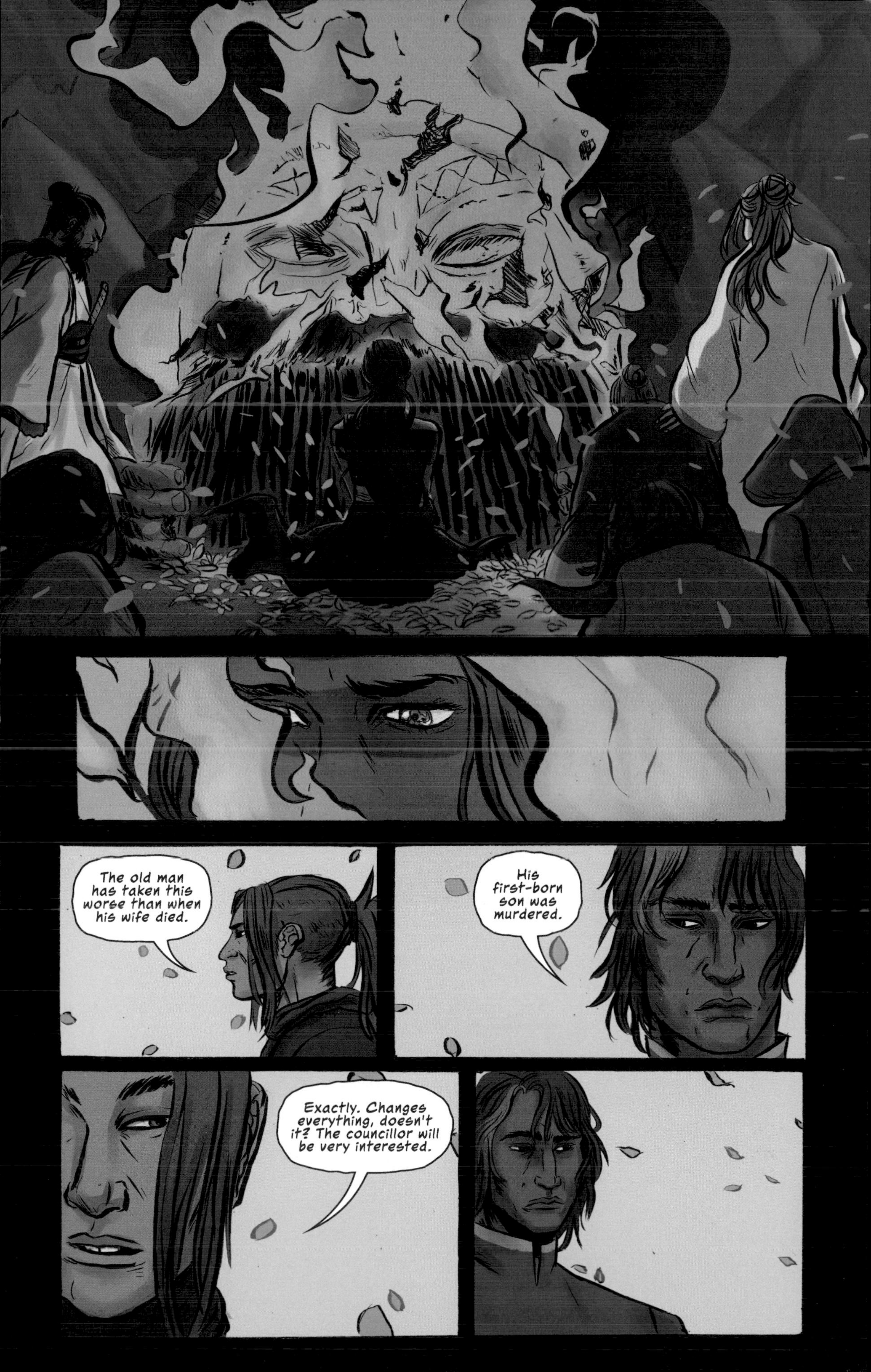
The old man has taken this worse than when his wife died.
His first-born son was murdered.
Exactly. Changes everything, doesn't it? The councillor will be very interested.

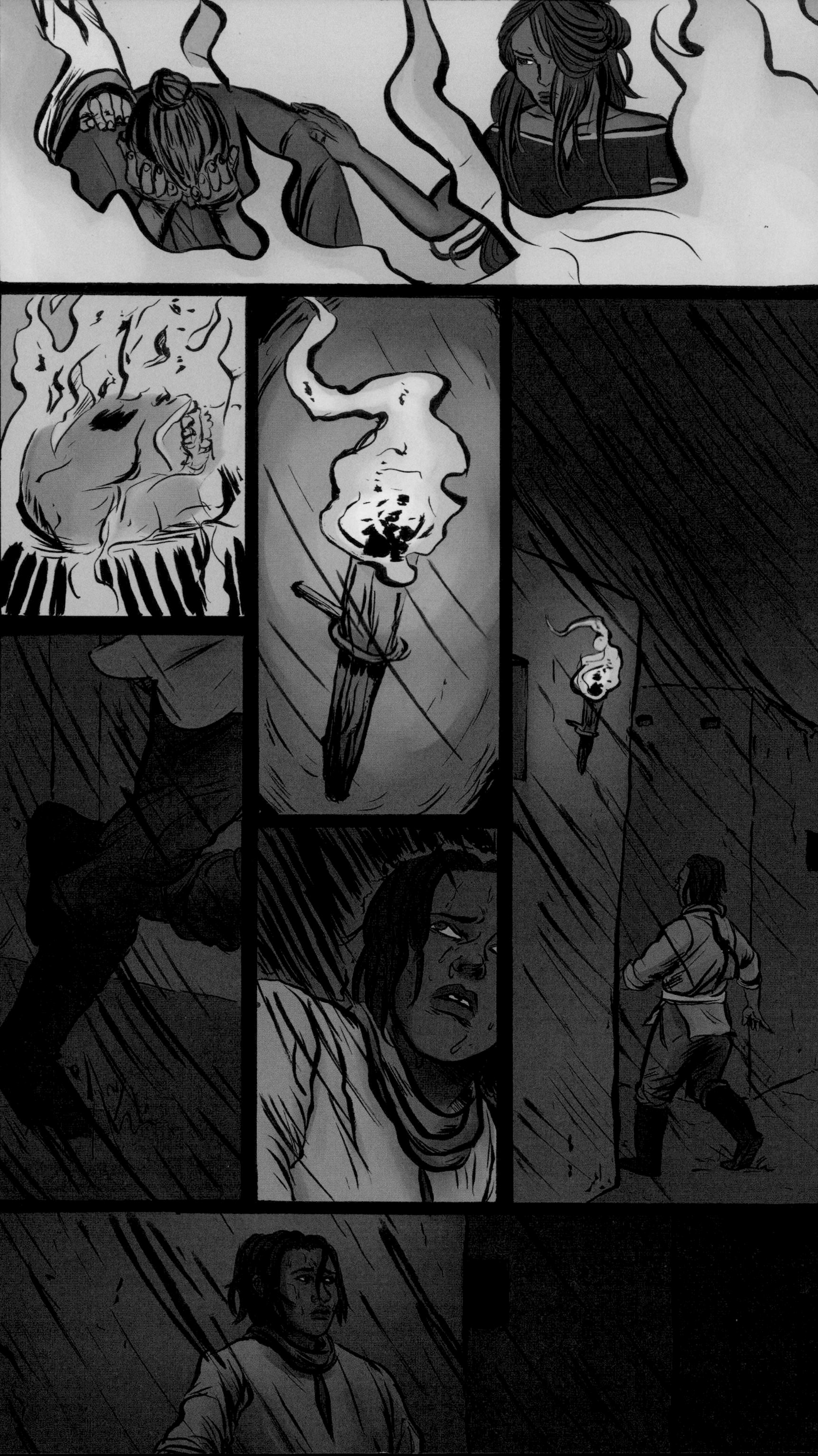

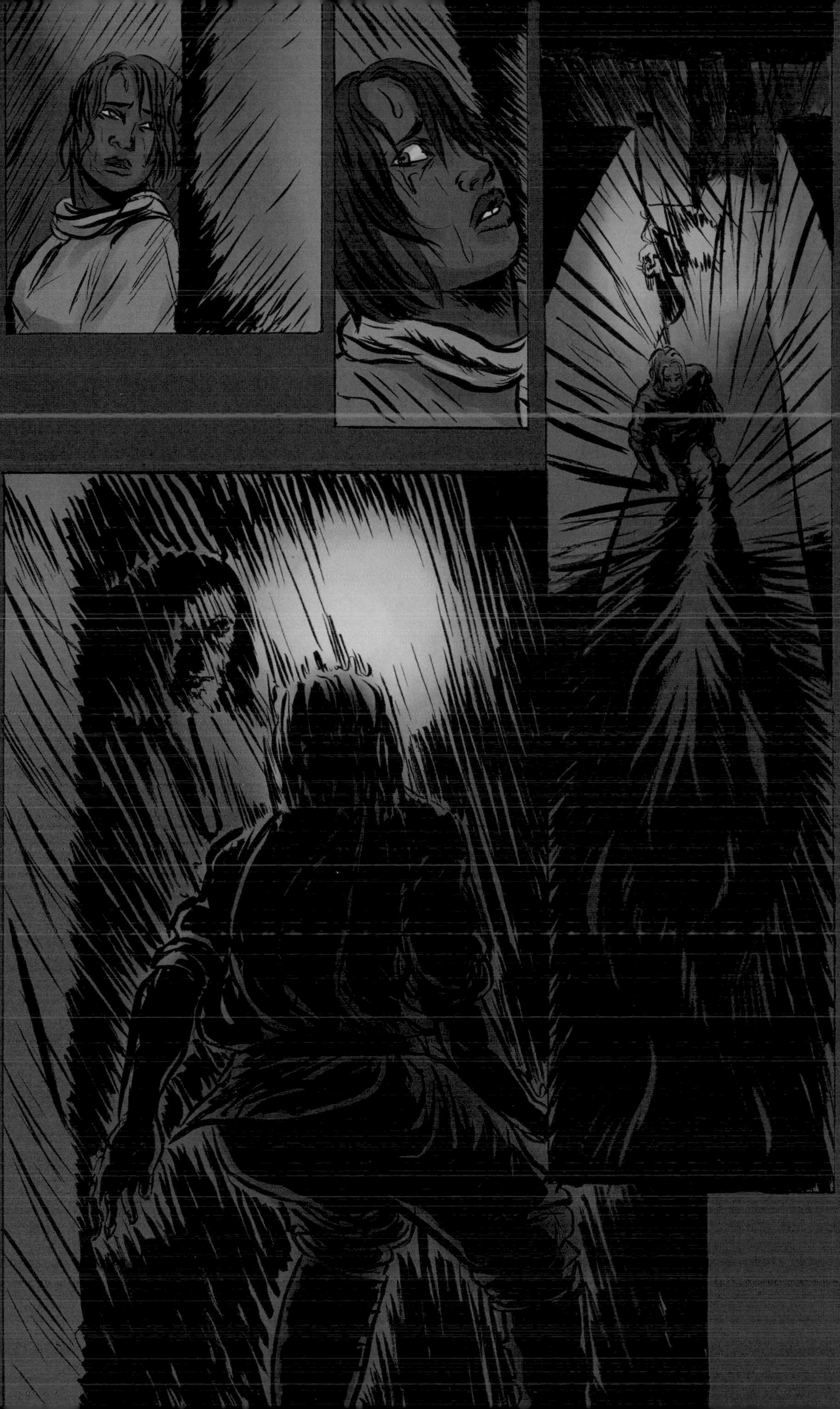

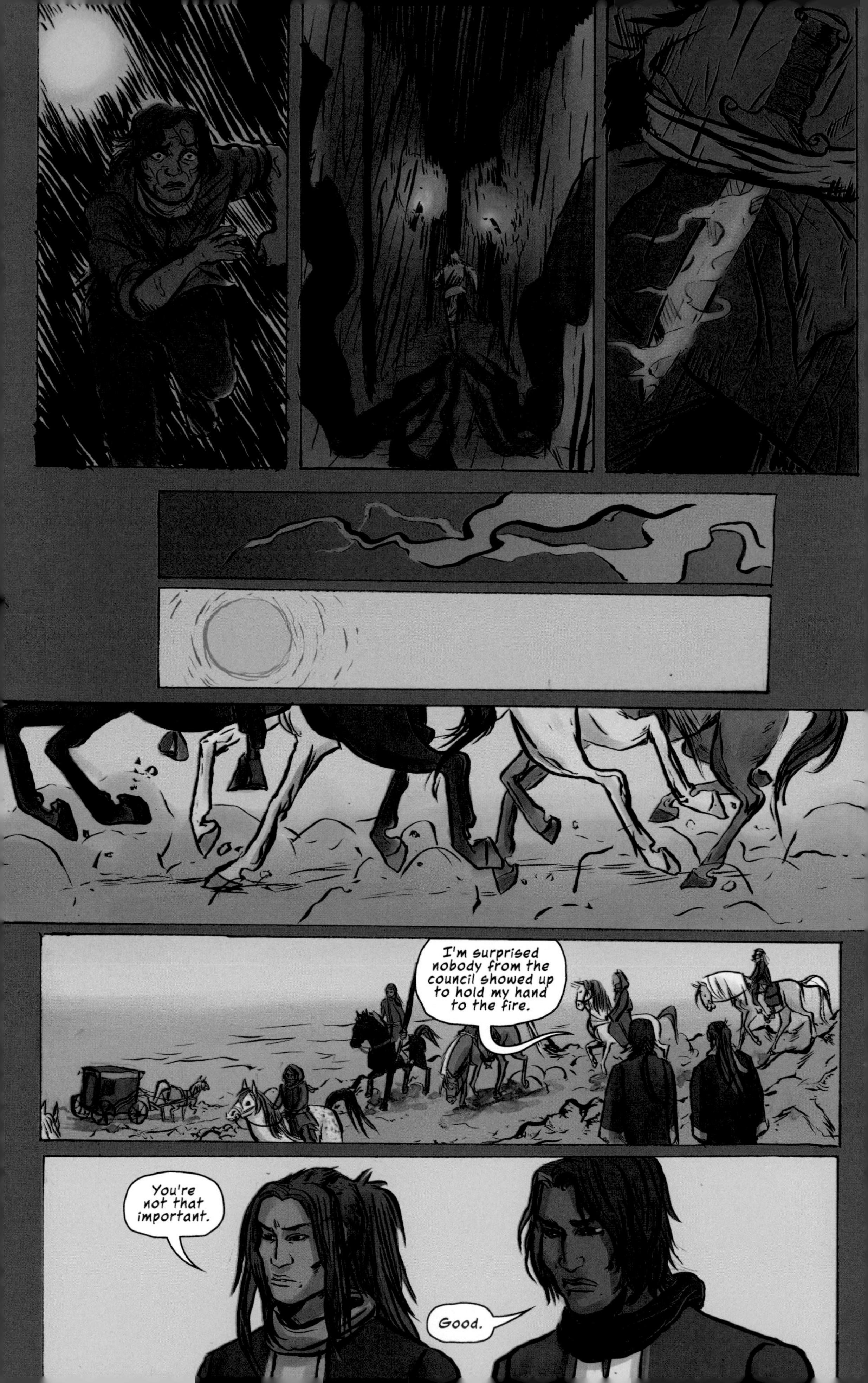
I'm surprised nobody from the council showed up to hold my hand to the fire.
You're not that important.
Good.

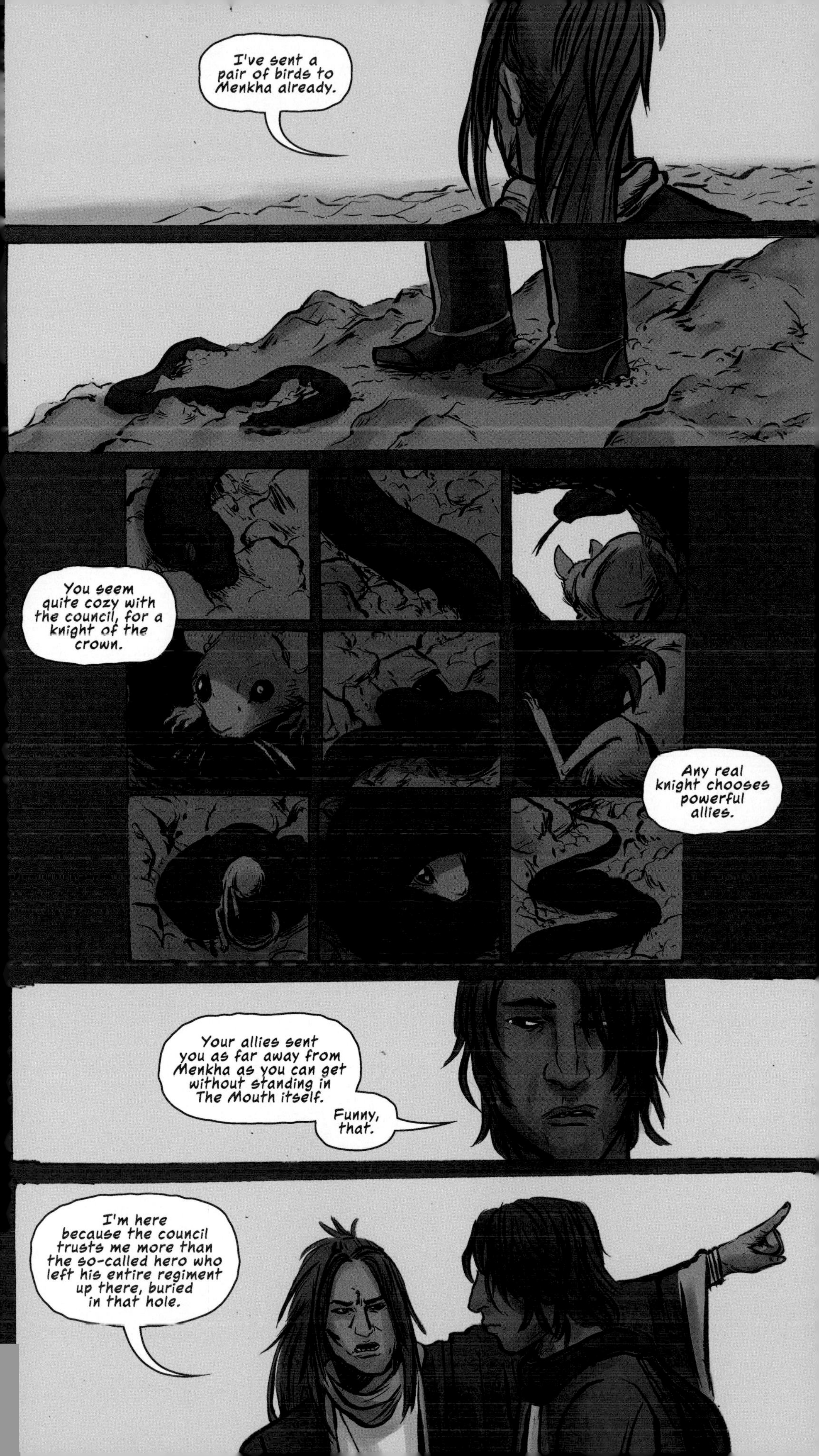

I've sent a pair of birds to Menkha already.
You seem quite cozy with the council, for a knight of the crown.
Any real knight chooses powerful allies.
Your allies sent you as far away from Menkha as you can get without standing in The Mouth itself.
Funny, that.
I'm here because the council trusts me more than the so-called hero who left his entire regiment up there, buried in that hole.

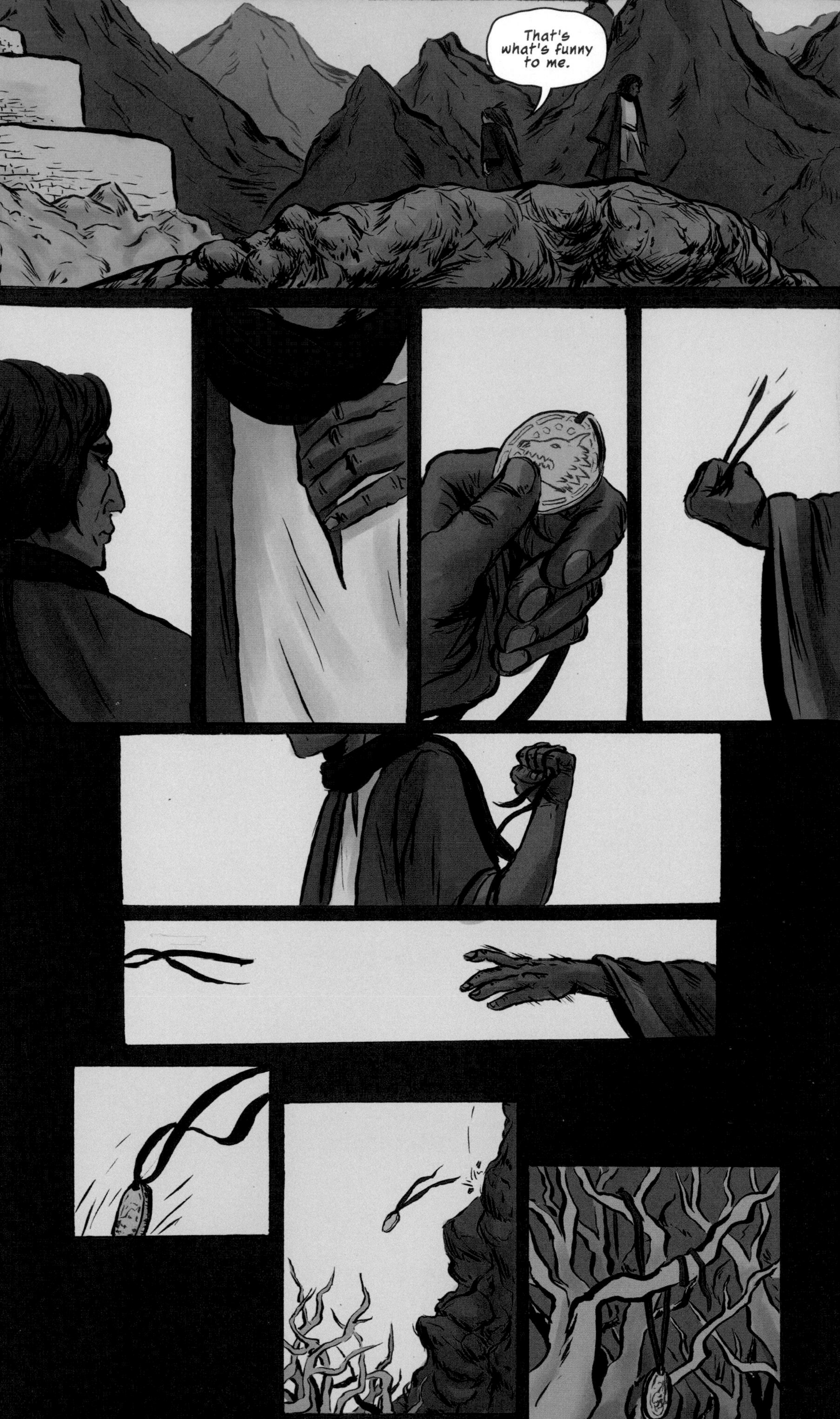
That's what's funny to me.

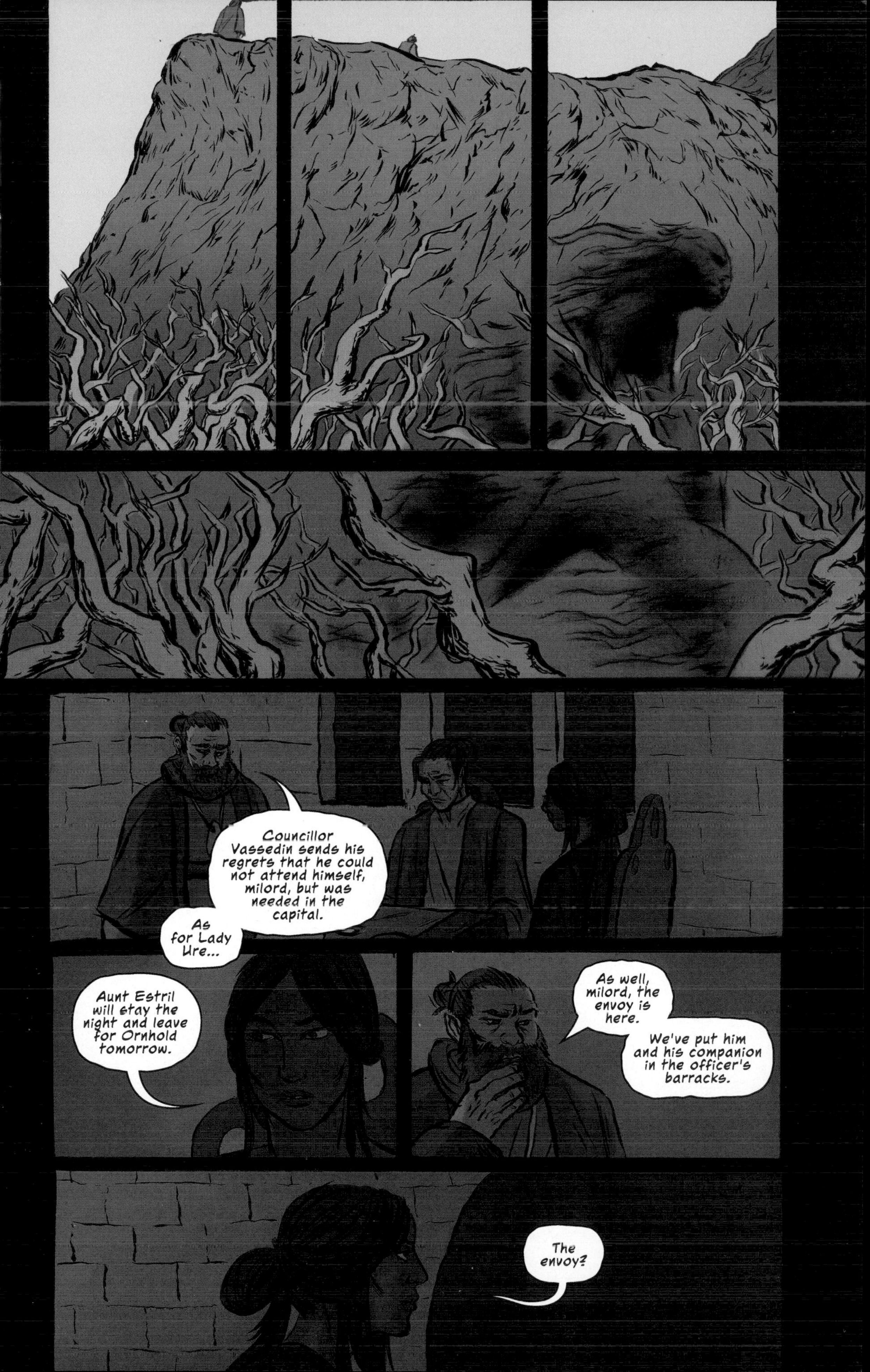
Councillor Vassedin sends his regrets that he could not attend himself, milord, but was needed in the capital.
As for Lady Ure...
Aunt Estril will stay the night and leave for Ornhold tomorrow.
As well, milord, the envoy is here.
We've put him and his companion in the officer's barracks.
The envoy?

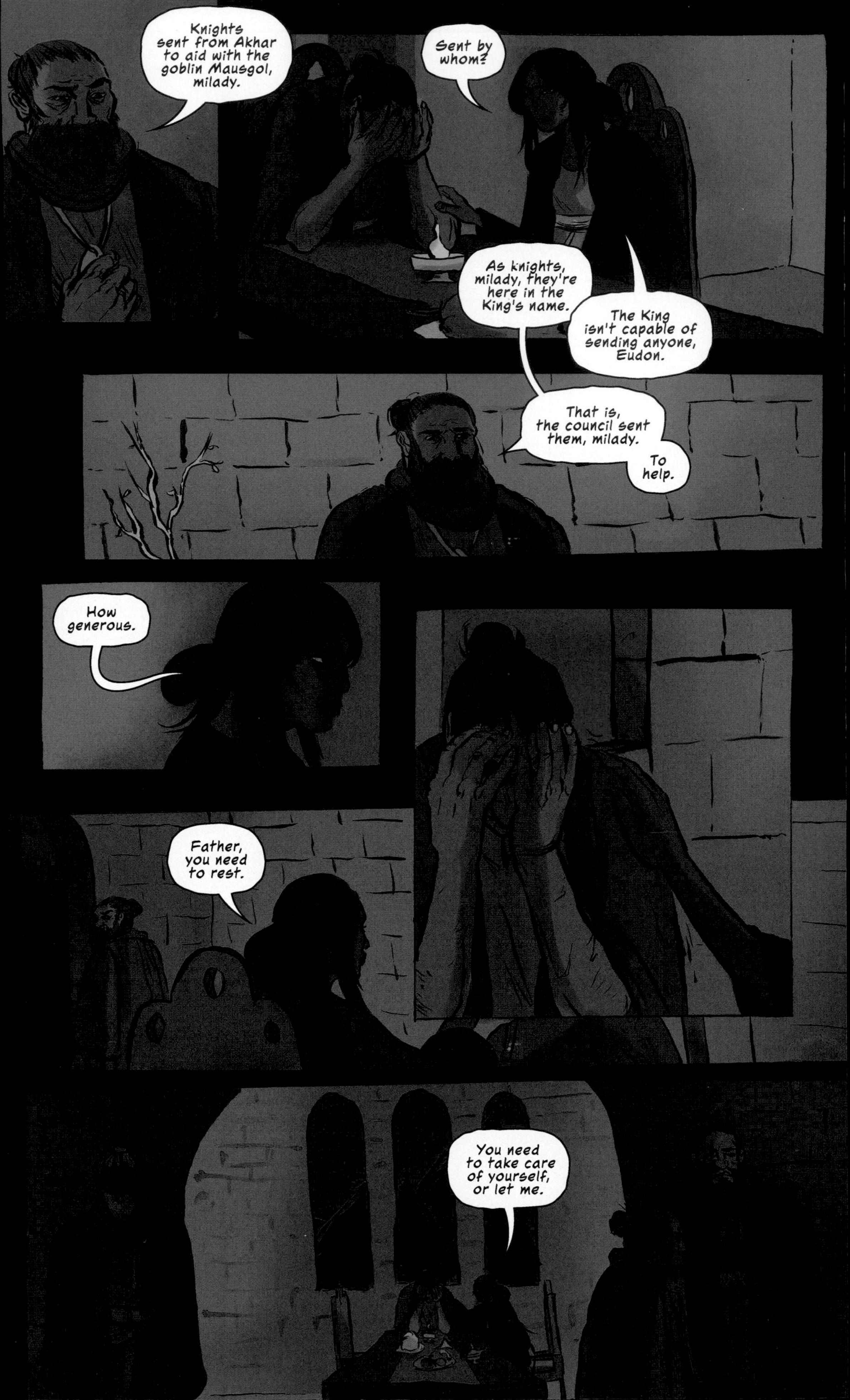
Knights sent from Akhar to aid with the goblin Mausgol, milady.
Sent by whom?
As knights, milady, they're here in the King's name.
The King isn't capable of sending anyone, Eudon.
That is, the council sent them, milady.
To help.
How generous.
Father, you need to rest.
You need to take care of yourself, or let me.

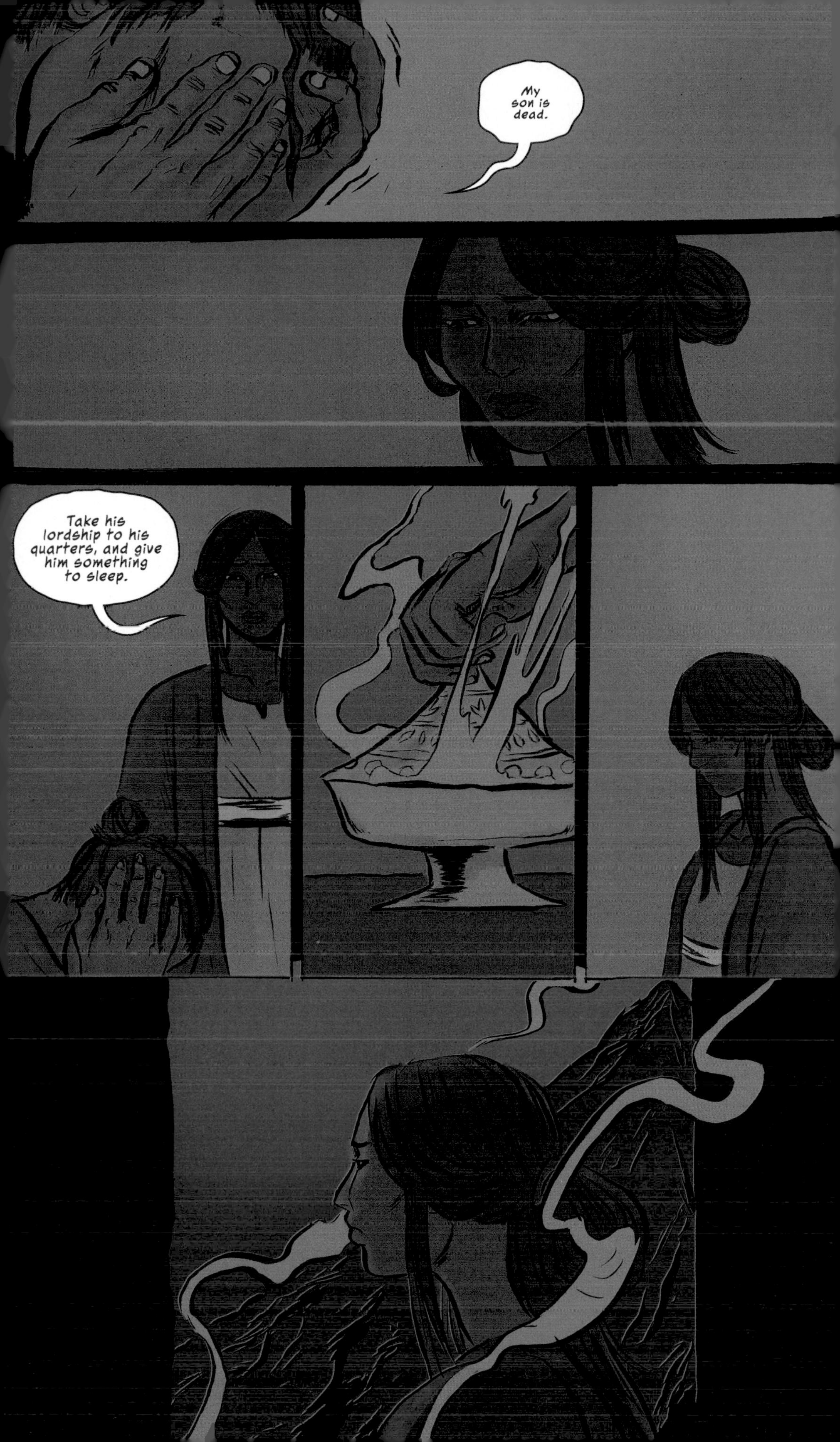
My son is dead.
Take his lordship to his quarters, and give him something to sleep.

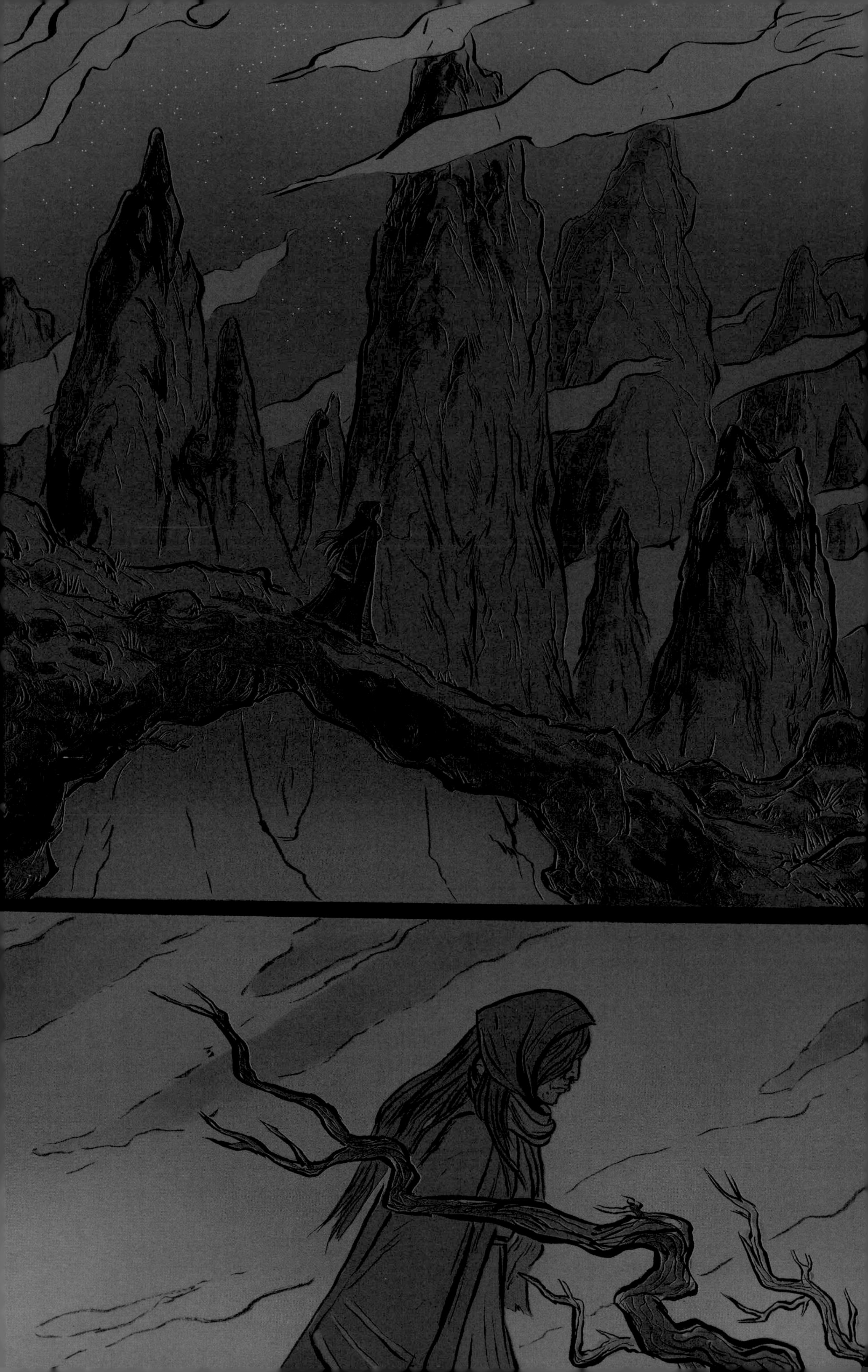

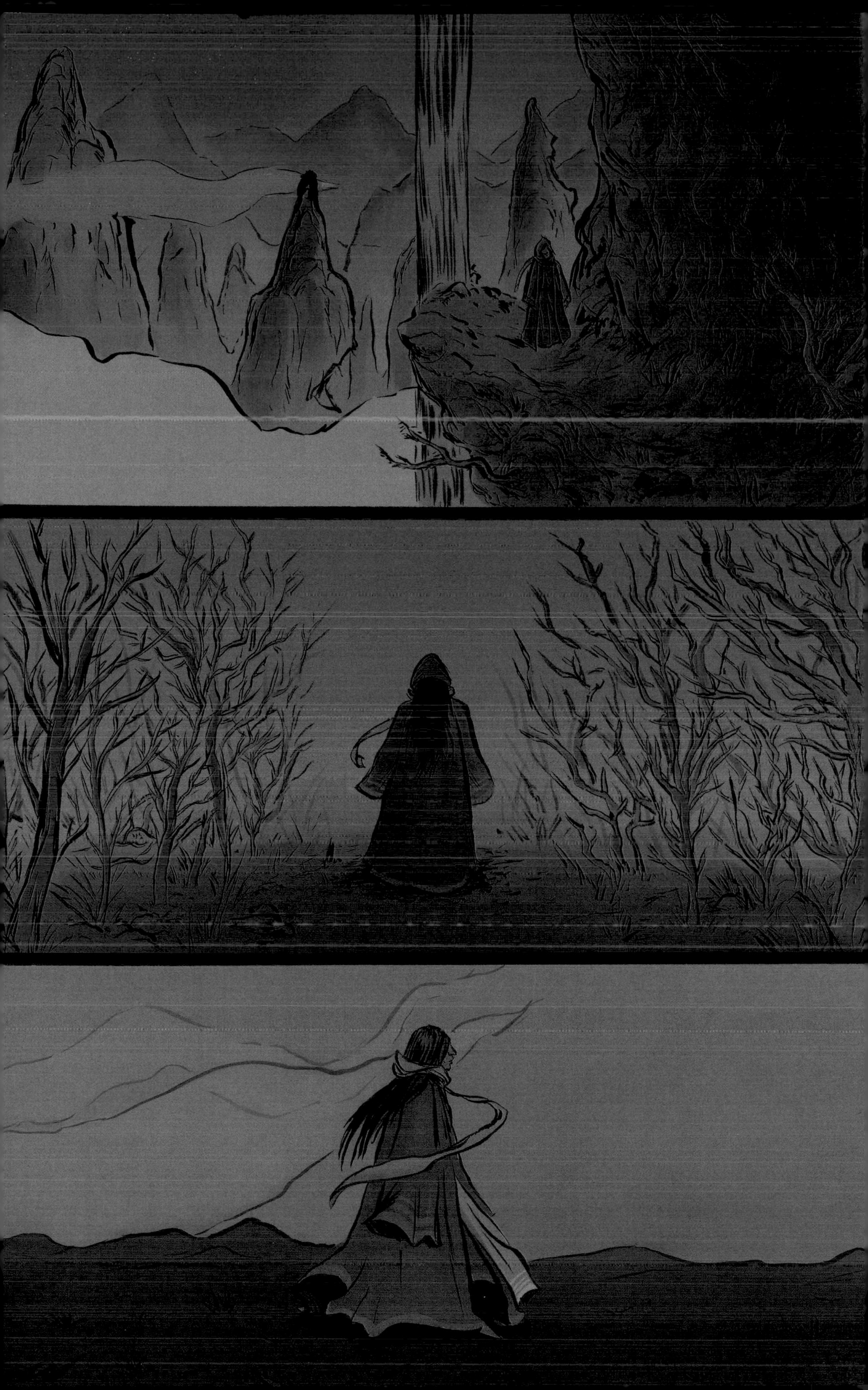

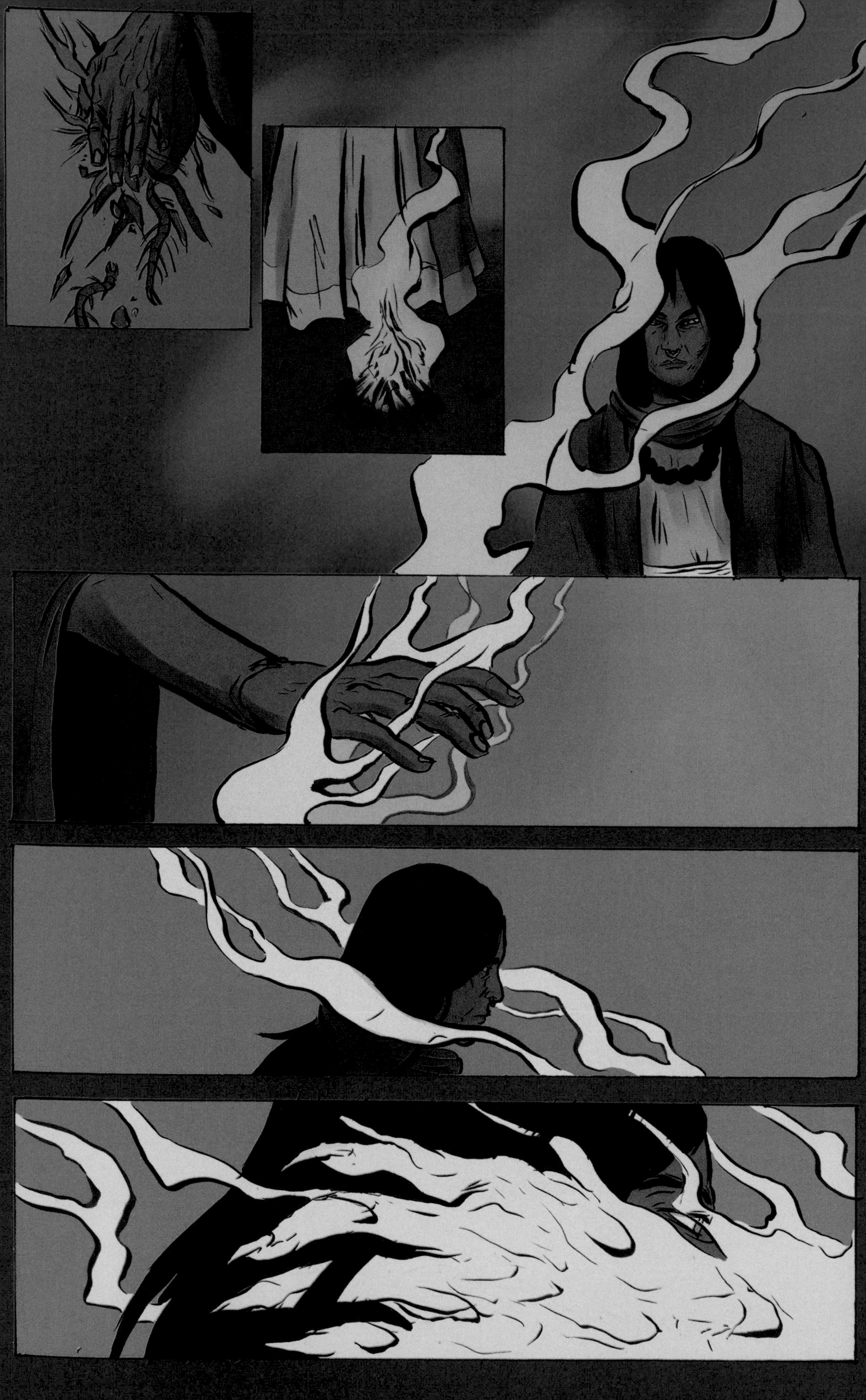

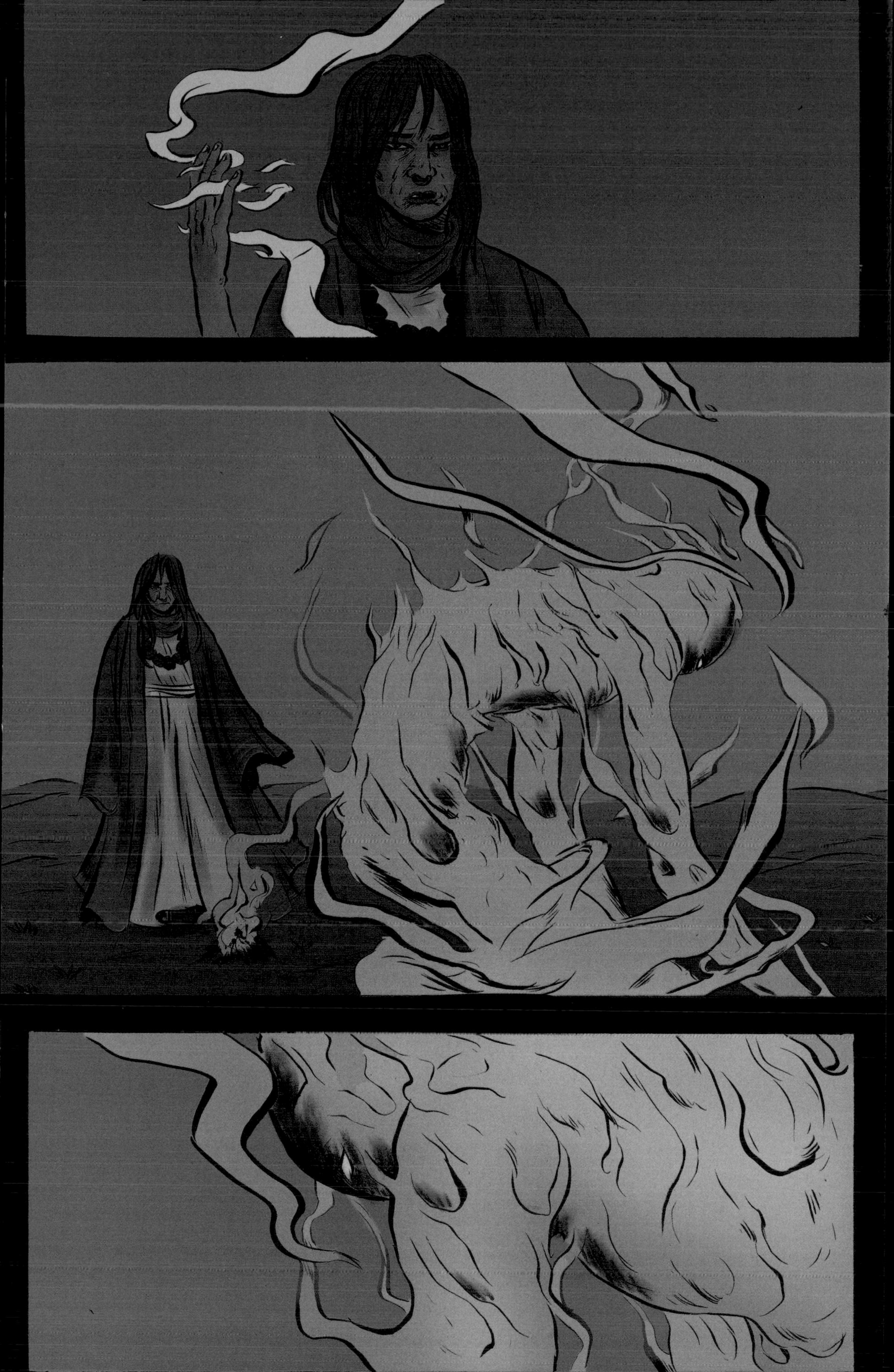

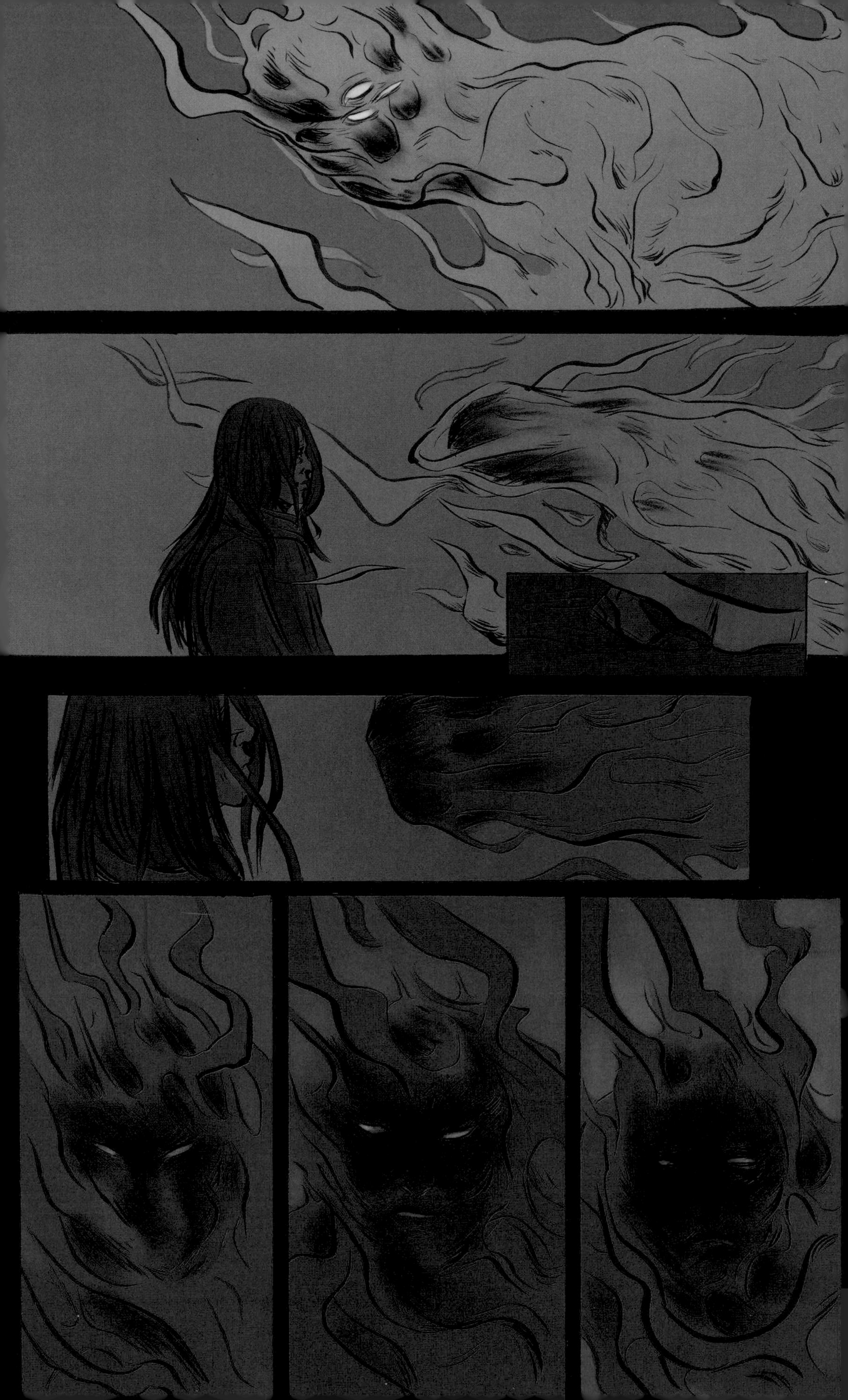

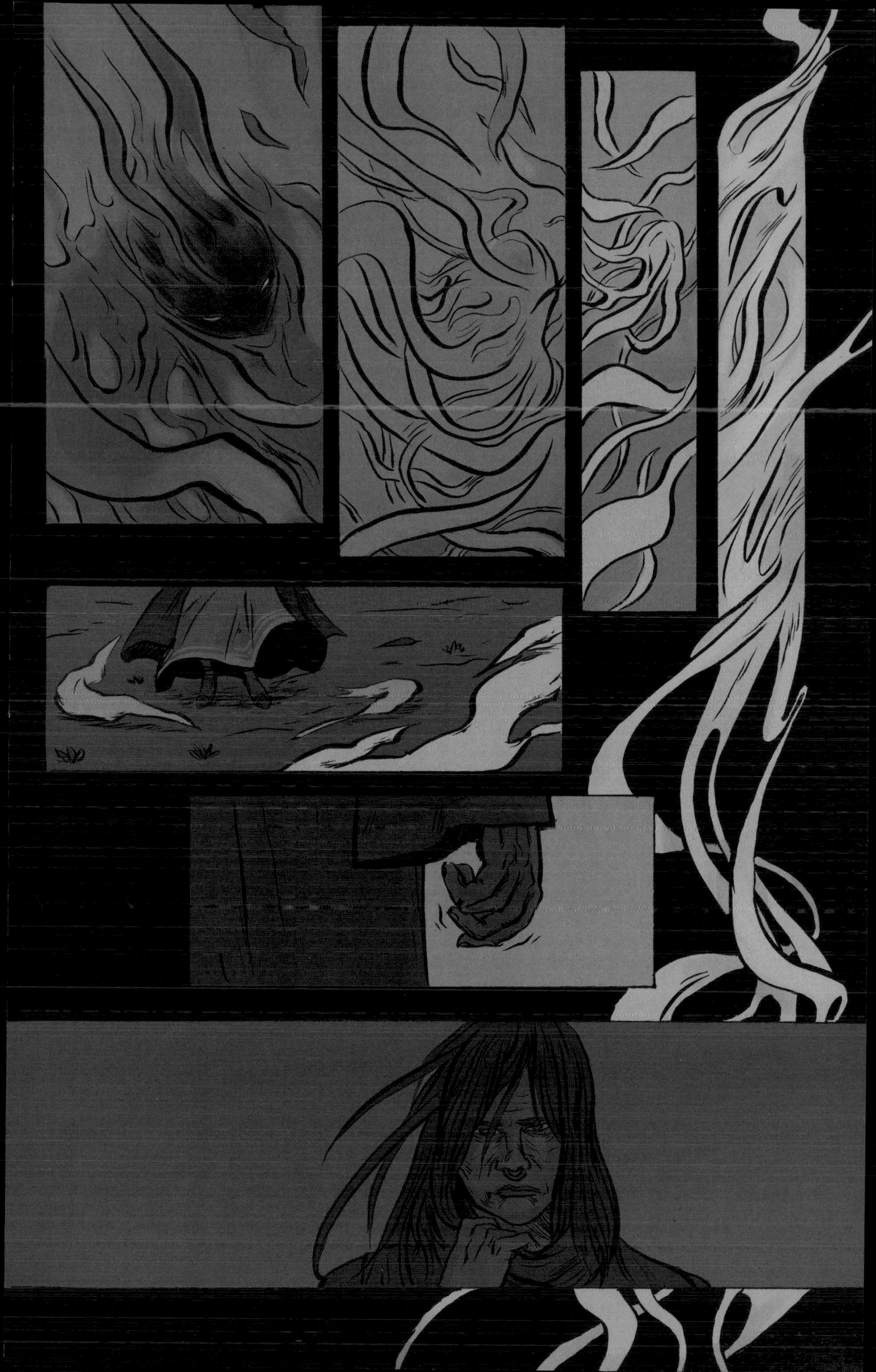

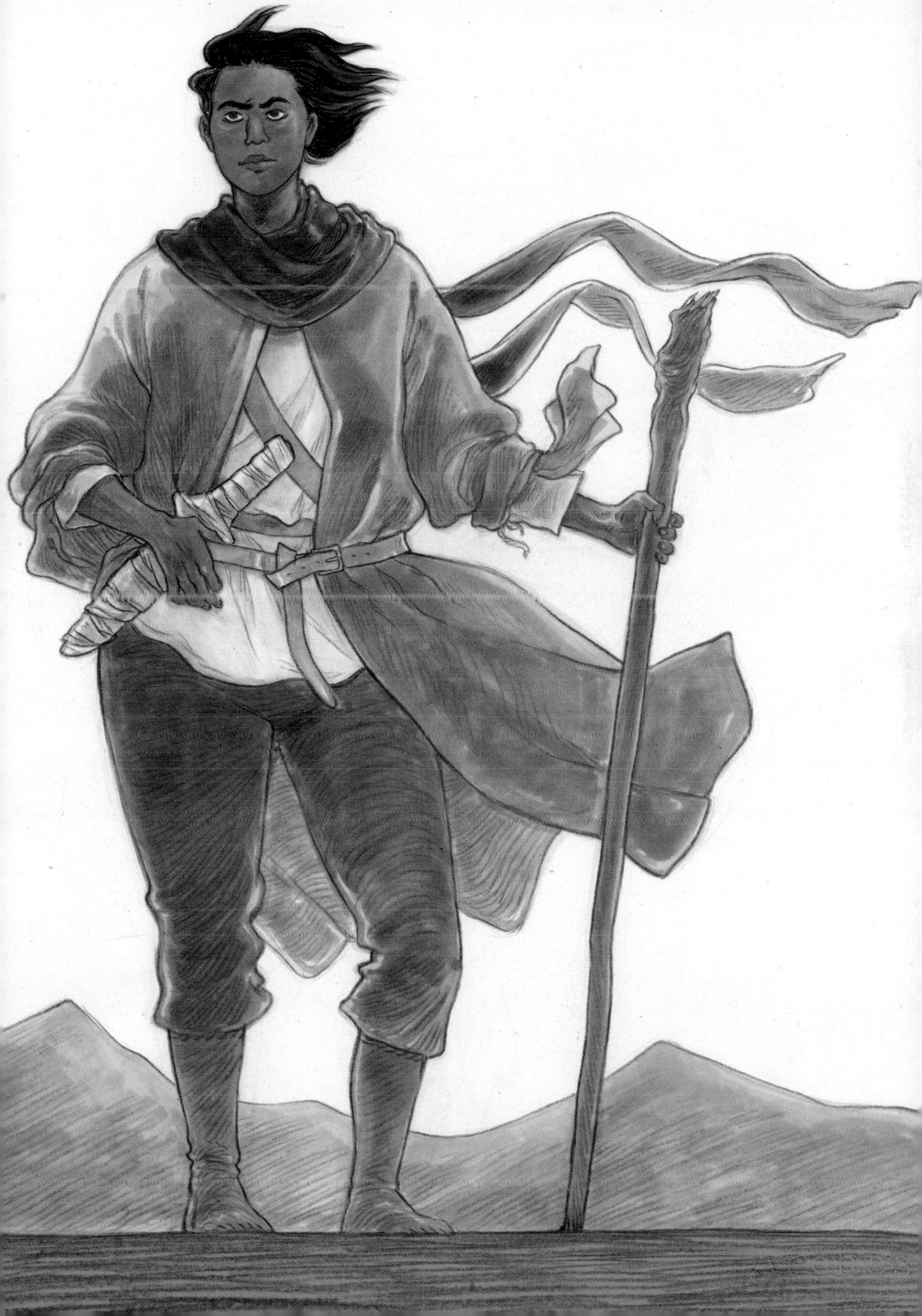

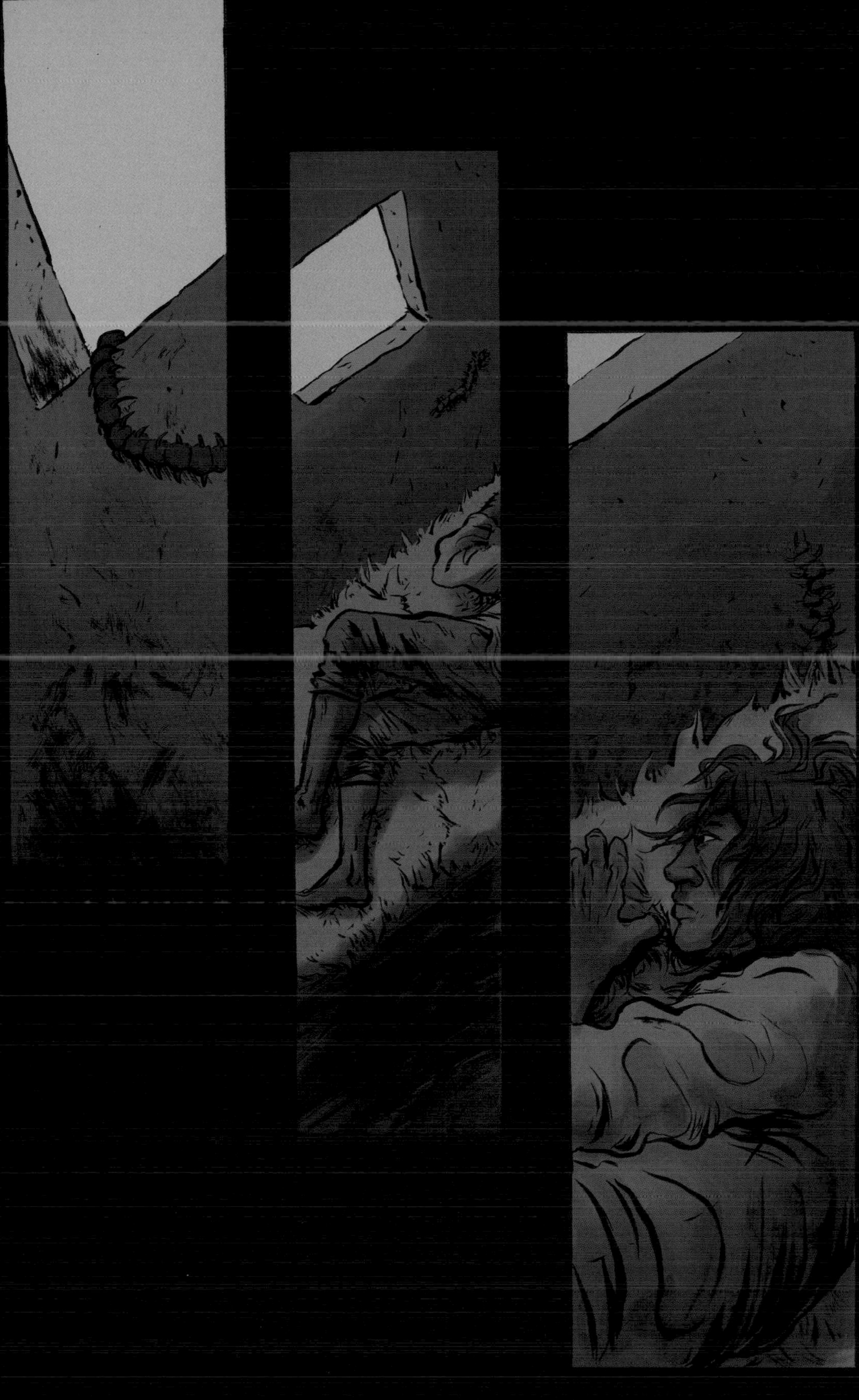

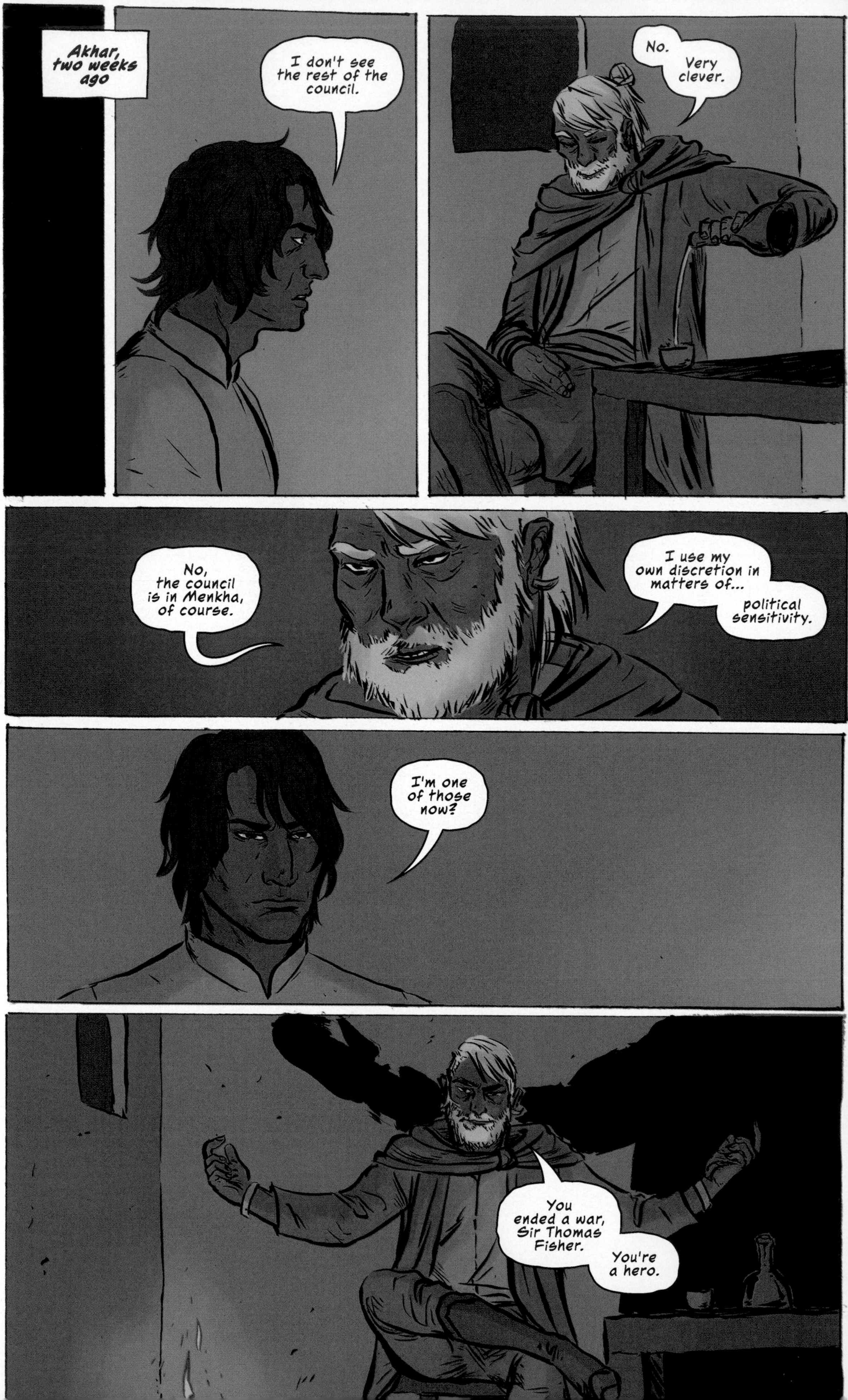
Akhar, two weeks ago
I don't see the rest of the council.
No.
Very clever.
No, the council is in Menkha, of course.
I use my own discretion in matters of...
political sensitivity.
I'm one of those now?
You ended a war, Sir Thomas Fisher.
You're a hero.

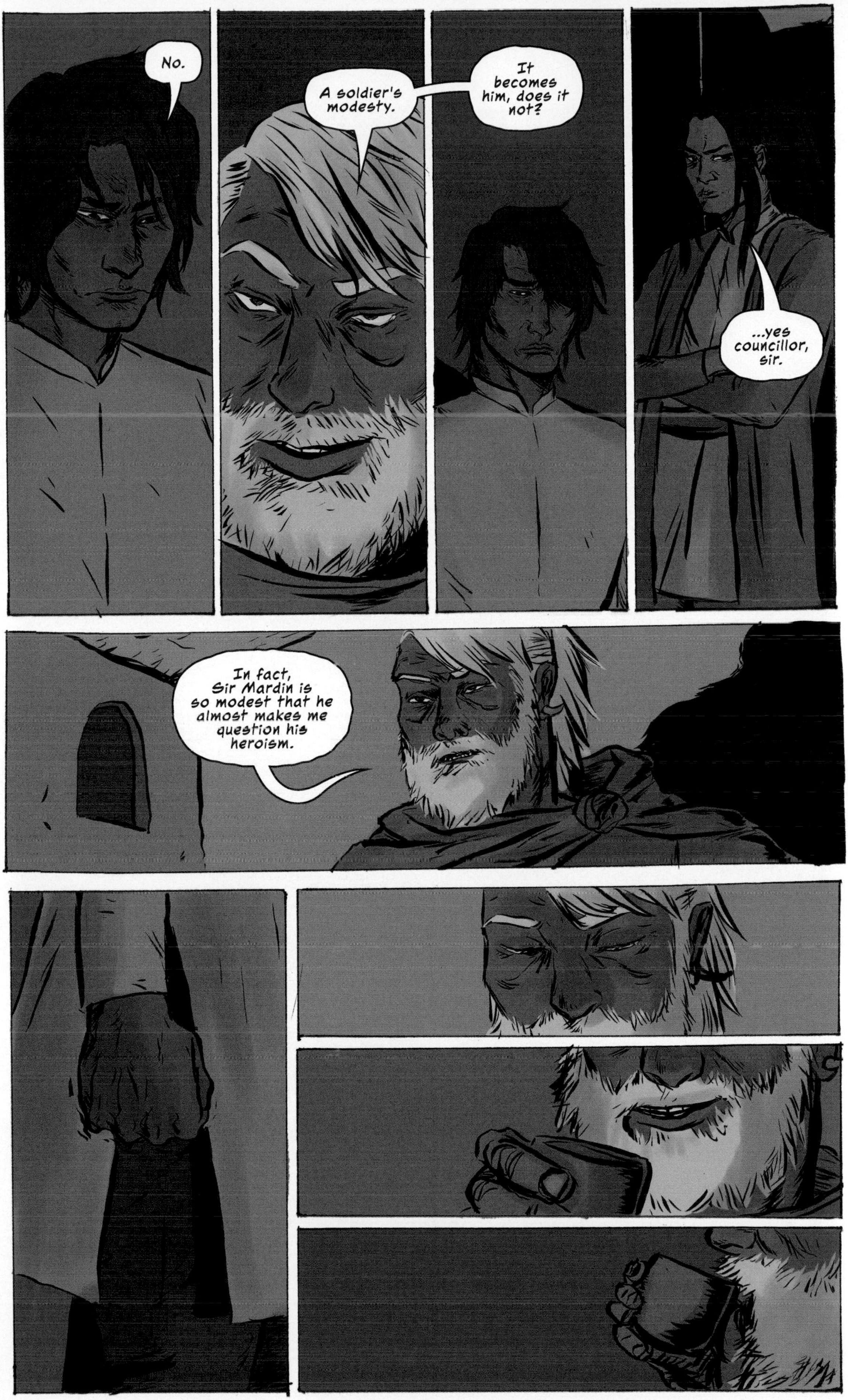
No.
A soldier's modesty.
It becomes him, does it not?
...yes councillor, sir.
In fact, Sir Mardin is so modest that he almost makes me question his heroism.

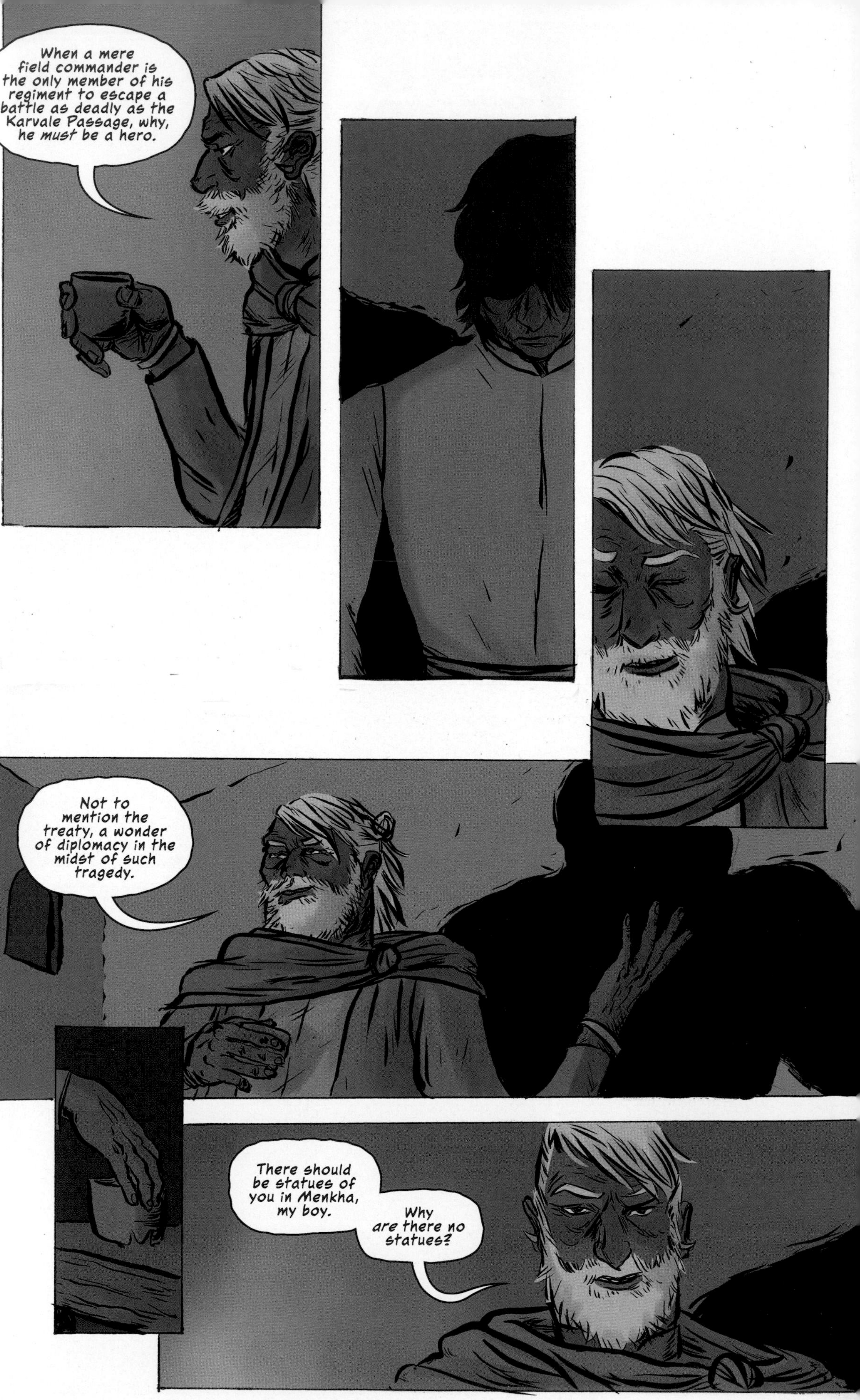
When a mere field commander is the only member of his regiment to escape a battle as deadly as the Karvale Passage, why, he *must* be a hero.
Not to mention the treaty, a wonder of diplomacy in the midst of such tragedy.
There should be statues of you in Menkha, my boy.
Why are there no statues?

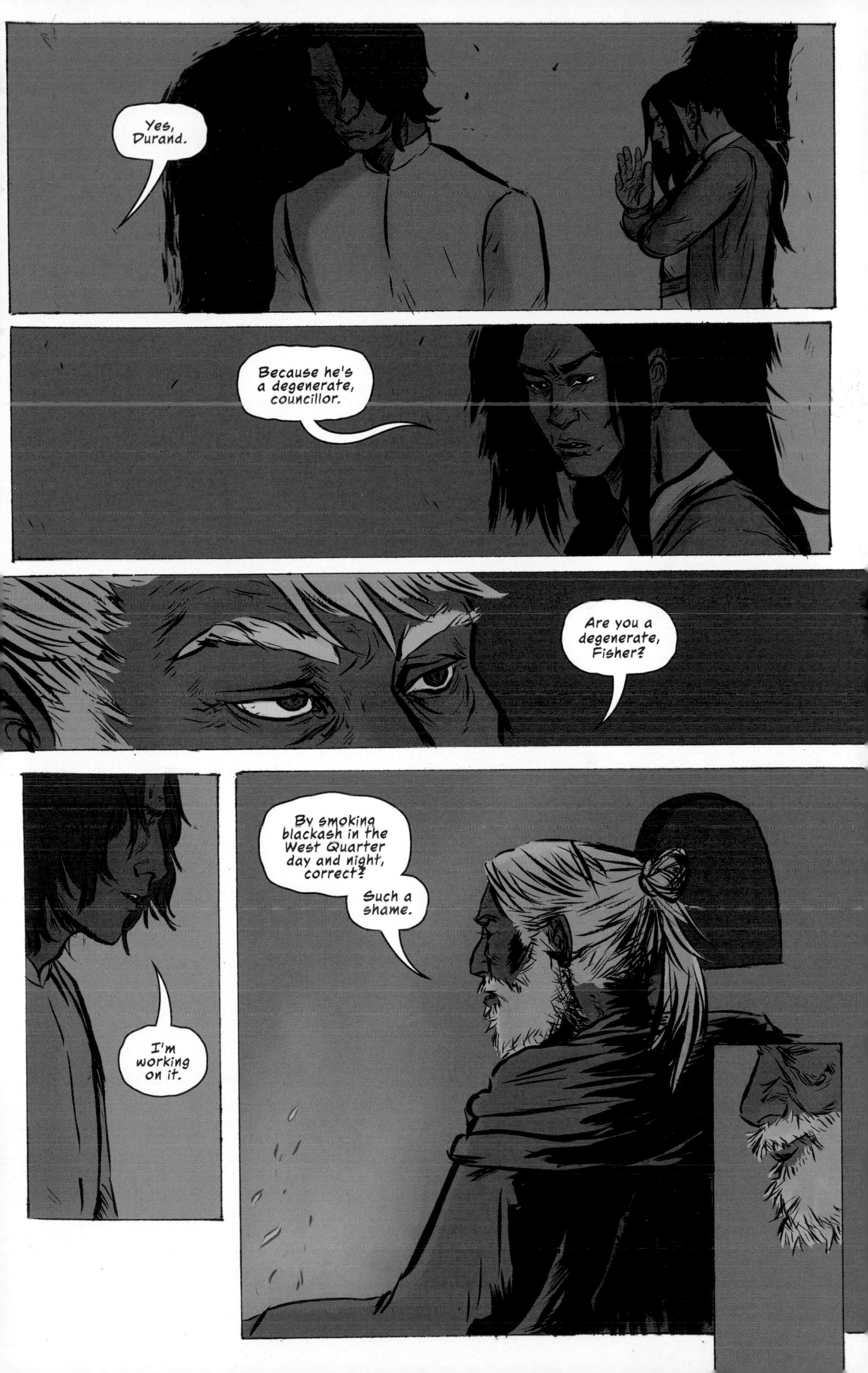
Yes, Durand.
Because he's a degenerate, councillor.
Are you a degenerate, Fisher?
I'm working on it.
By smoking blackash in the West Quarter day and night, correct?
Such a shame.

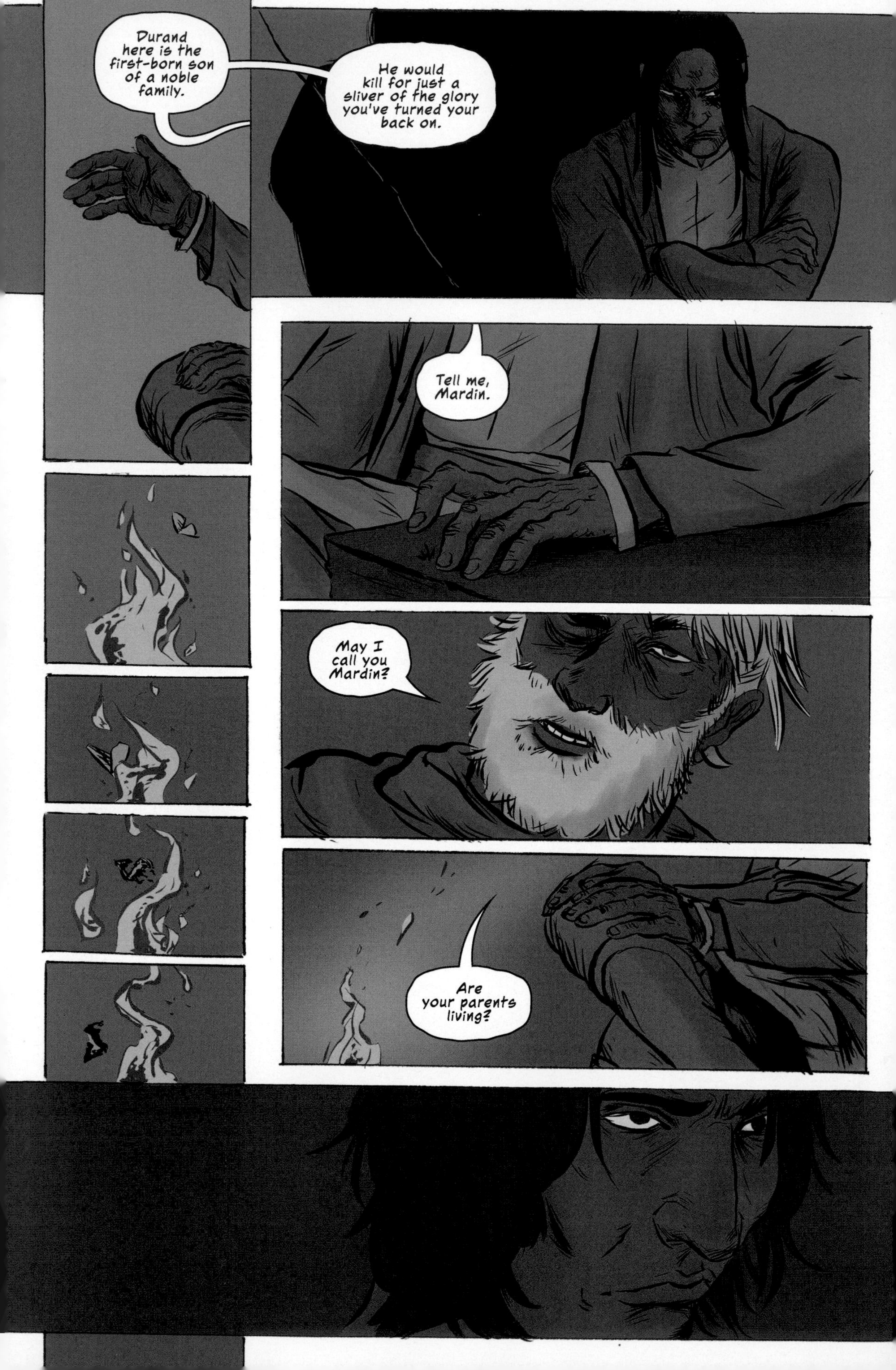
Durand here is the first-born son of a noble family.
He would kill for just a sliver of the glory you've turned your back on.
Tell me, Mardin.
May I call you Mardin?
Are your parents living?

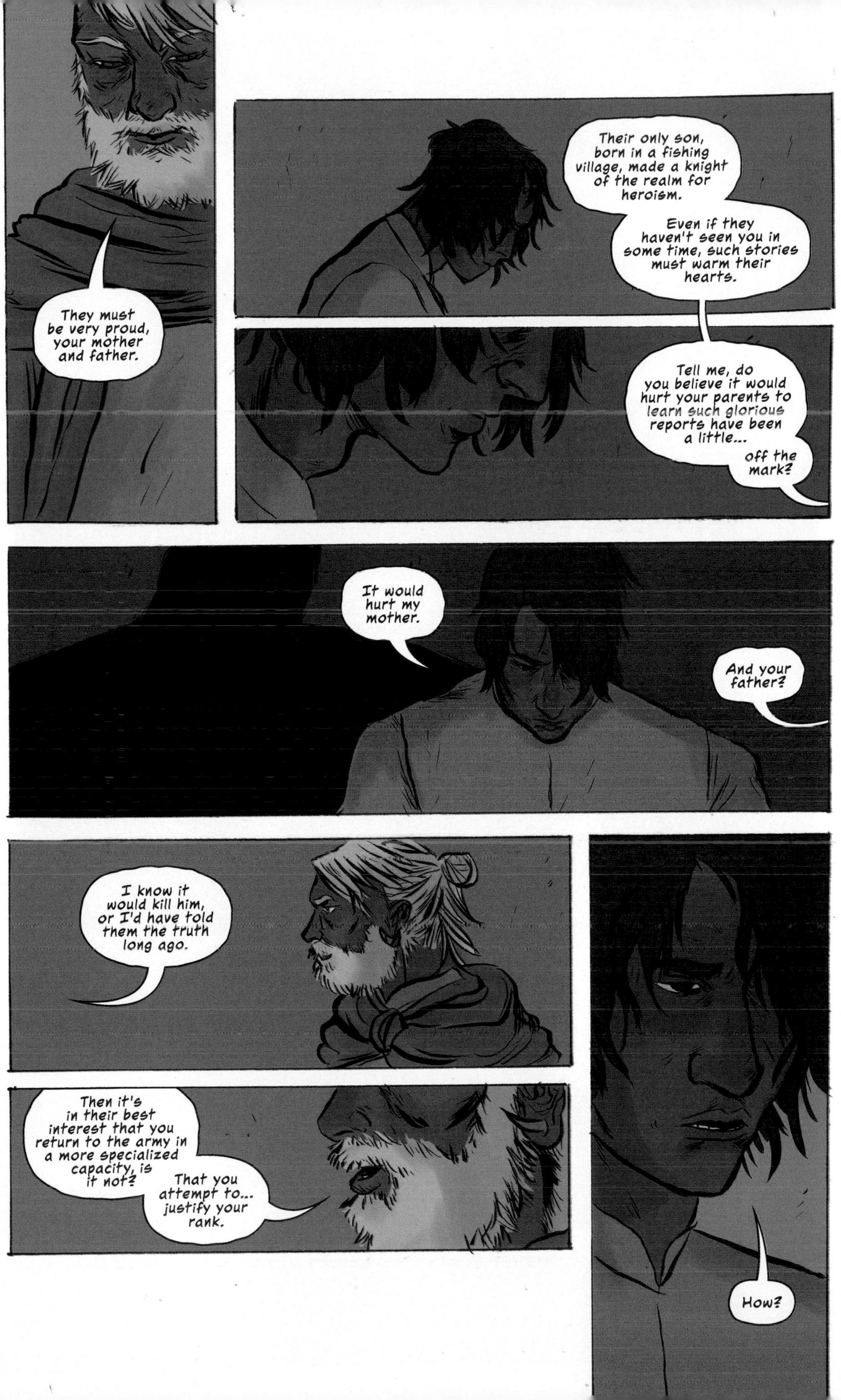
They must be very proud, your mother and father.
Their only son, born in a fishing village, made a knight of the realm for heroism.
Even if they haven't seen you in some time, such stories must warm their hearts.
Tell me, do you believe it would hurt your parents to learn such glorious reports have been a little...
off the mark?
It would hurt my mother.
And your father?
I know it would kill him, or I'd have told them the truth long ago.
Then it's in their best interest that you return to the army in a more specialized capacity, is it not?
That you attempt to... justify your rank.
How?

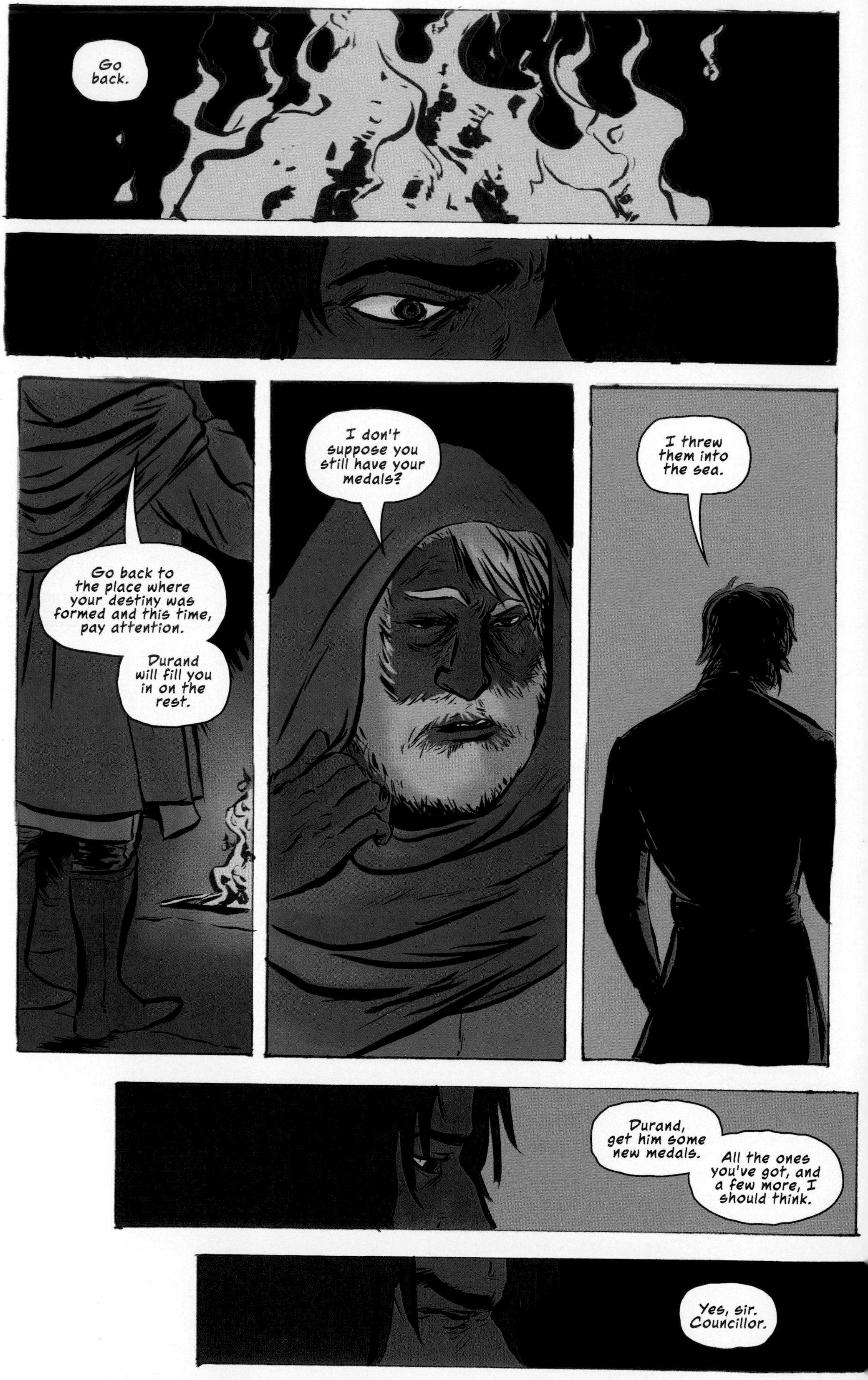

Go back.
Go back to the place where your destiny was formed and this time, pay attention.
Durand will fill you in on the rest.
I don't suppose you still have your medals?
I threw them into the sea.
Durand, get him some new medals.
All the ones you've got, and a few more, I should think.
Yes, sir. Councillor.

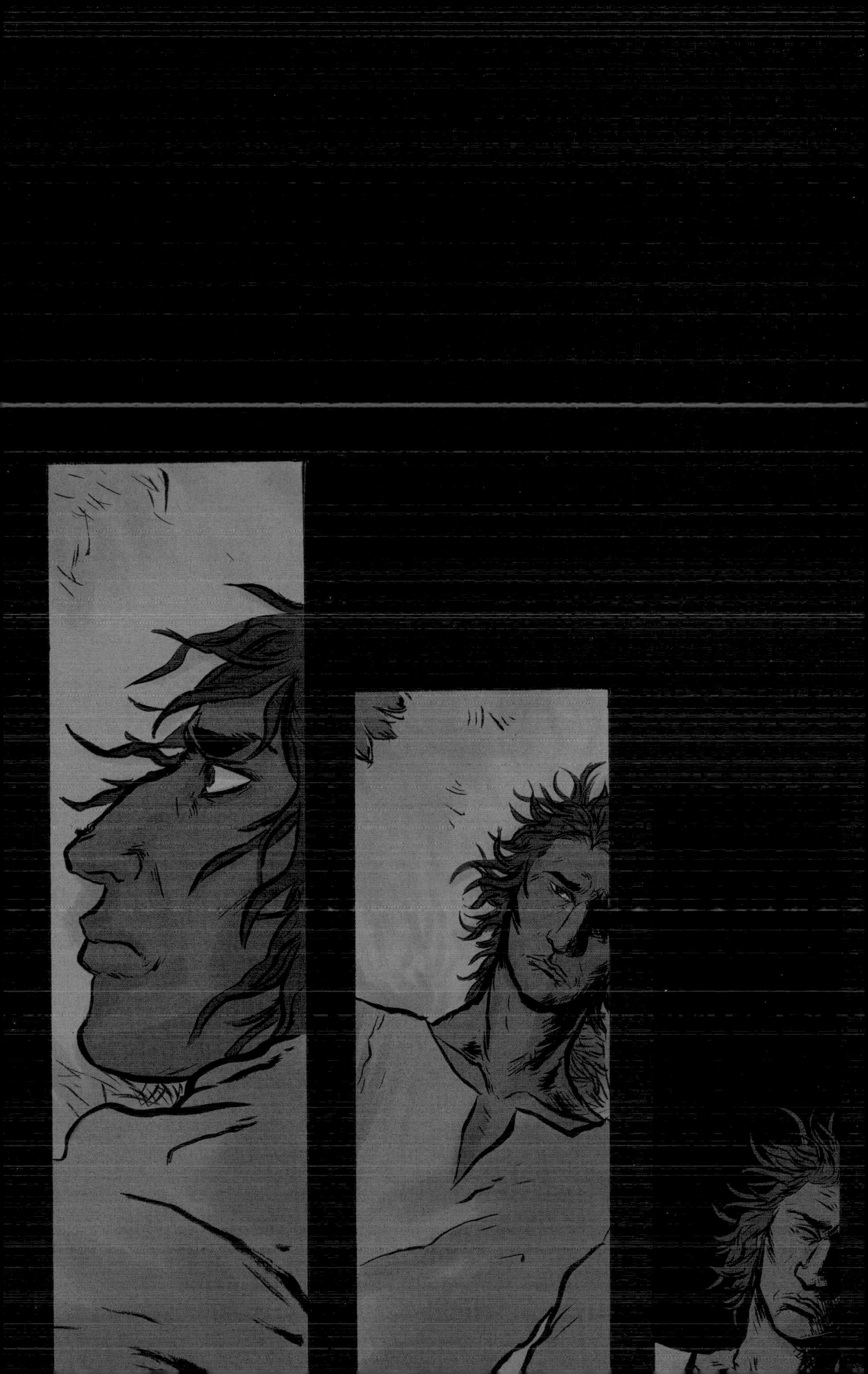

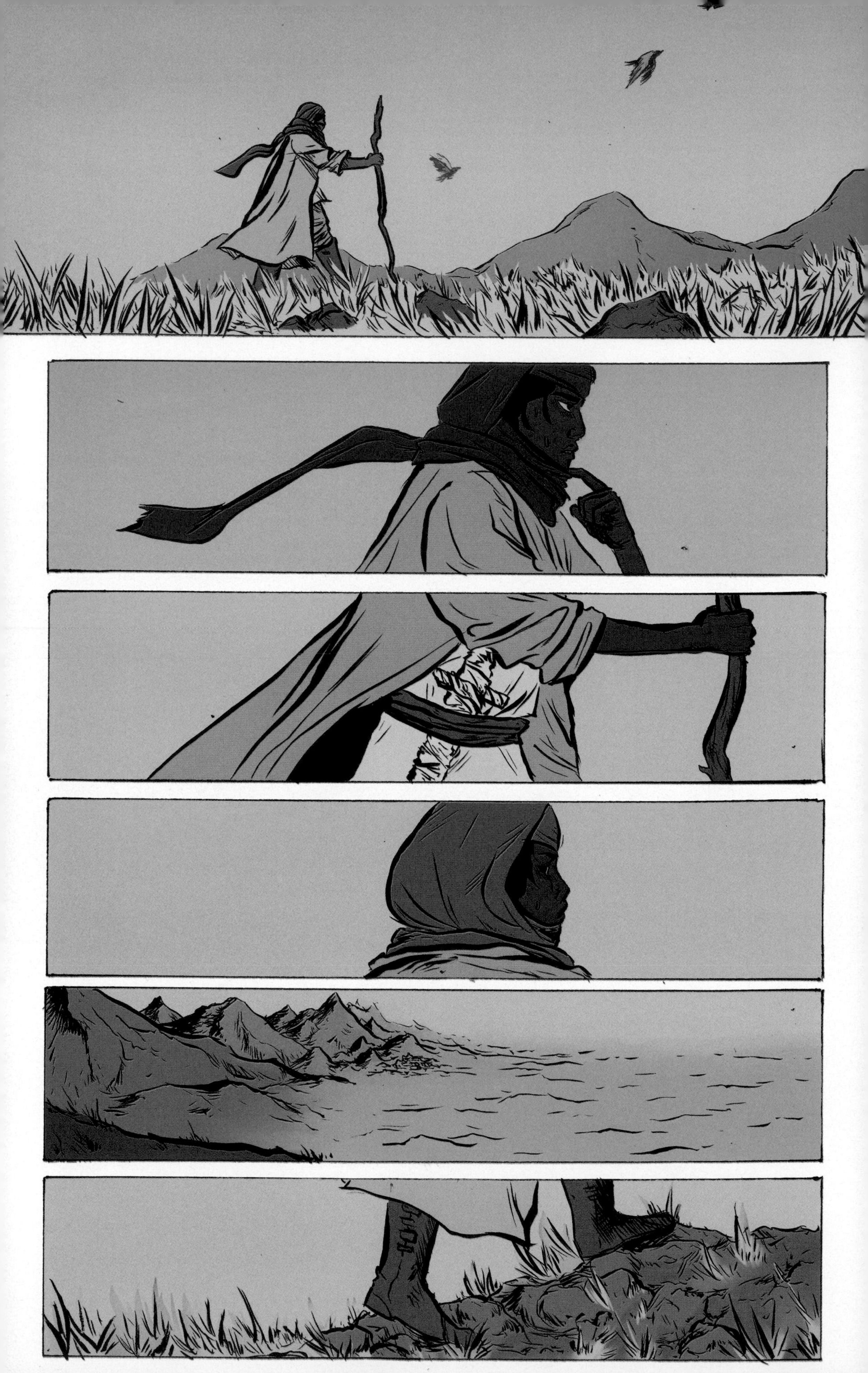

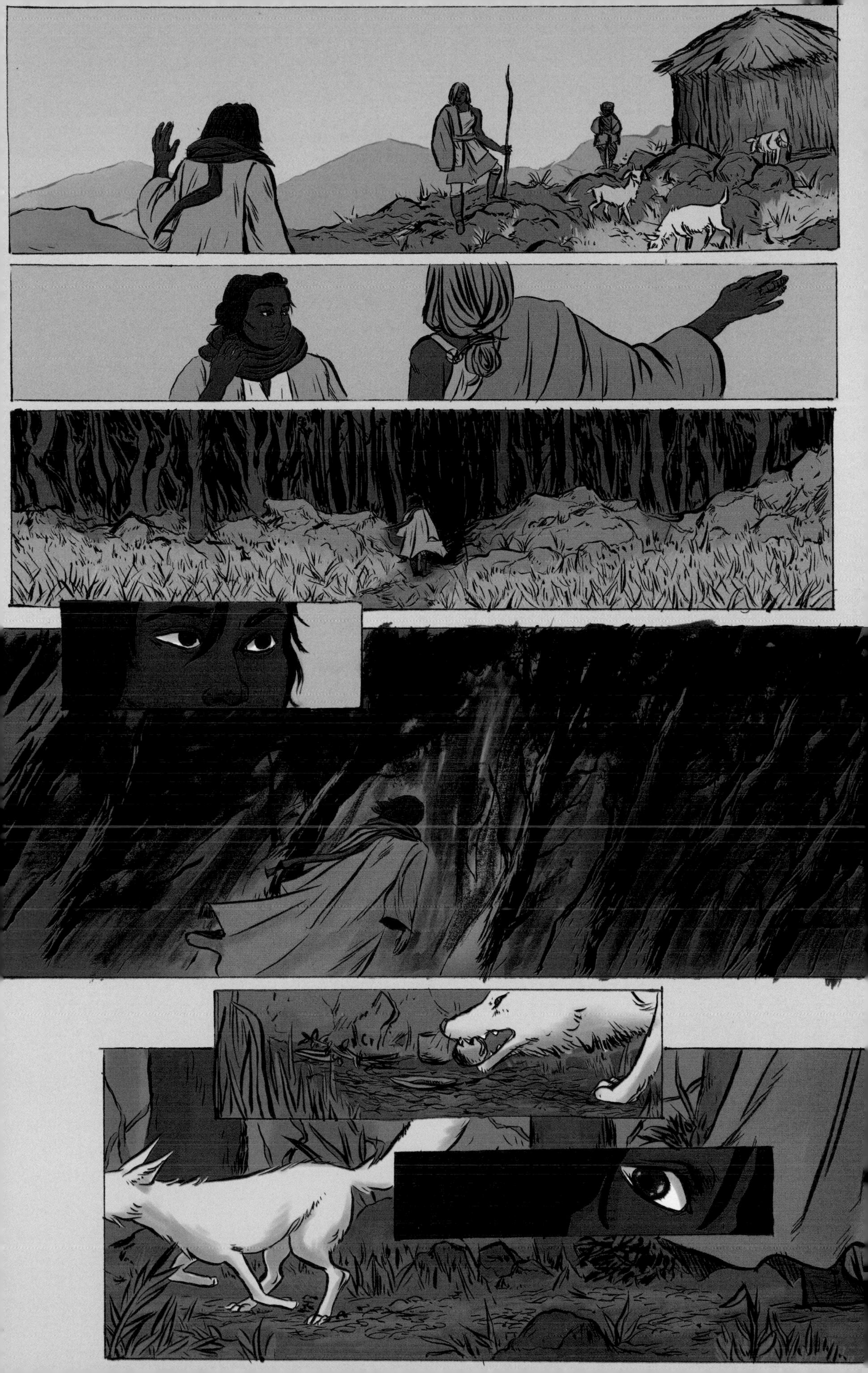

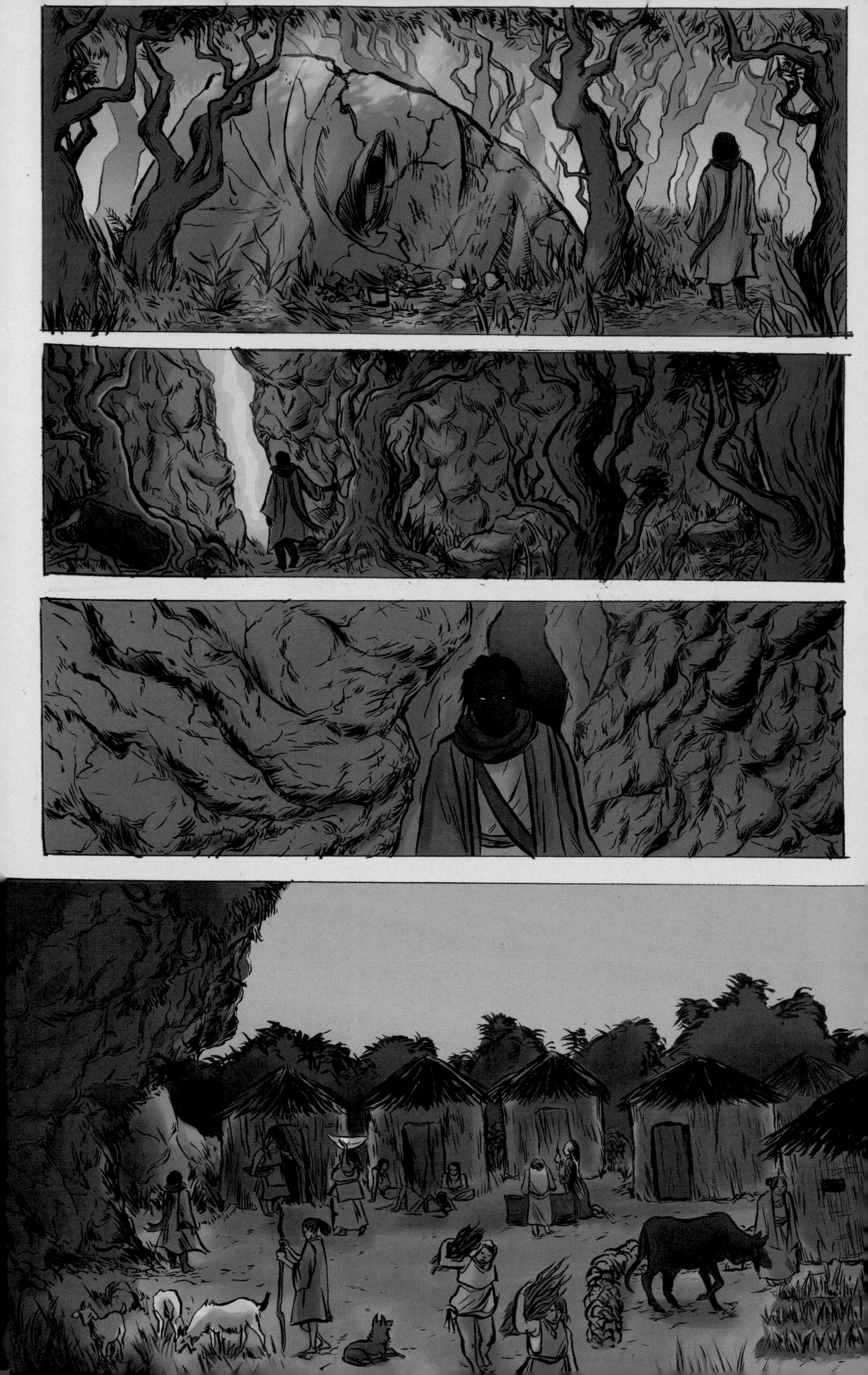

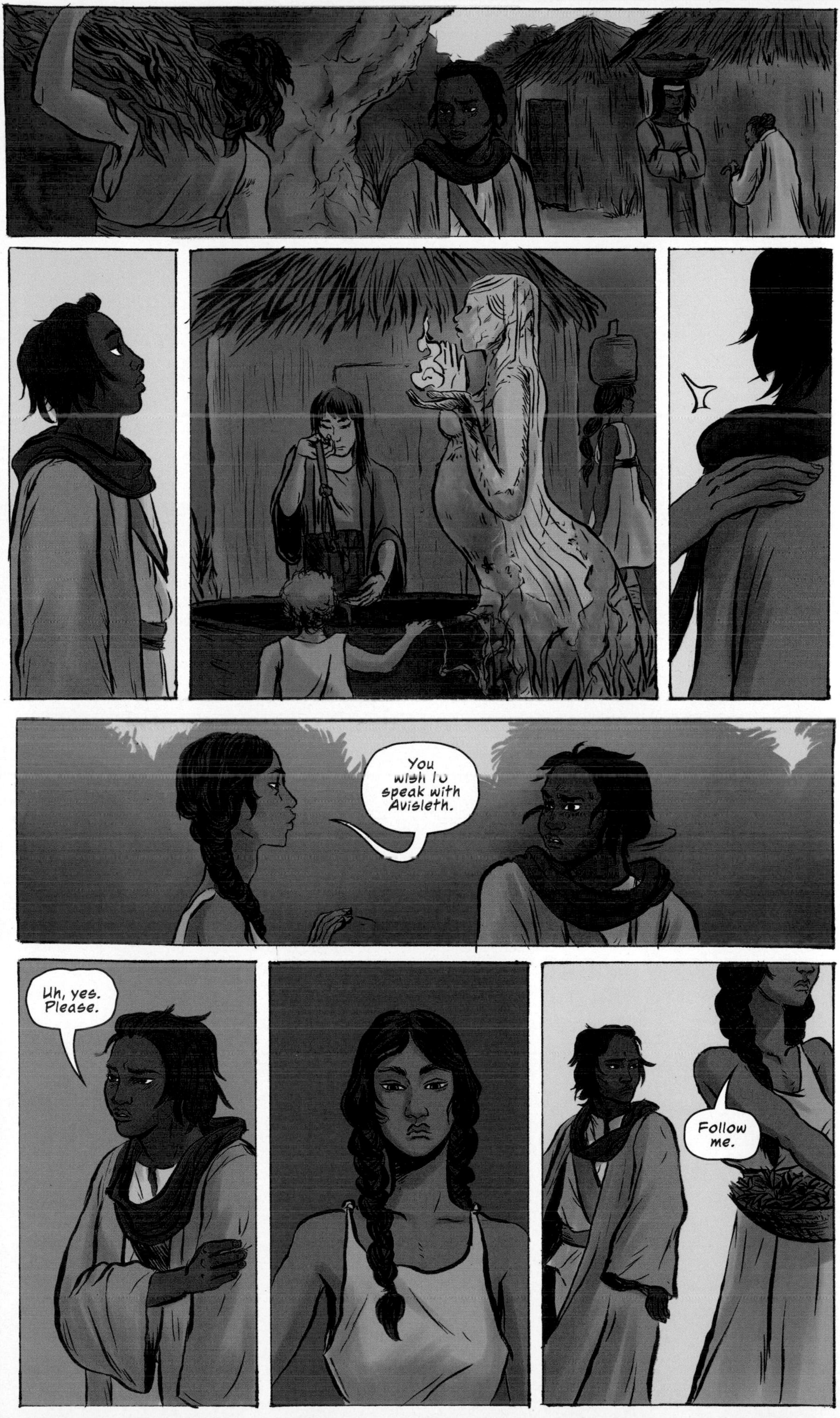
You wish to speak with Avisleth.
Uh, yes. Please.
Follow me.

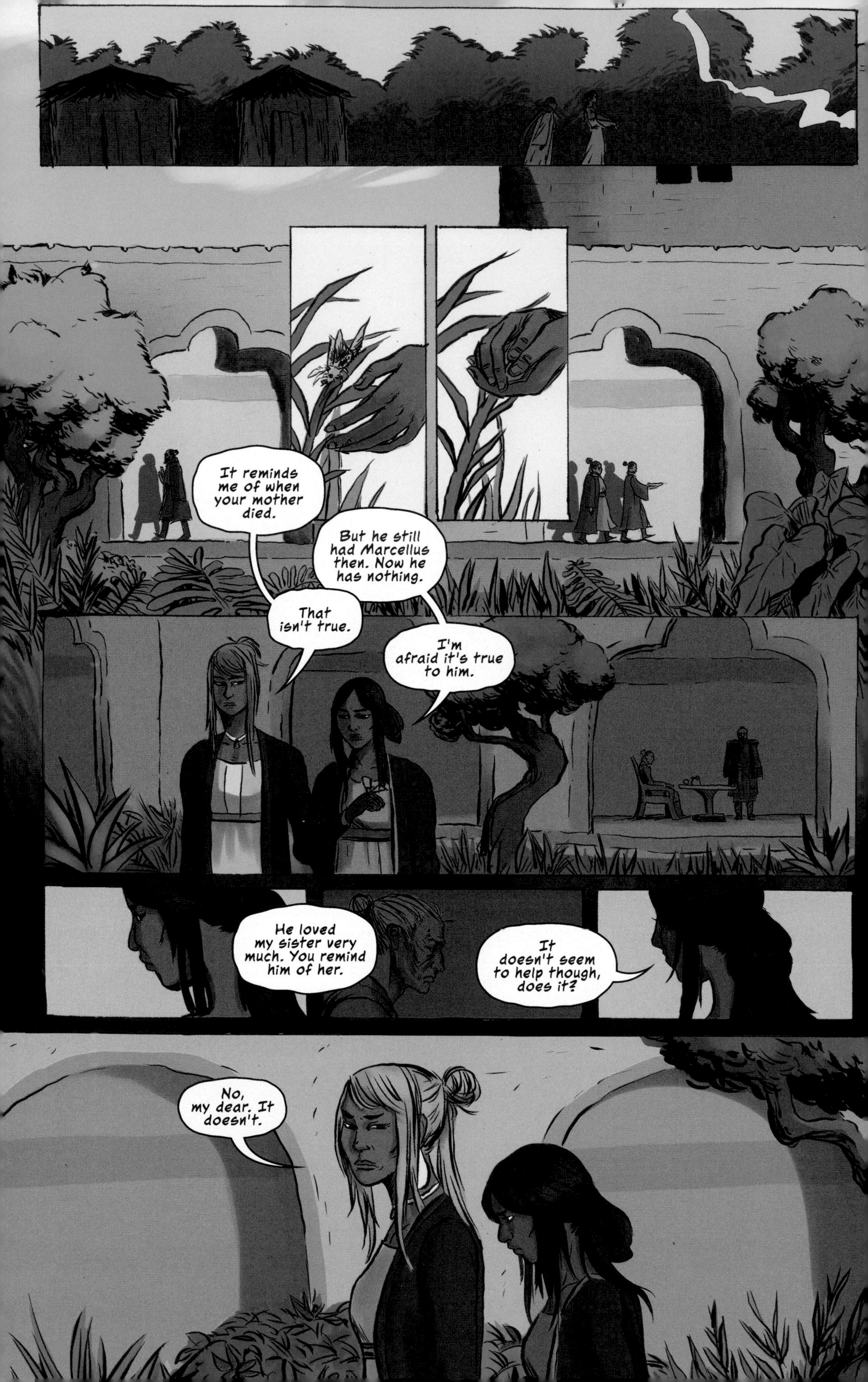
It reminds me of when your mother died.
But he still had Marcellus then. Now he has nothing.
That isn't true.
I'm afraid it's true to him.
He loved my sister very much. You remind him of her.
It doesn't seem to help though, does it?
No, my dear. It doesn't.

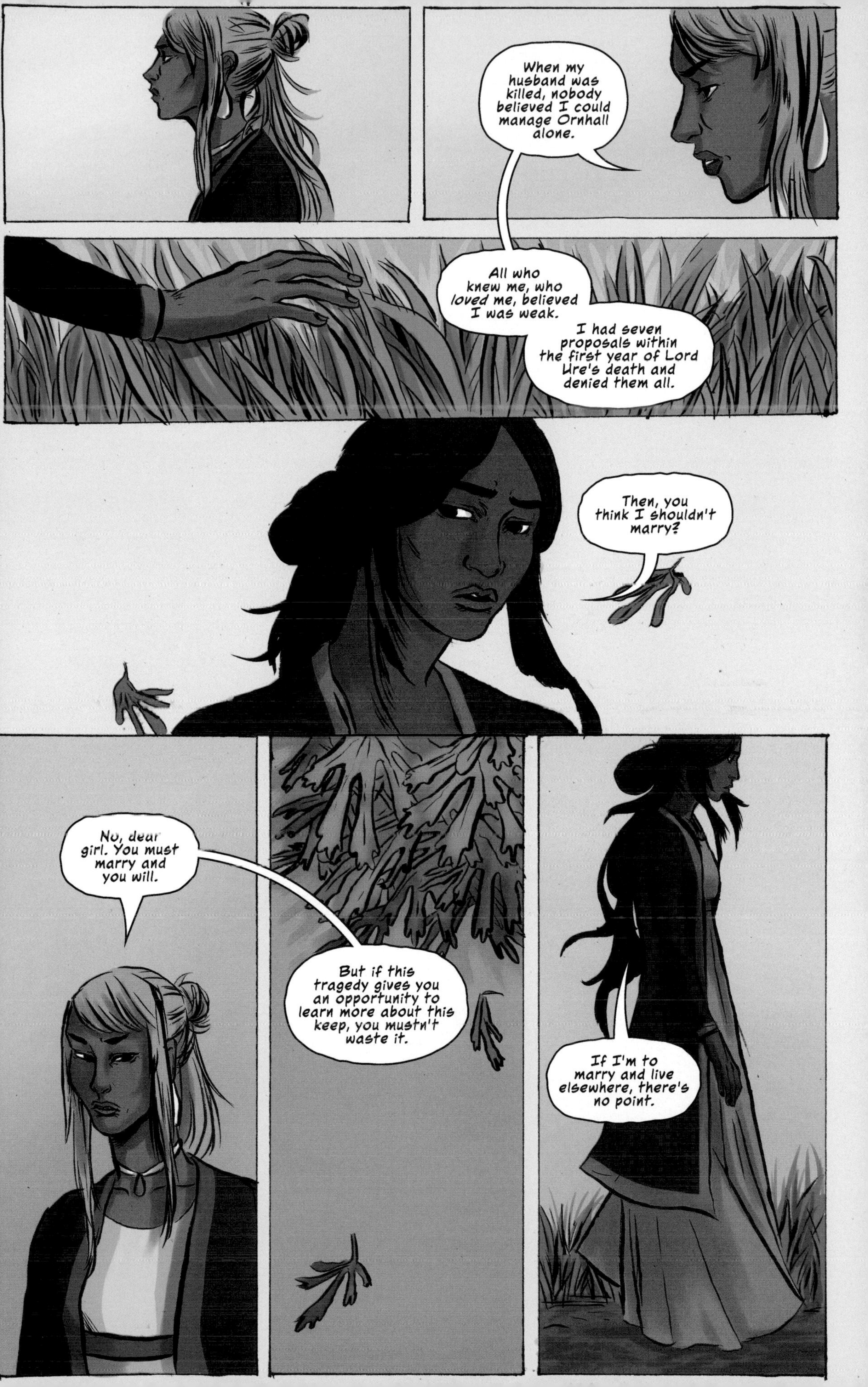
When my husband was killed, nobody believed I could manage Ornhall alone.
All who knew me, who loved me, believed I was weak.
I had seven proposals within the first year of Lord Ure's death and denied them all.
Then, you think I shouldn't marry?
No, dear girl. You must marry and you will.
But if this tragedy gives you an opportunity to learn more about this keep, you mustn't waste it.
If I'm to marry and live elsewhere, there's no point.

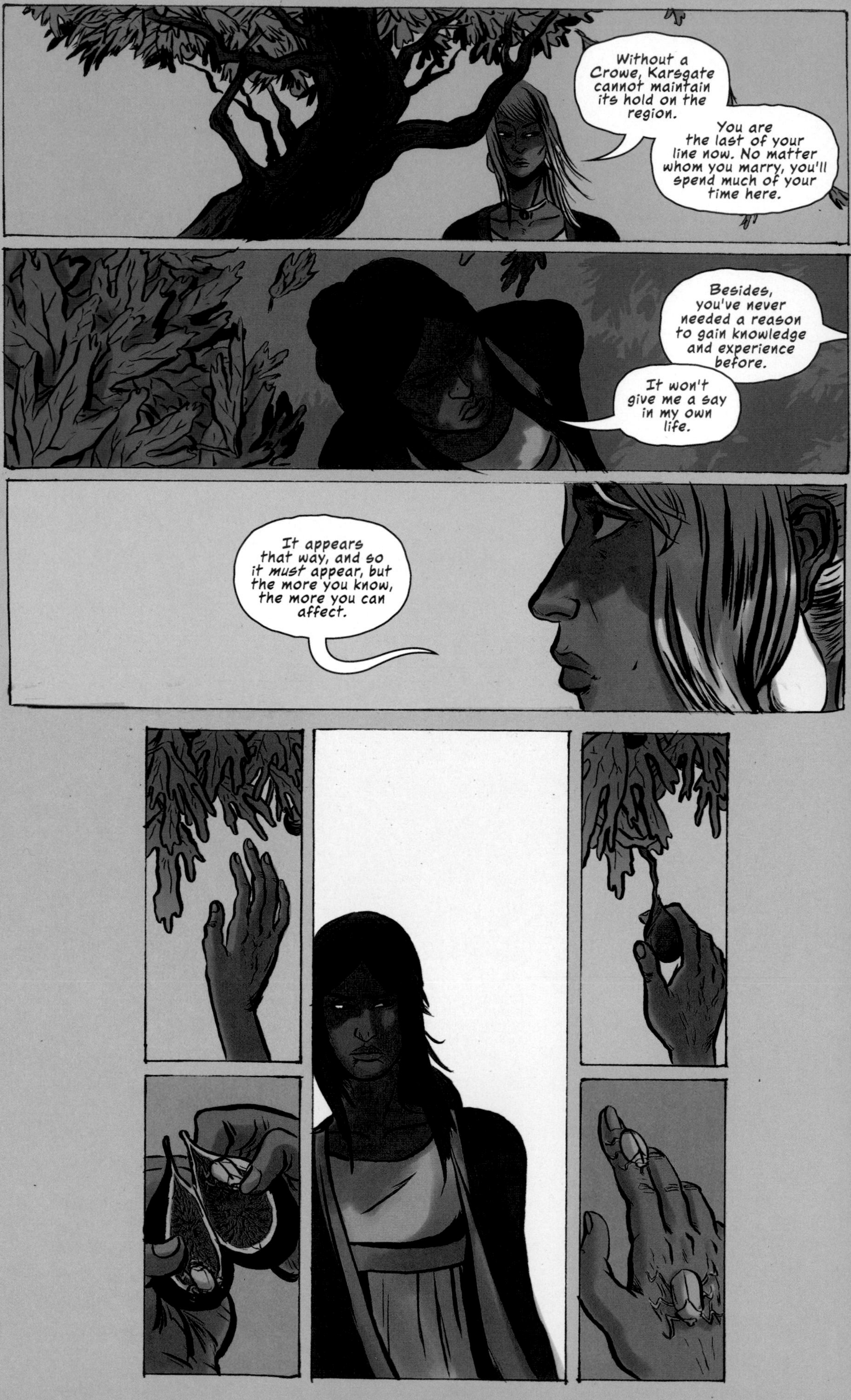
Without a Crowe, Karsgate cannot maintain its hold on the region.
You are the last of your line now. No matter whom you marry, you'll spend much of your time here.
Besides, you've never needed a reason to gain knowledge and experience before.
It won't give me a say in my own life.
It appears that way, and so it *must* appear, but the more you know, the more you can affect.

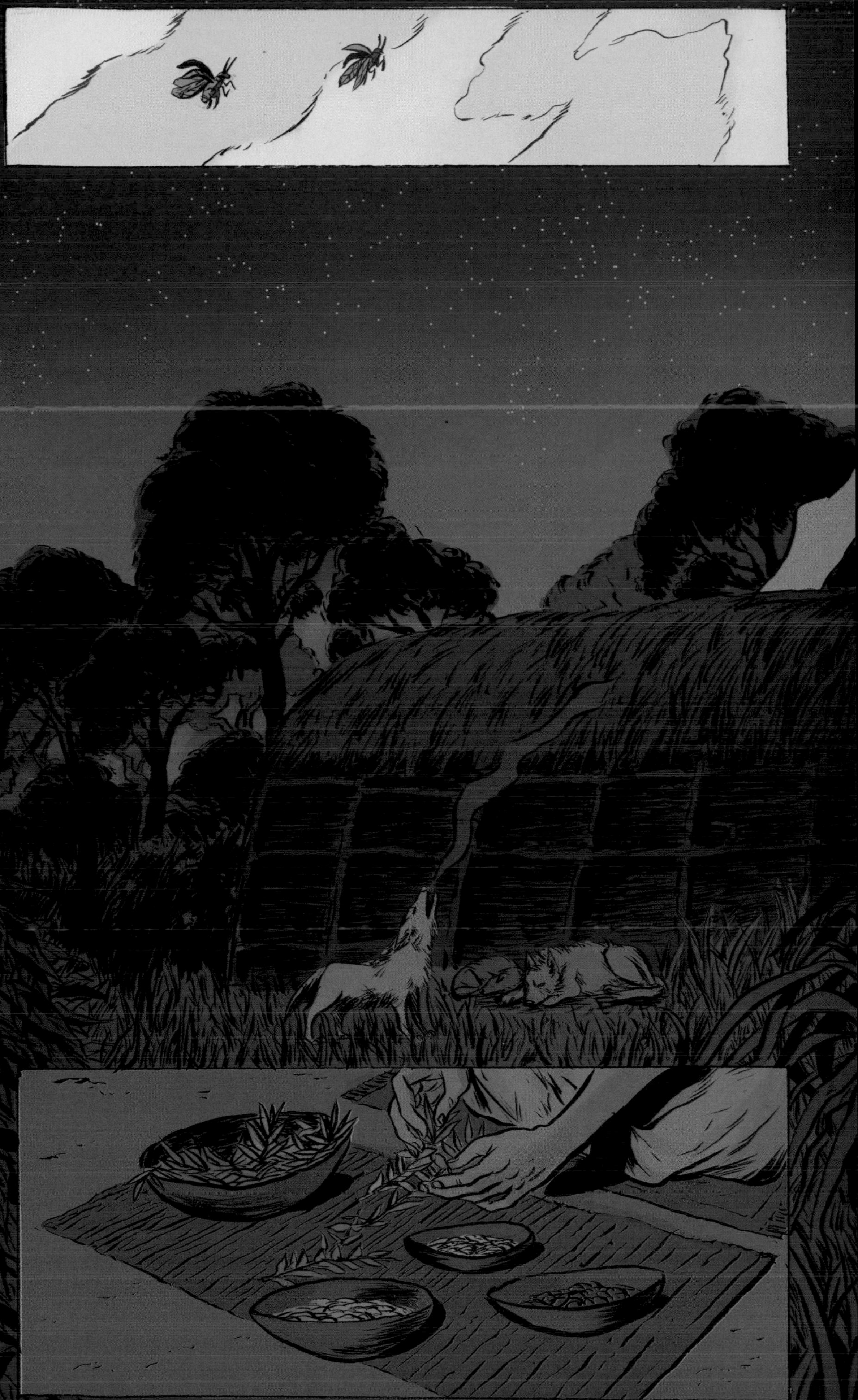

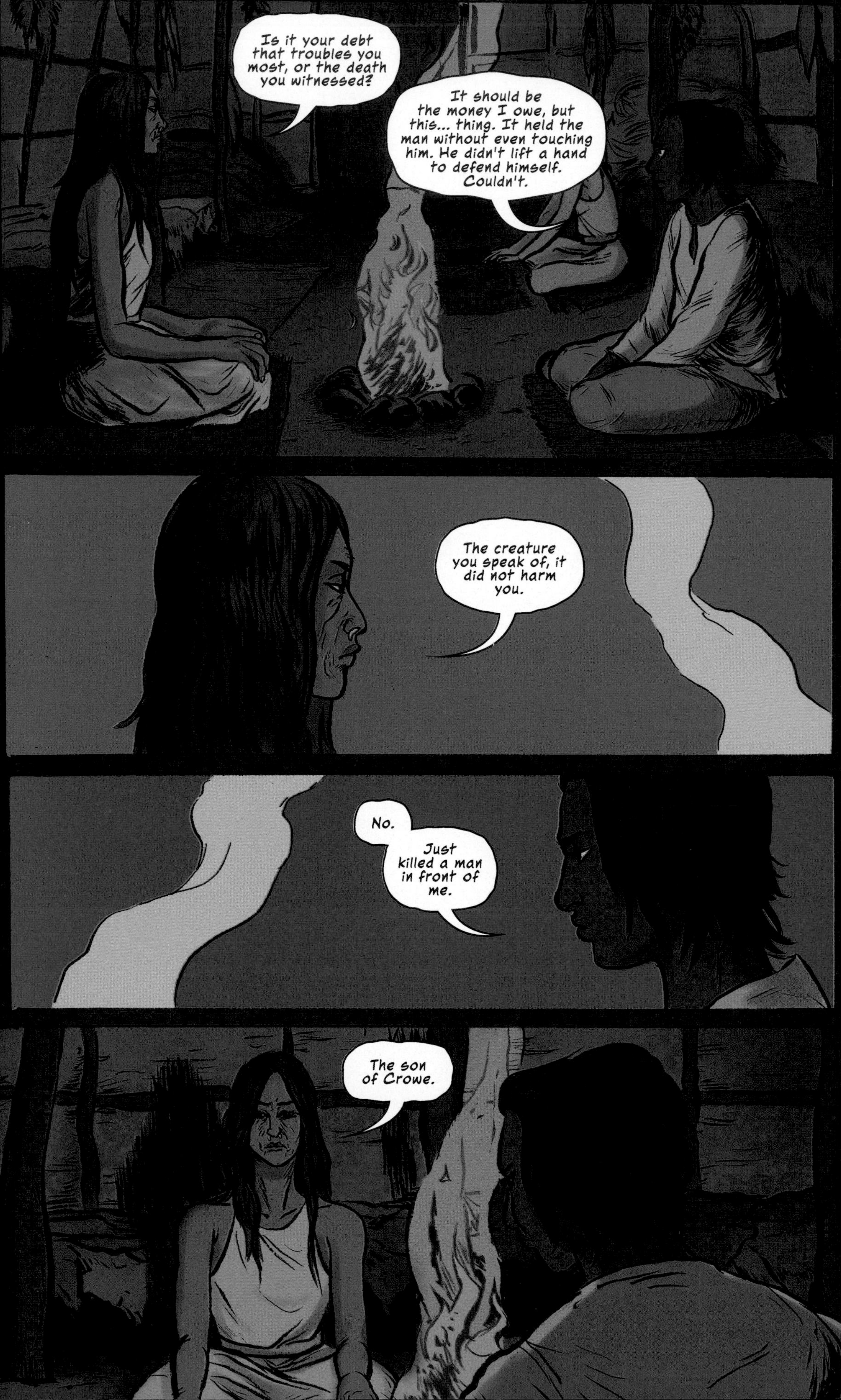
Is it your debt that troubles you most, or the death you witnessed?
It should be the money I owe, but this... thing. It held the man without even touching him. He didn't lift a hand to defend himself. Couldn't.
The creature you speak of, it did not harm you.
No.
Just killed a man in front of me.
The son of Crowe.

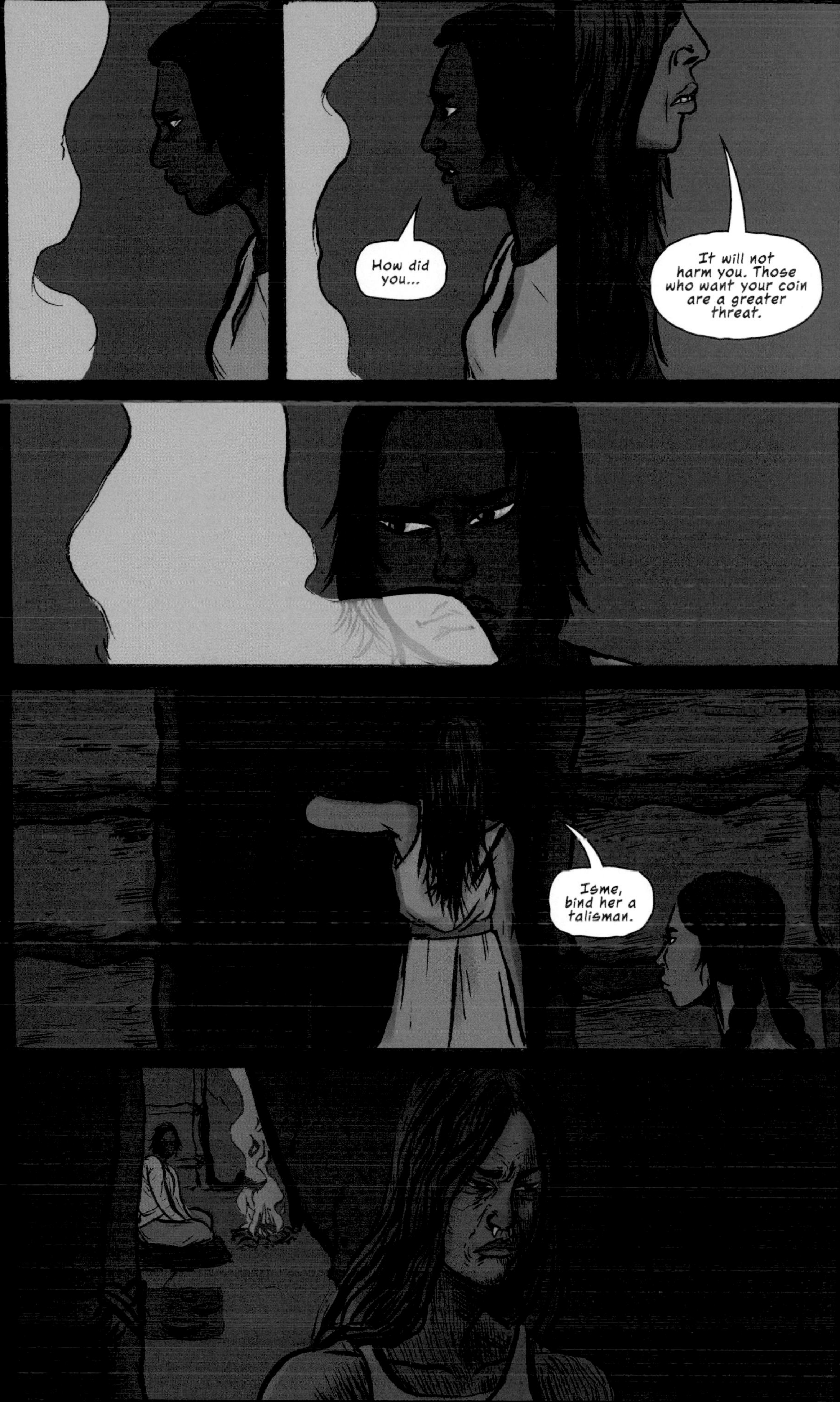
How did you...
It will not harm you. Those who want your coin are a greater threat.
Isme, bind her a talisman.

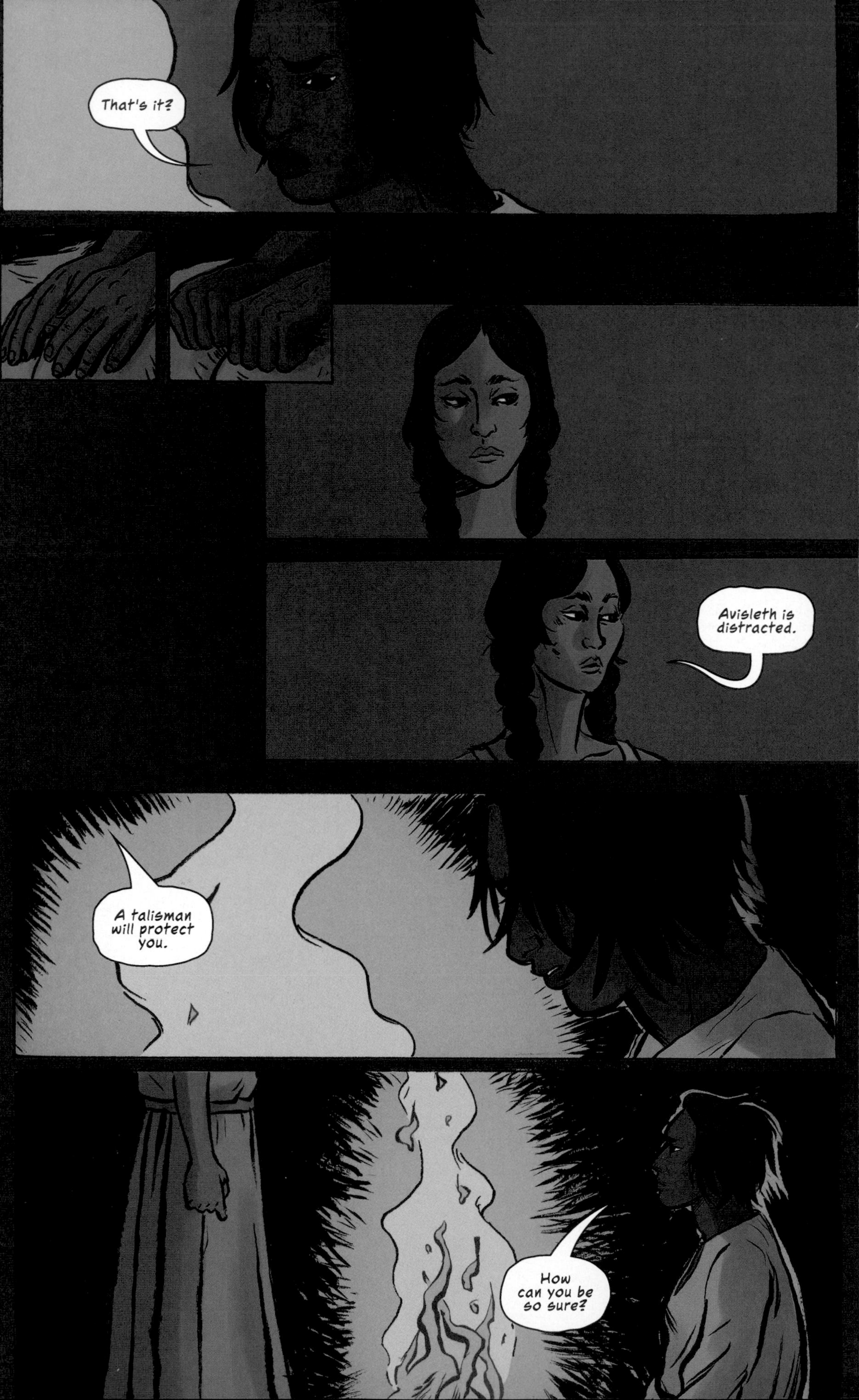
That's it?
Avisleth is distracted.
A talisman will protect you.
How can you be so sure?

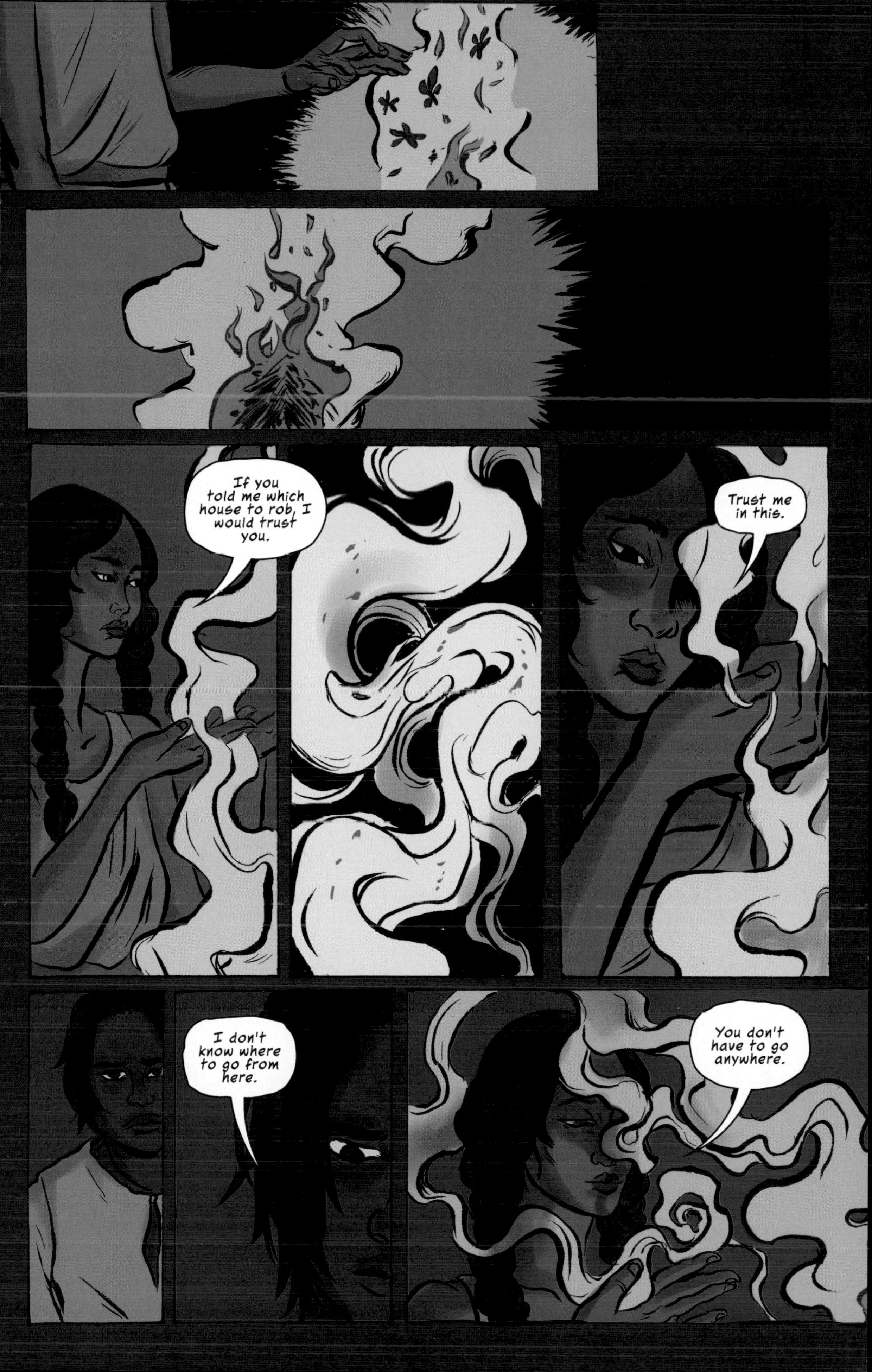
If you told me which house to rob, I would trust you.
Trust me in this.
I don't know where to go from here.
You don't have to go anywhere.

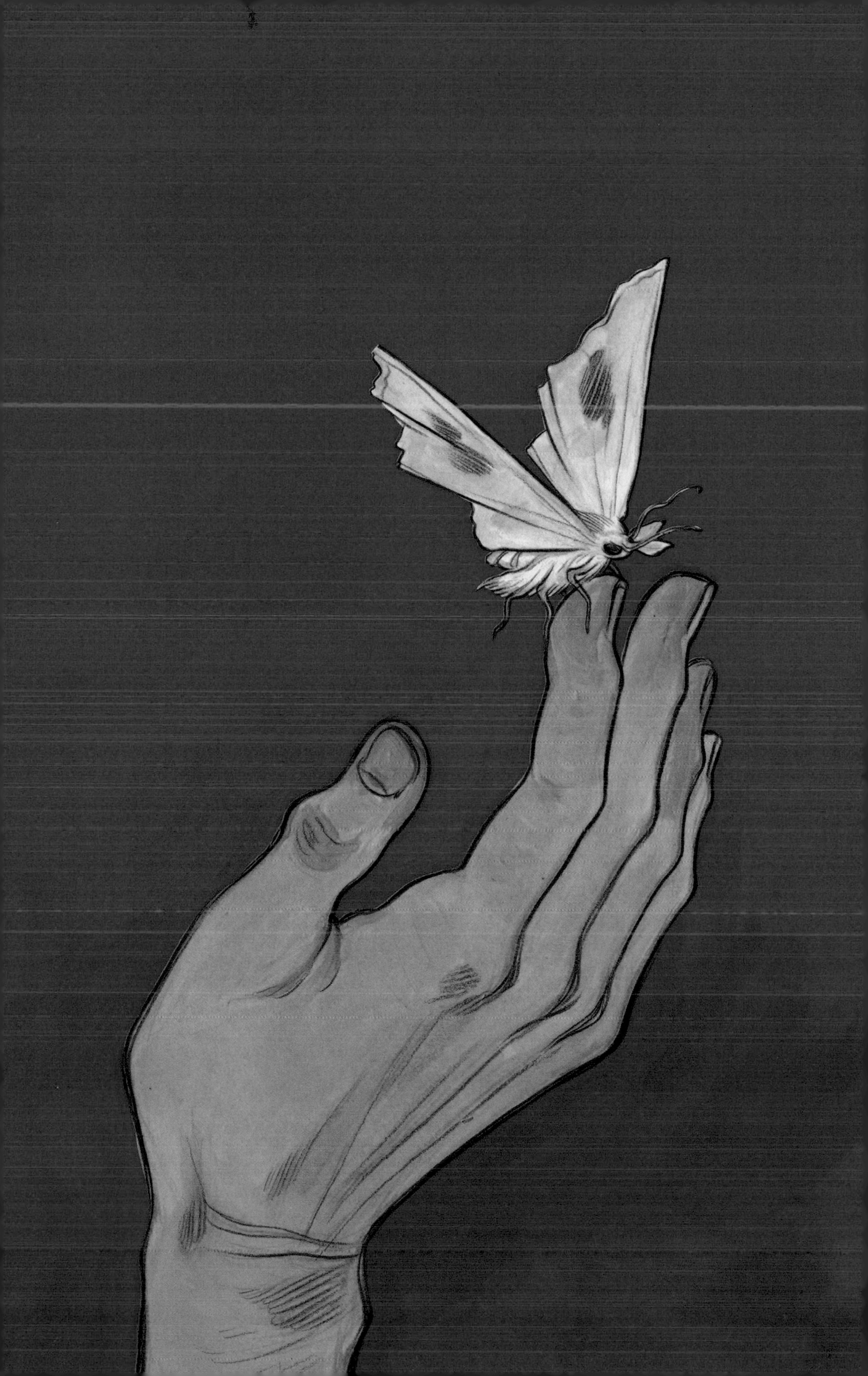

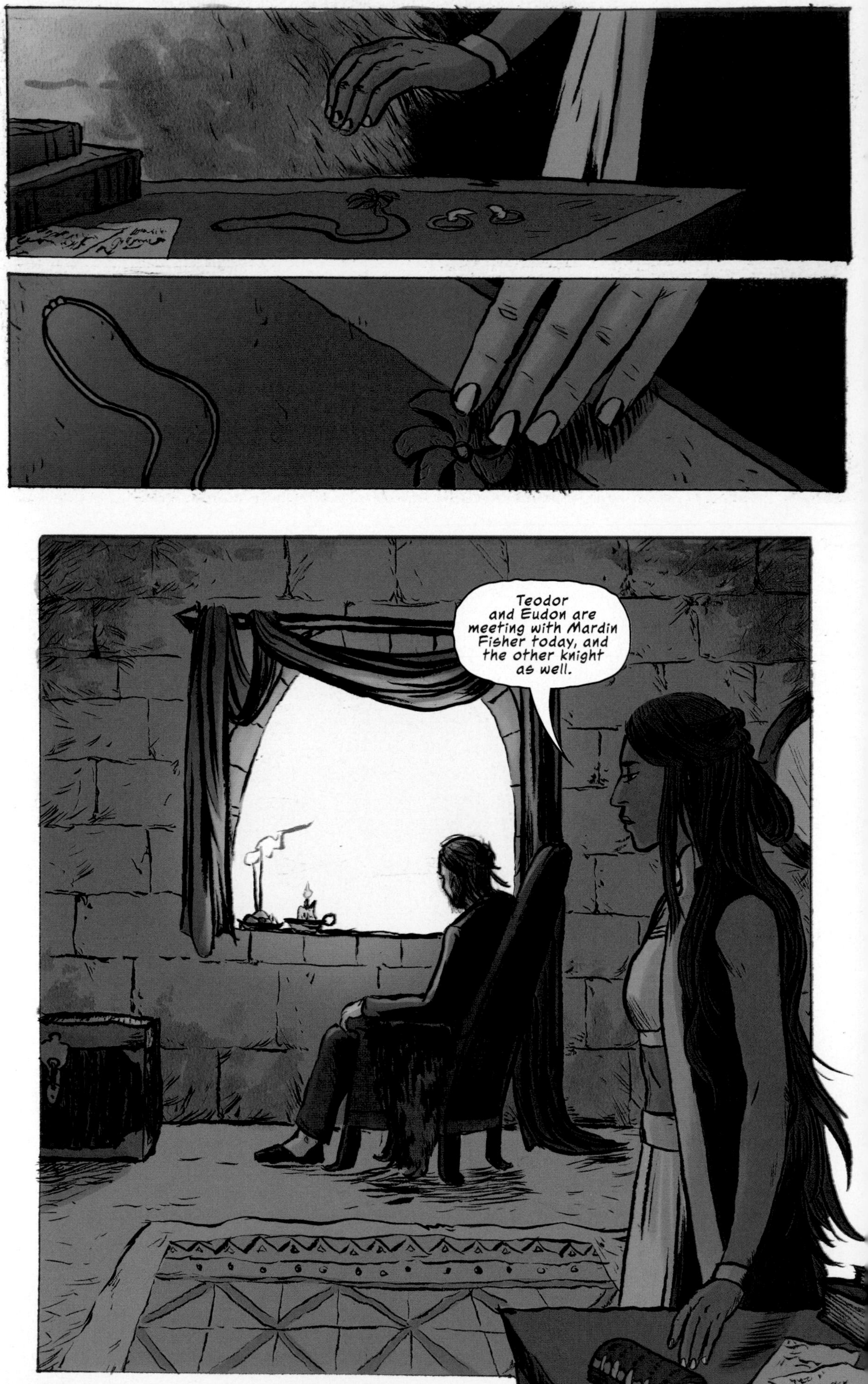
Teodor and Eudon are meeting with Mardin Fisher today, and the other knight as well.

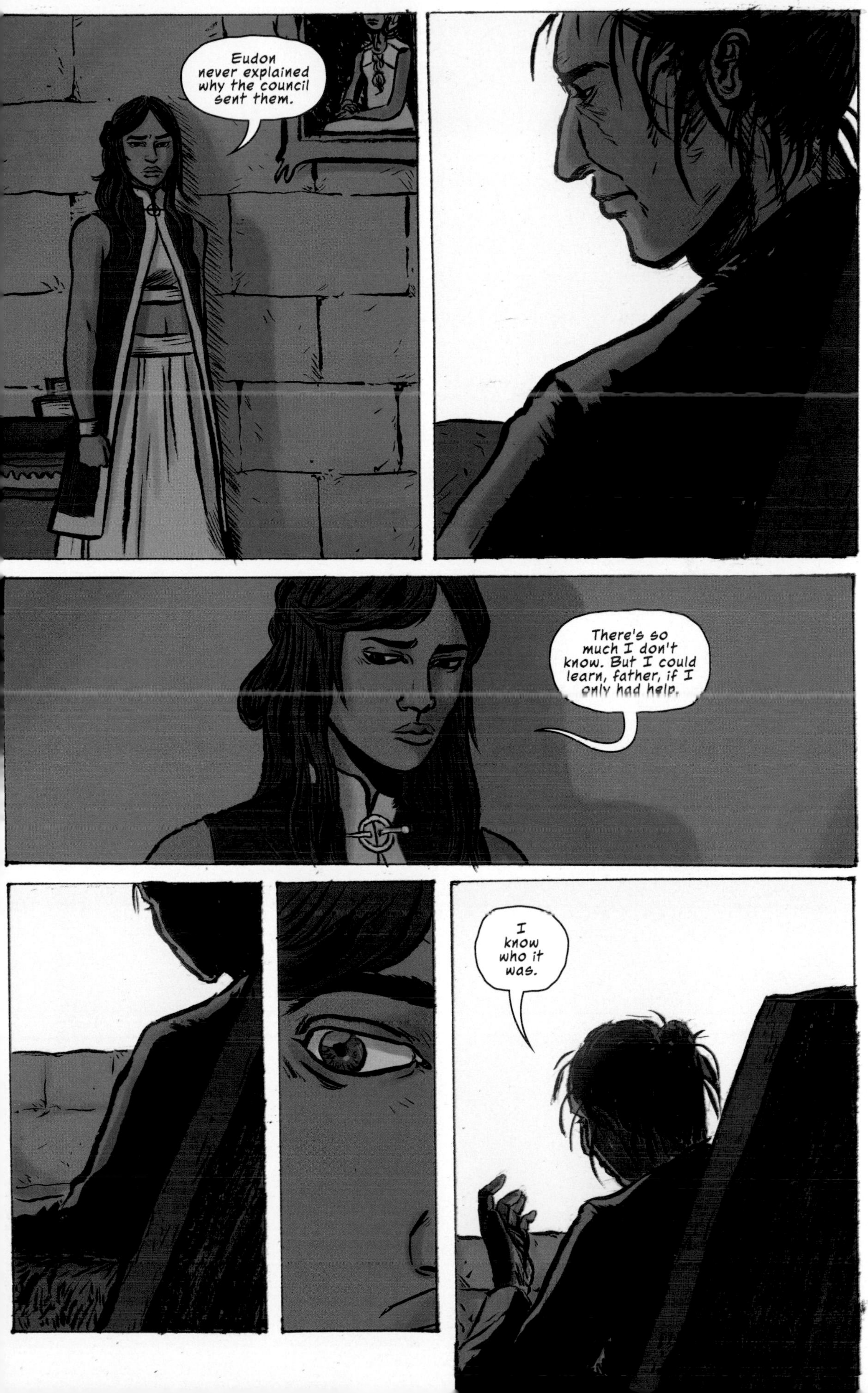
Eudon never explained why the council sent them.
There's so much I don't know. But I could learn, father, if I only had help.
I know who it was.

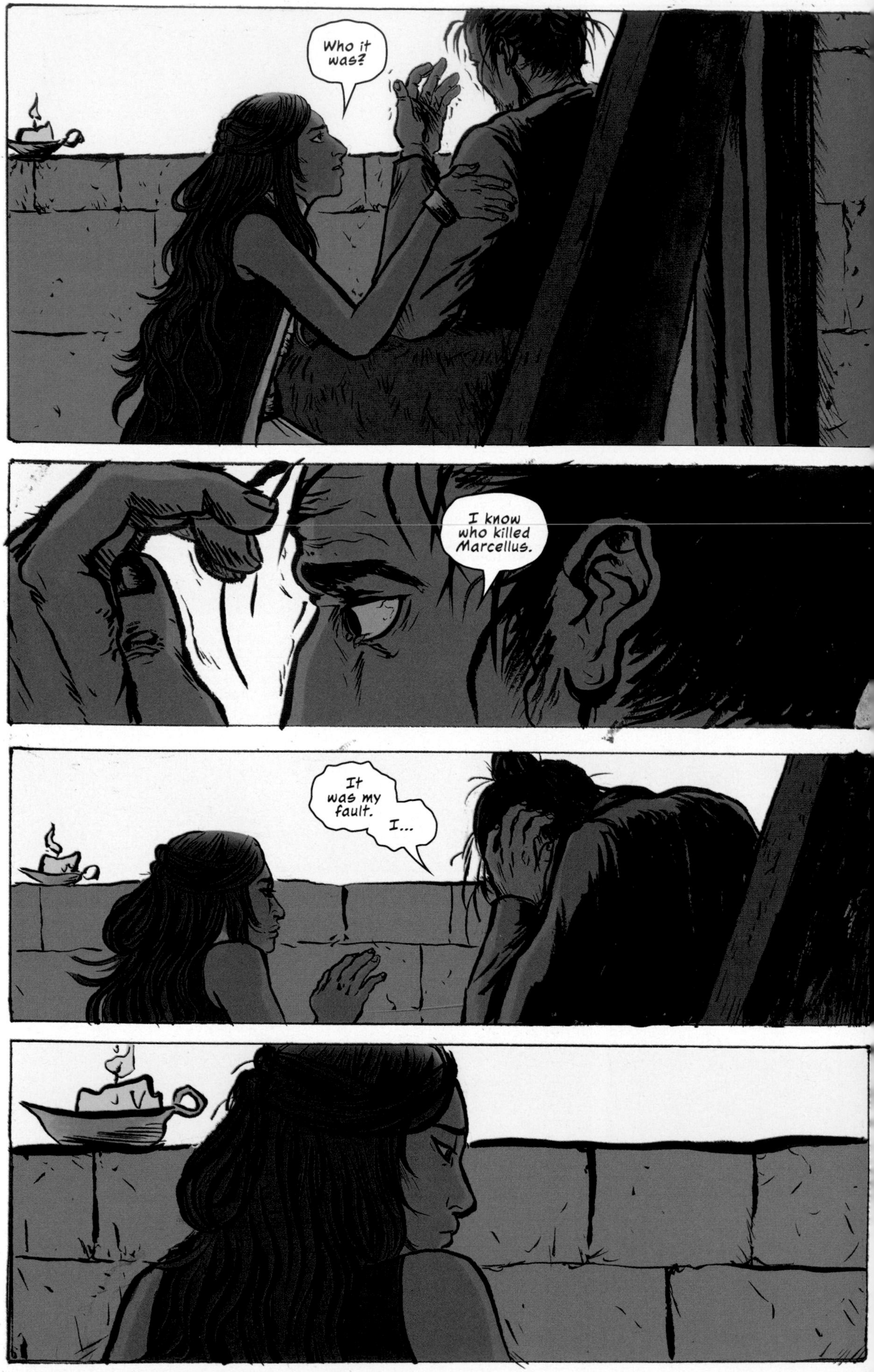
Who it was?
I know who killed Marcellus.
It was my fault.
I...

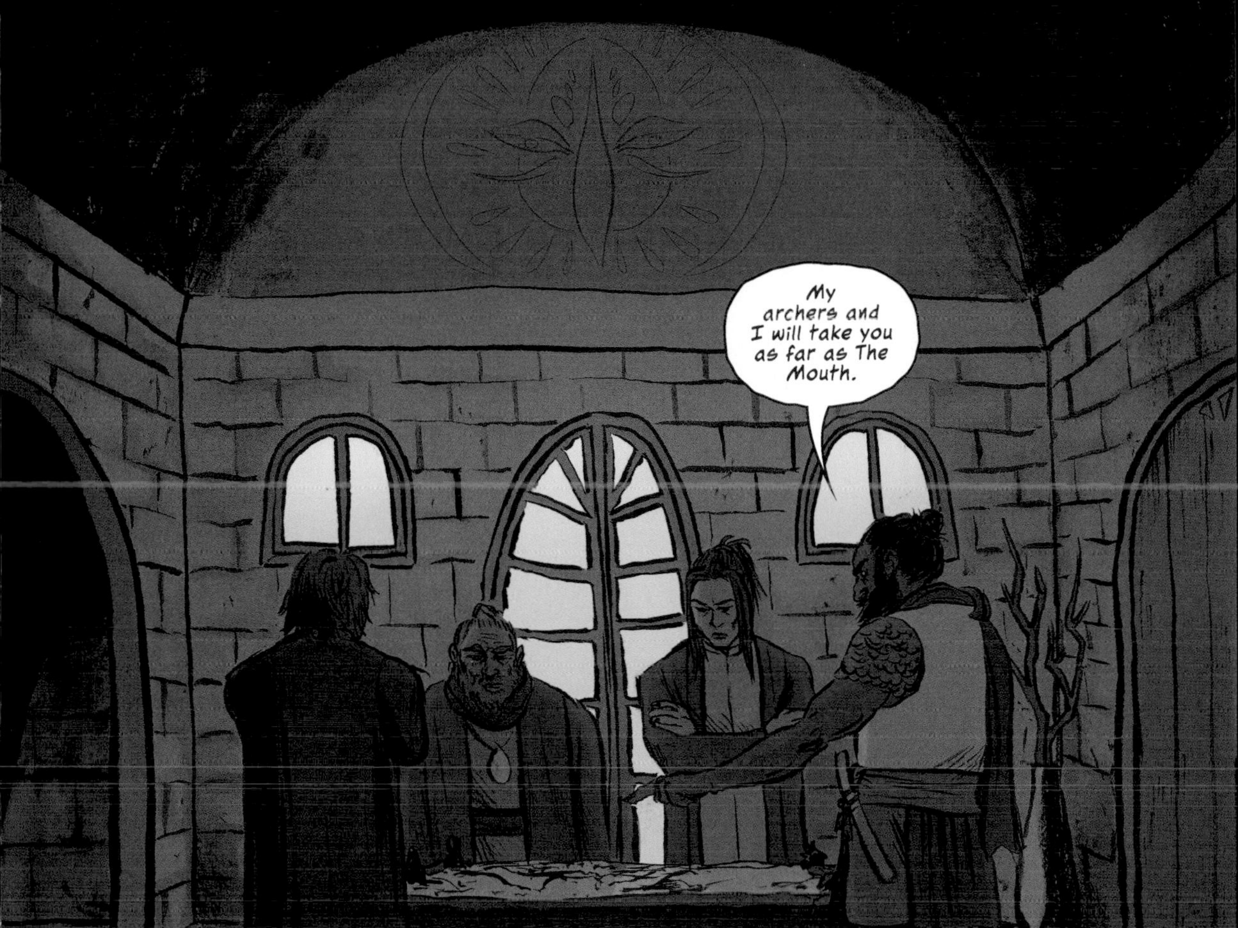
My archers and I will take you as far as The Mouth.

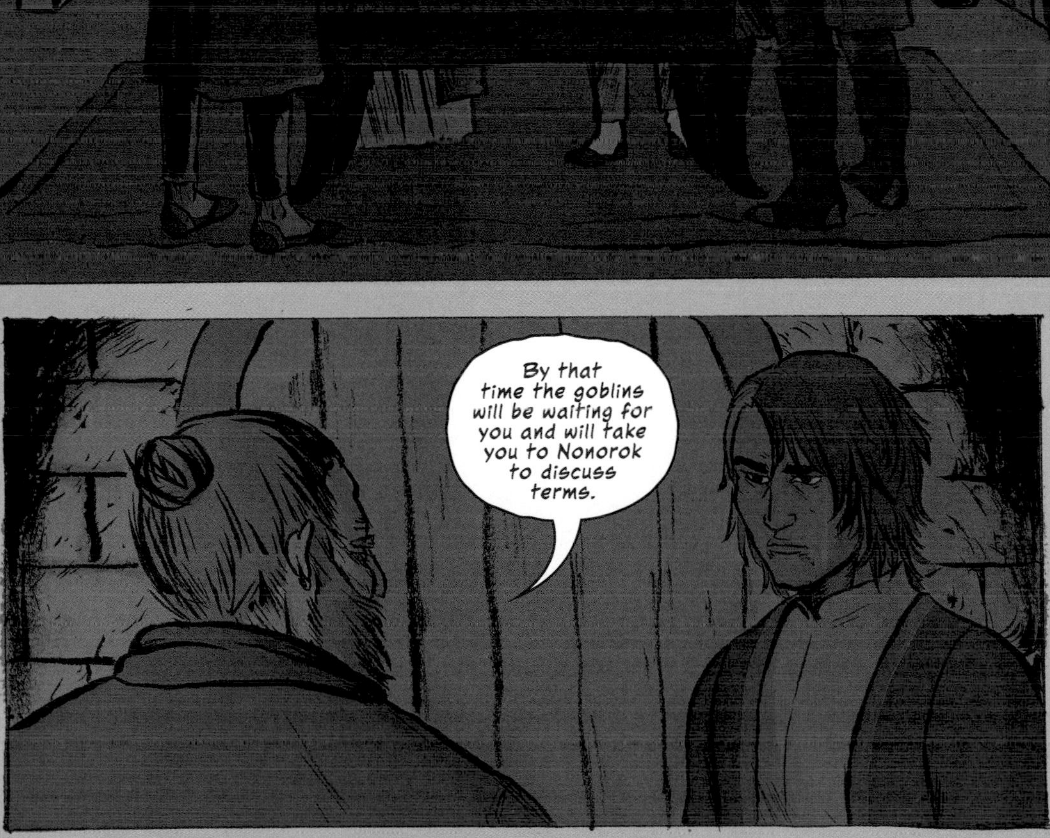
By that time the goblins will be waiting for you and will take you to Nonorok to discuss terms.

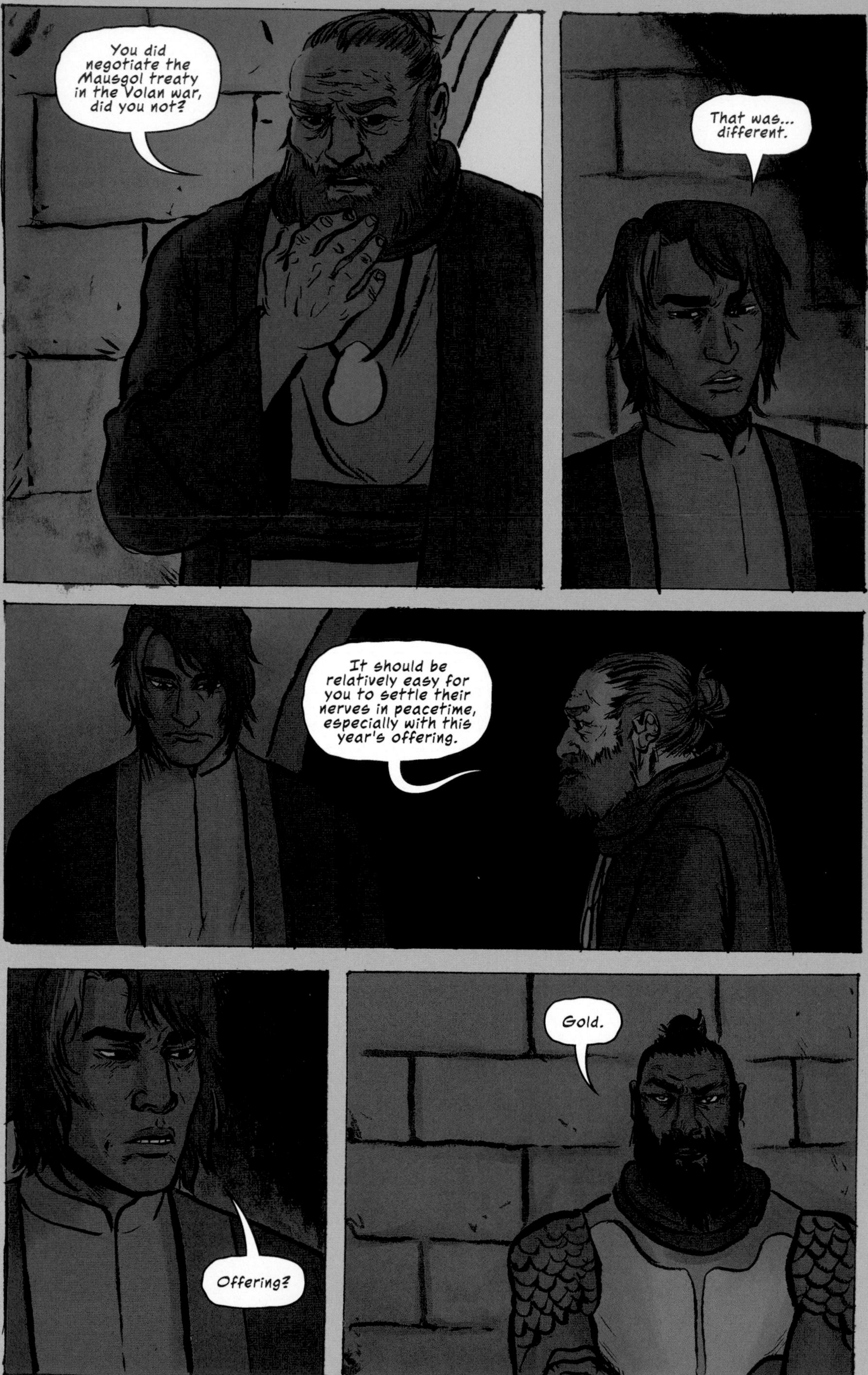
You did negotiate the Mausgol treaty in the Volan war, did you not?
That was... different.
It should be relatively easy for you to settle their nerves in peacetime, especially with this year's offering.
Offering?
Gold.

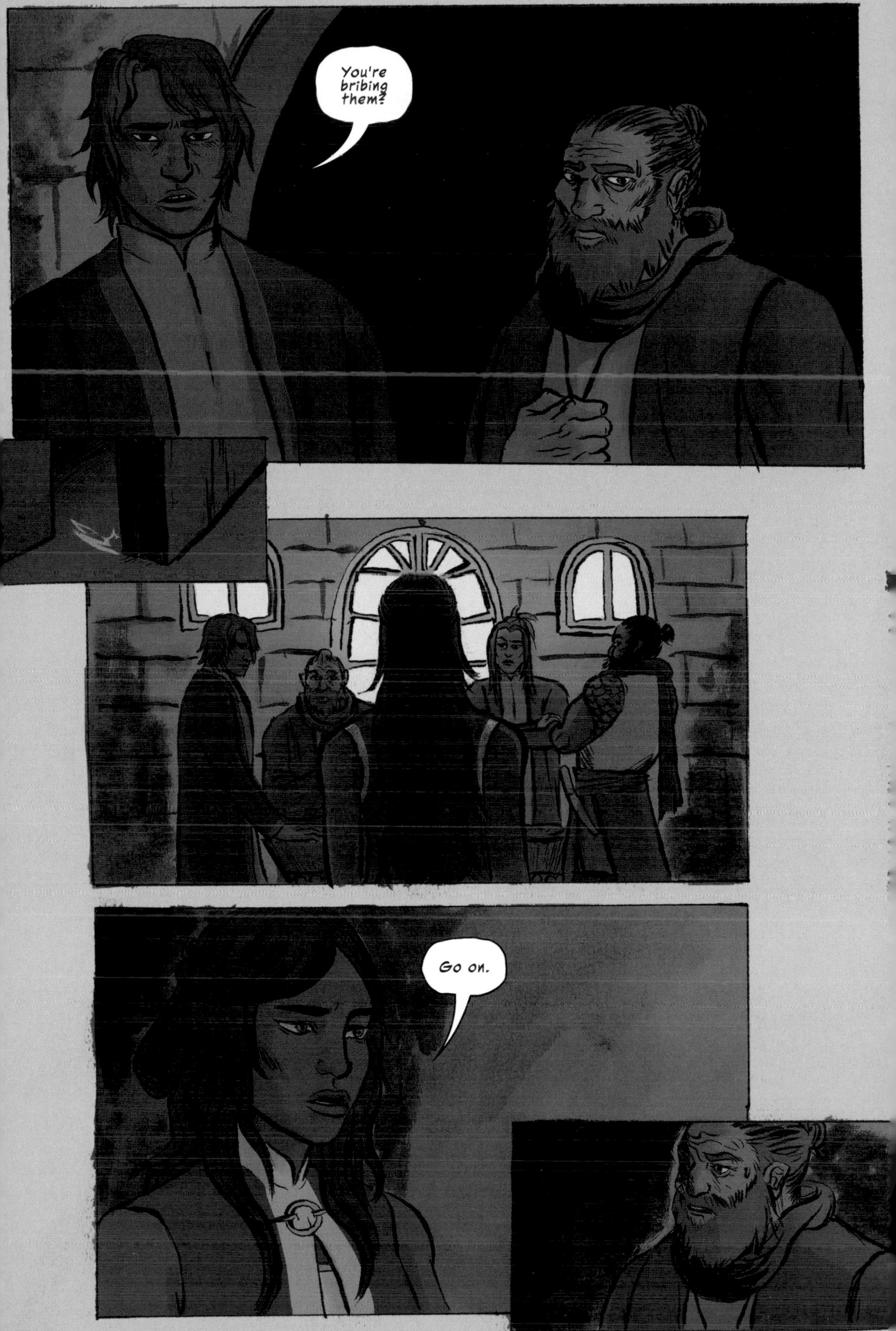
You're bribing them?
Go on.

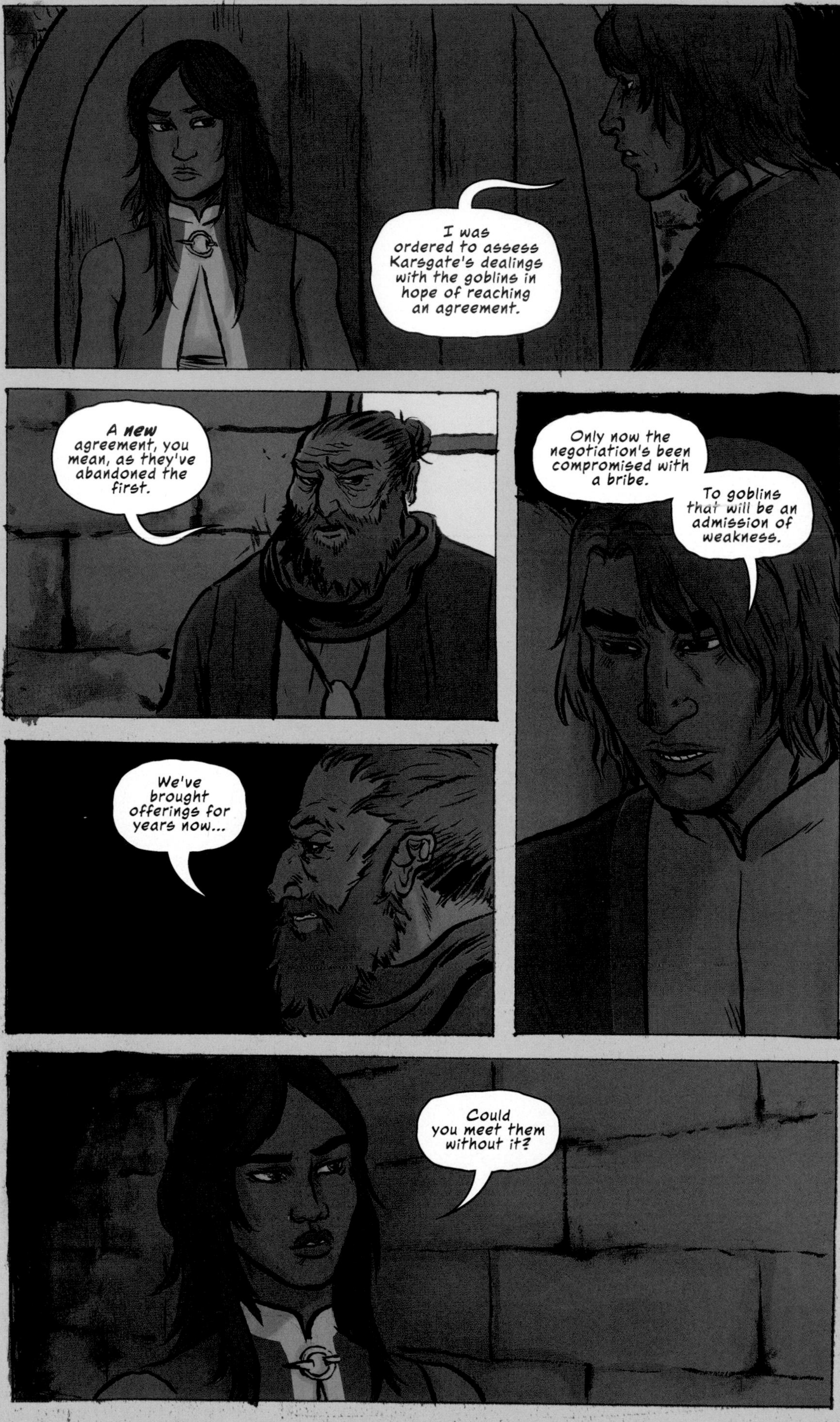
I was ordered to assess Karsgate's dealings with the goblins in hope of reaching an agreement.
A **new** agreement, you mean, as they've abandoned the first.
We've brought offerings for years now...
Only now the negotiation's been compromised with a bribe.
To goblins that will be an admission of weakness.
Could you meet them without it?

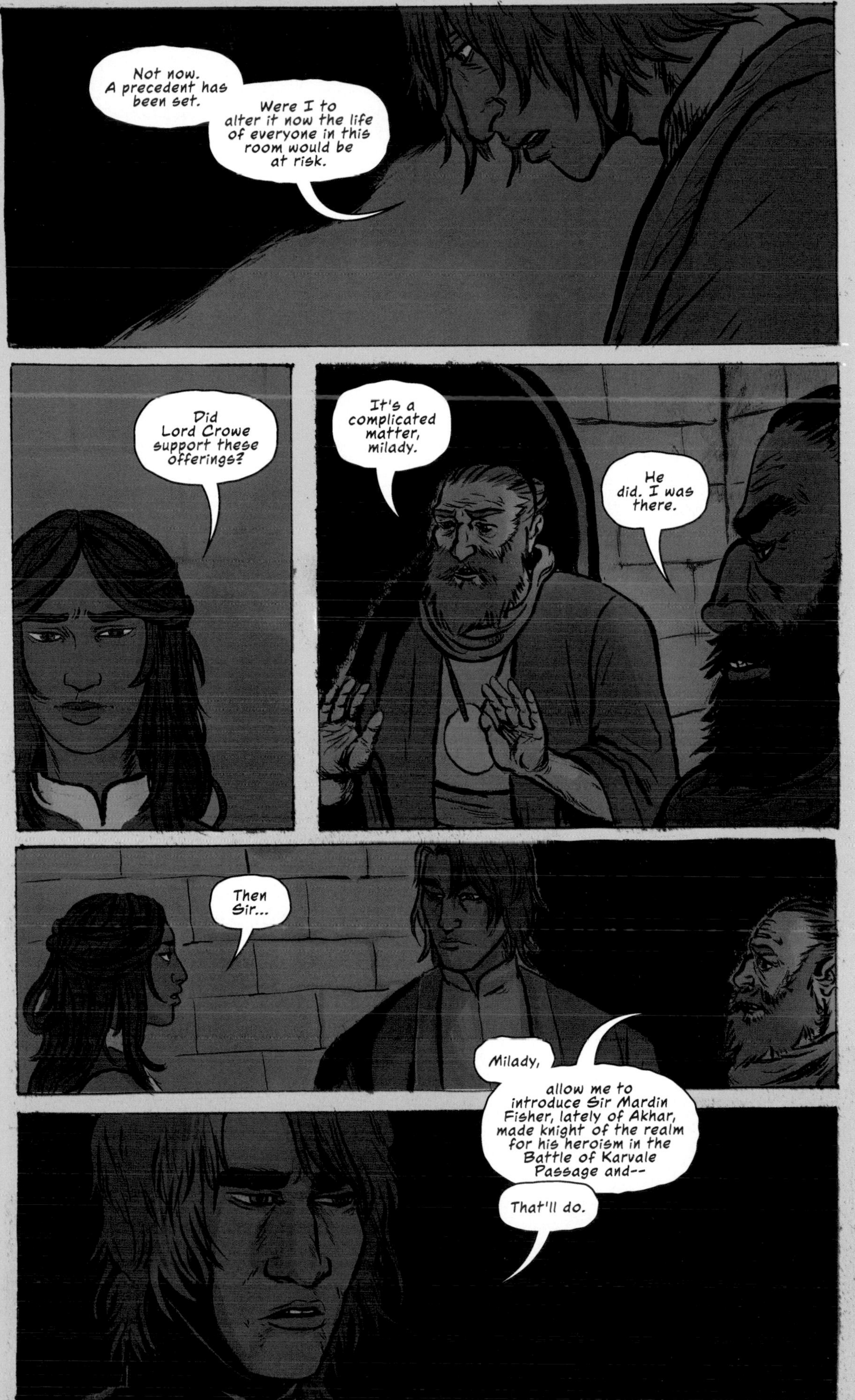
Not now. A precedent has been set.
Were I to alter it now the life of everyone in this room would be at risk.
Did Lord Crowe support these offerings?
It's a complicated matter, milady.
He did. I was there.
Then Sir...
Milady,
allow me to introduce Sir Mardin Fisher, lately of Akhar, made knight of the realm for his heroism in the Battle of Karvale Passage and--
That'll do.

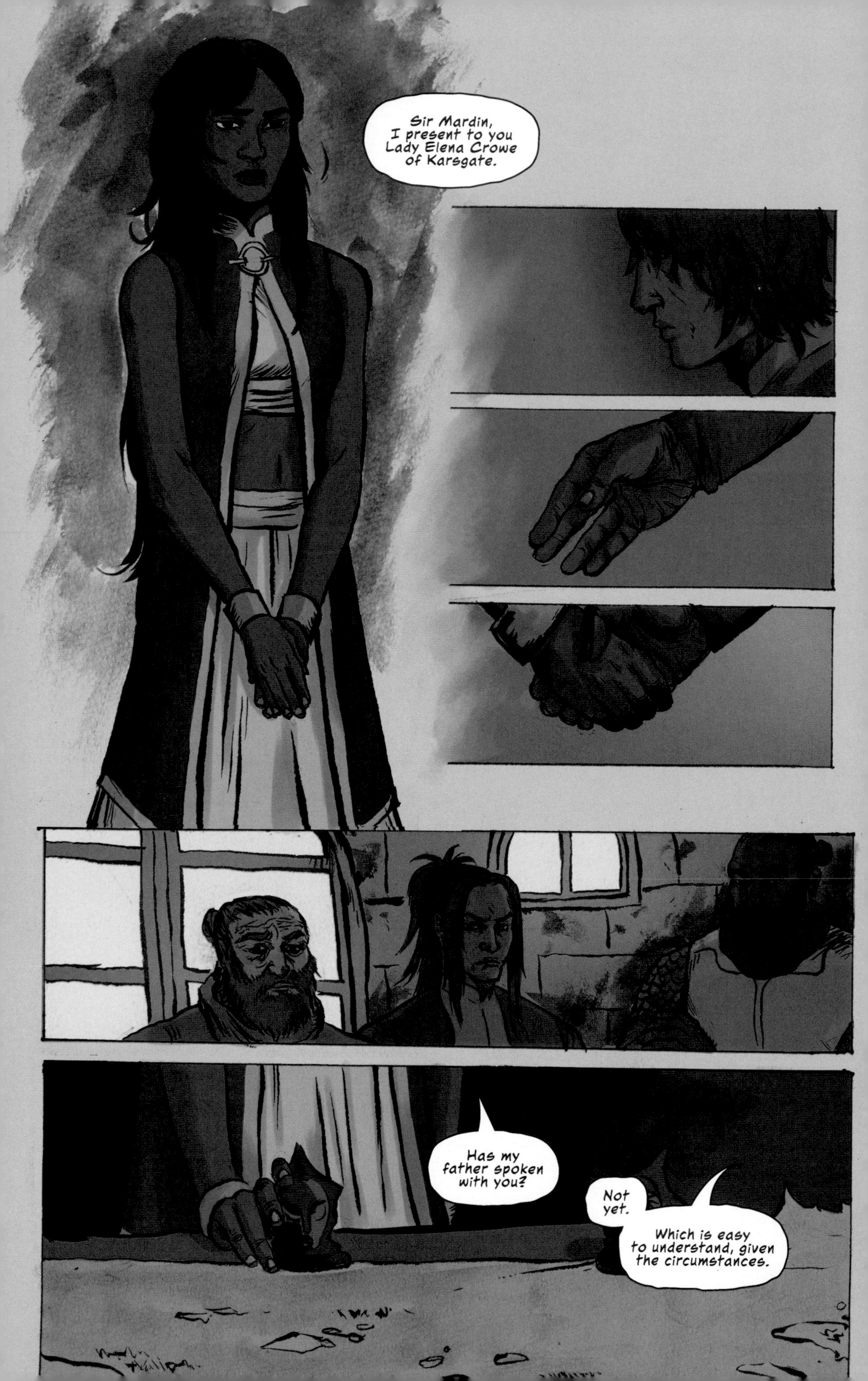
Sir Mardin, I present to you Lady Elena Crowe of Karsgate.
Has my father spoken with you?
Not yet.
Which is easy to understand, given the circumstances.

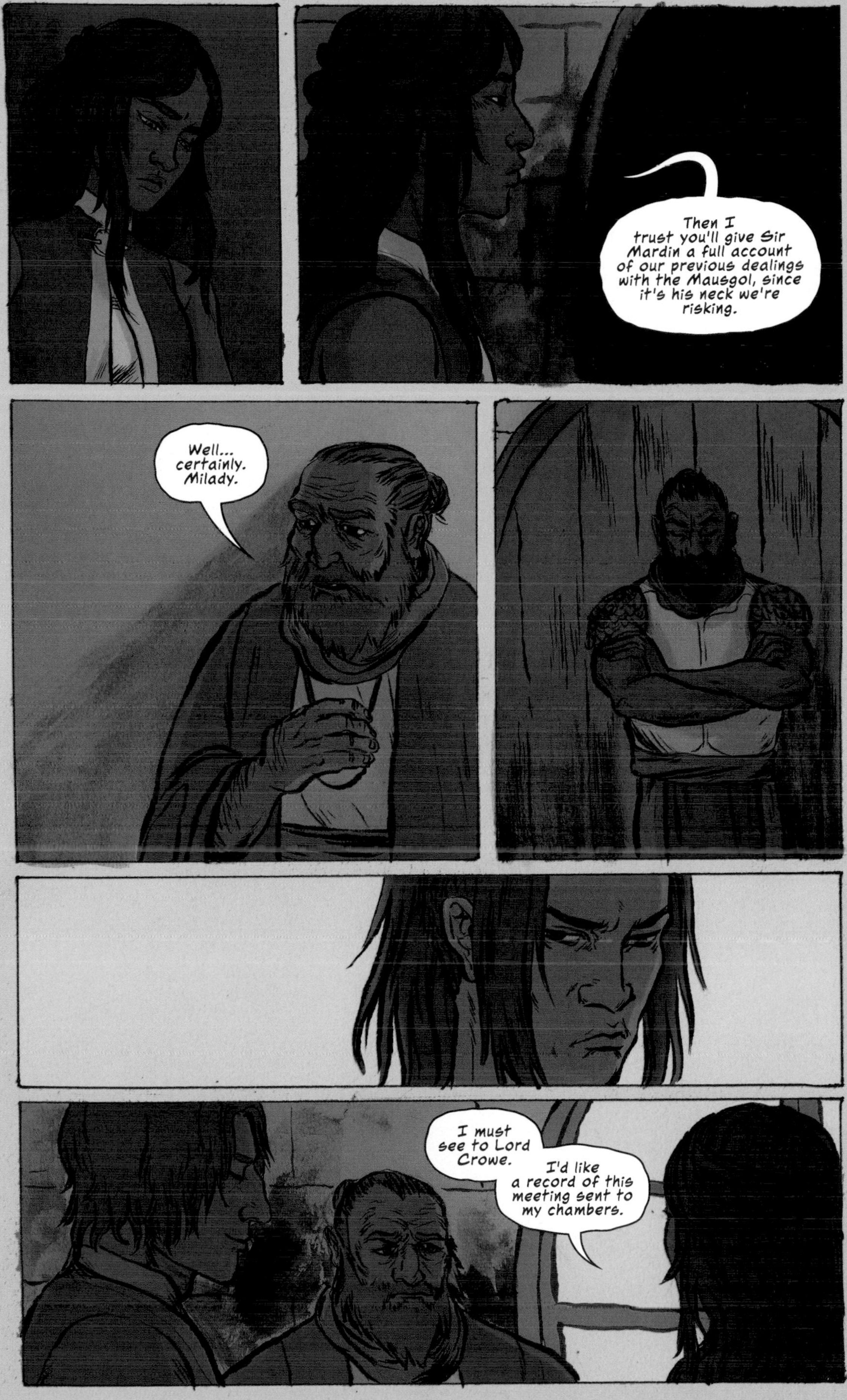
Then I trust you'll give Sir Mardin a full account of our previous dealings with the Mausgol, since it's his neck we're risking.
Well... certainly. Milady.
I must see to Lord Crowe.
I'd like a record of this meeting sent to my chambers.

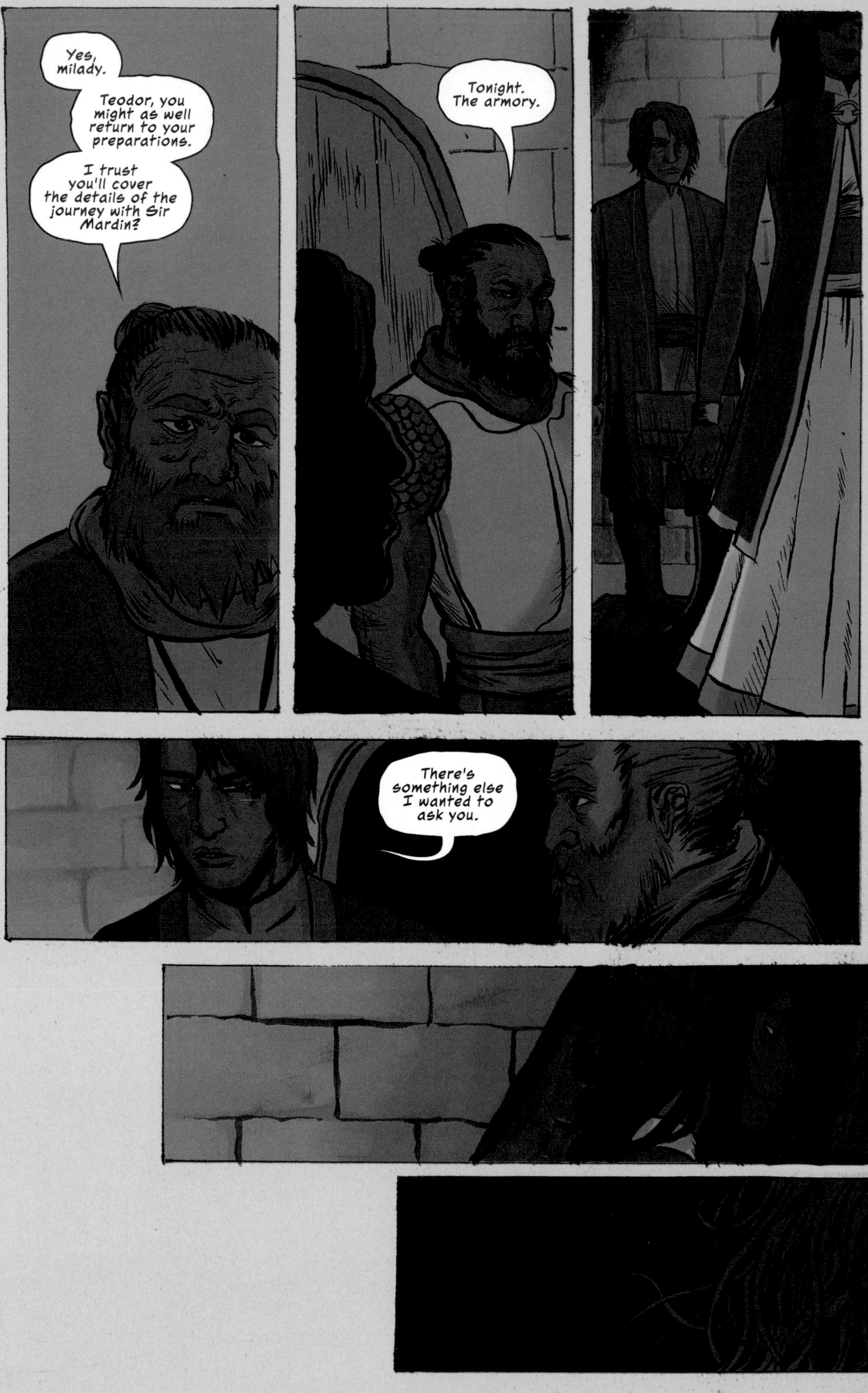
Yes, milady.
Teodor, you might as well return to your preparations.
I trust you'll cover the details of the journey with Sir Mardin?
Tonight. The armory.
There's something else I wanted to ask you.

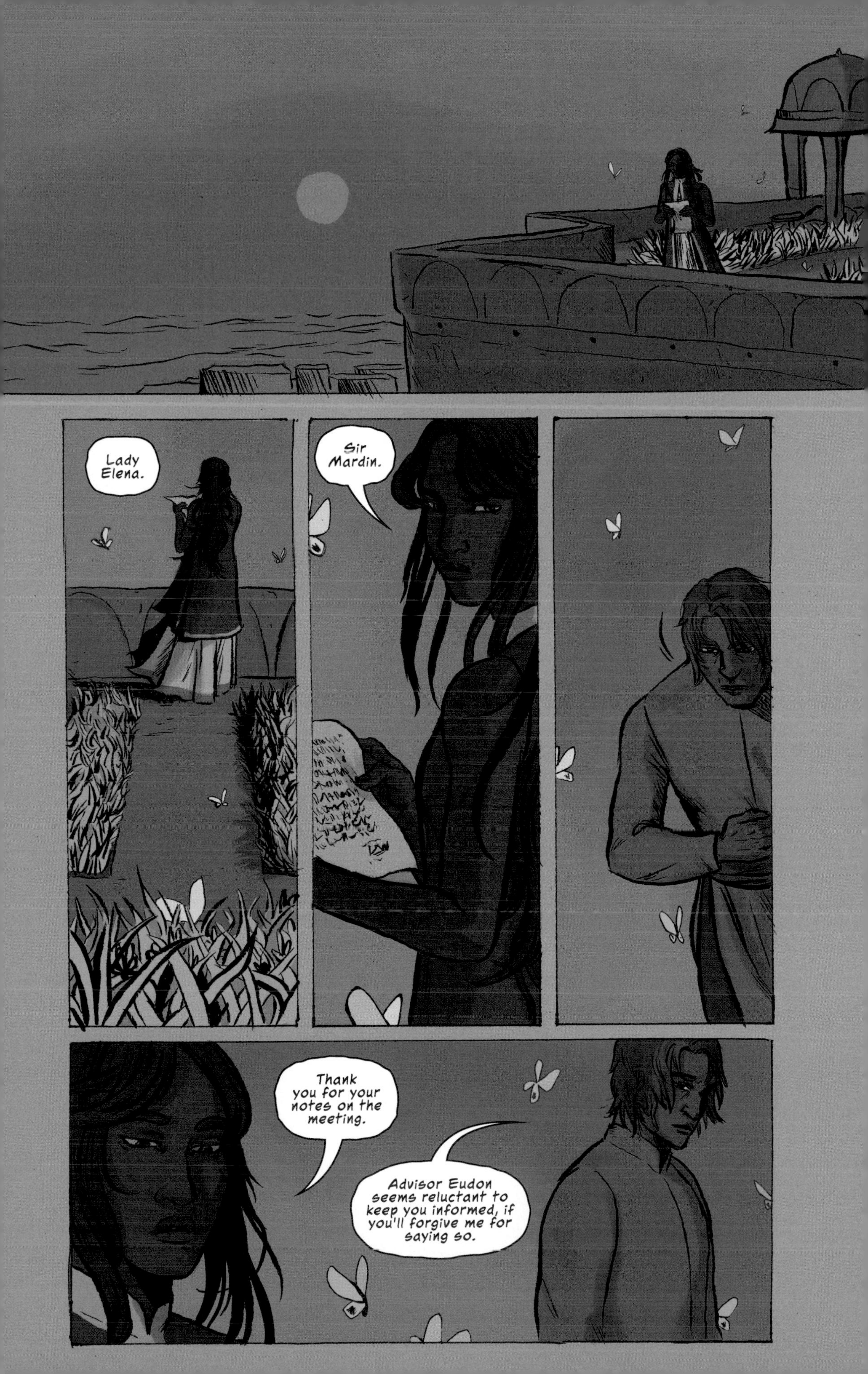
Lady Elena.
Sir Mardin.
Thank you for your notes on the meeting.
Advisor Eudon seems reluctant to keep you informed, if you'll forgive me for saying so.

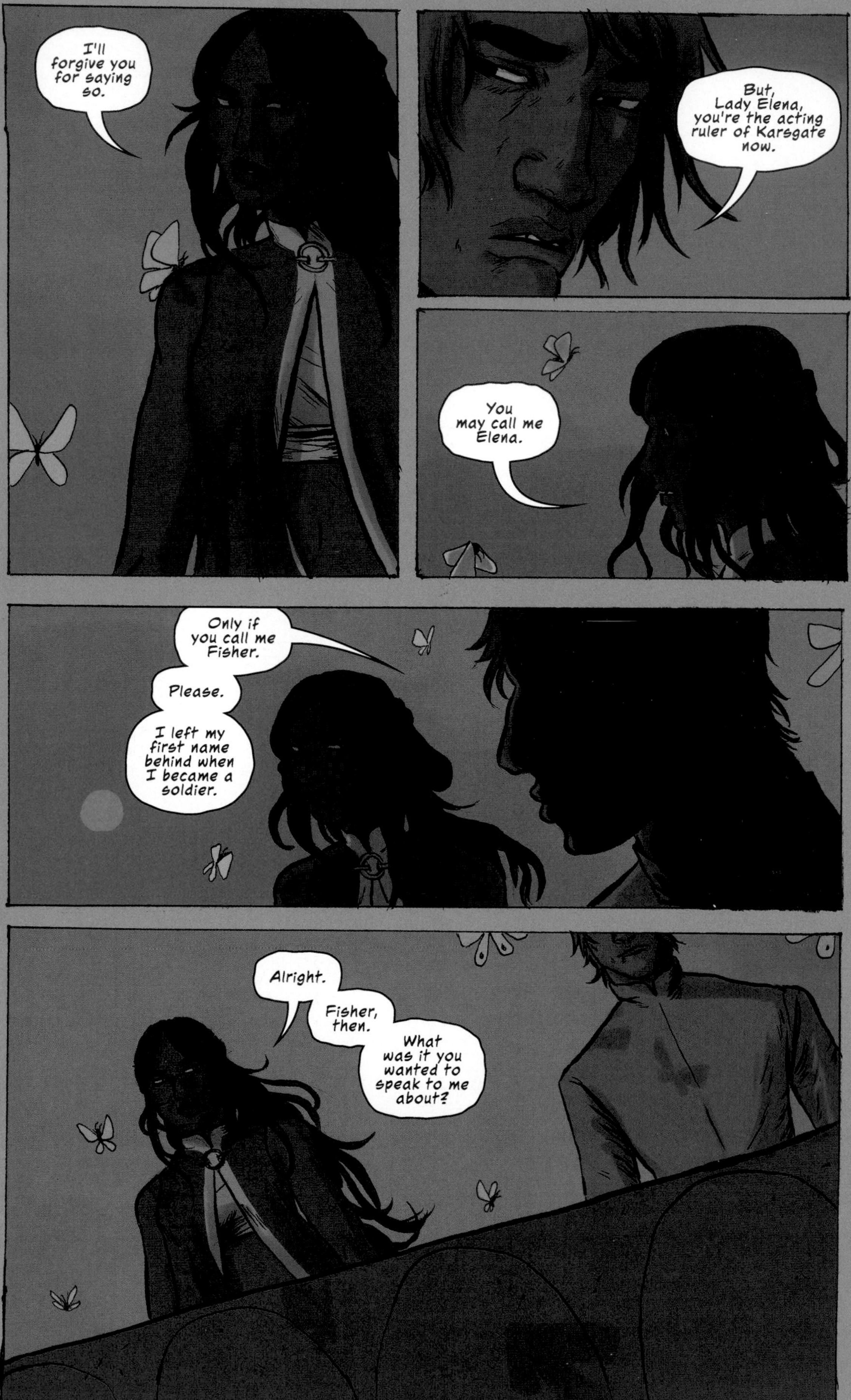
I'll forgive you for saying so.
But, Lady Elena, you're the acting ruler of Karsgate now.
You may call me Elena.
Only if you call me Fisher.
Please.
I left my first name behind when I became a soldier.
Alright.
Fisher, then.
What was it you wanted to speak to me about?

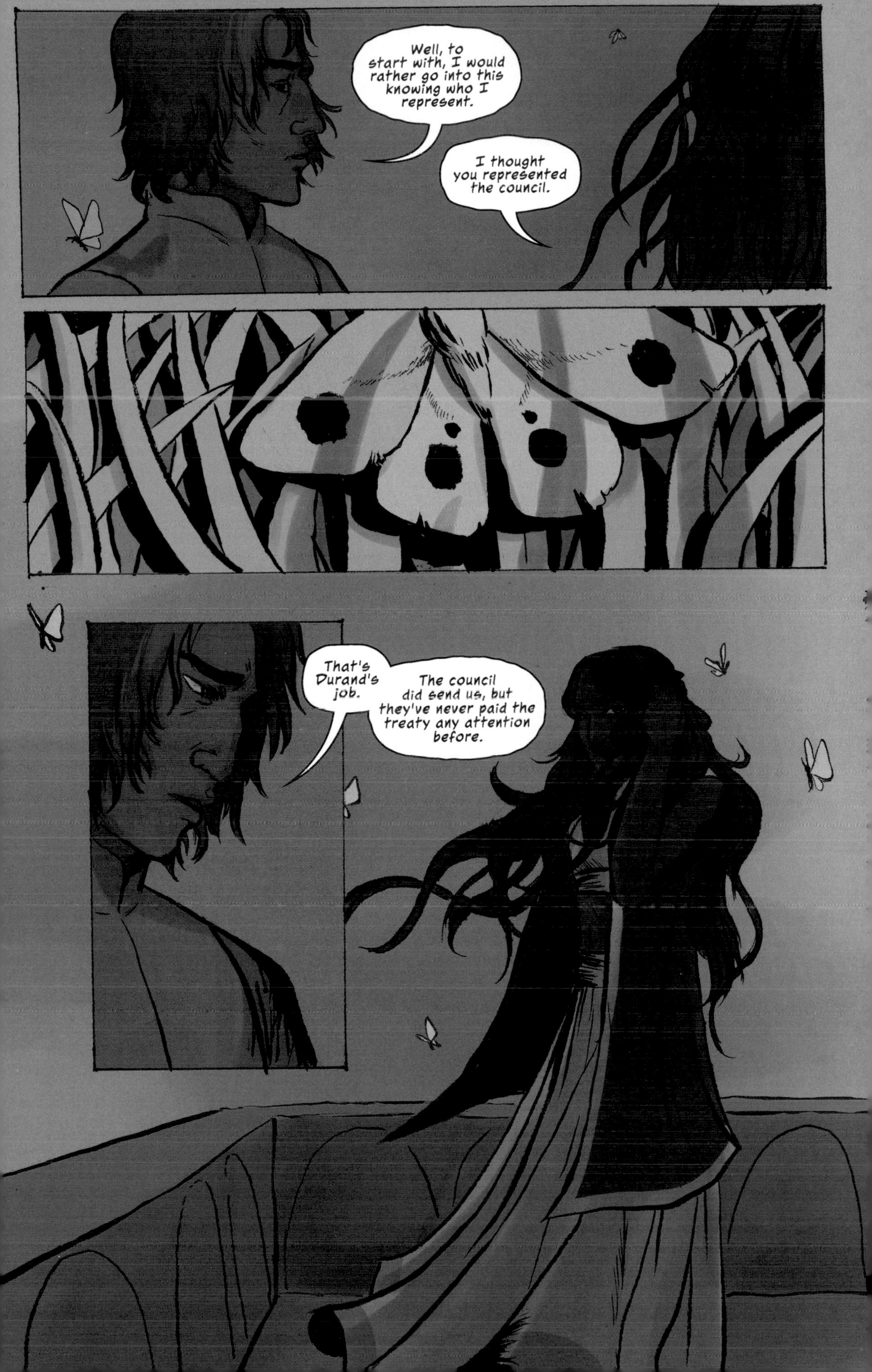
Well, to start with, I would rather go into this knowing who I represent.
I thought you represented the council.
That's Durand's job.
The council did send us, but they've never paid the treaty any attention before.

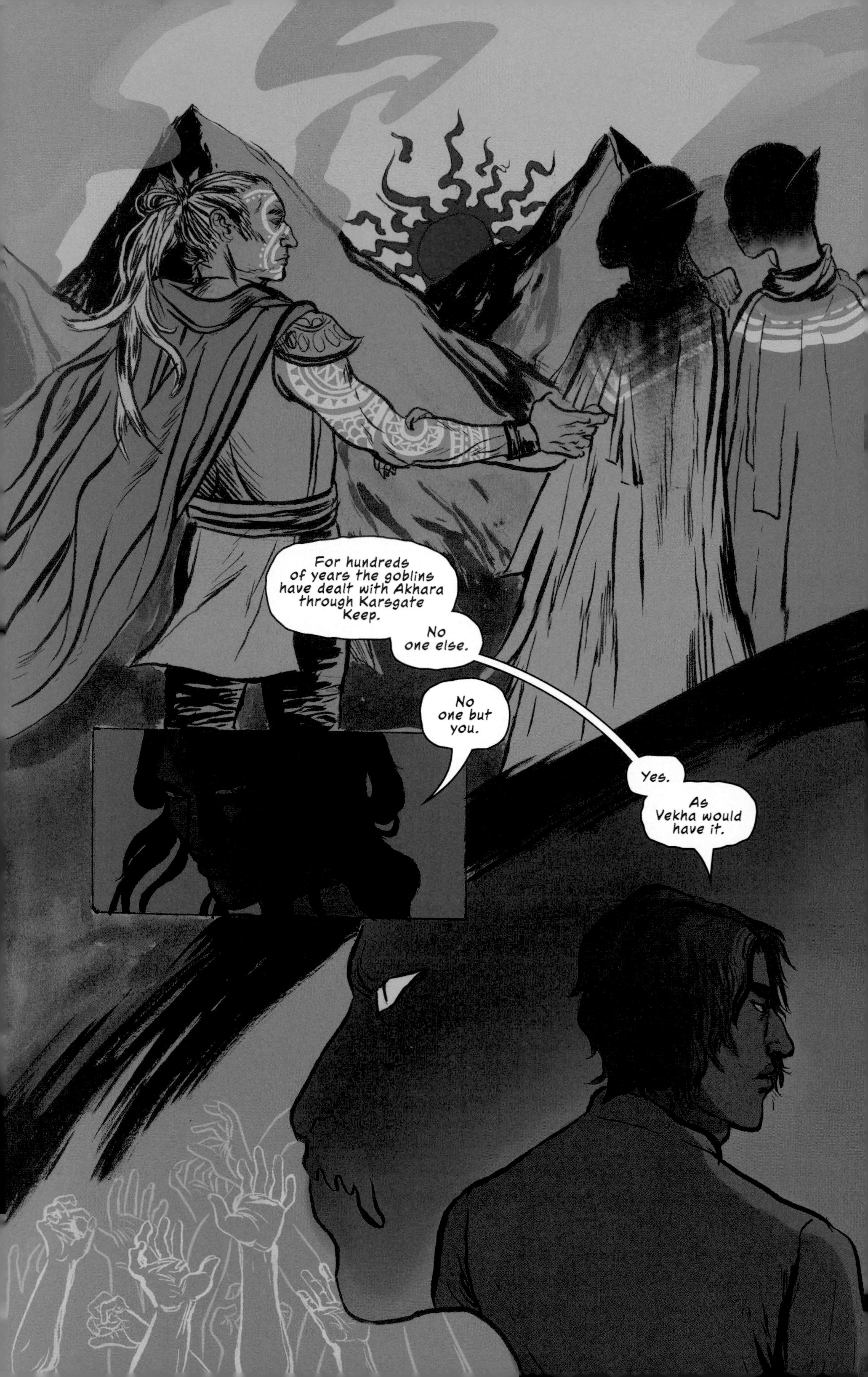
For hundreds of years the goblins have dealt with Akhara through Karsgate Keep.
No one else.
No one but you.
Yes.
As Vekha would have it.

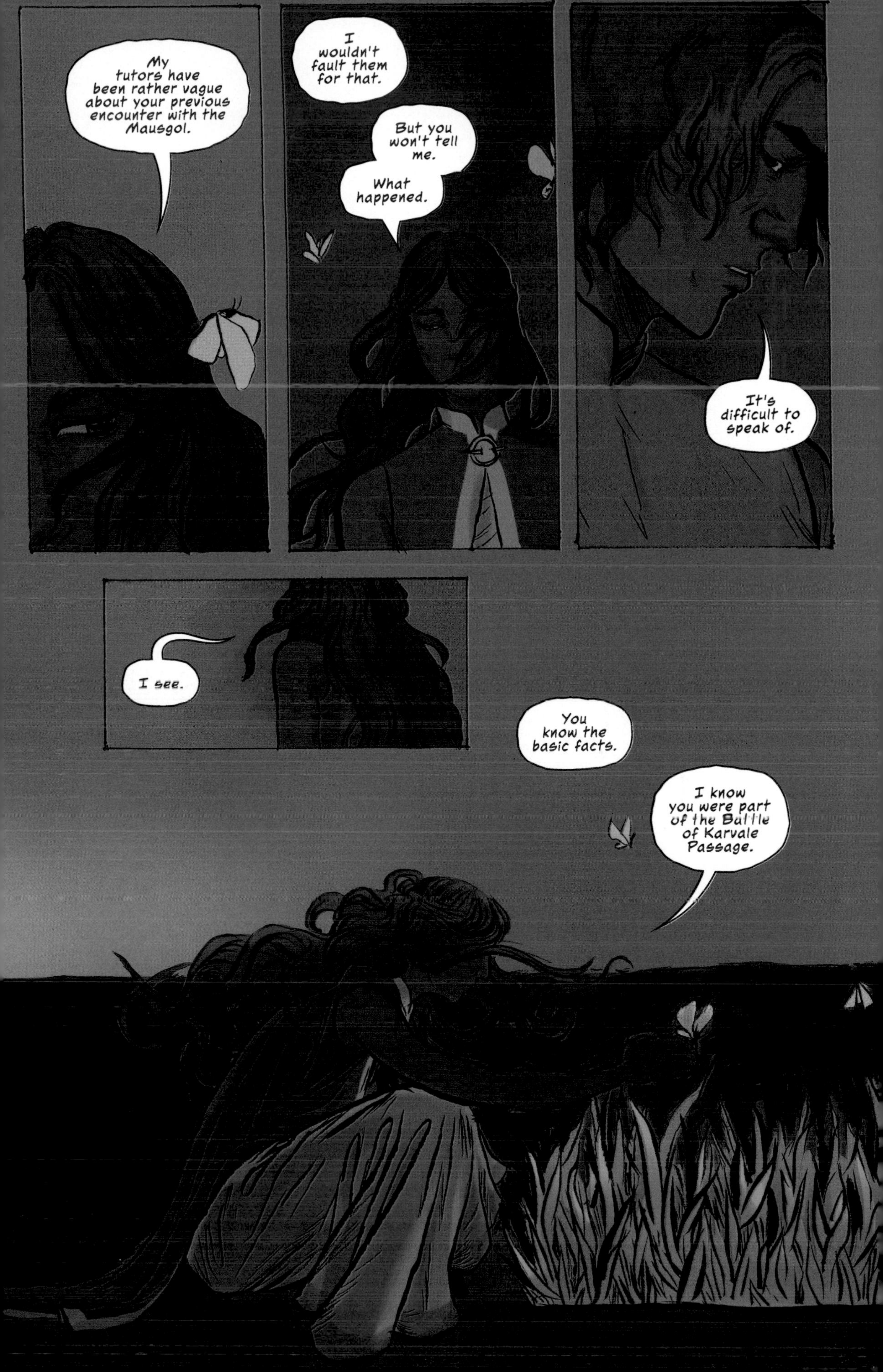
My tutors have been rather vague about your previous encounter with the Mausgol.
I wouldn't fault them for that.
But you won't tell me.
What happened.
It's difficult to speak of.
I see.
You know the basic facts.
I know you were part of the Bartle of Karvale Passage.

I know you rose from field commander to acting sergeant in that time.
That your meeting with the goblins resulted in the treaty that ended the war with Vol--
and that the rest of your regiment was lost within the mountain.
You're a hero.
Let's stick with fact.

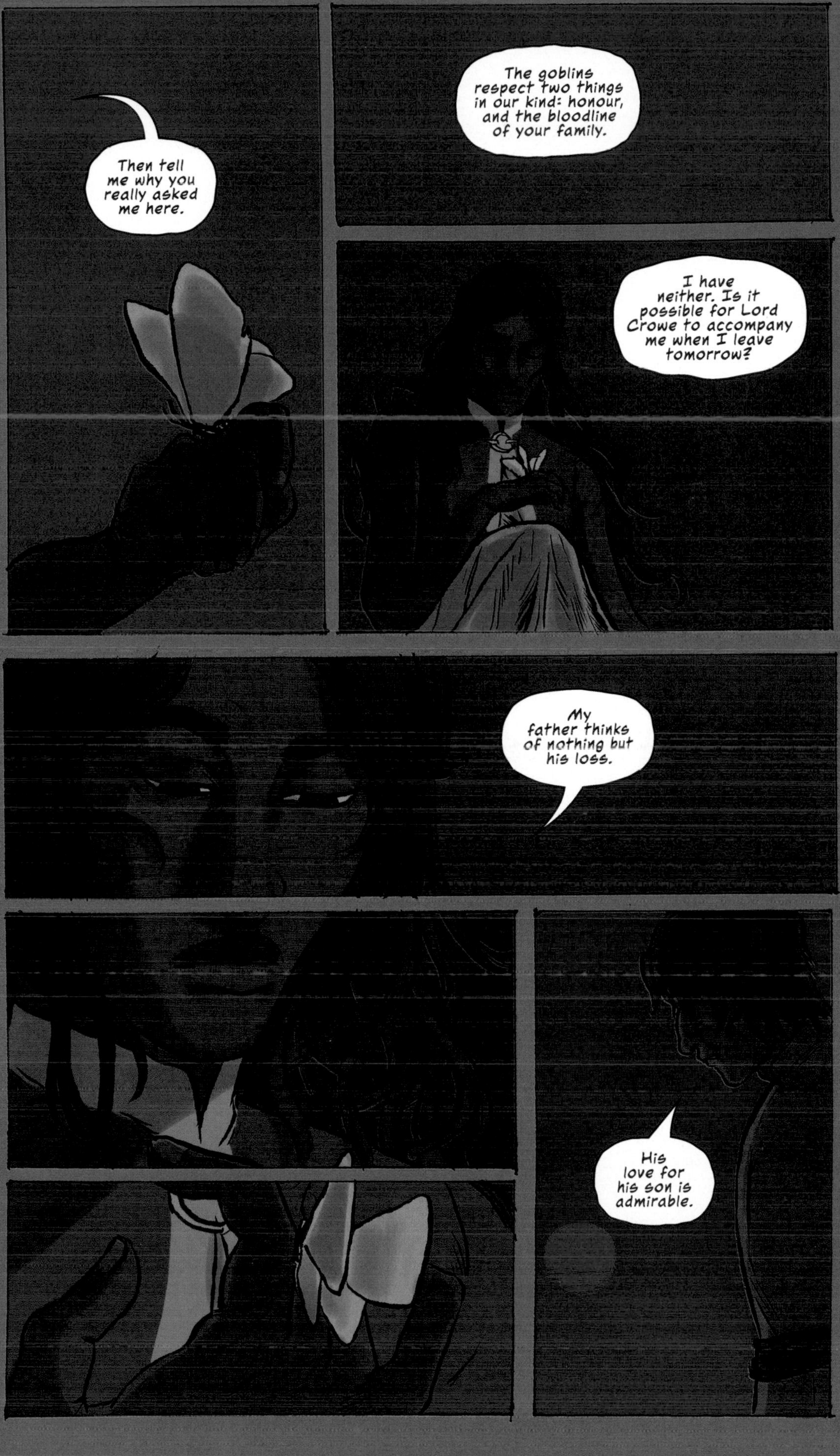
Then tell me why you really asked me here.
The goblins respect two things in our kind: honour, and the bloodline of your family.
I have neither. Is it possible for Lord Crowe to accompany me when I leave tomorrow?
My father thinks of nothing but his loss.
His love for his son is admirable.

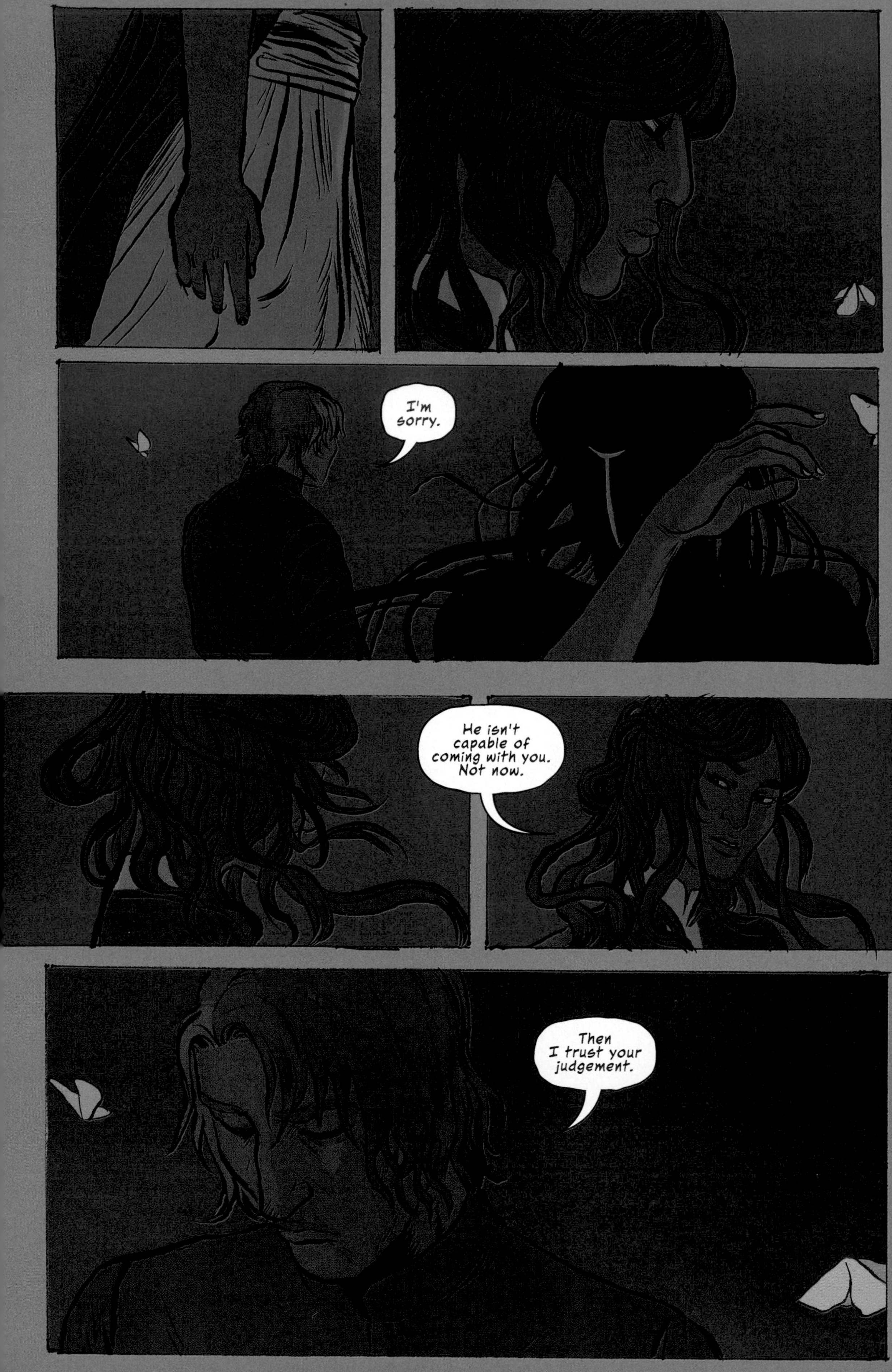
I'm sorry.
He isn't capable of coming with you. Not now.
Then I trust your judgement.

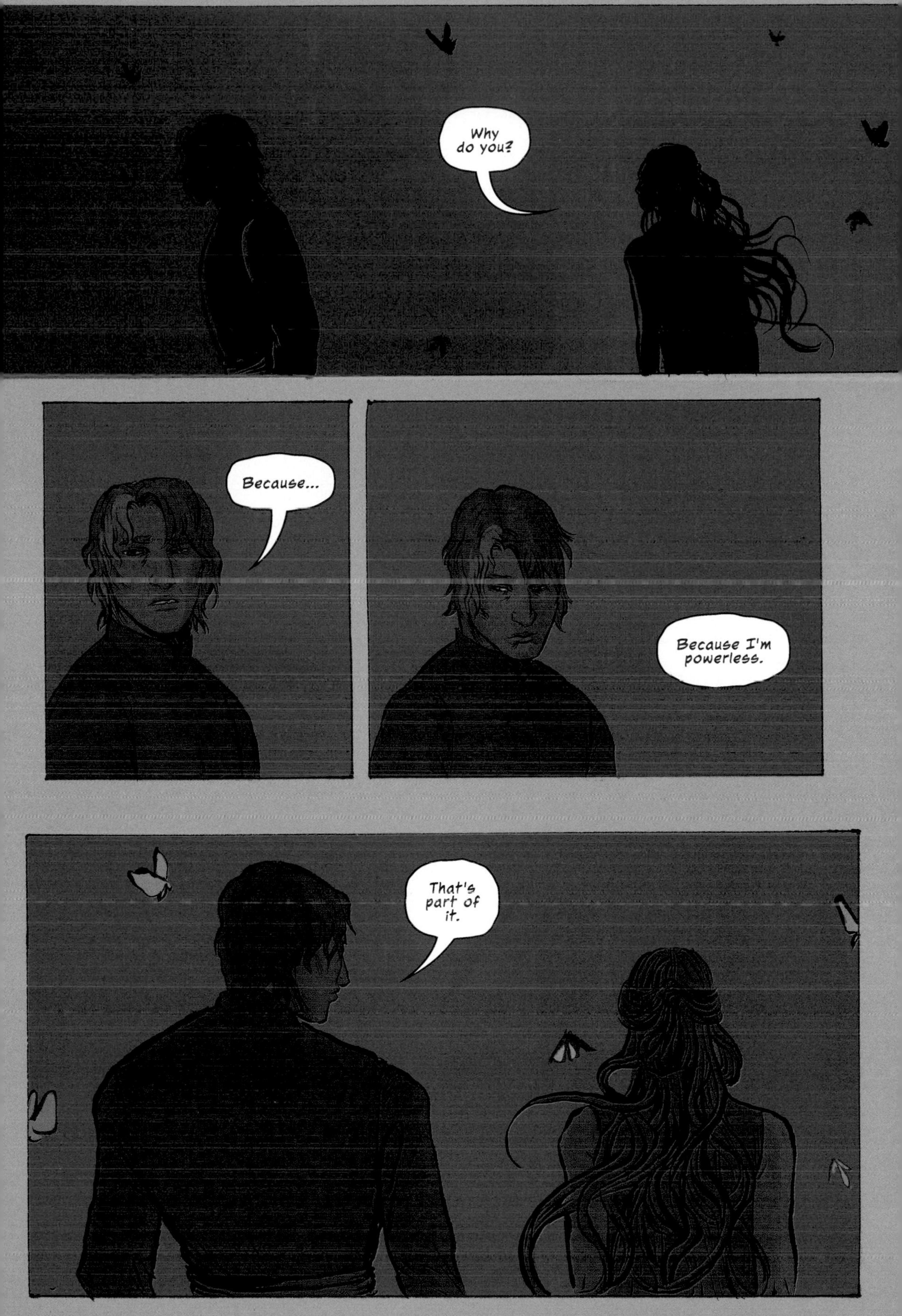
Why do you?
Because...
Because I'm powerless.
That's part of it.

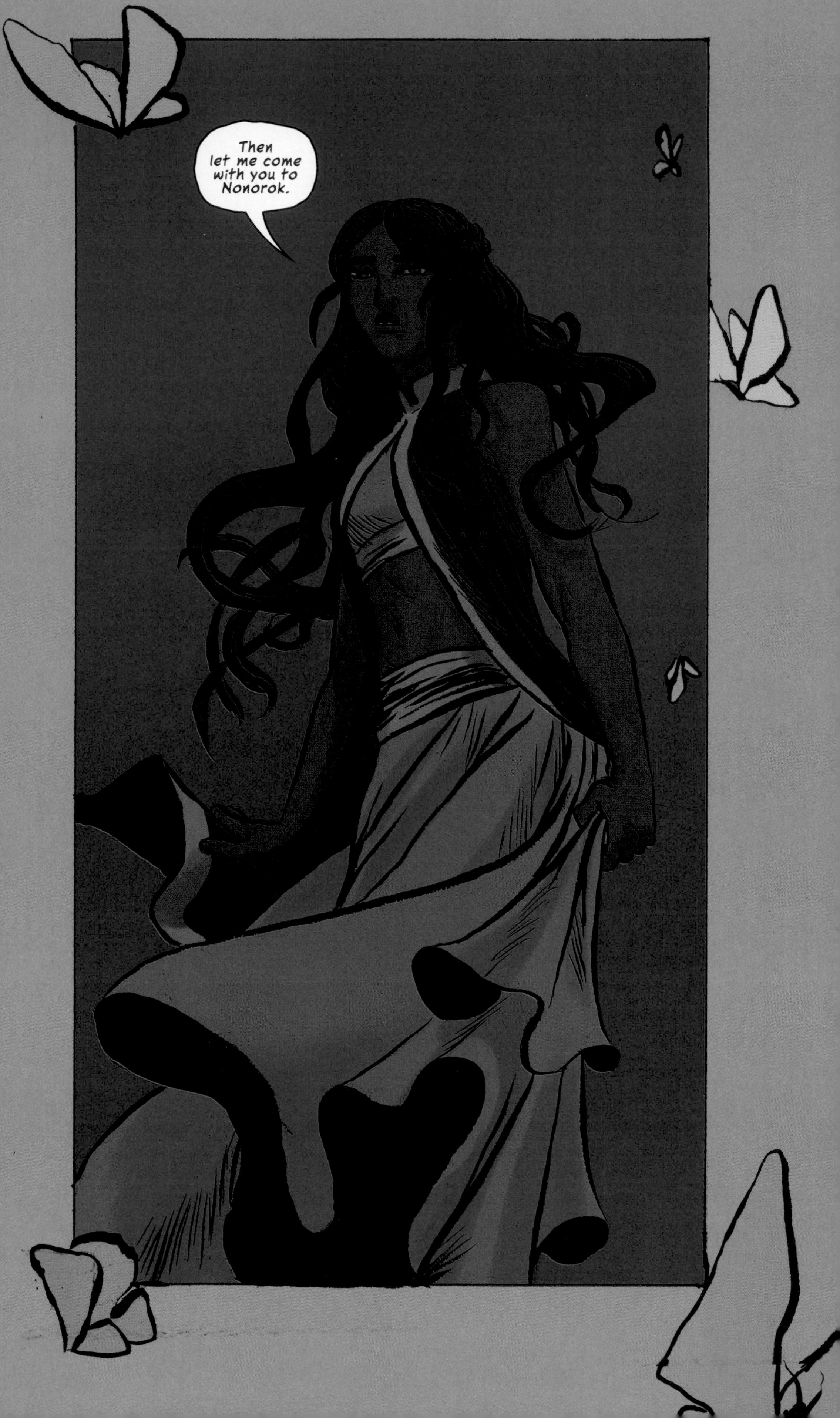
Then let me come with you to Nonorok.

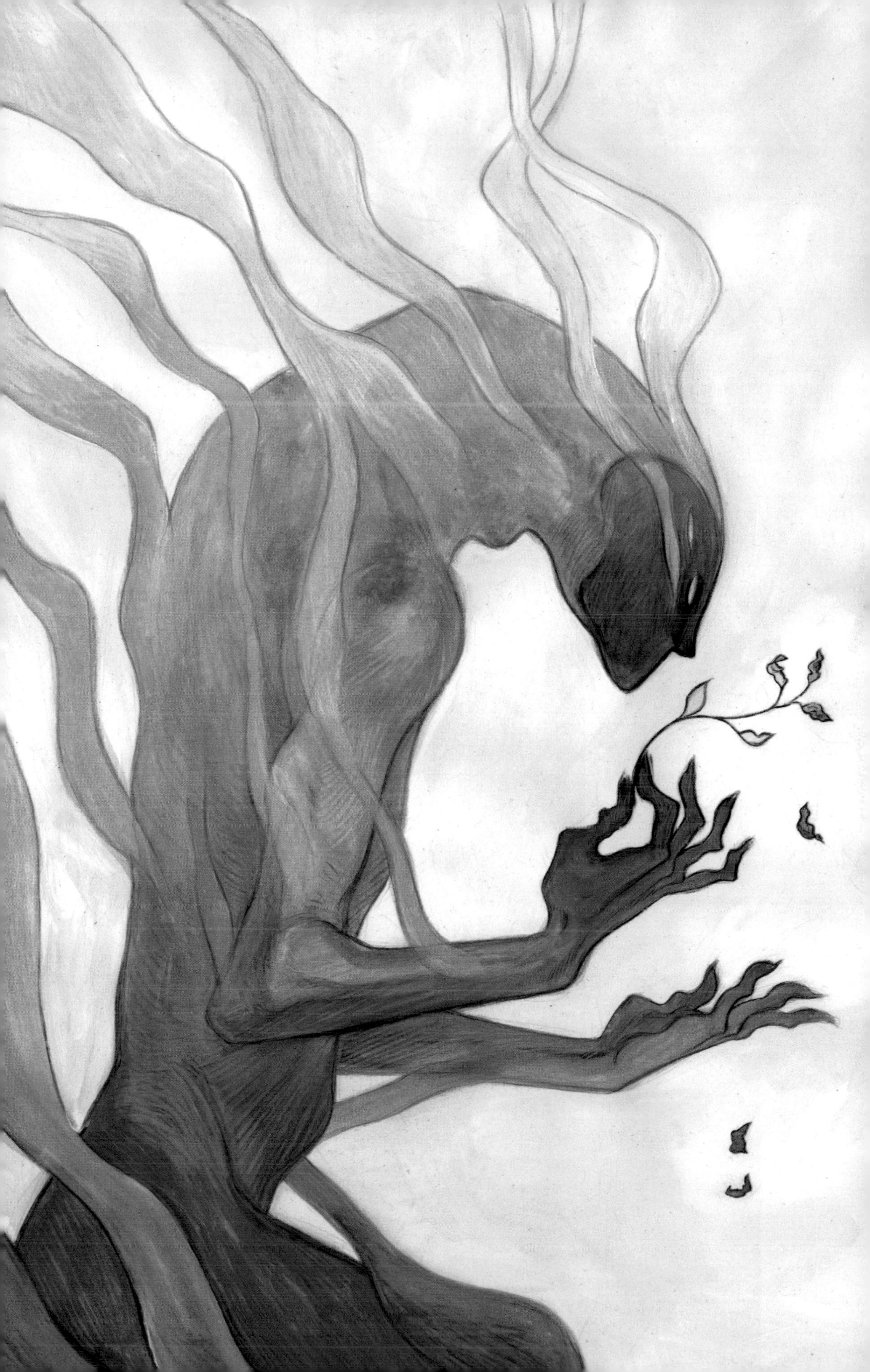

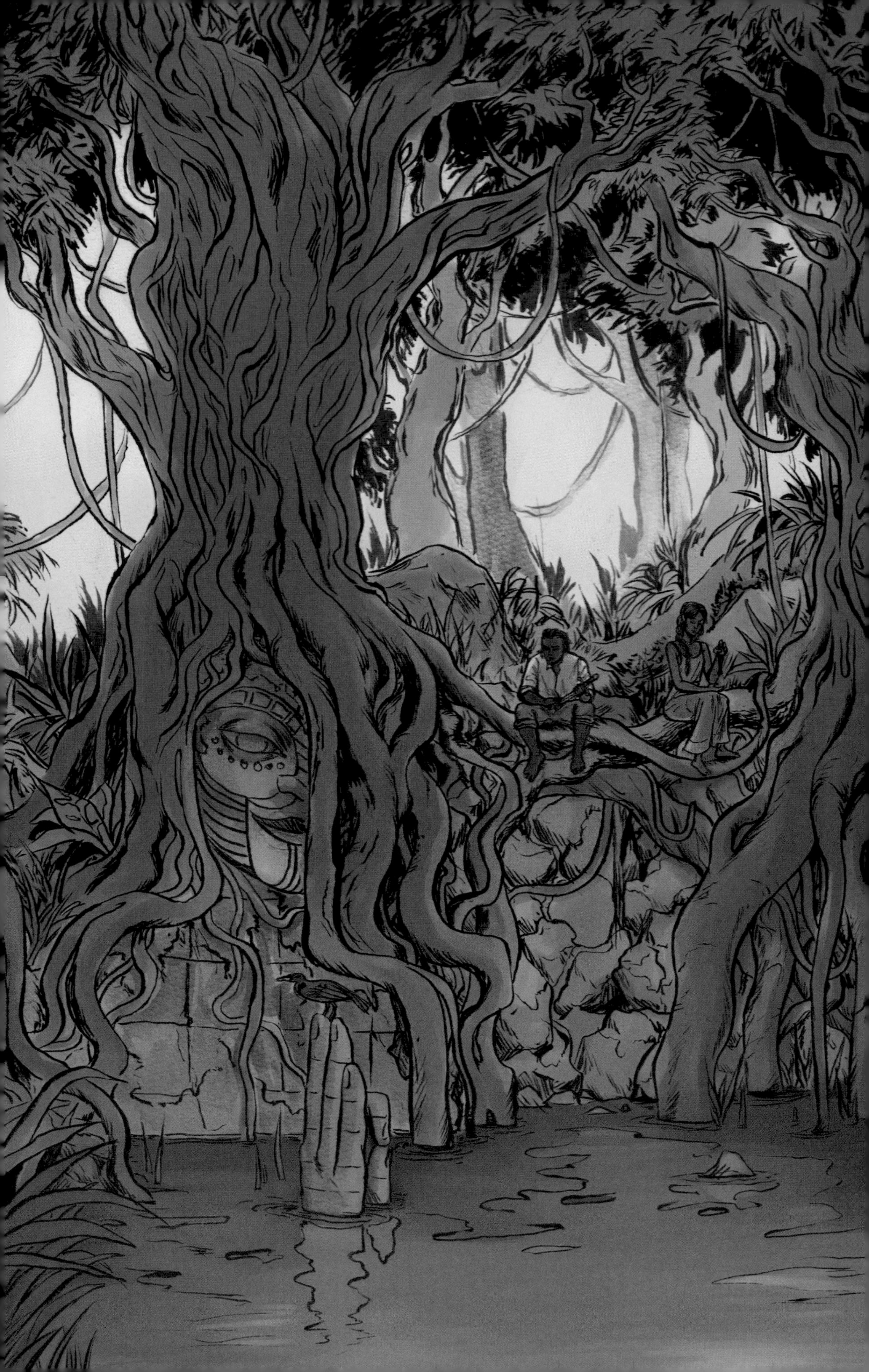

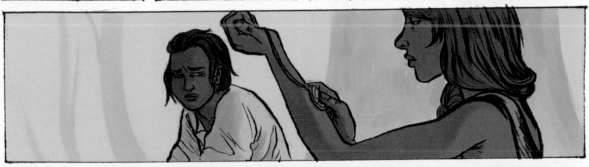

She knew the creature was Lord Crowe's son without my telling her. How?

I no longer question how Avisleth knows all she does. It keeps me from learning from her.

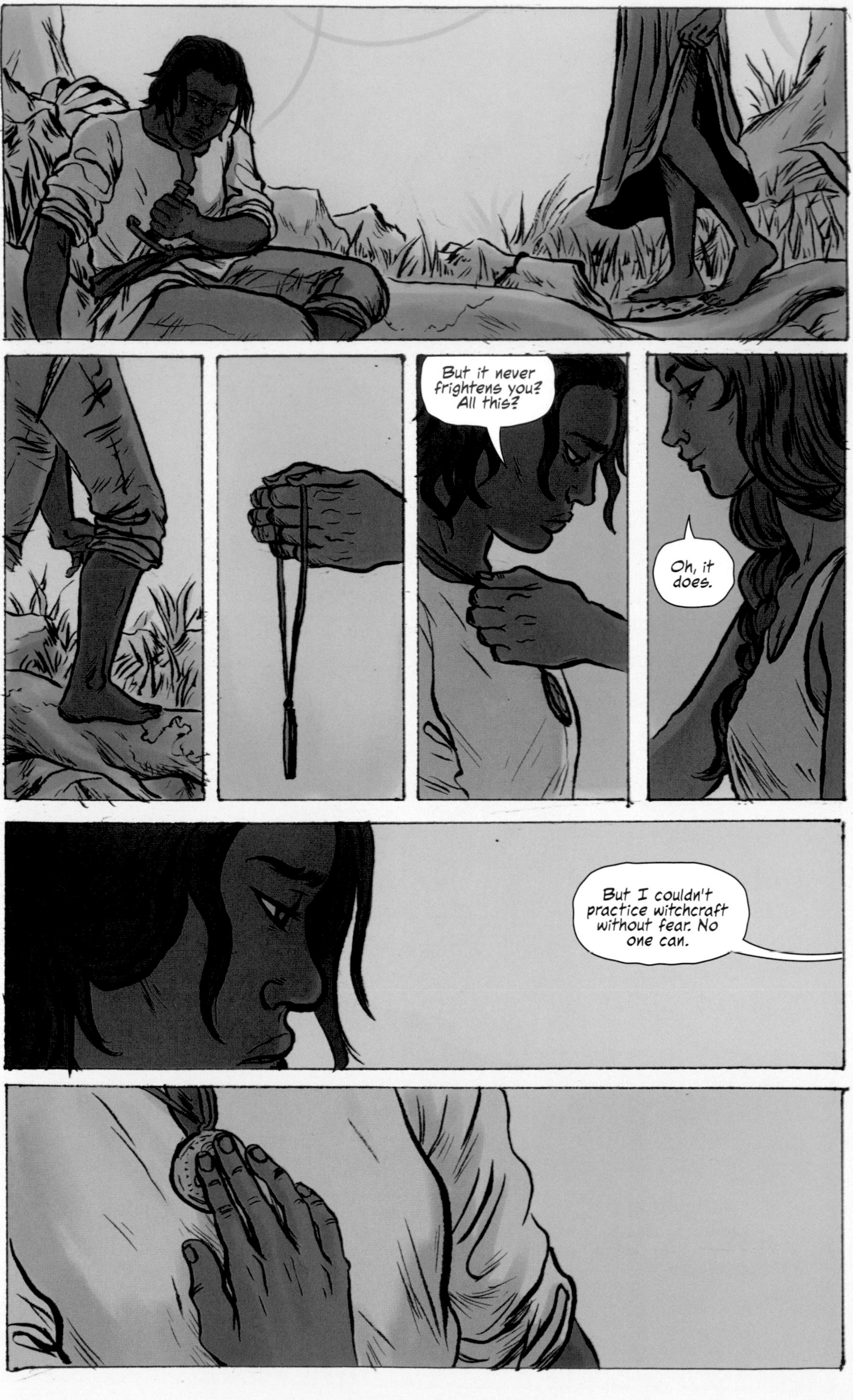
But it never frightens you? All this?
Oh, it does.
But I couldn't practice witchcraft without fear. No one can.

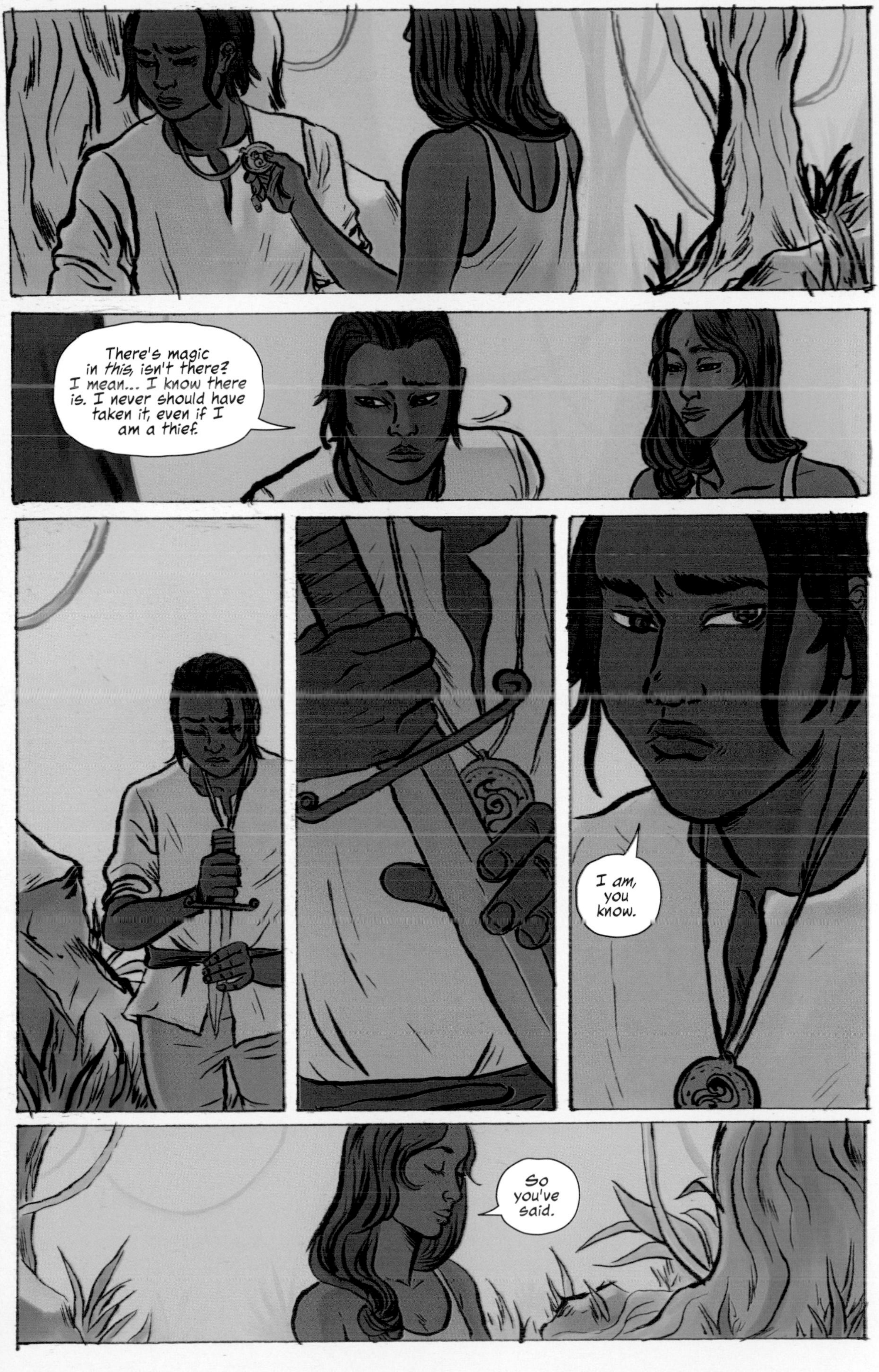
There's magic in *this,* isn't there? I mean... I know there is. I never should have taken it, even if I am a thief.
I am, you know.
So you've said.

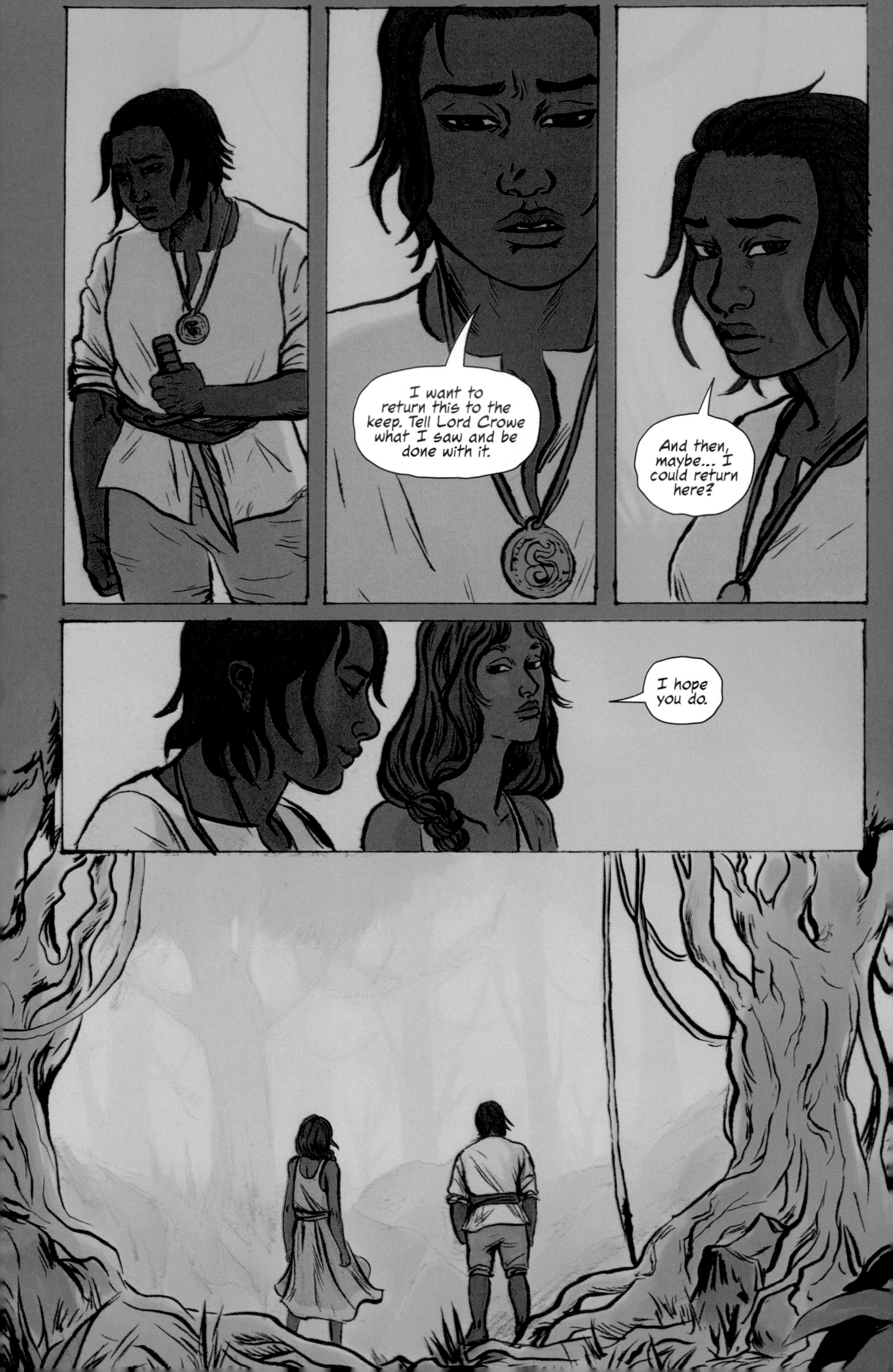
I want to return this to the keep. Tell Lord Crowe what I saw and be done with it.
And then, maybe... I could return here?
I hope you do.

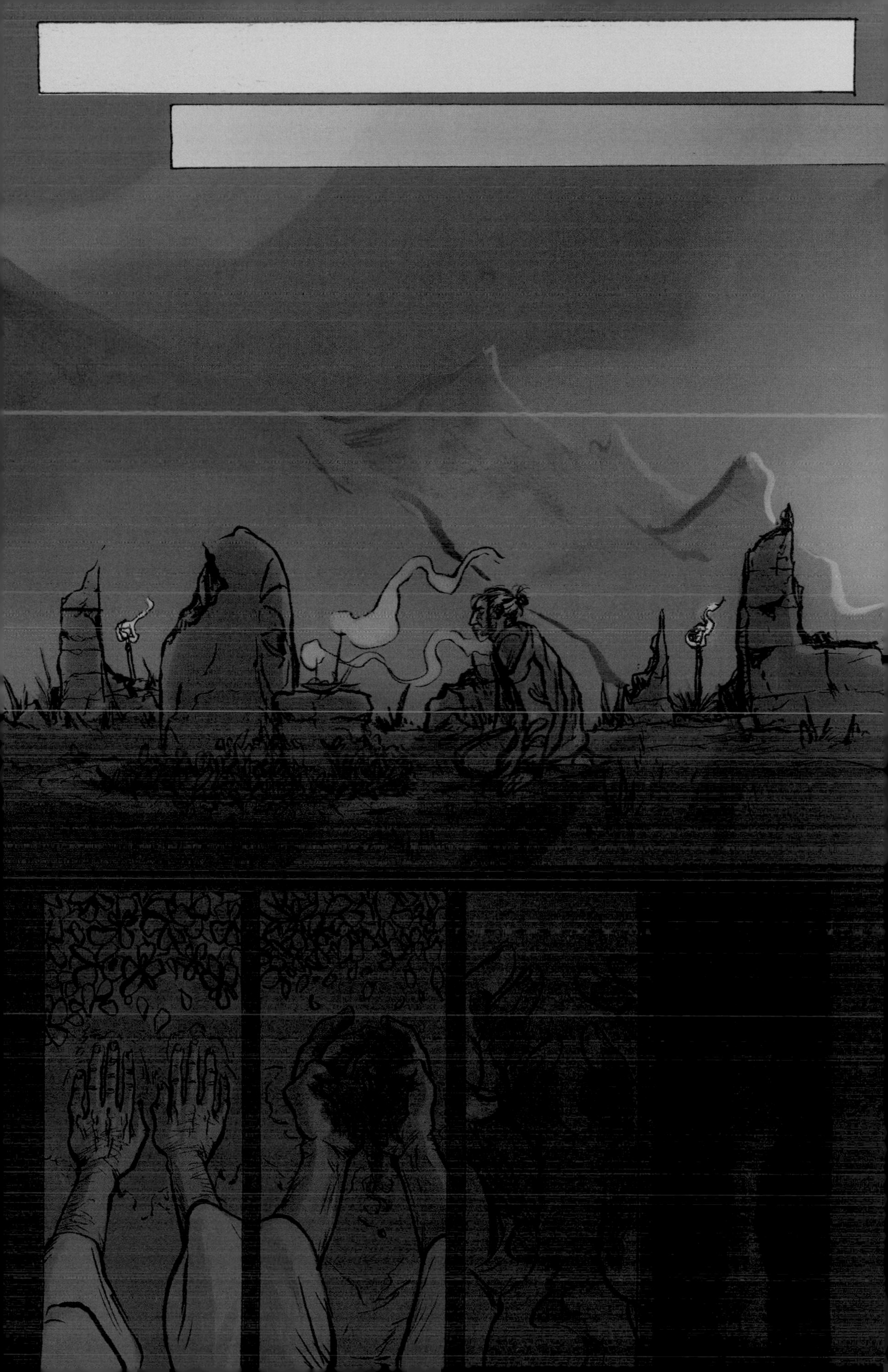

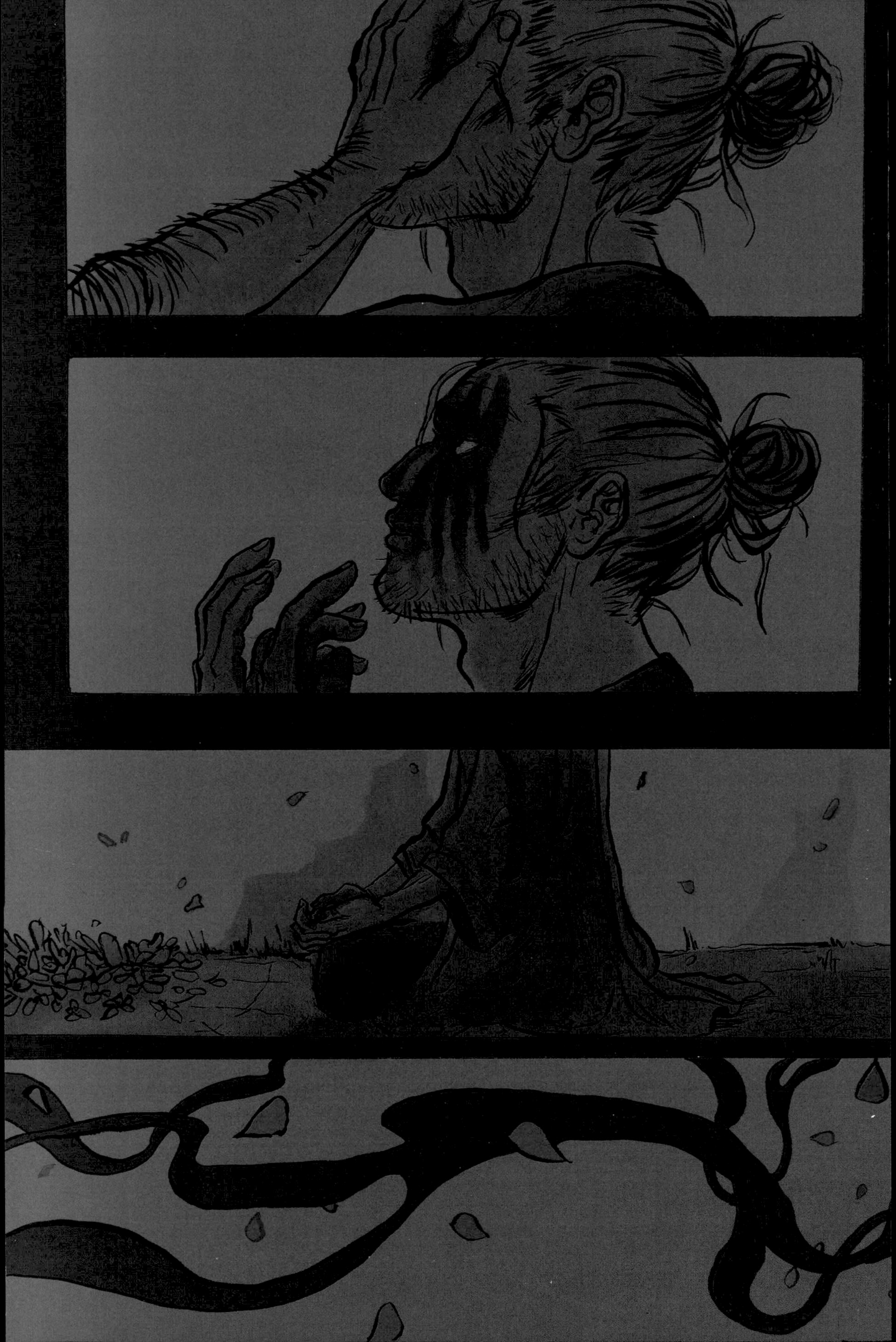

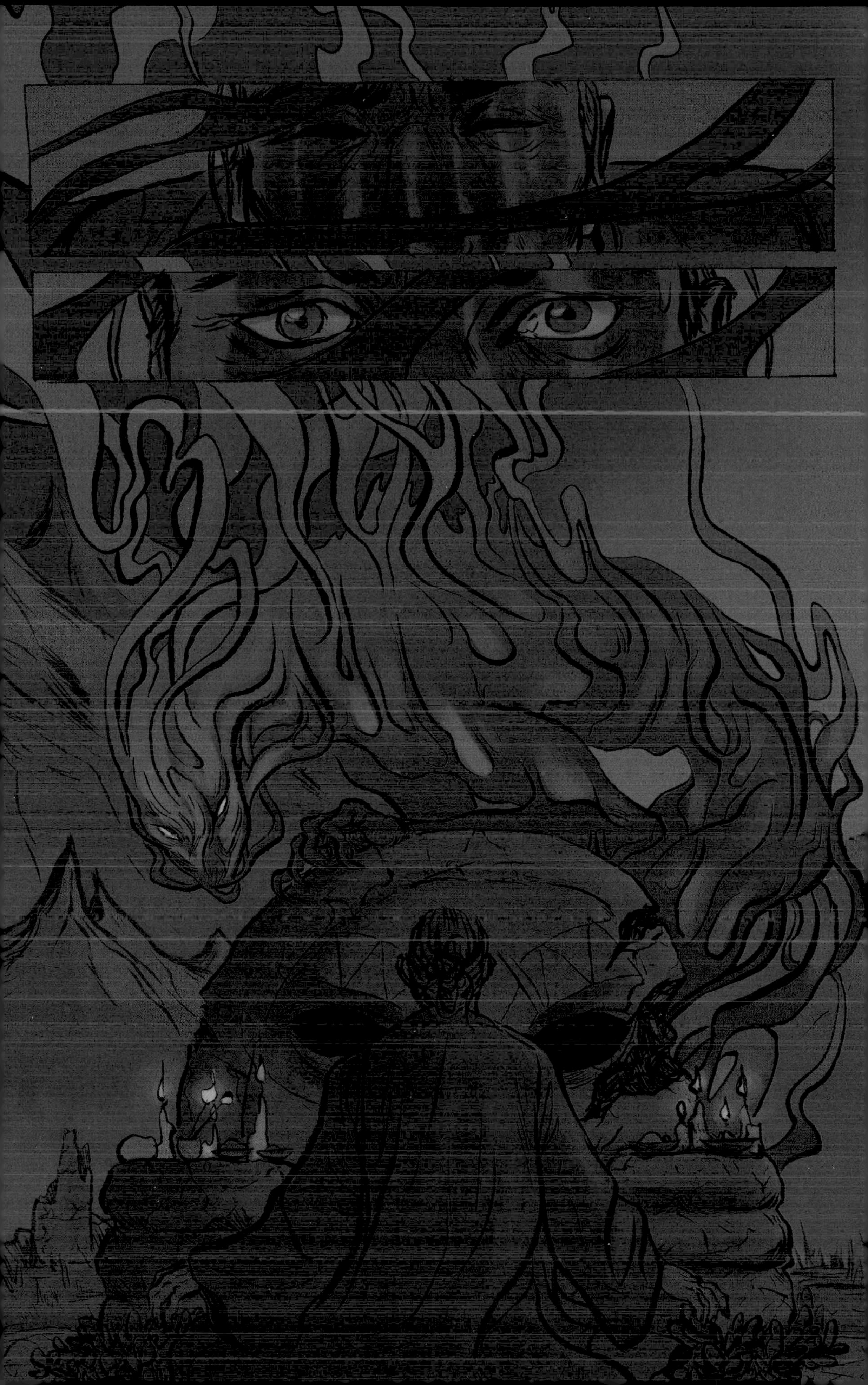

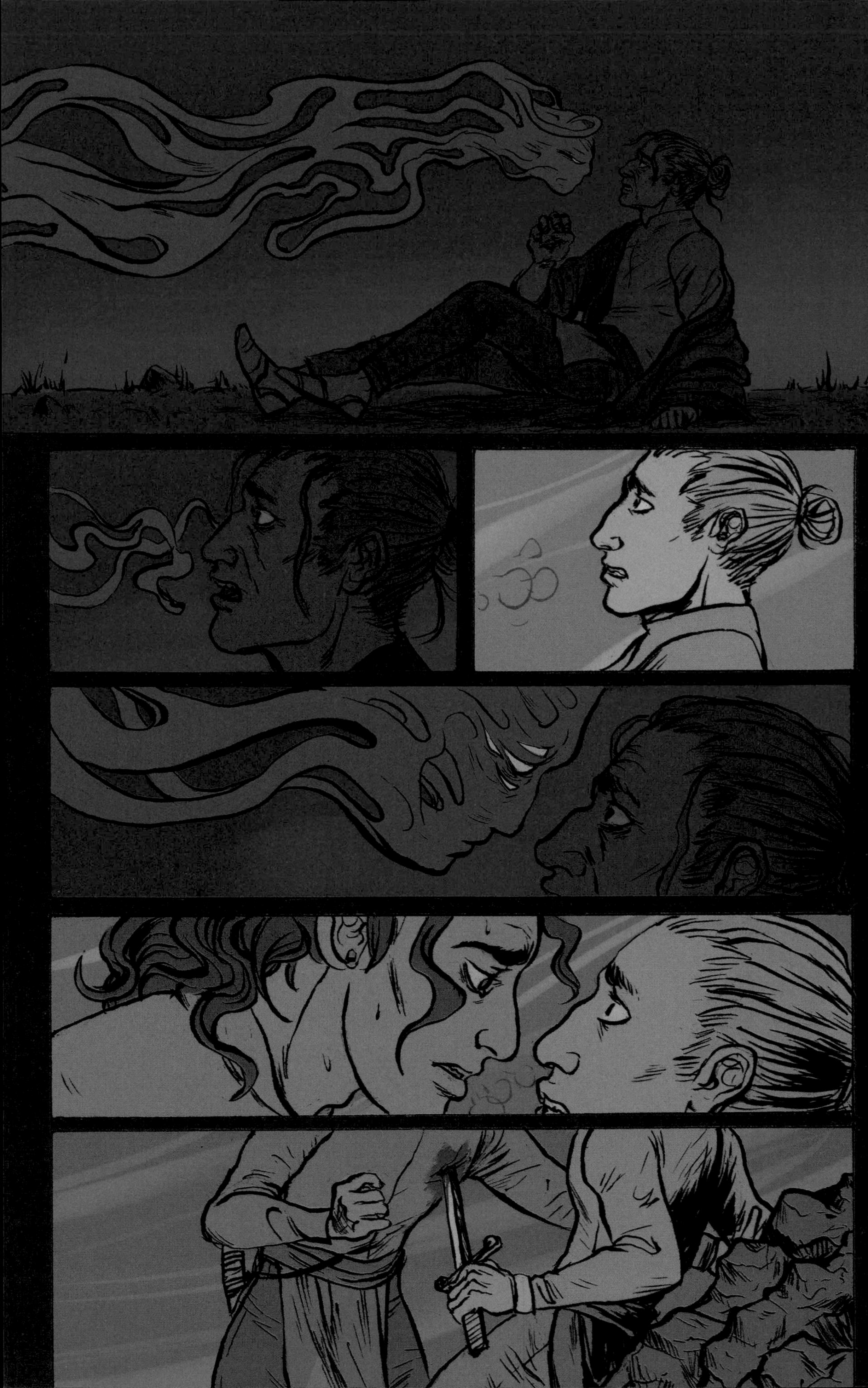

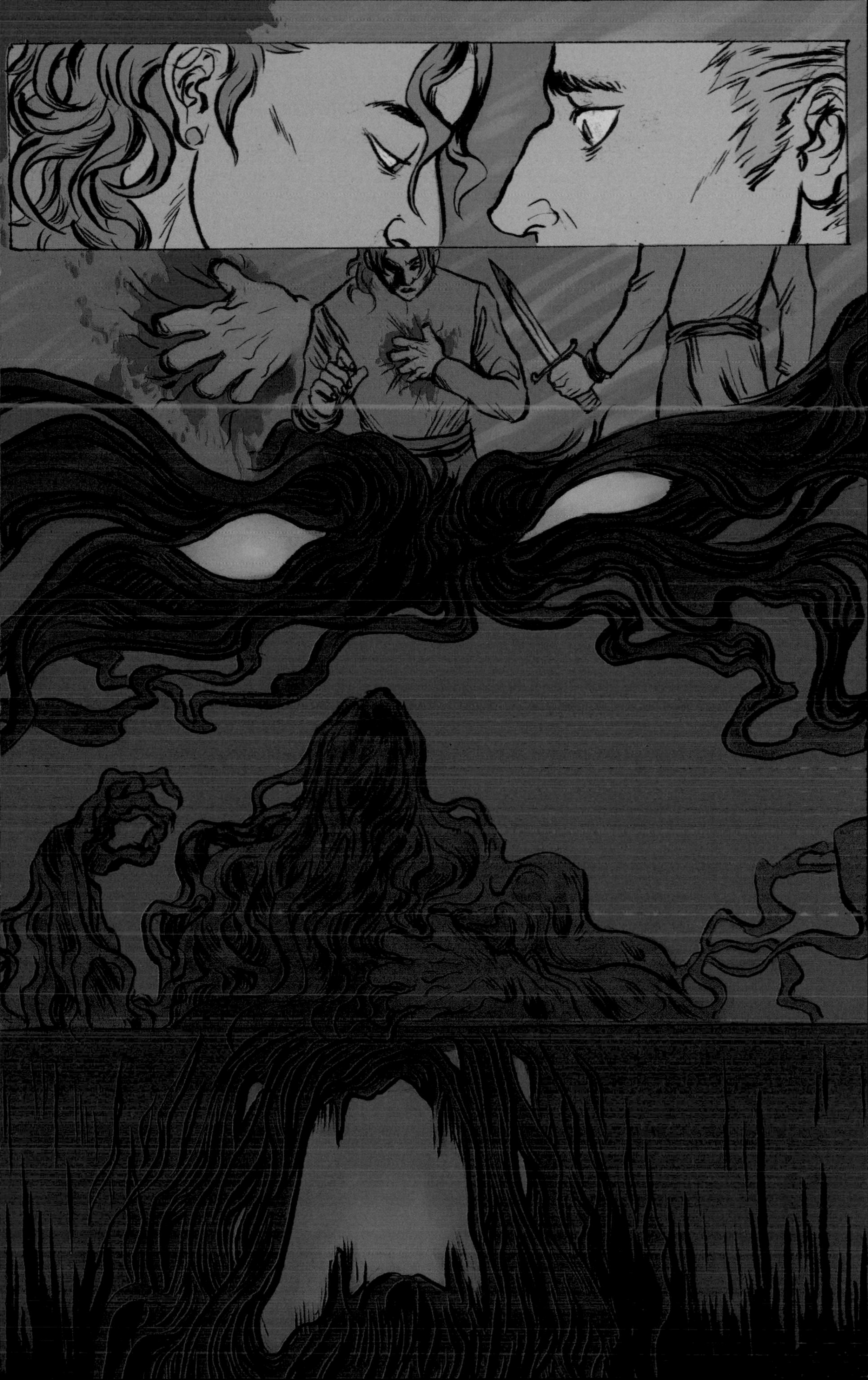

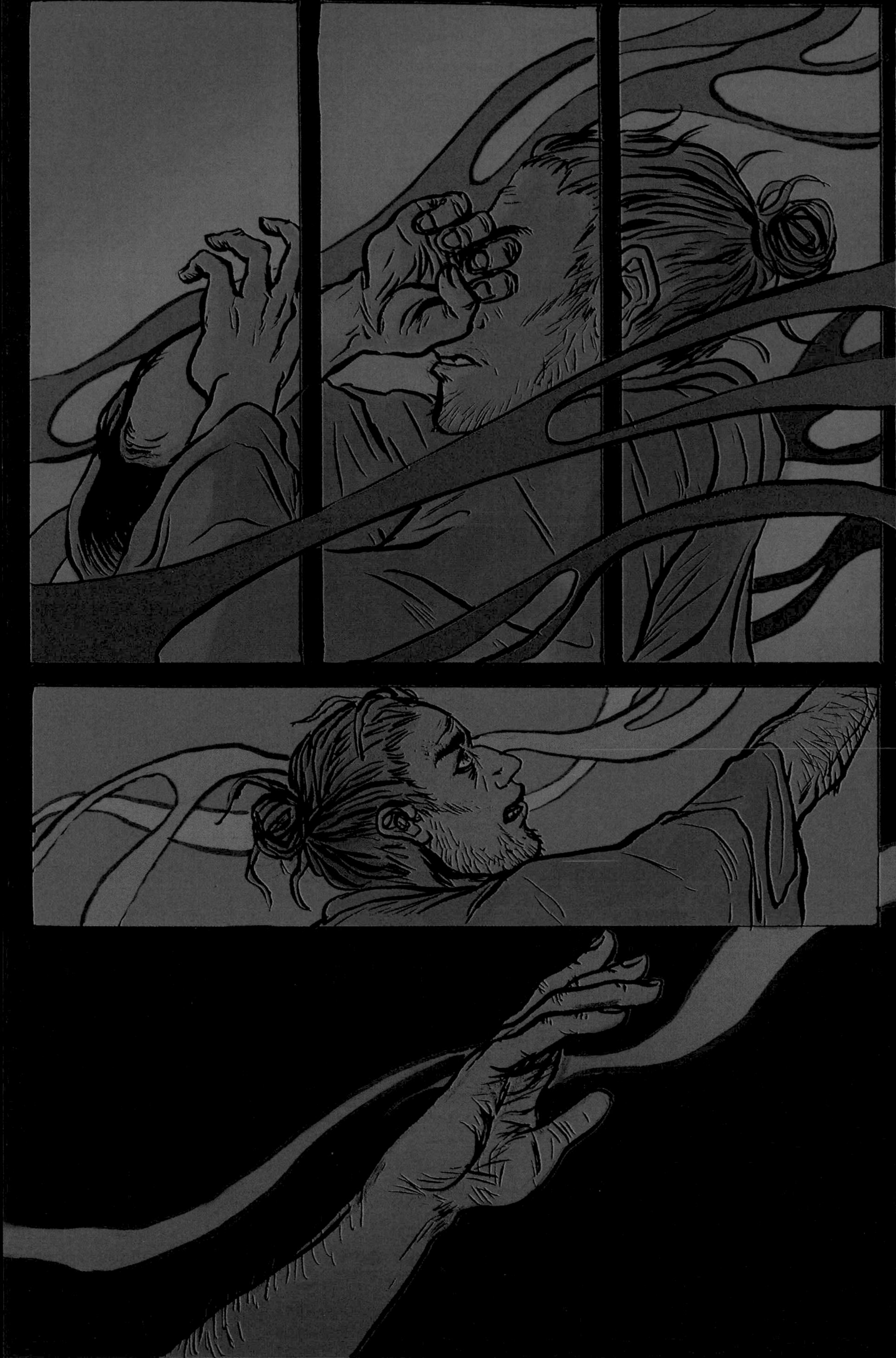

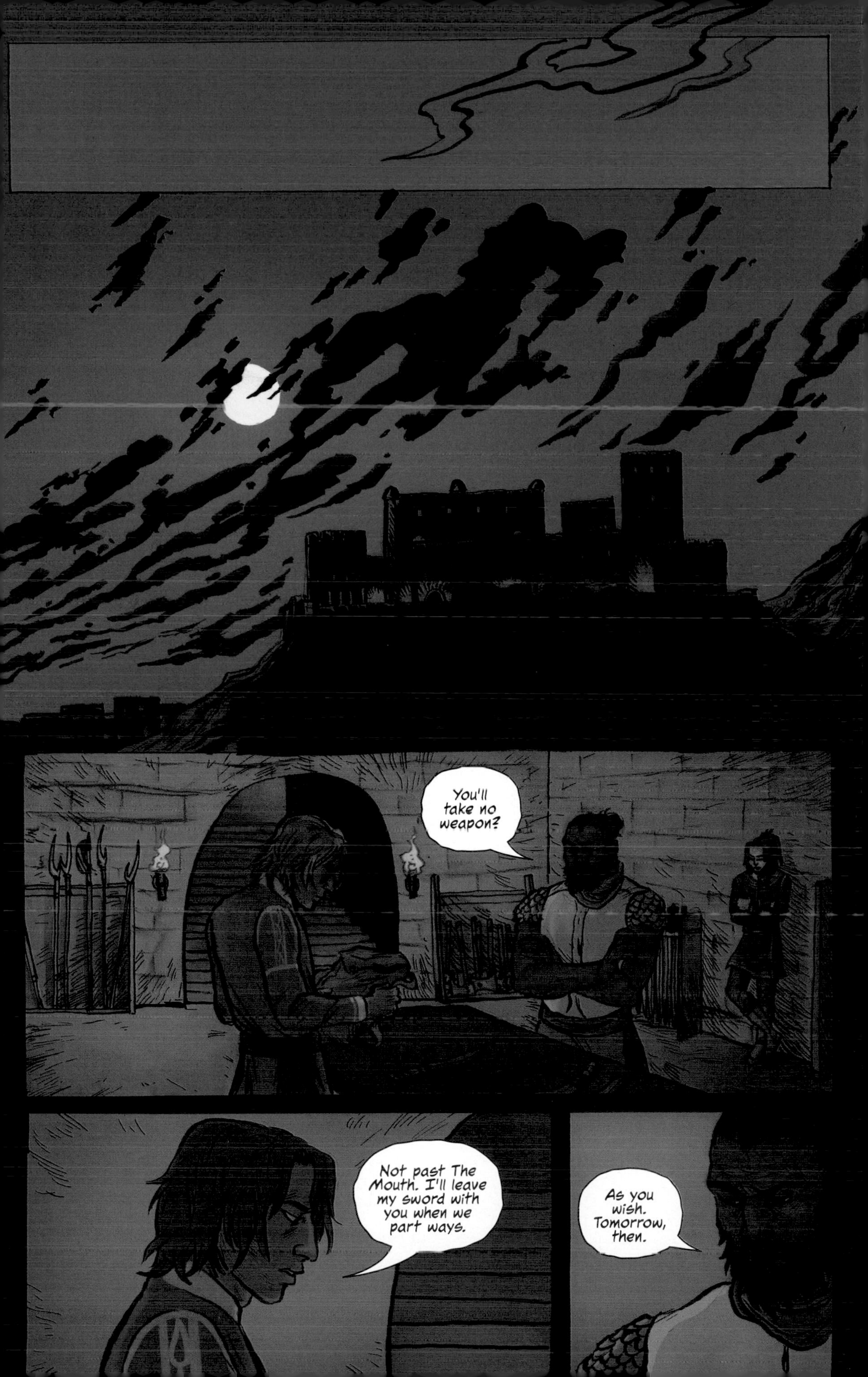
You'll take no weapon?
Not past The Mouth. I'll leave my sword with you when we part ways.
As you wish. Tomorrow, then.

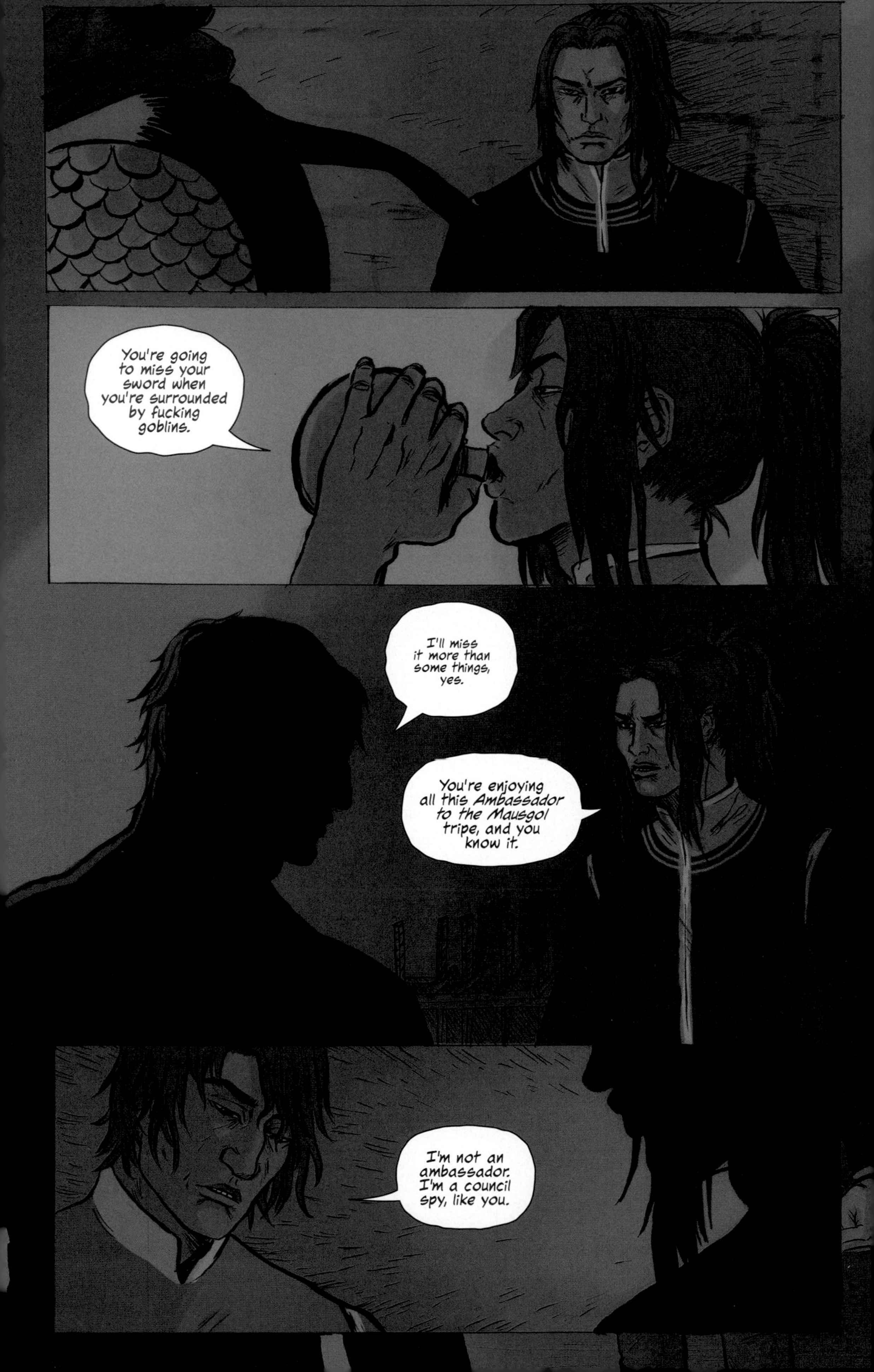
You're going to miss your sword when you're surrounded by fucking goblins.
I'll miss it more than some things, yes.
You're enjoying all this *Ambassador to the Mausgol* tripe, and you know it.
I'm not an ambassador. I'm a council spy, like you.

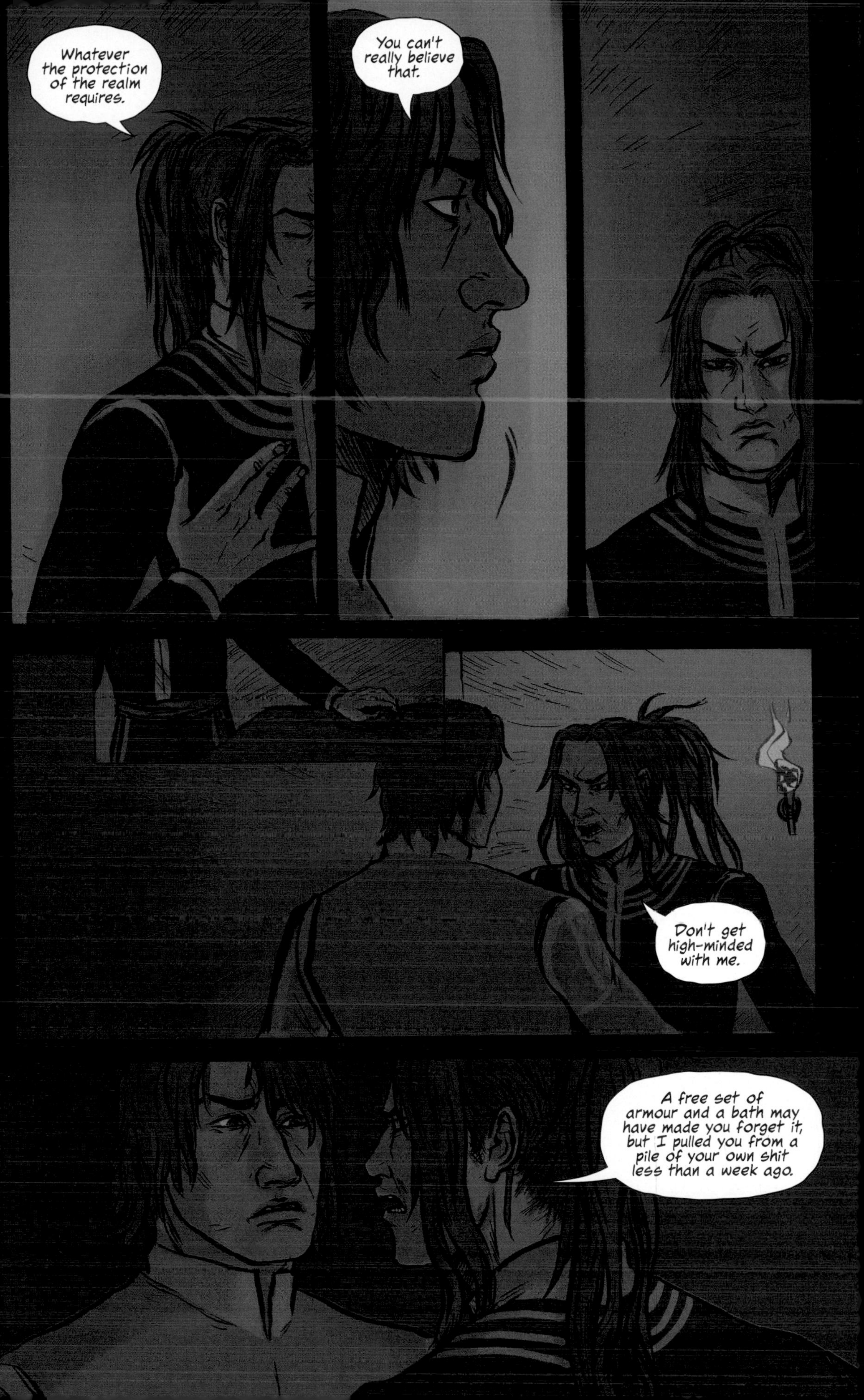
Whatever the protection of the realm requires.
You can't really believe that.
Don't get high-minded with me.
A free set of armour and a bath may have made you forget it, but I pulled you from a pile of your own shit less than a week ago.

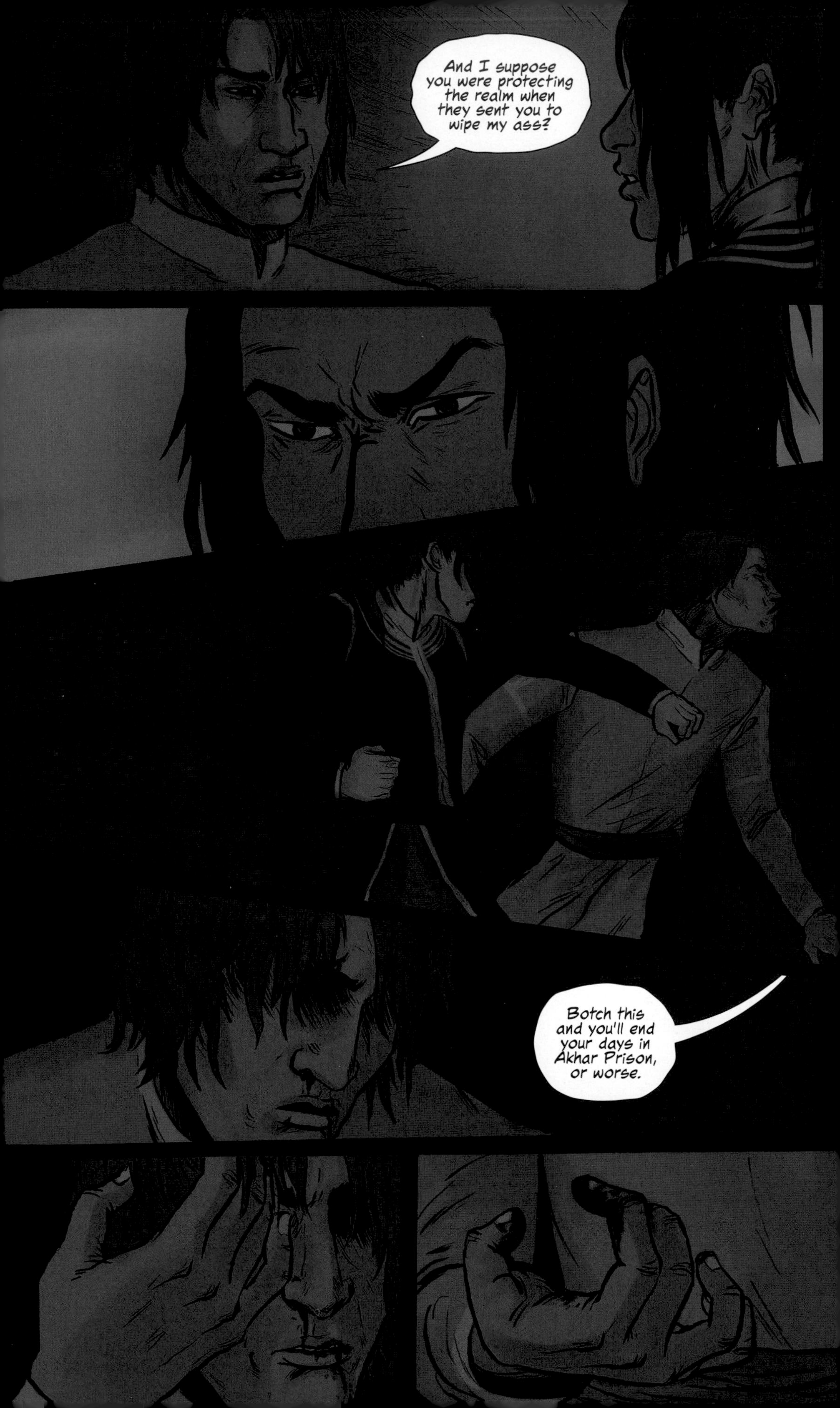
And I suppose you were protecting the realm when they sent you to wipe my ass?
Botch this and you'll end your days in Akhar Prison, or worse.

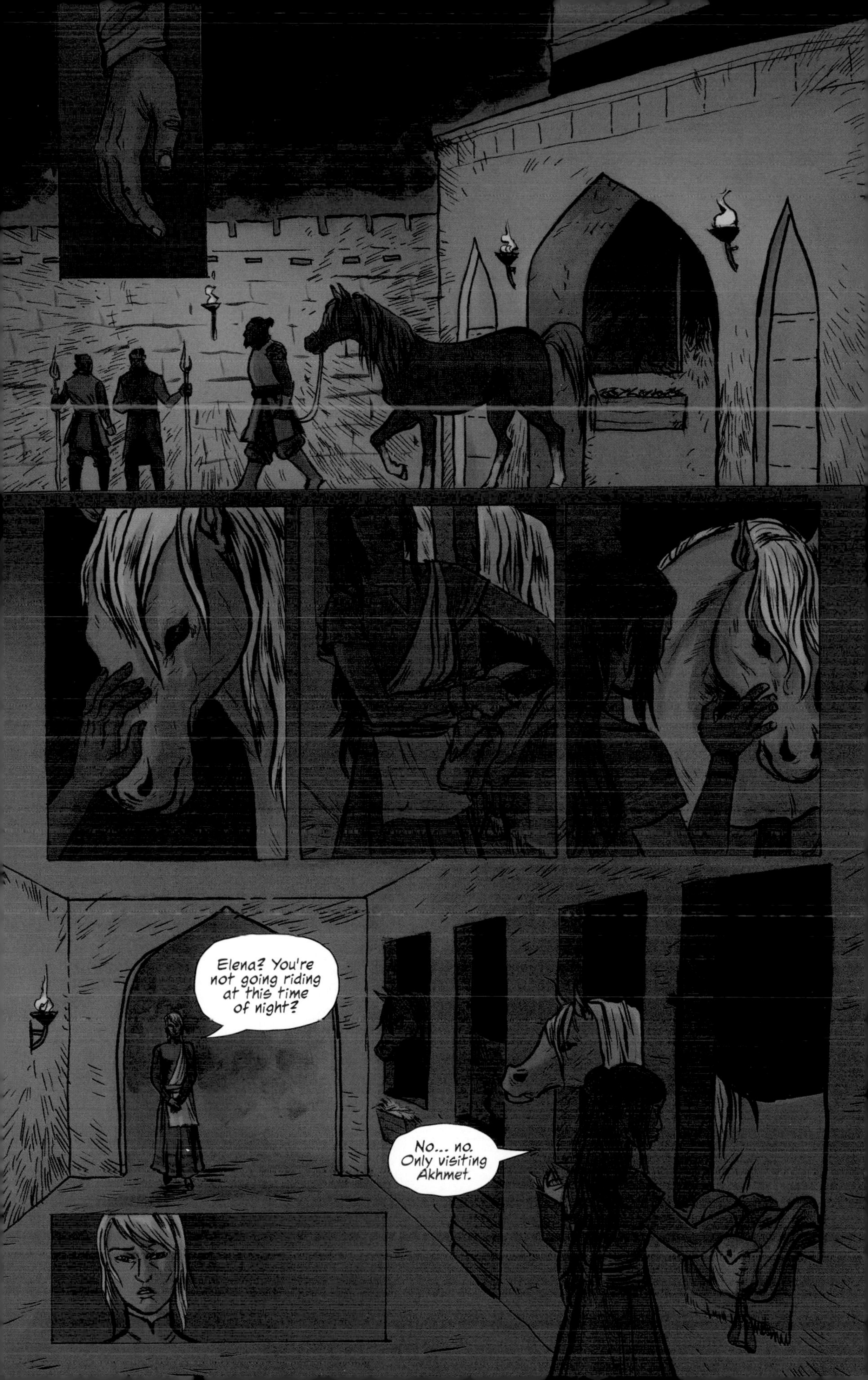
Elena? You're not going riding at this time of night?
No... no. Only visiting Akhmet.

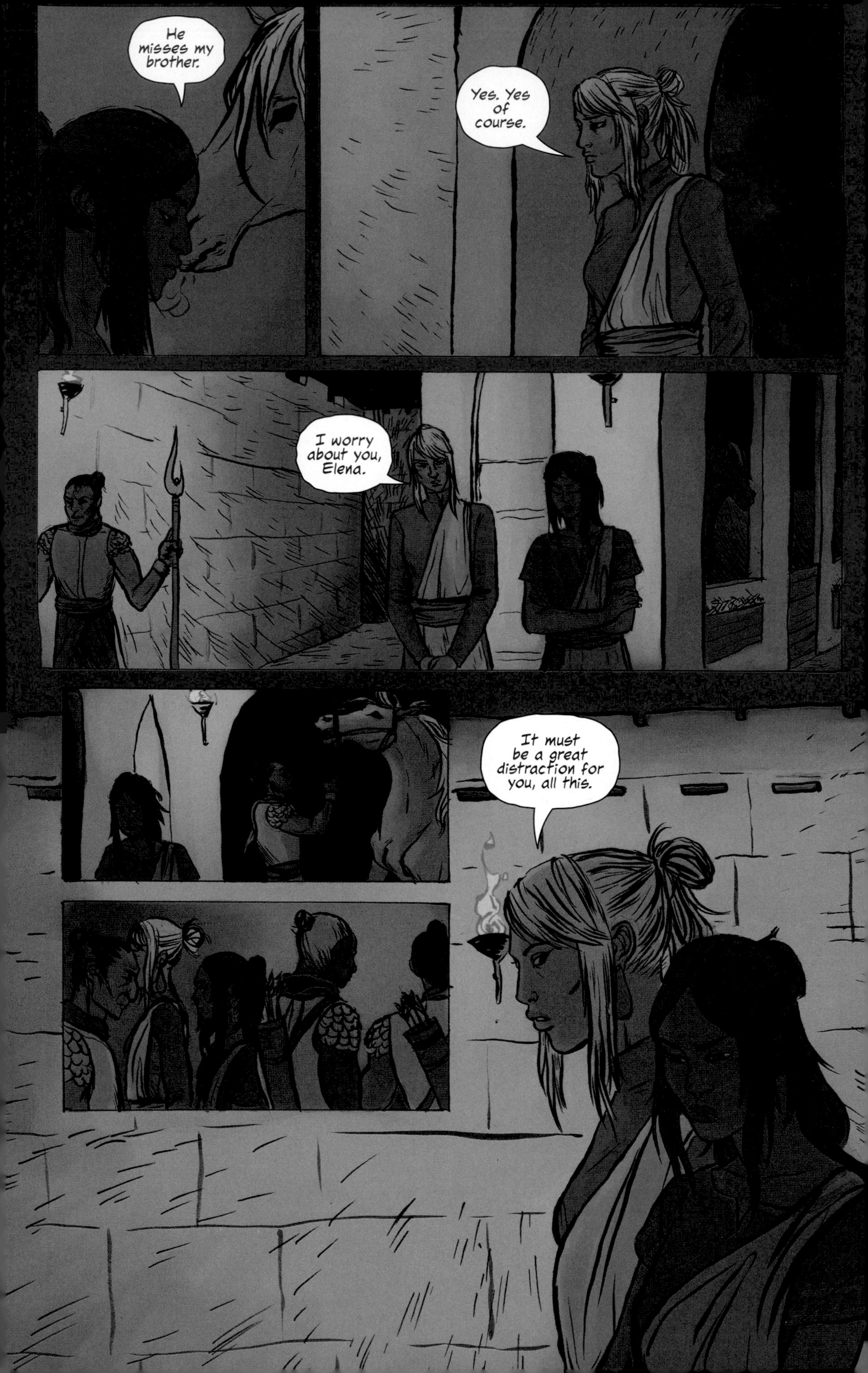
He misses my brother.
Yes. Yes of course.
I worry about you, Elena.
It must be a great distraction for you, all this.

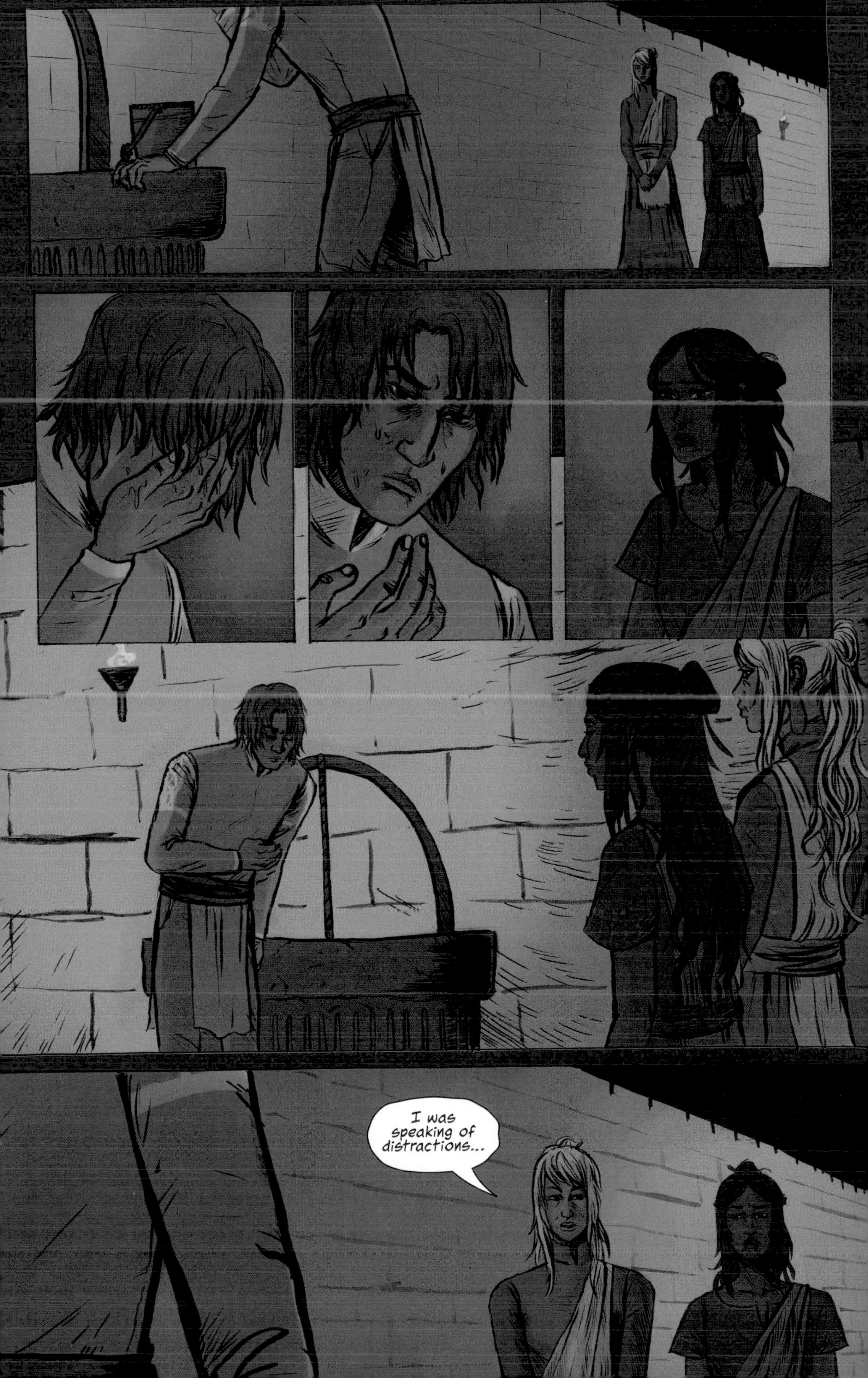
I was speaking of distractions...

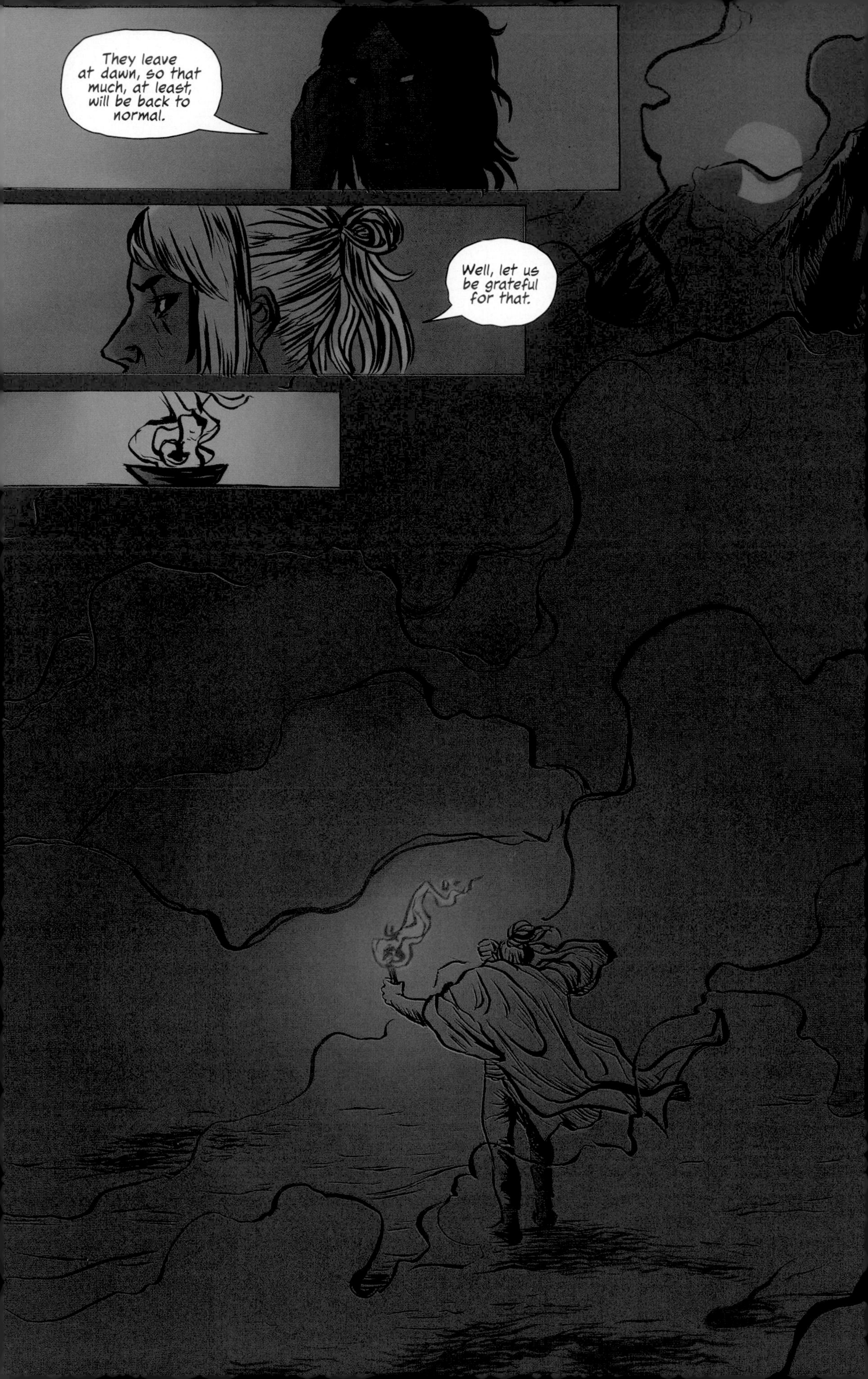
They leave at dawn, so that much, at least, will be back to normal.
Well, let us be grateful for that.

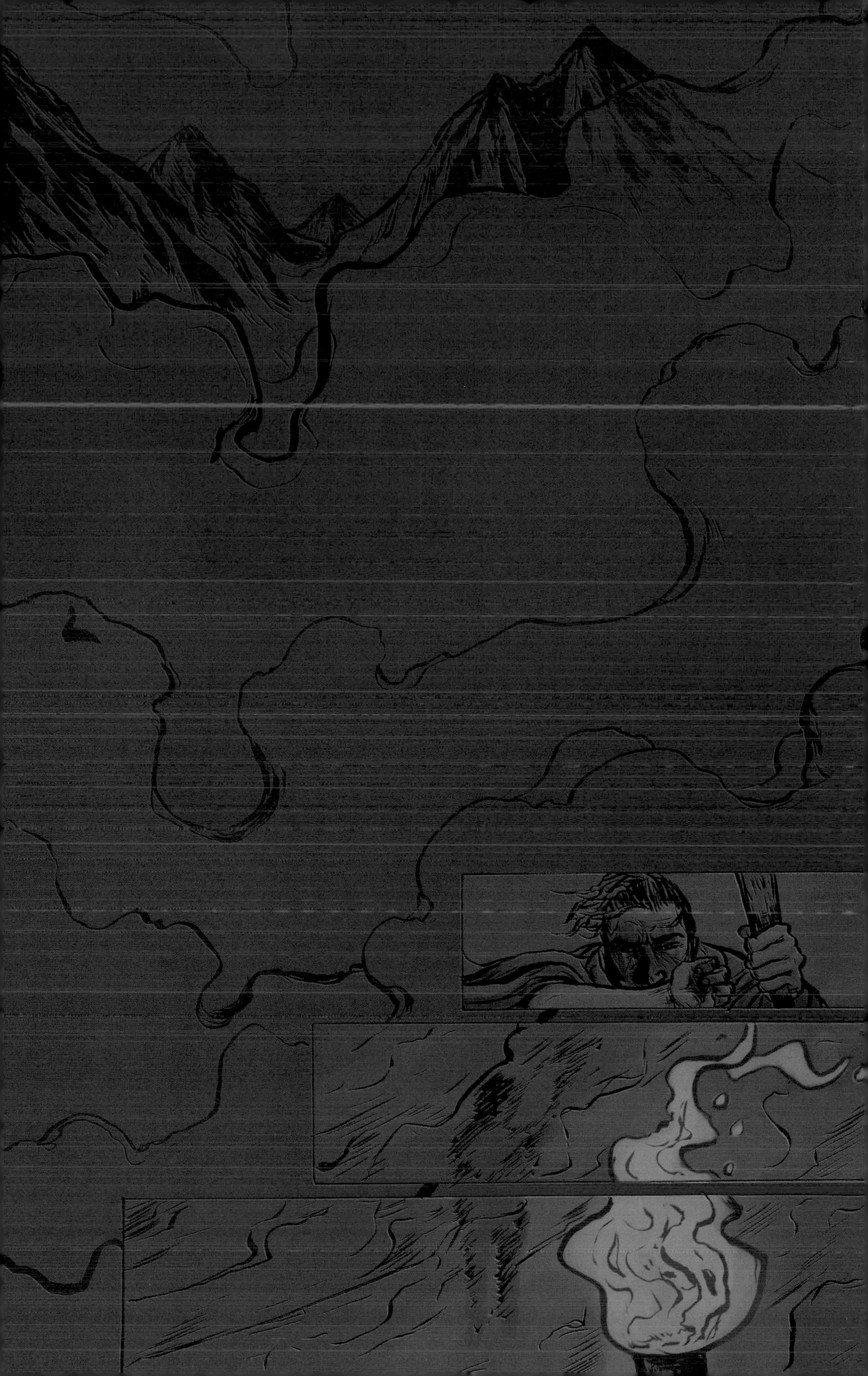

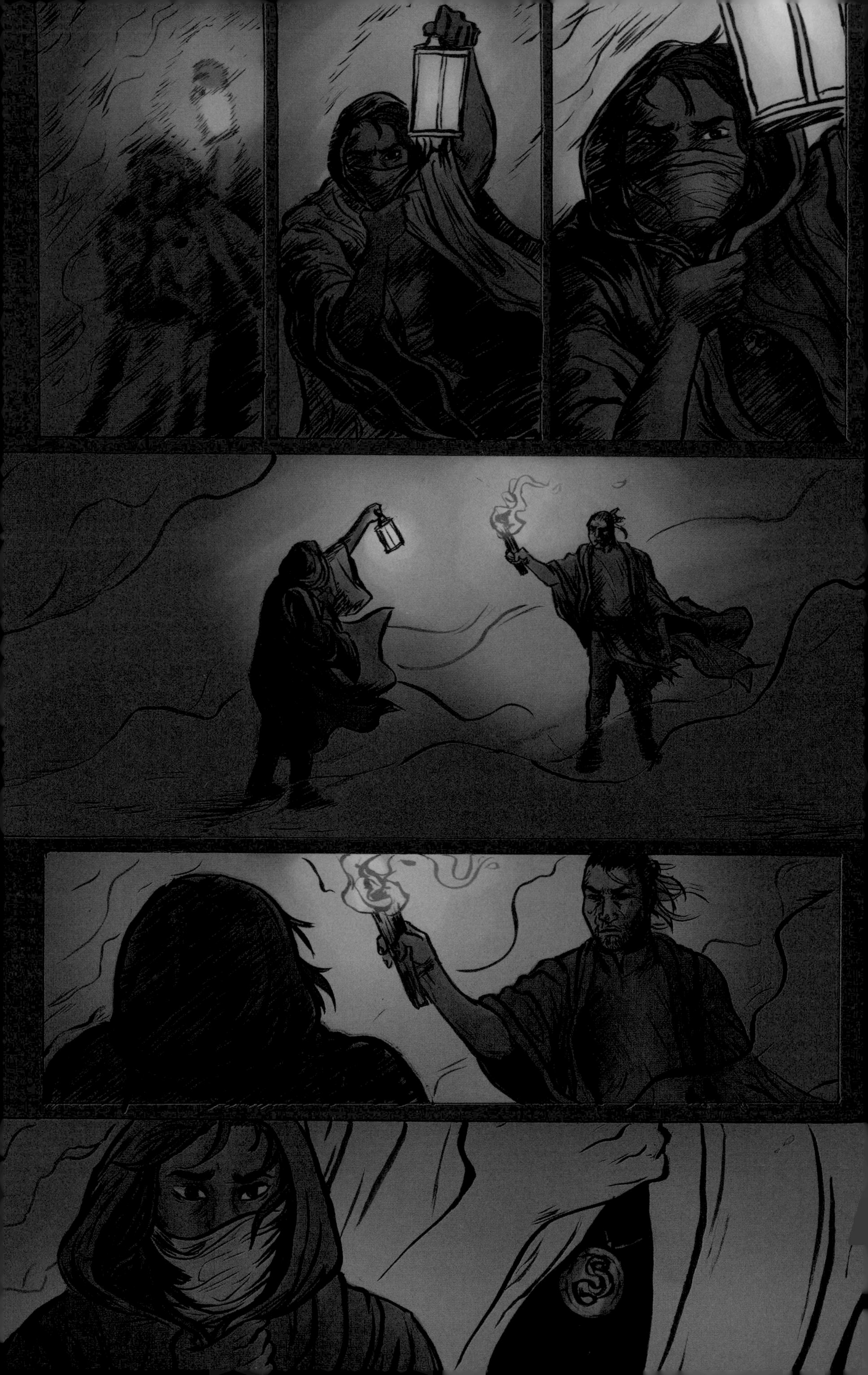

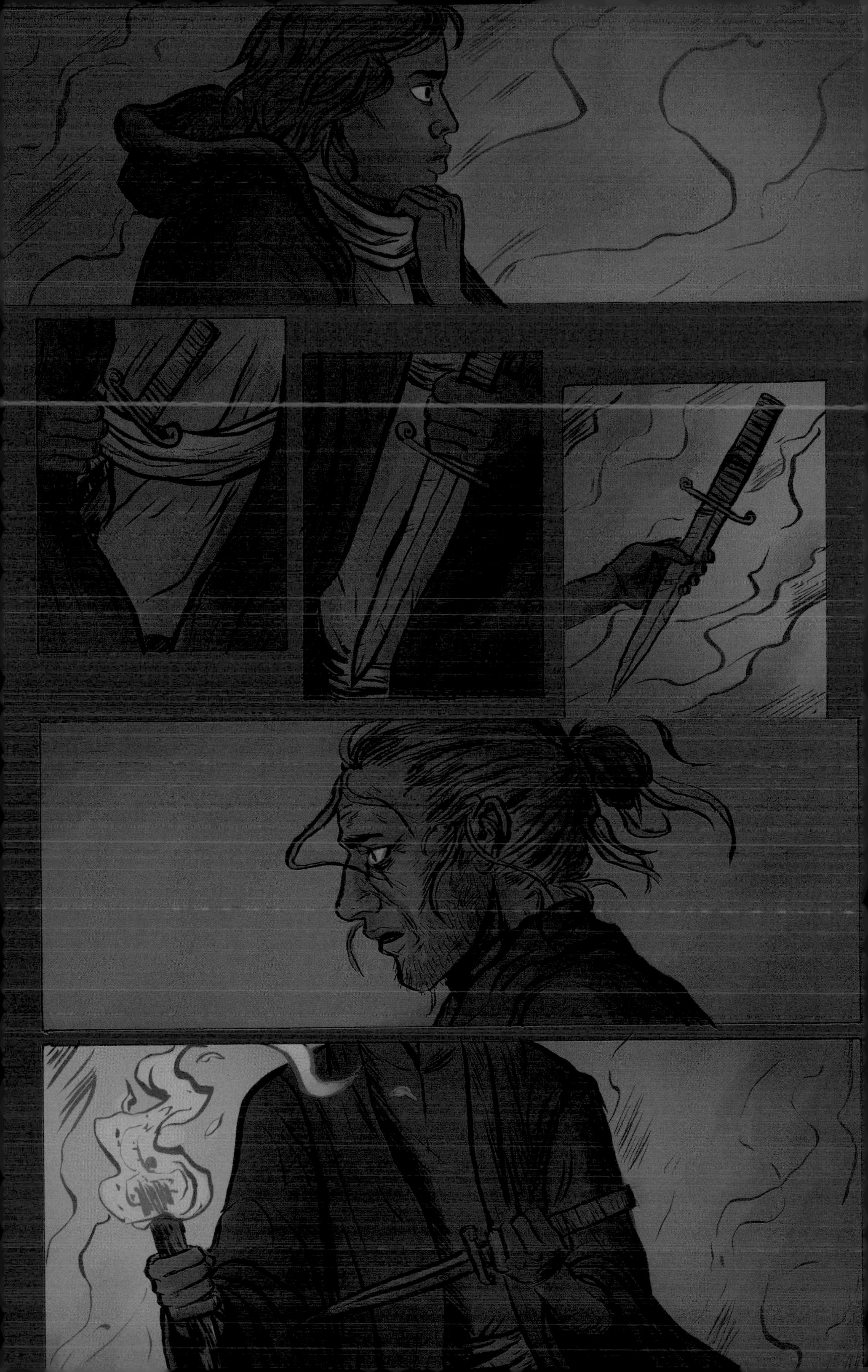

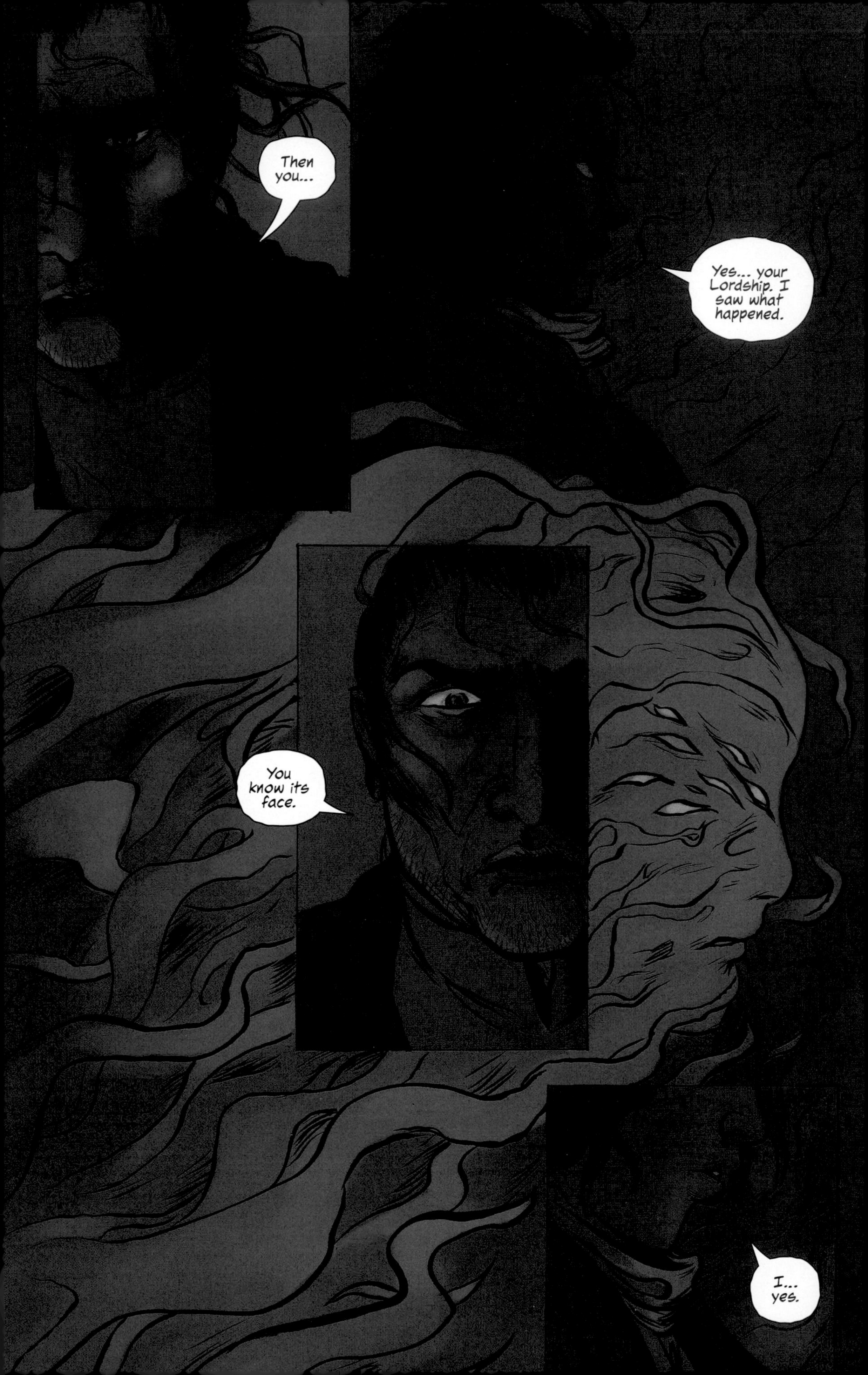
Then you...
Yes... your Lordship. I saw what happened.
You know its face.
I... yes.

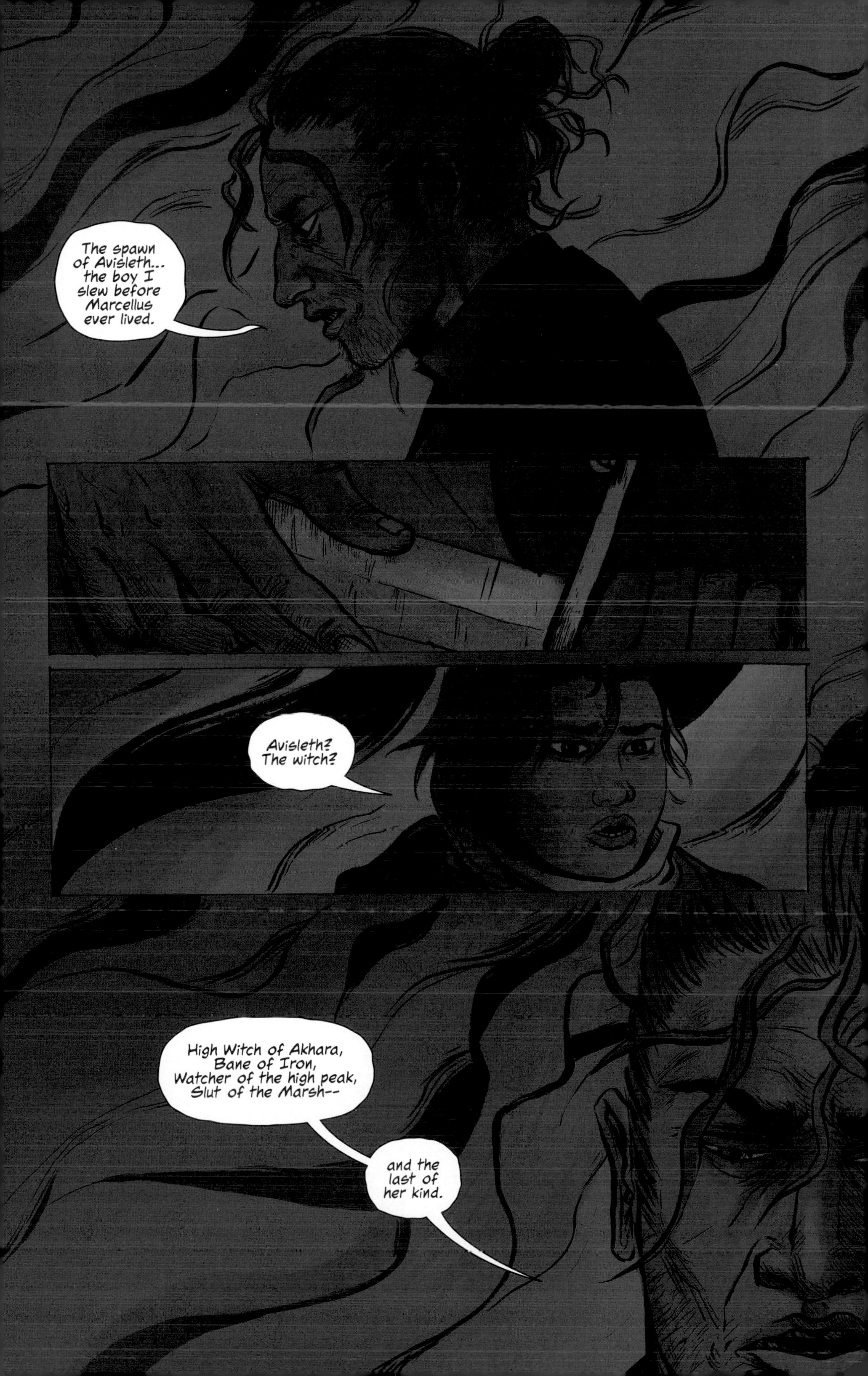
The spawn of Avisleth... the boy I slew before Marcellus ever lived.
Avisleth? The witch?
High Witch of Akhara, Bane of Iron, Watcher of the high peak, Slut of the Marsh--
and the last of her kind.

I don't understand.
Blood is owed now, each to each. To make an end...
My lord?
Is everything...

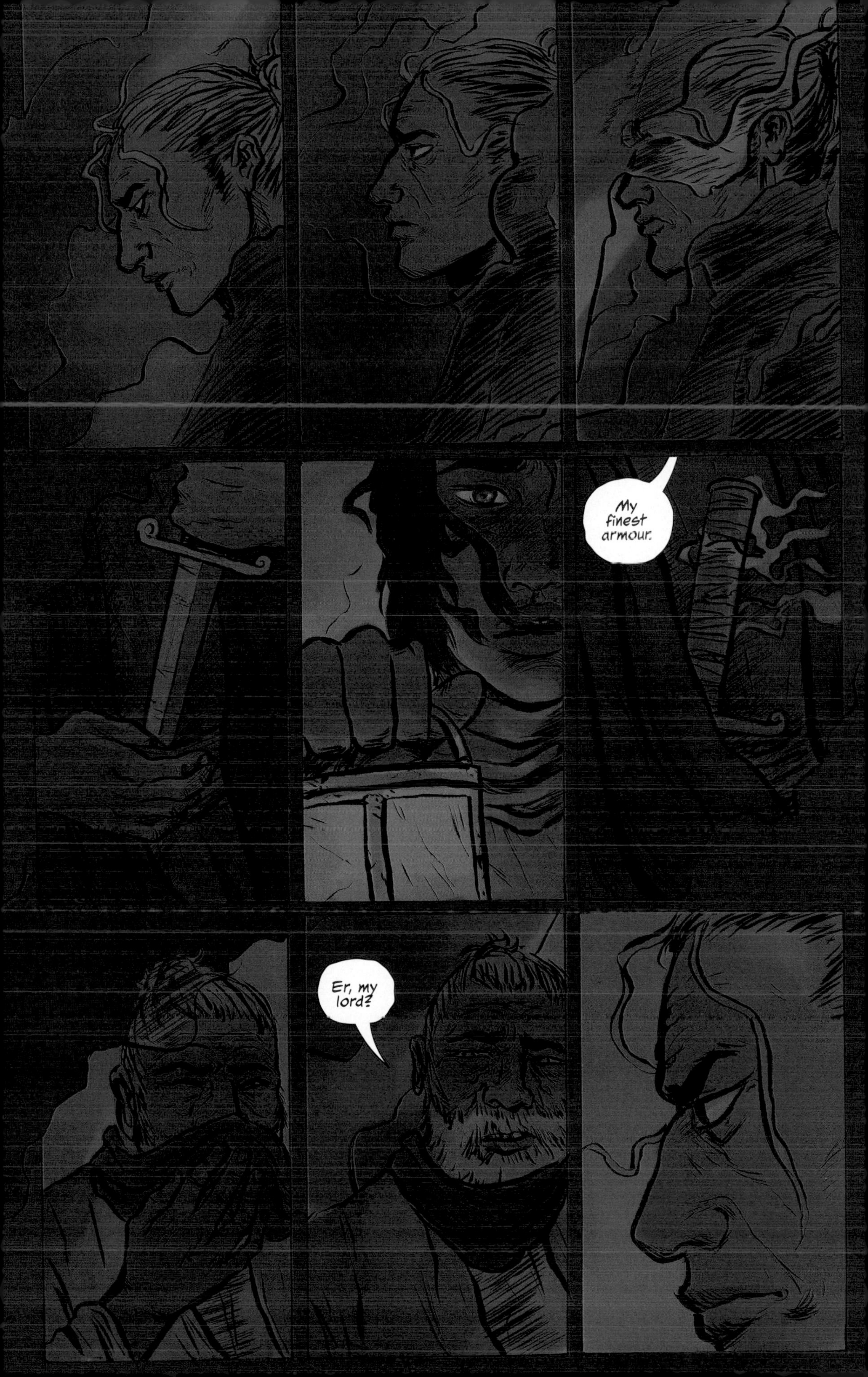
My finest armour.
Er, my lord?

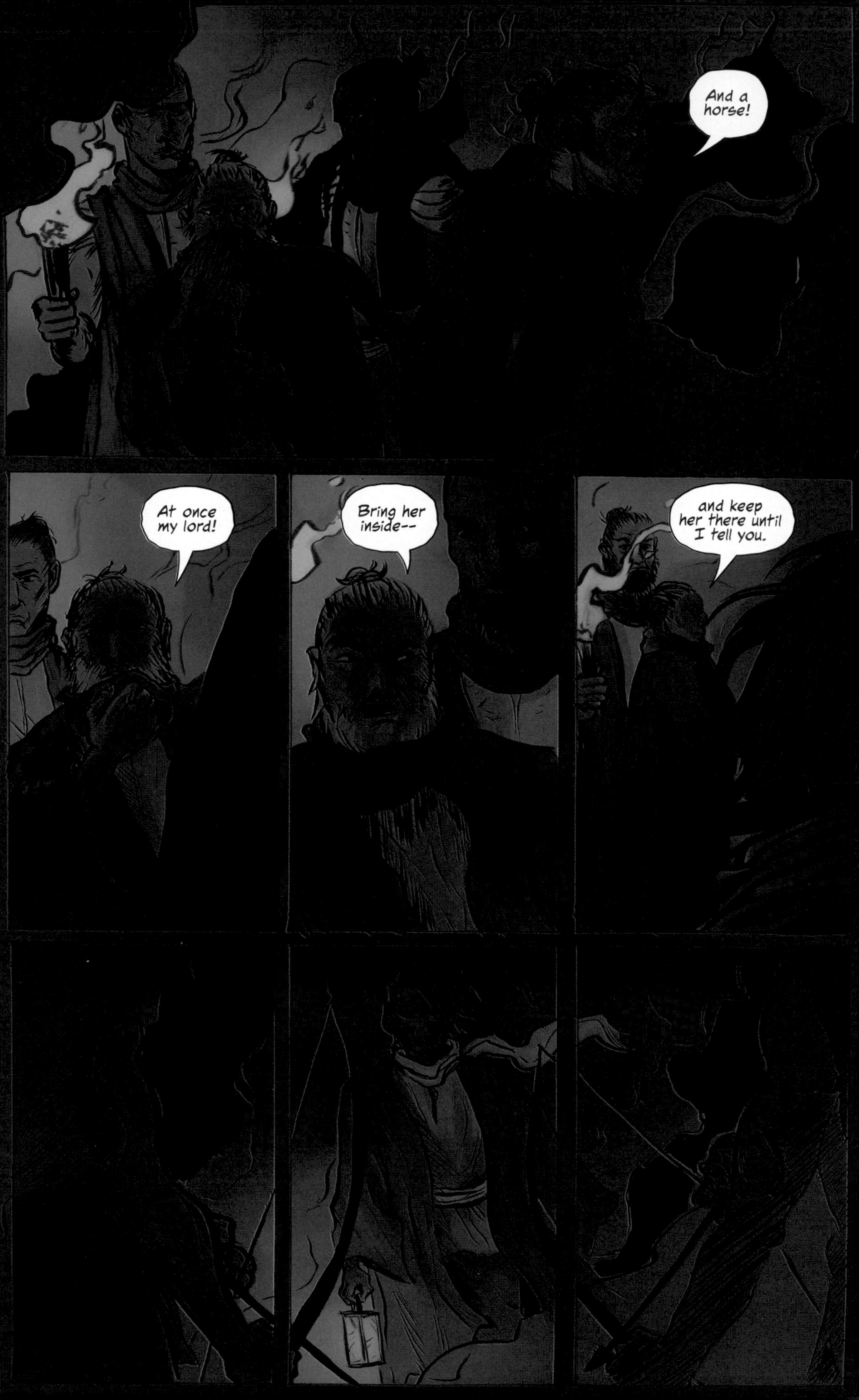
And a horse!
At once my lord!
Bring her inside--
and keep her there until I tell you.

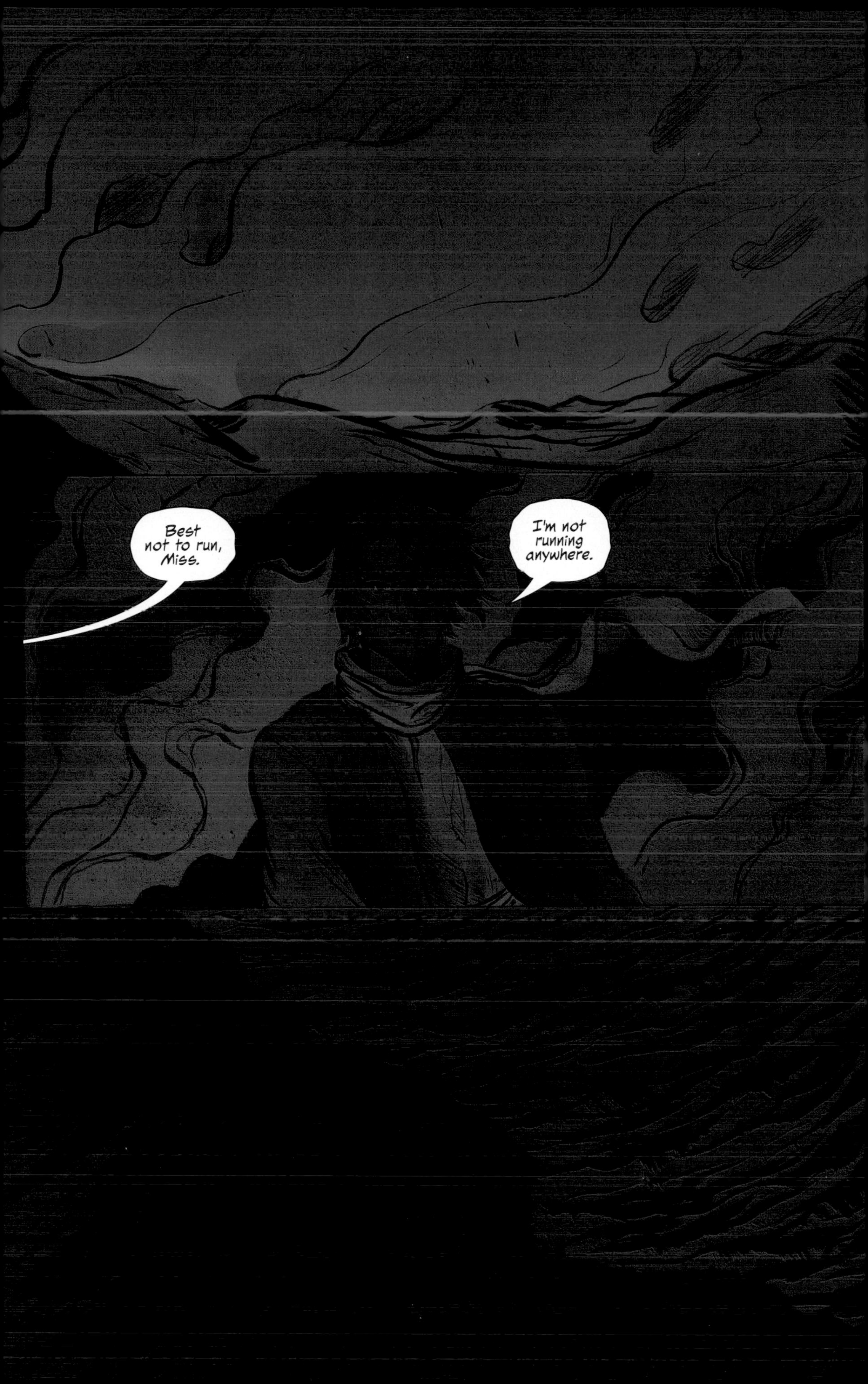
Best not to run, Miss.
I'm not running anywhere.

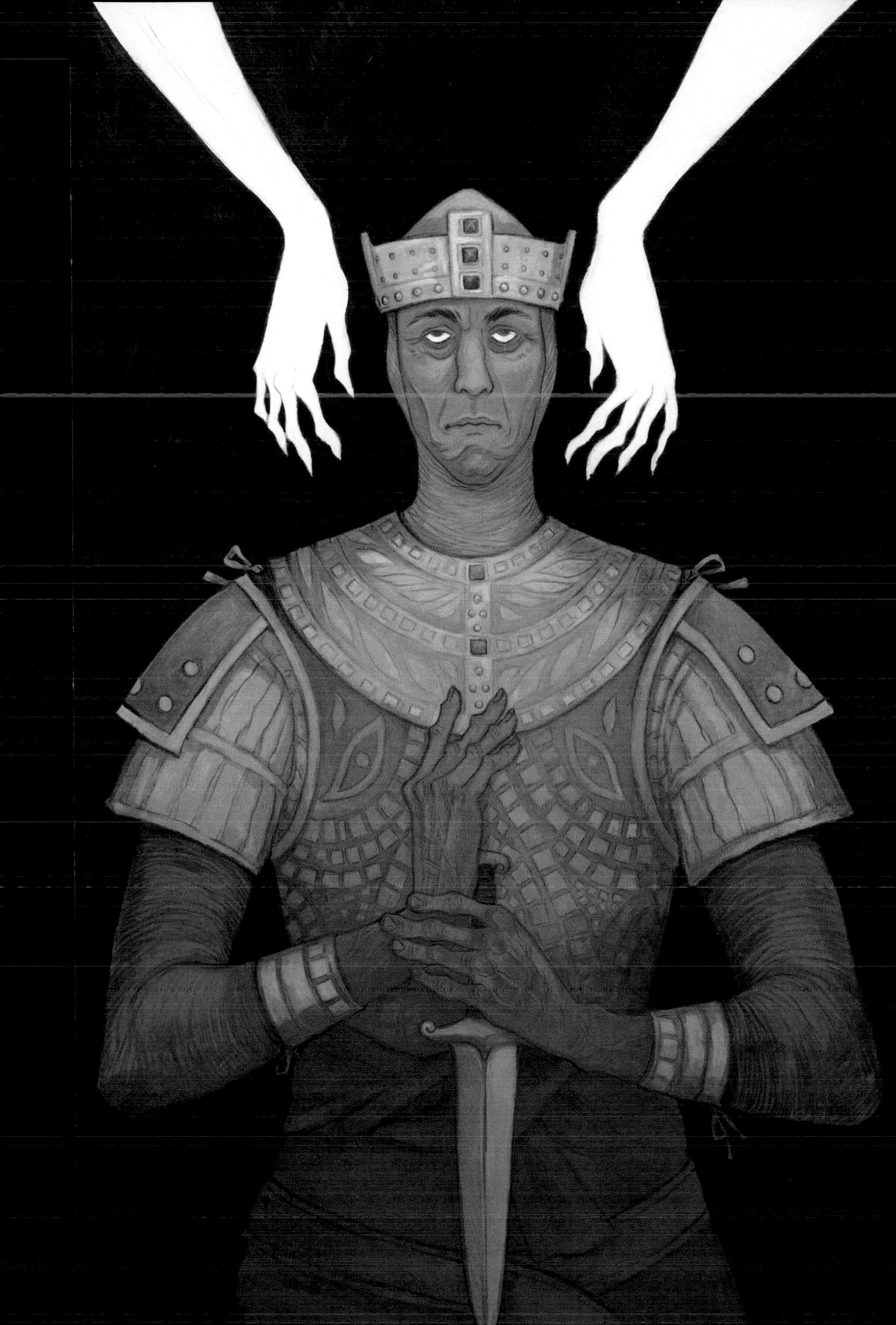

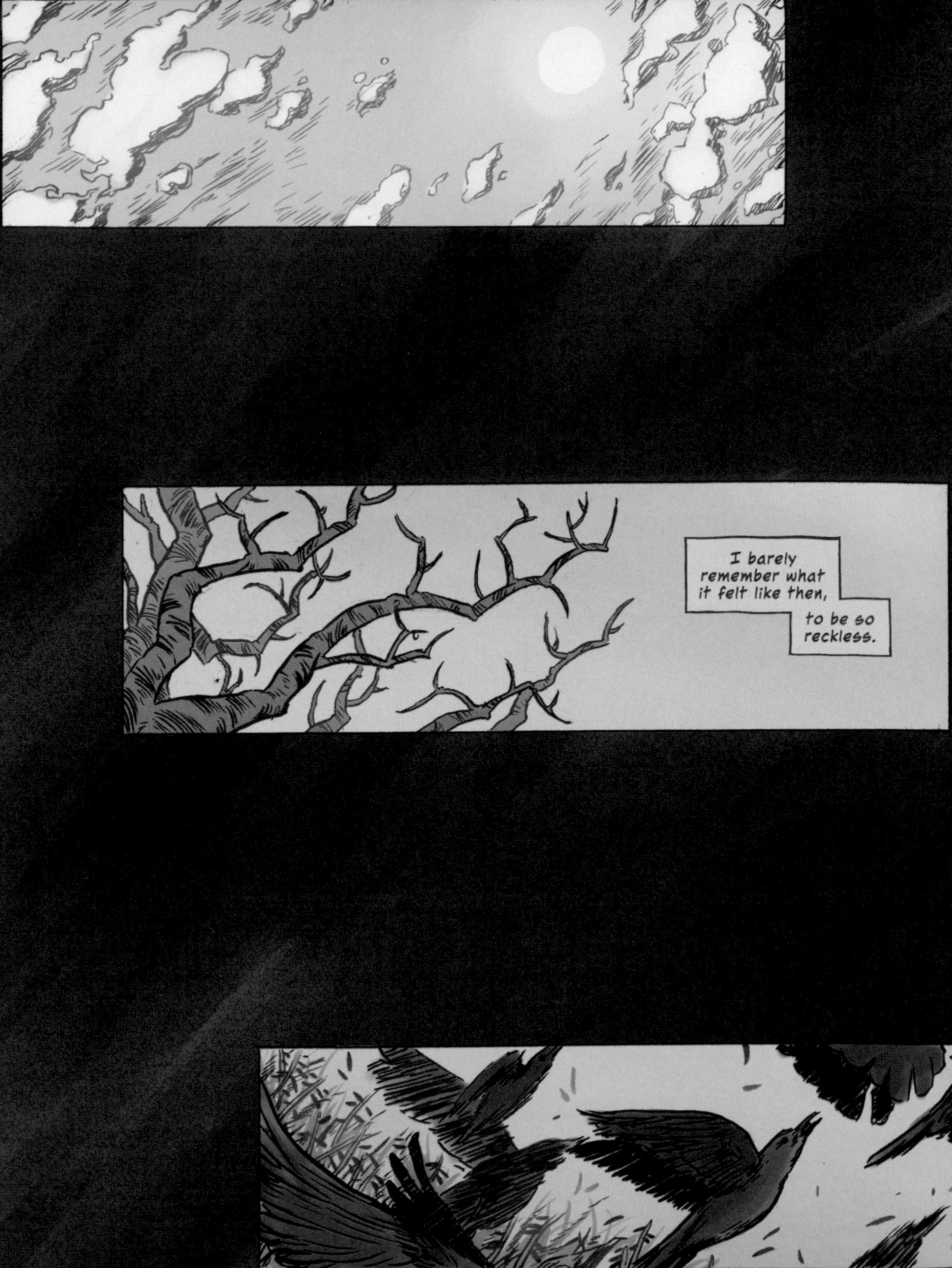
I barely remember what it felt like then,
to be so reckless.

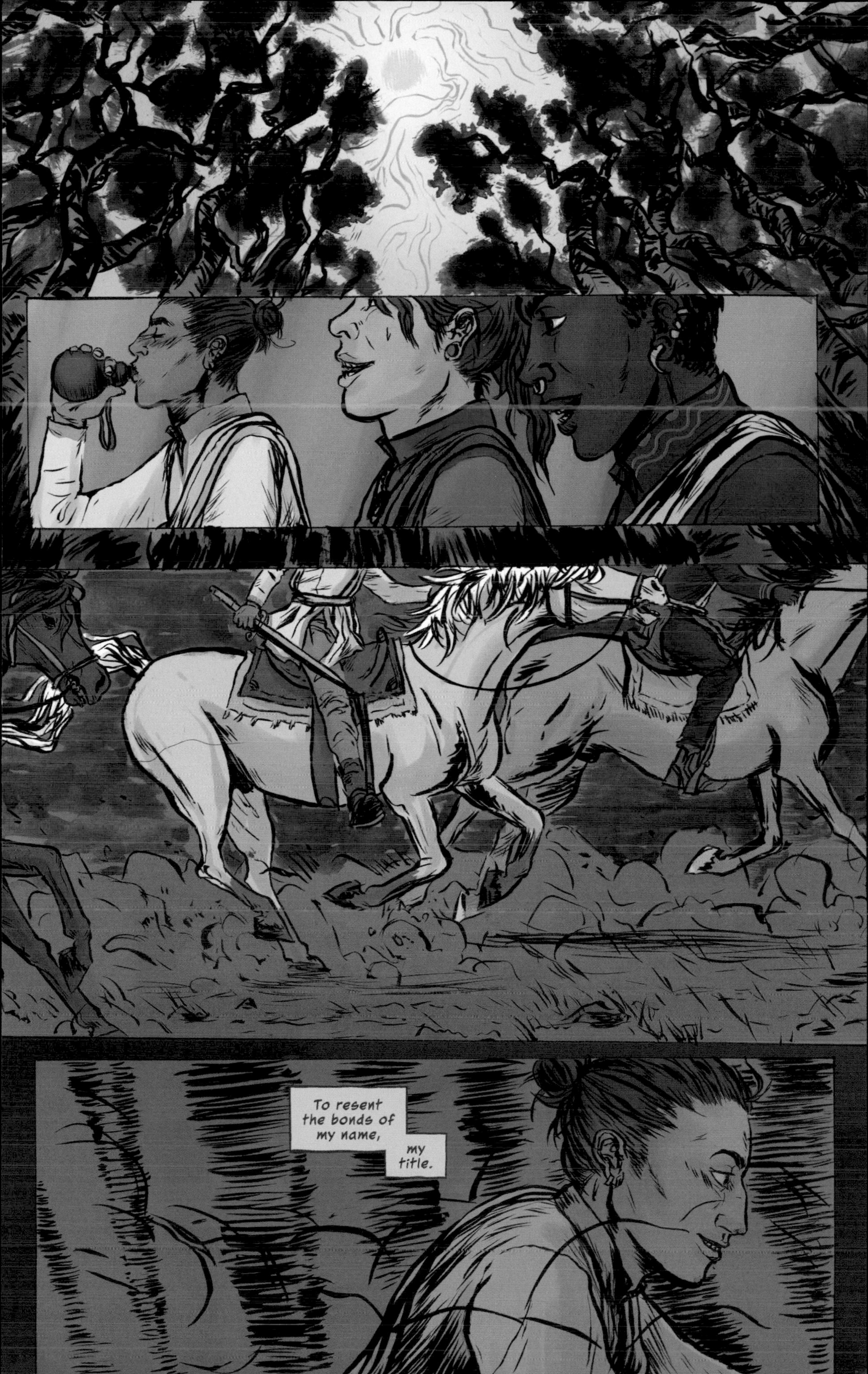
To resent the bonds of my name,
my title.

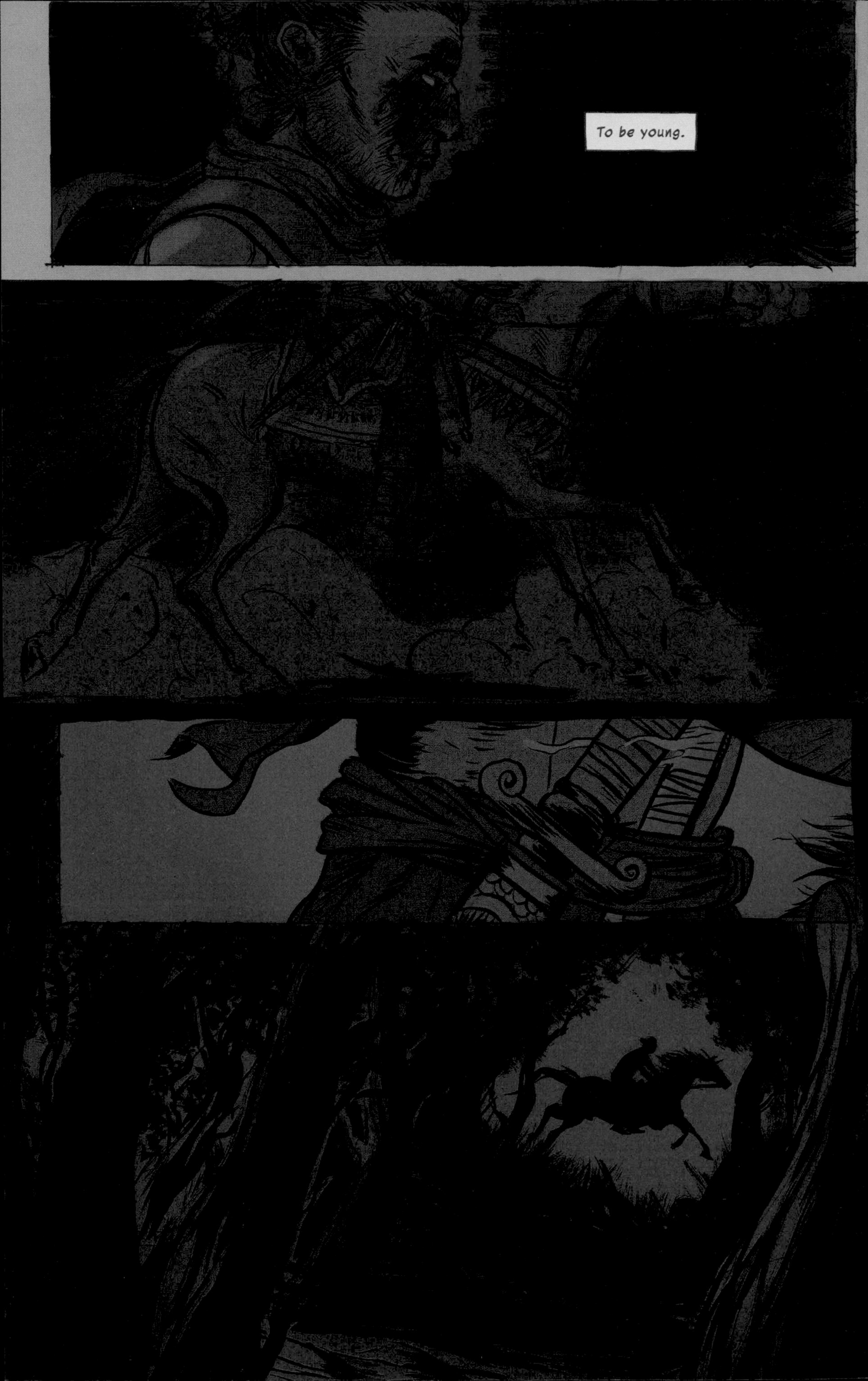
To be young.

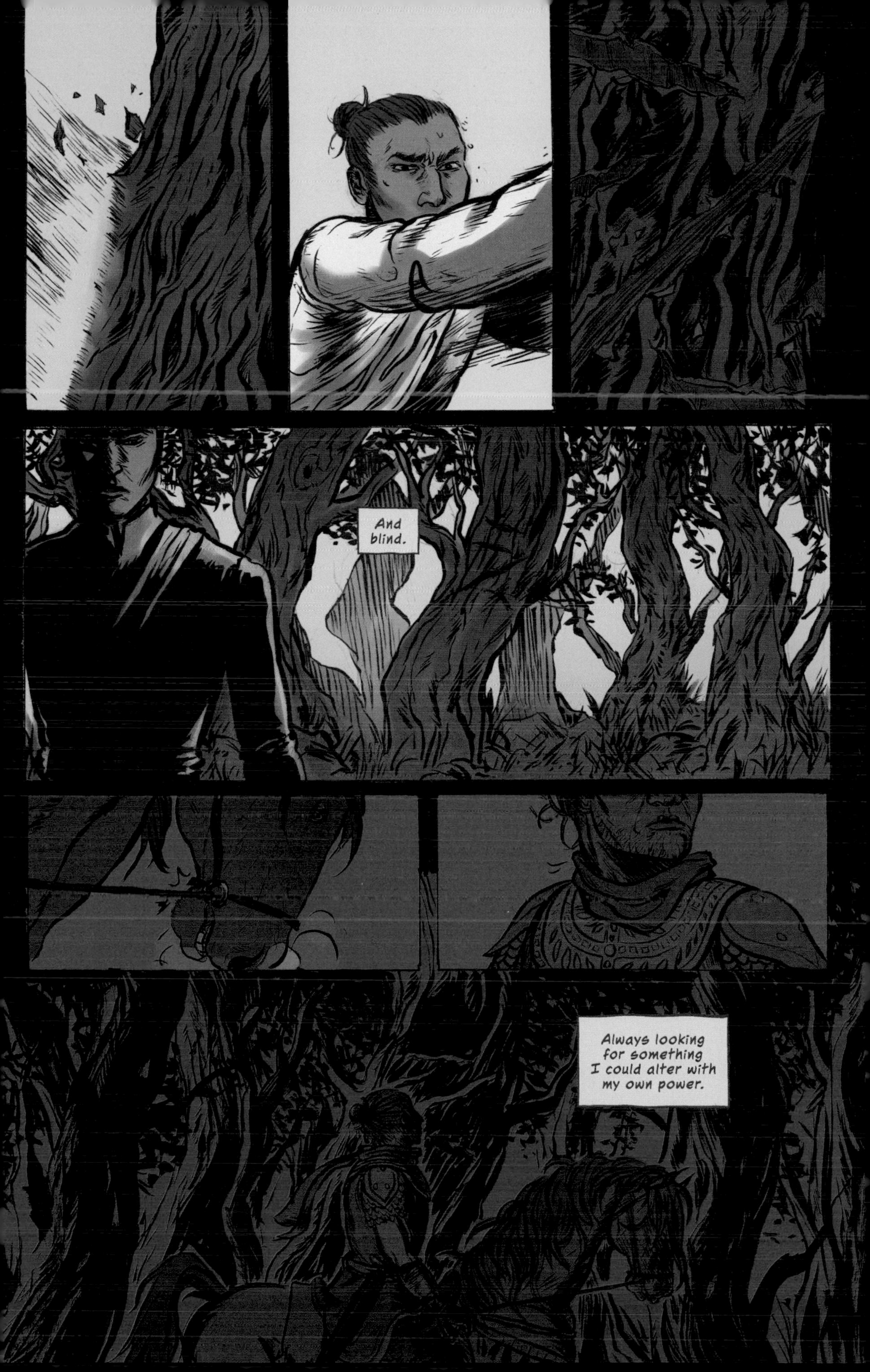
And blind.
Always looking for something I could alter with my own power.

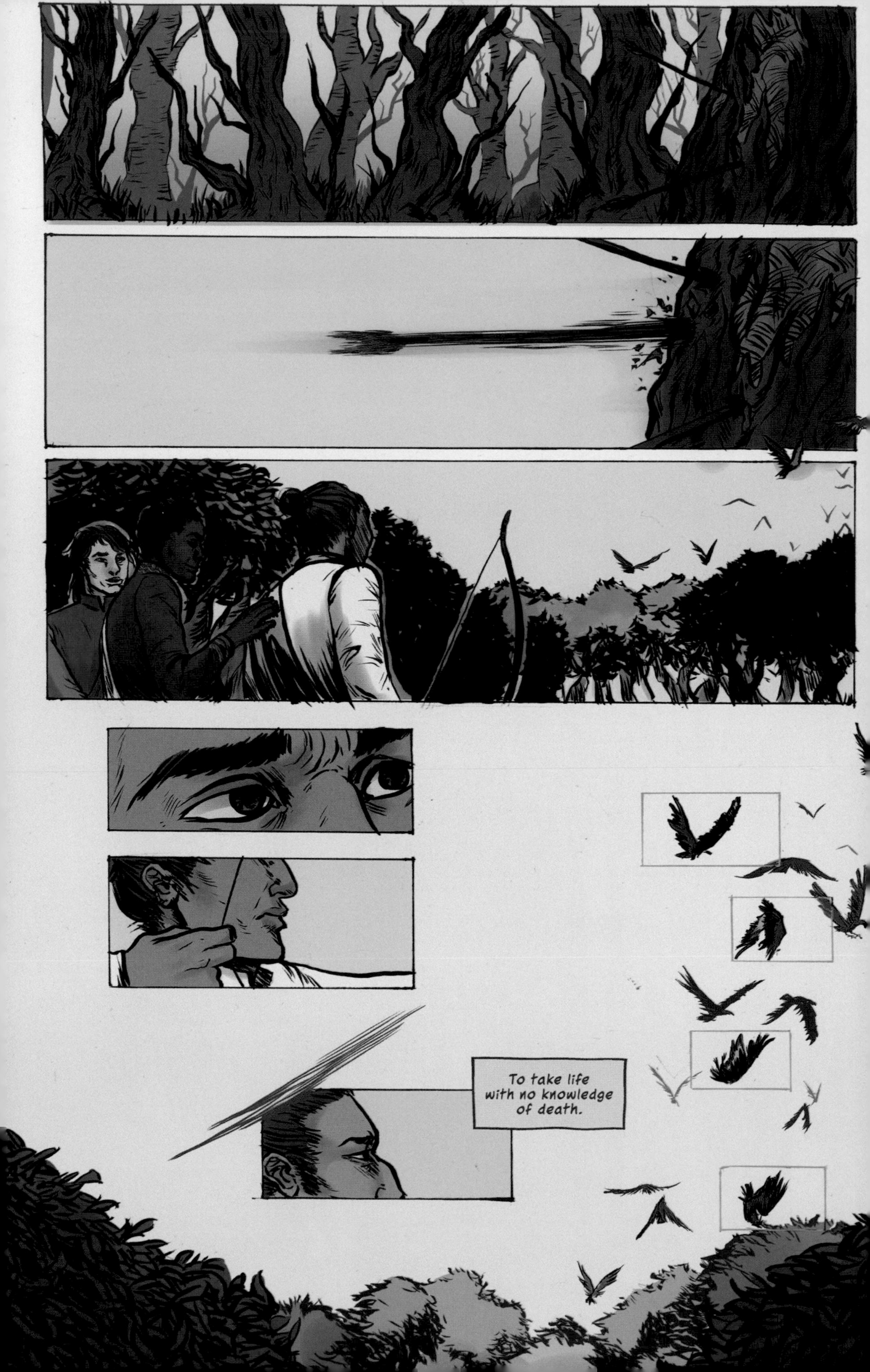
To take life
with no knowledge
of death.

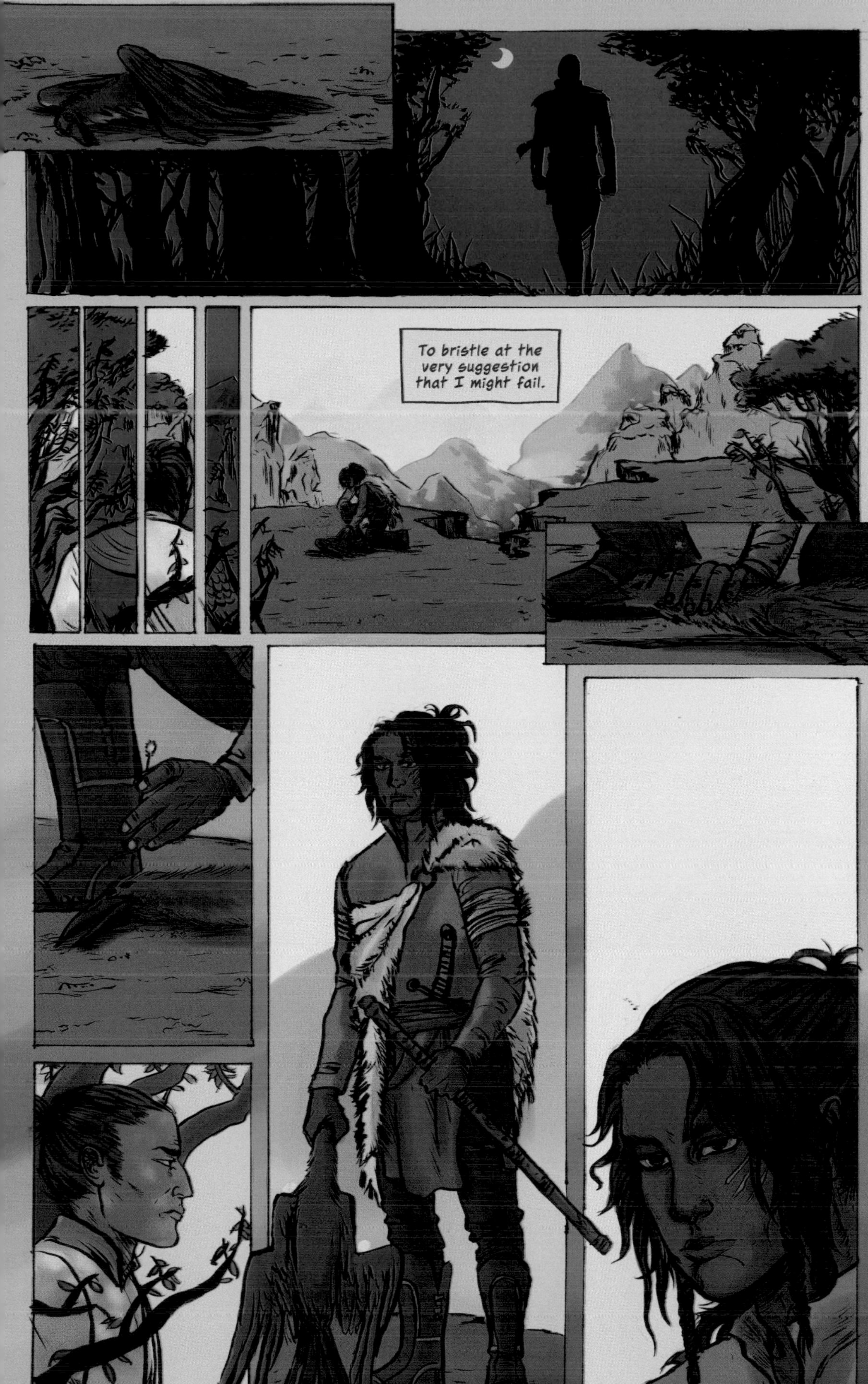
To bristle at the very suggestion that I might fail.

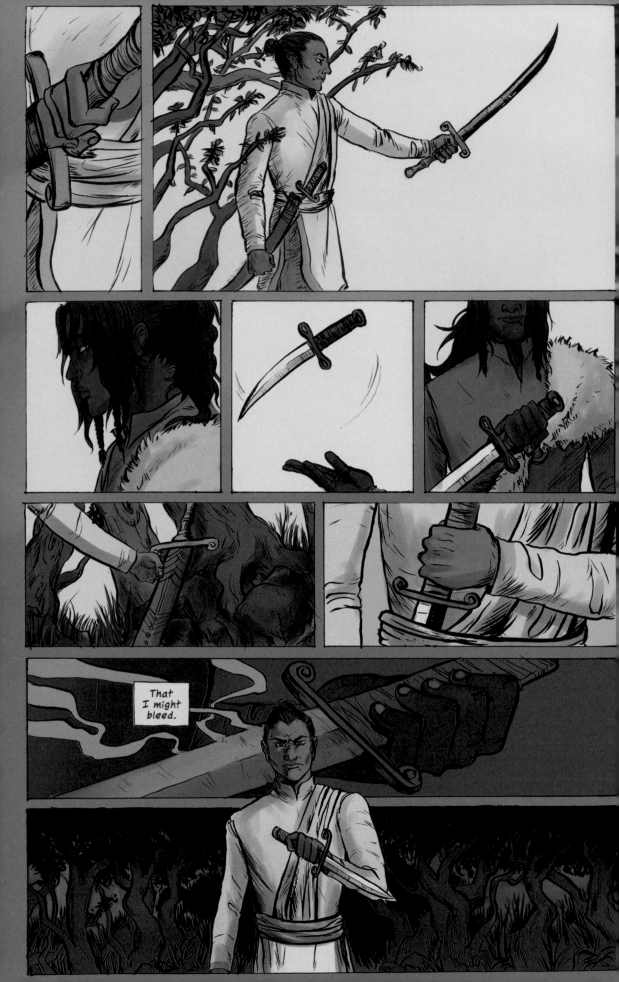

That I might bleed.

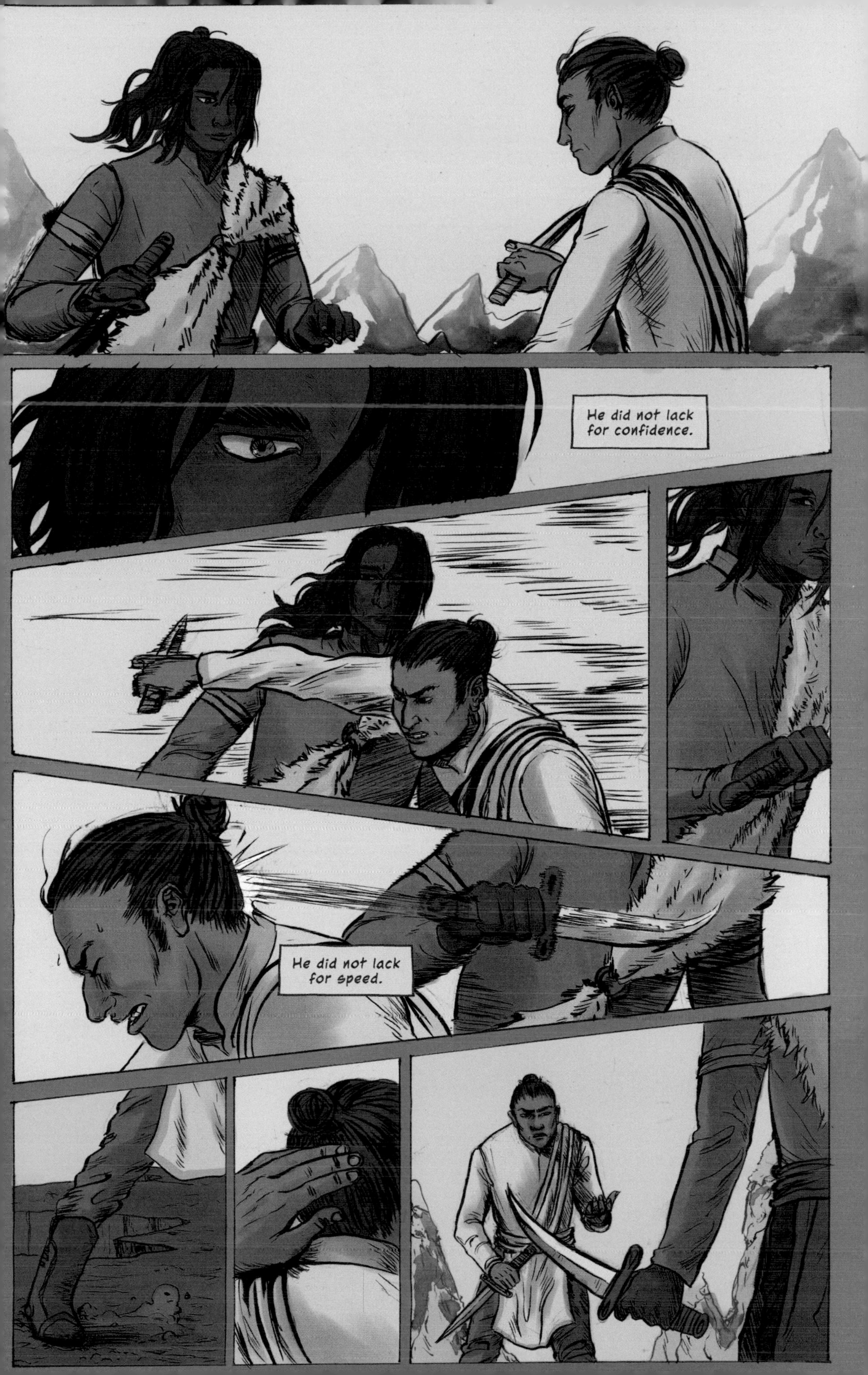
He did not lack
for confidence.
He did not lack
for speed.

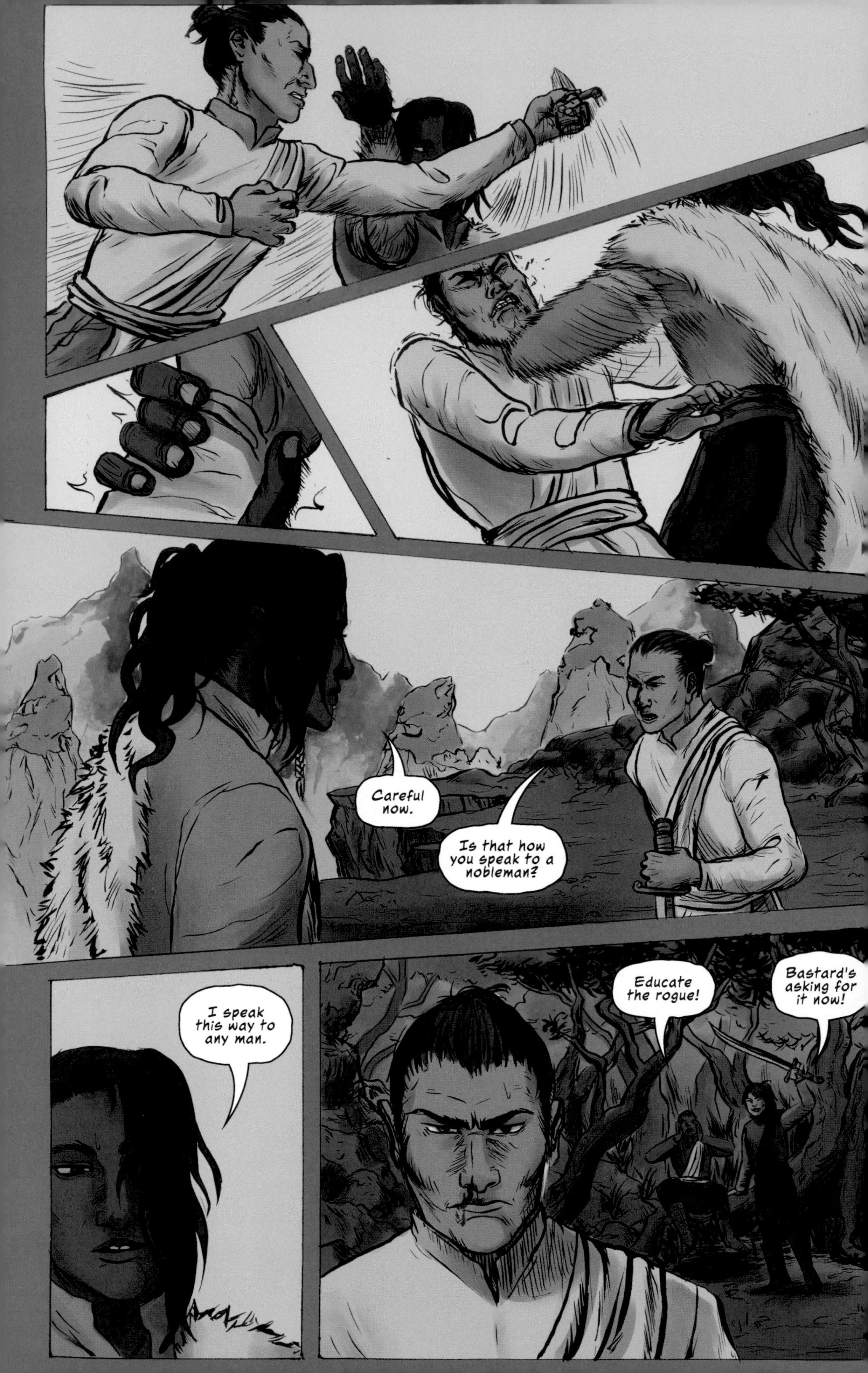
Careful now.
Is that how you speak to a nobleman?
I speak this way to any man.
Educate the rogue!
Bastard's asking for it now!

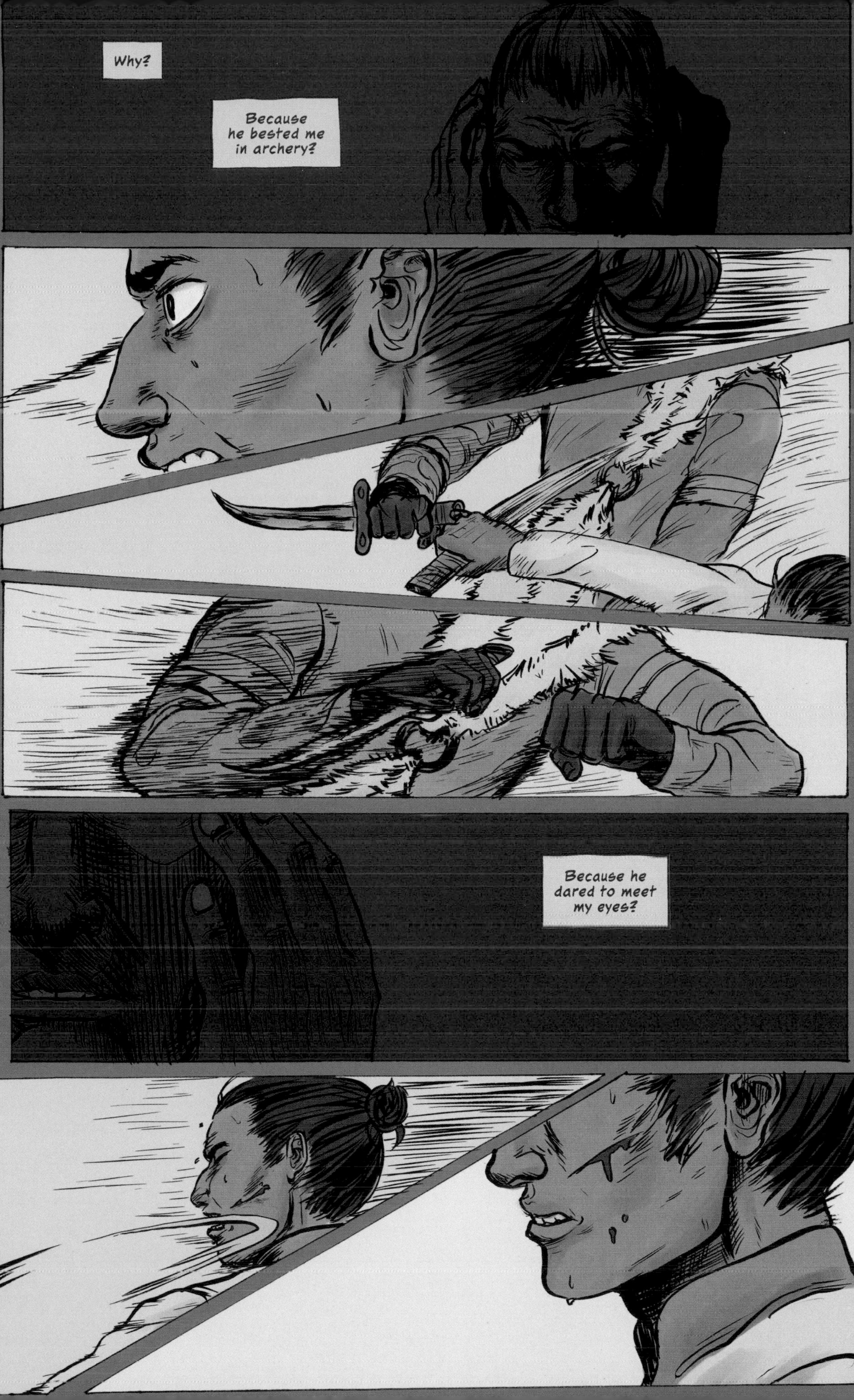
Why?
Because he bested me in archery?
Because he dared to meet my eyes?

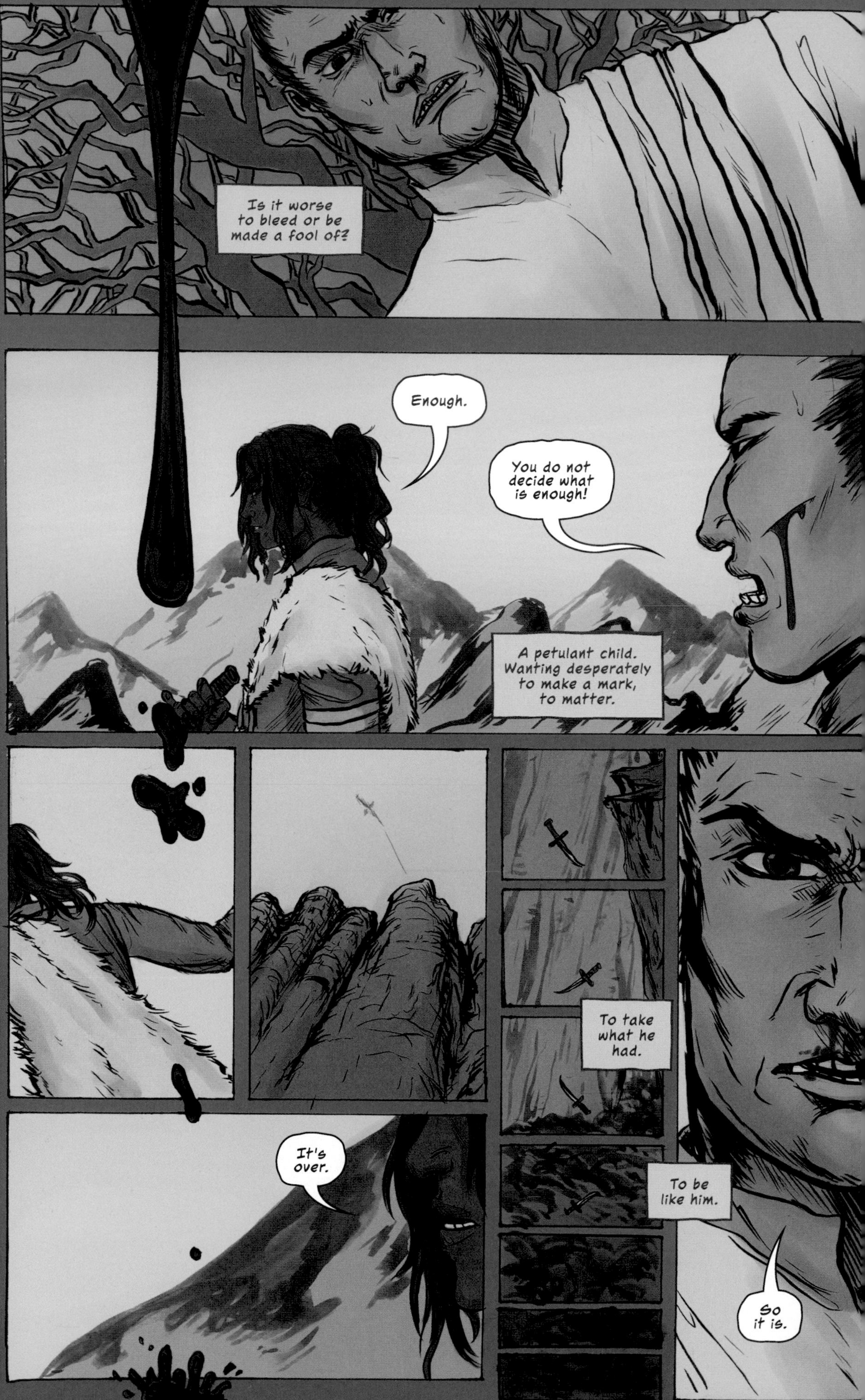
Is it worse to bleed or be made a fool of?
Enough.
You do not decide what is enough!
A petulant child. Wanting desperately to make a mark, to matter.
To take what he had.
It's over.
To be like him.
So it is.

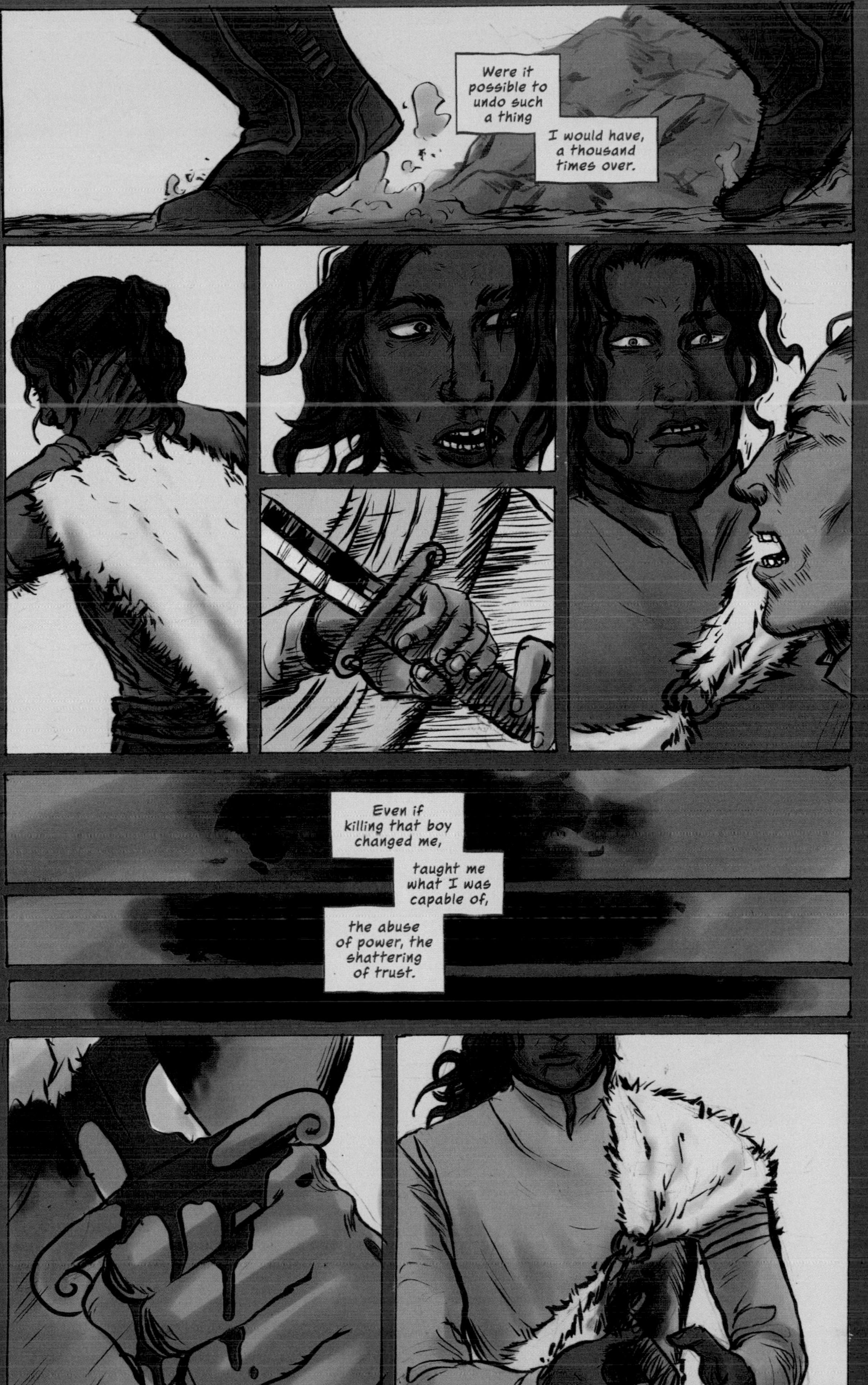
Were it possible to undo such a thing
I would have, a thousand times over.
Even if killing that boy changed me,
taught me what I was capable of,
the abuse of power, the shattering of trust.

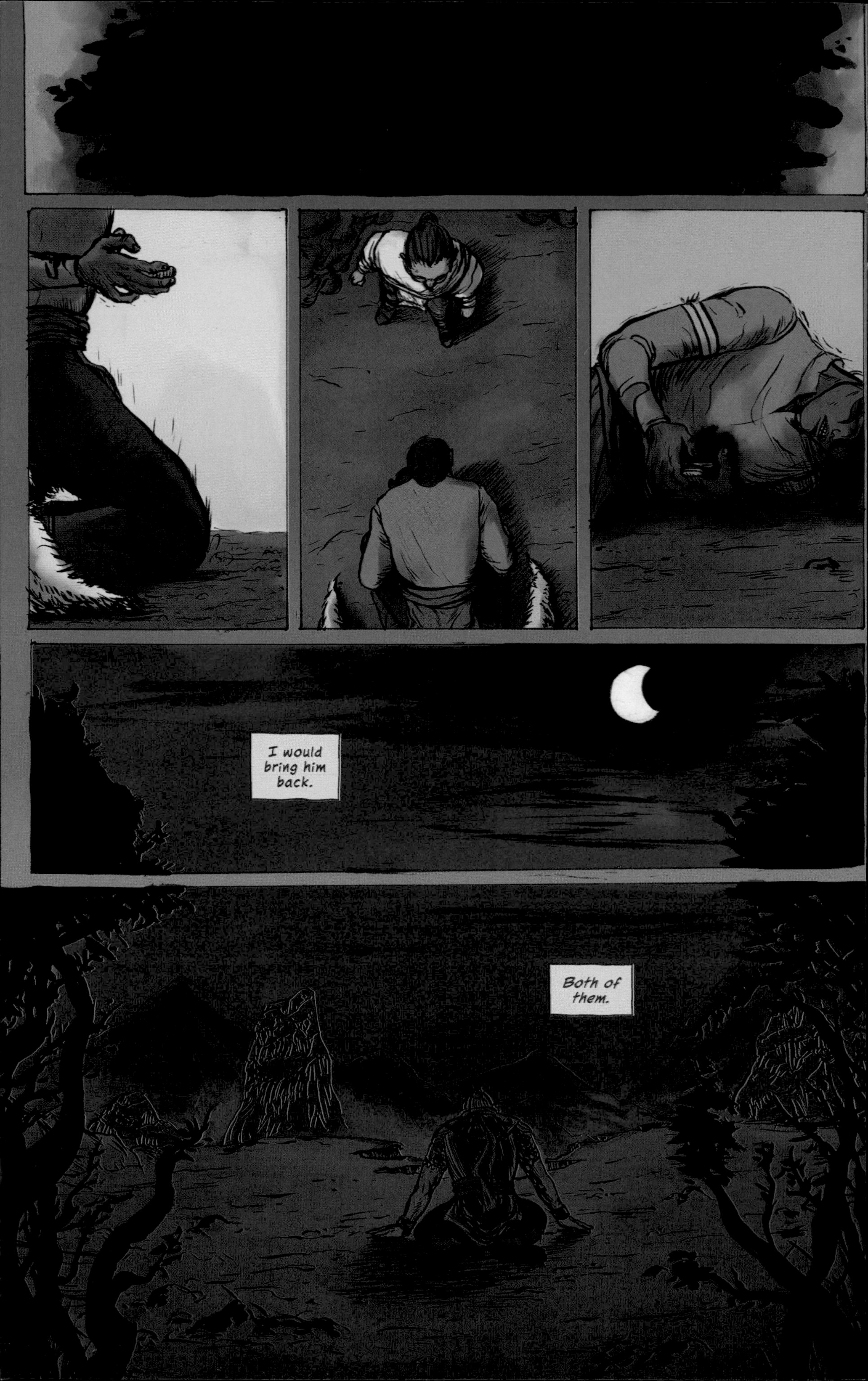
I would bring him back.
Both of them.

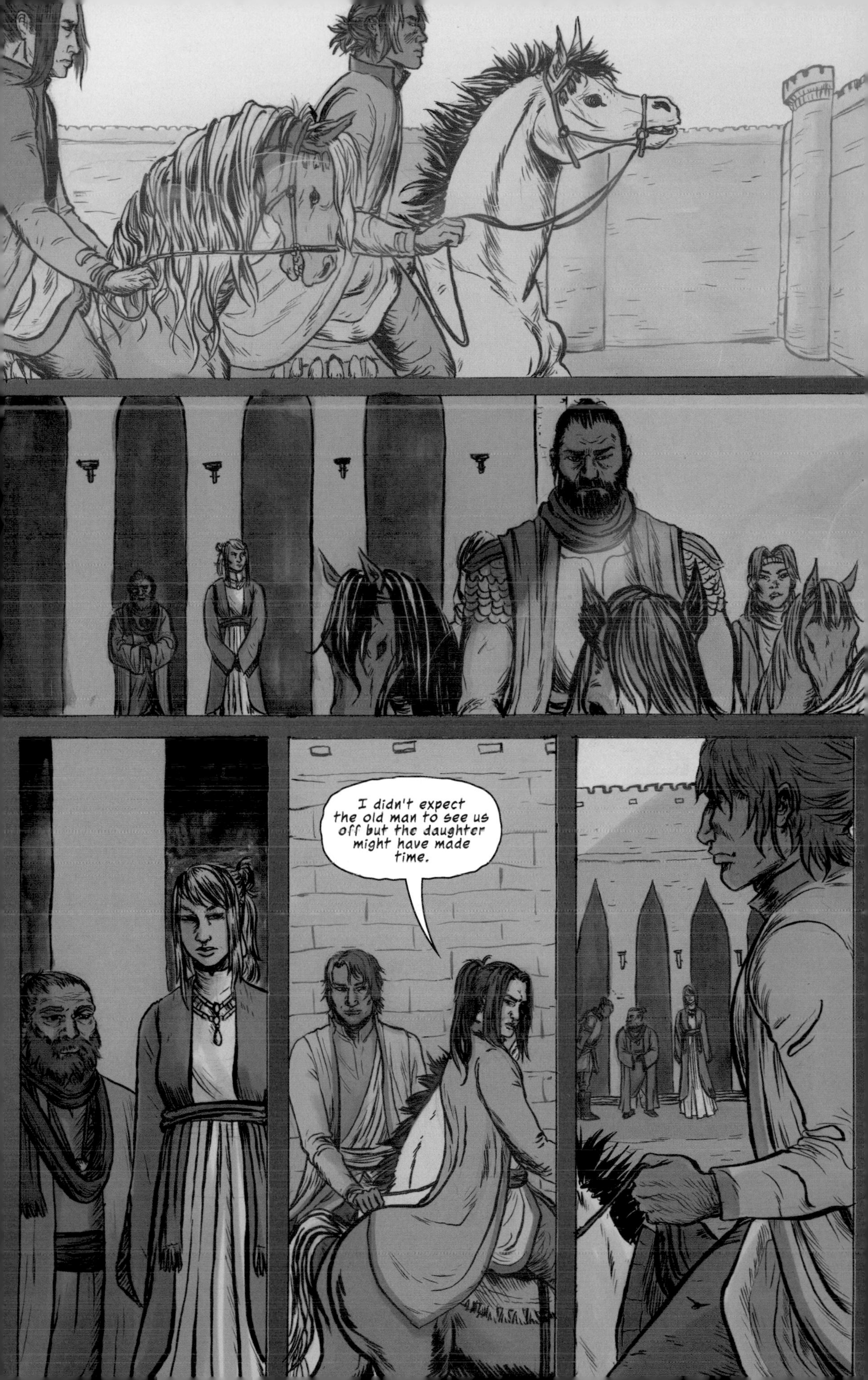
I didn't expect the old man to see us off but the daughter might have made time.

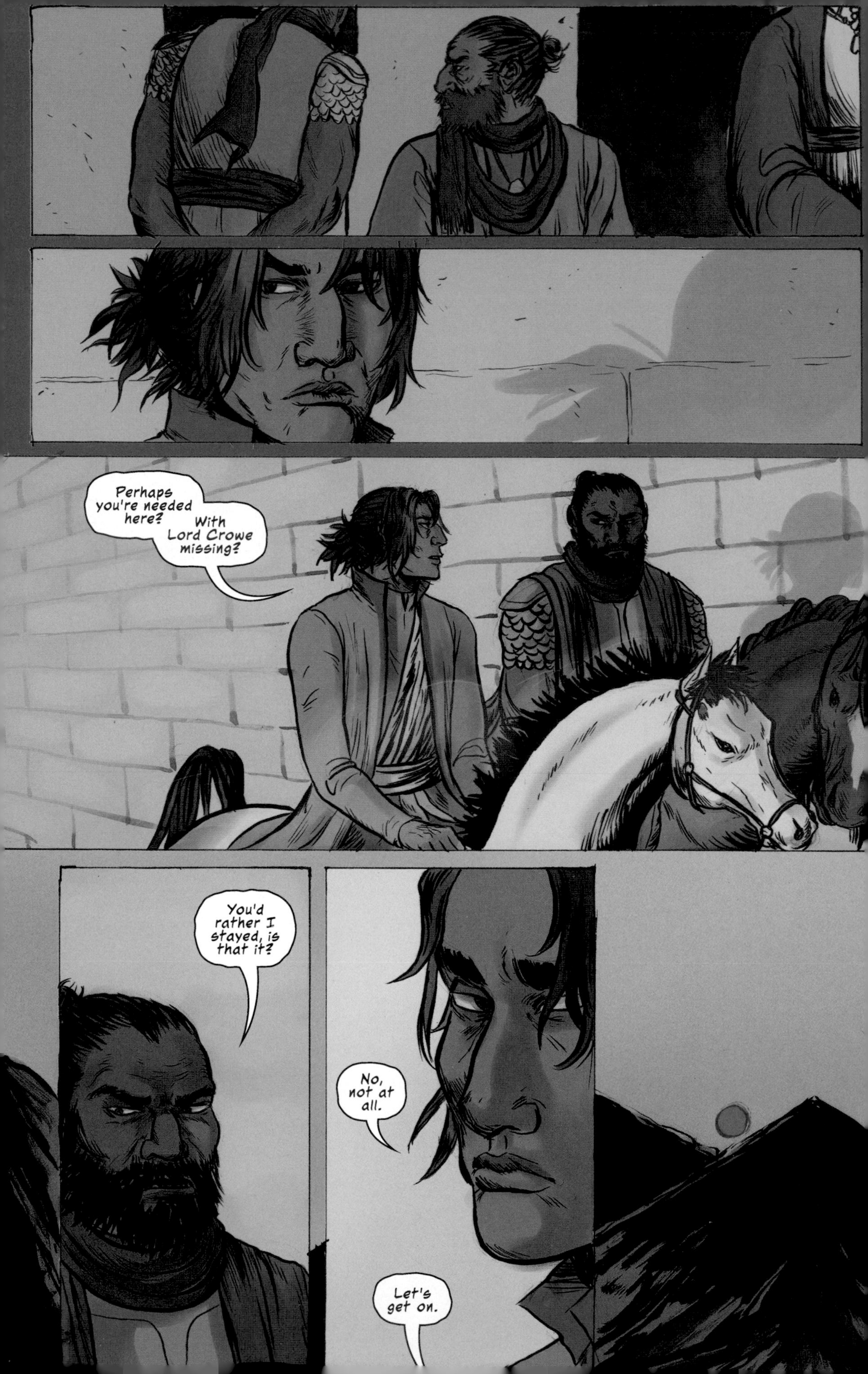
Perhaps you're needed here?
With Lord Crowe missing?
You'd rather I stayed, is that it?
No, not at all.
Let's get on.

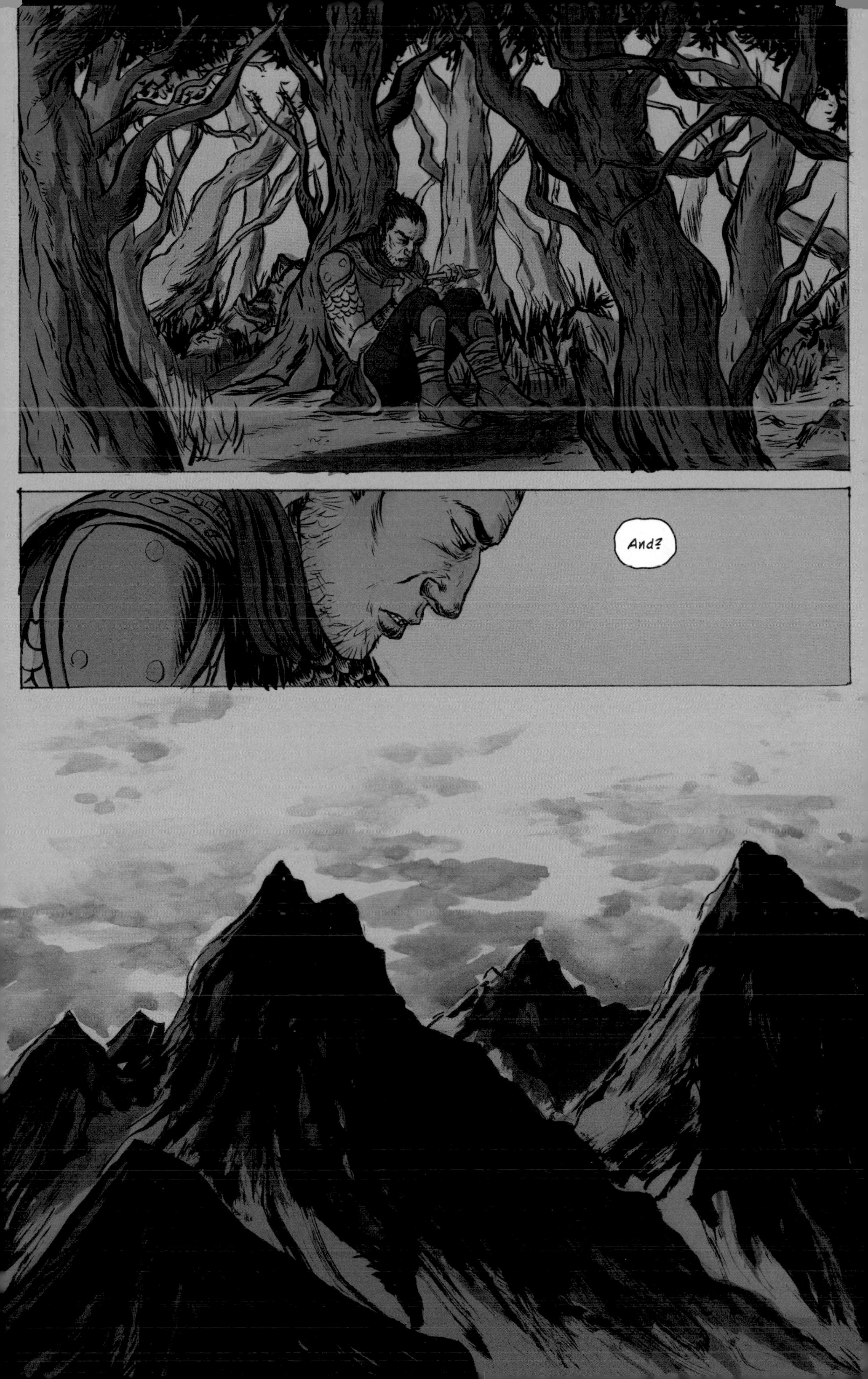
And?

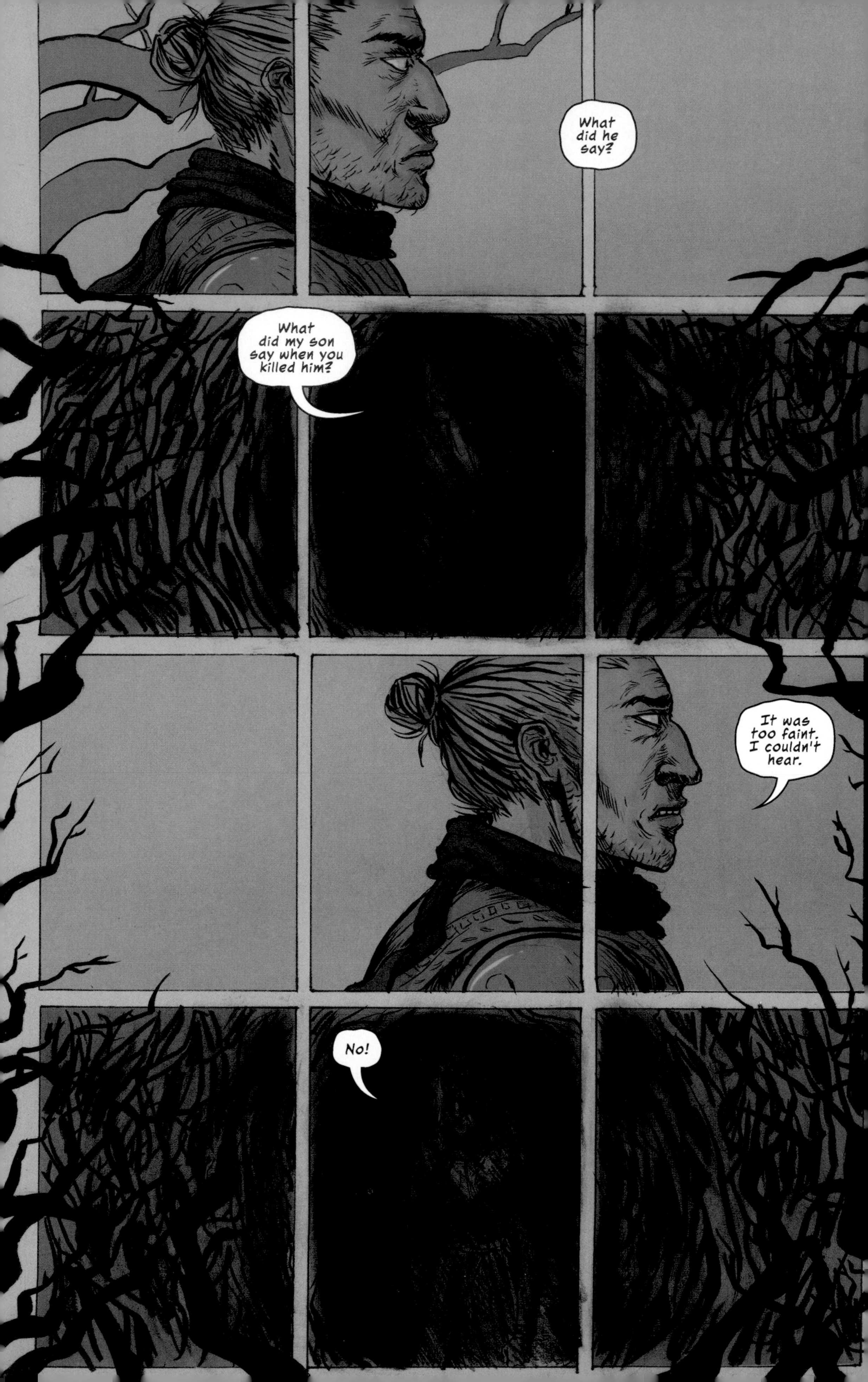
What did he say?
What did my son say when you killed him?
It was too faint. I couldn't hear.
No!

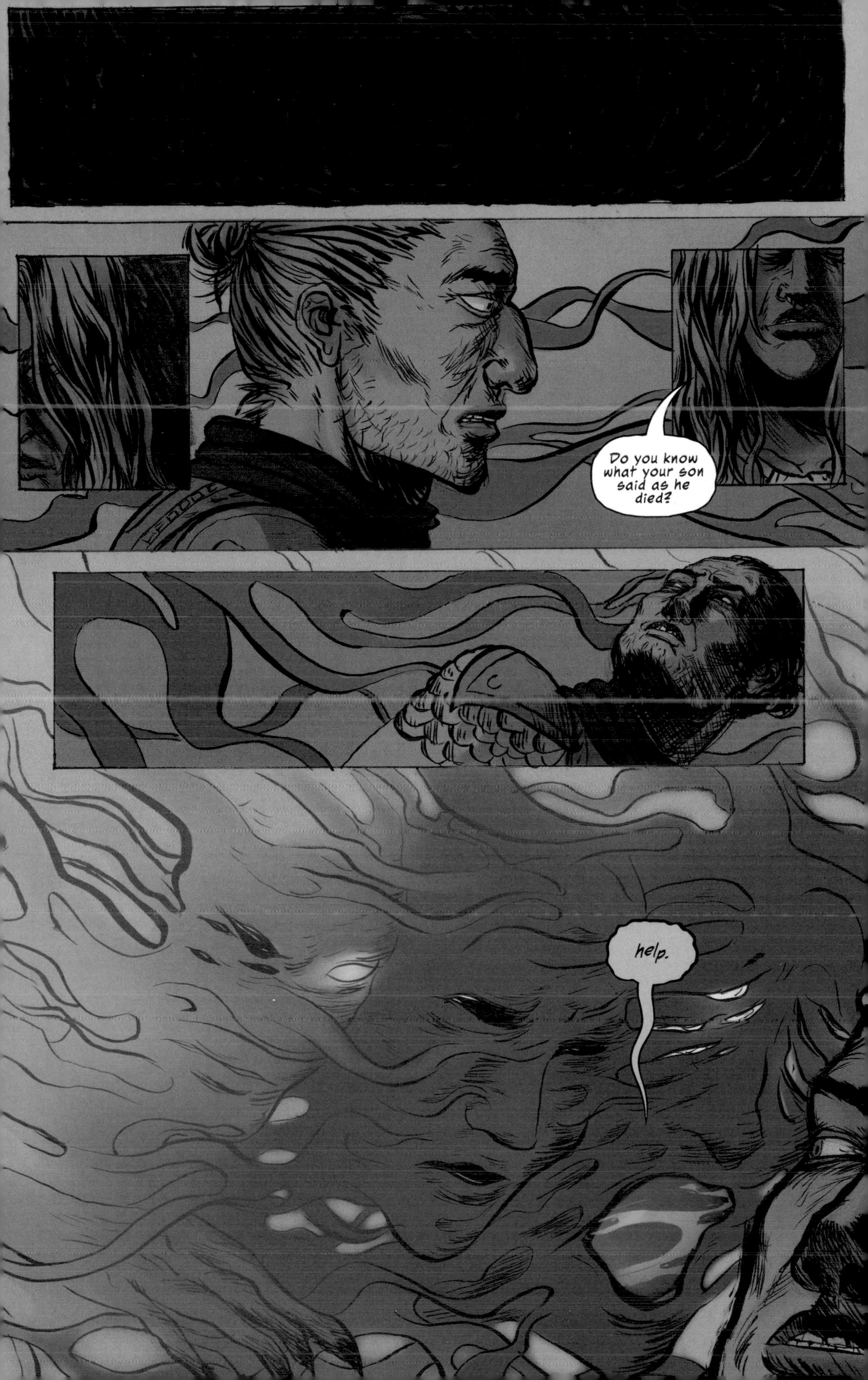
Do you know what your son said as he died?
help.

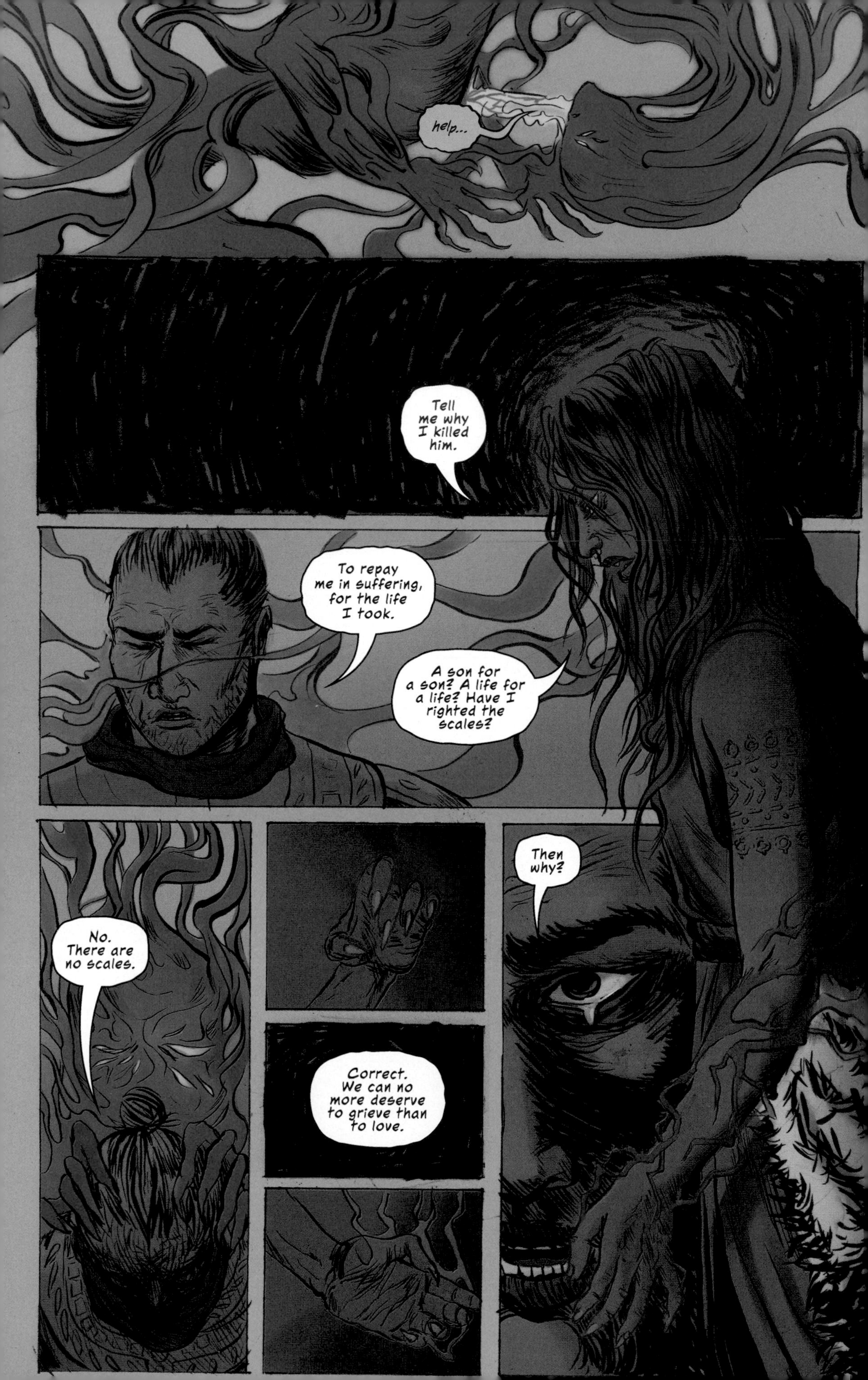
help...
Tell me why I killed him.
To repay me in suffering, for the life I took.
A son for a son? A life for a life? Have I righted the scales?
No. There are no scales.
Then why?
Correct. We can no more deserve to grieve than to love.

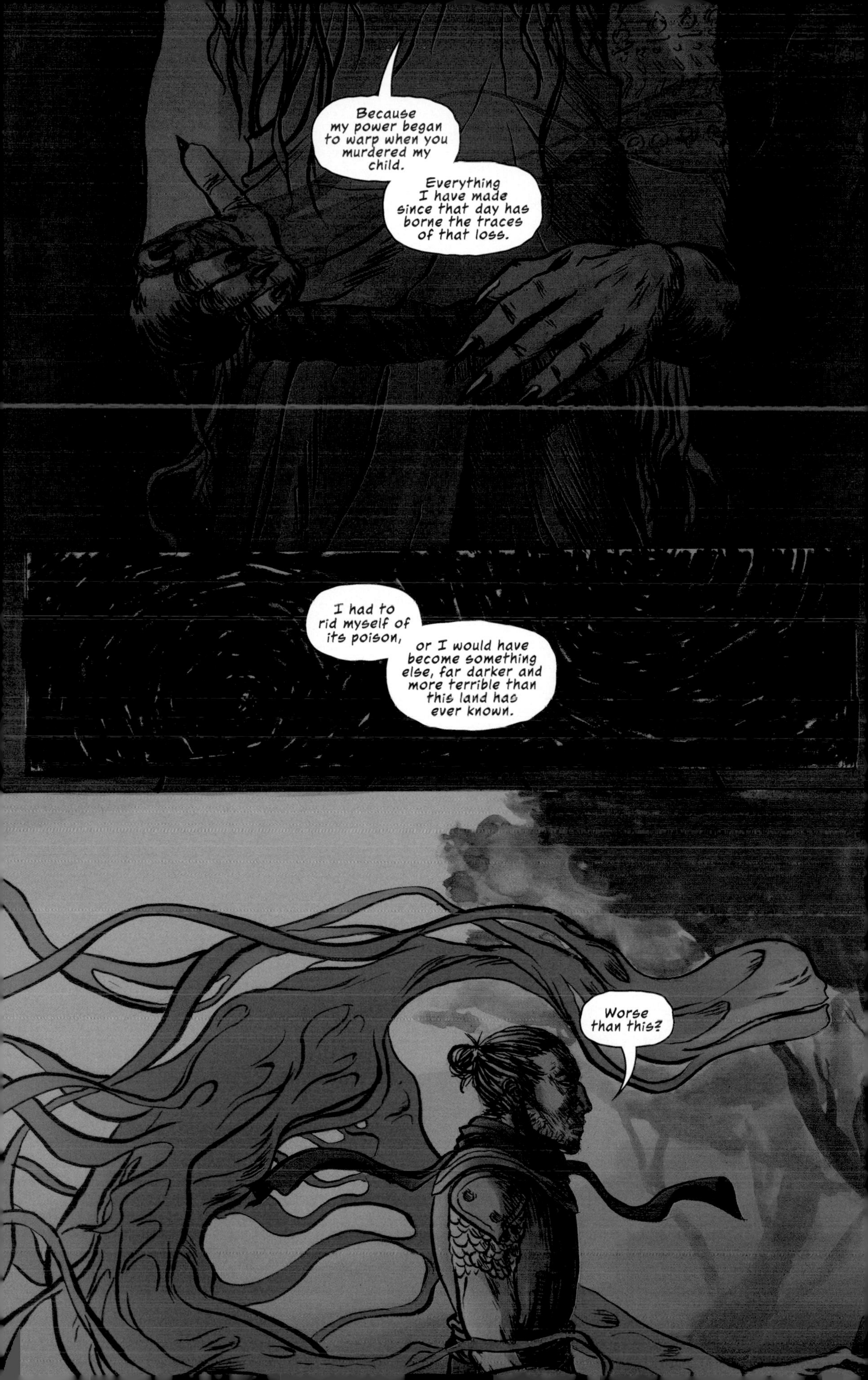
Because my power began to warp when you murdered my child.
Everything I have made since that day has borne the traces of that loss.
I had to rid myself of its poison,
or I would have become something else, far darker and more terrible than this land has ever known.
Worse than this?

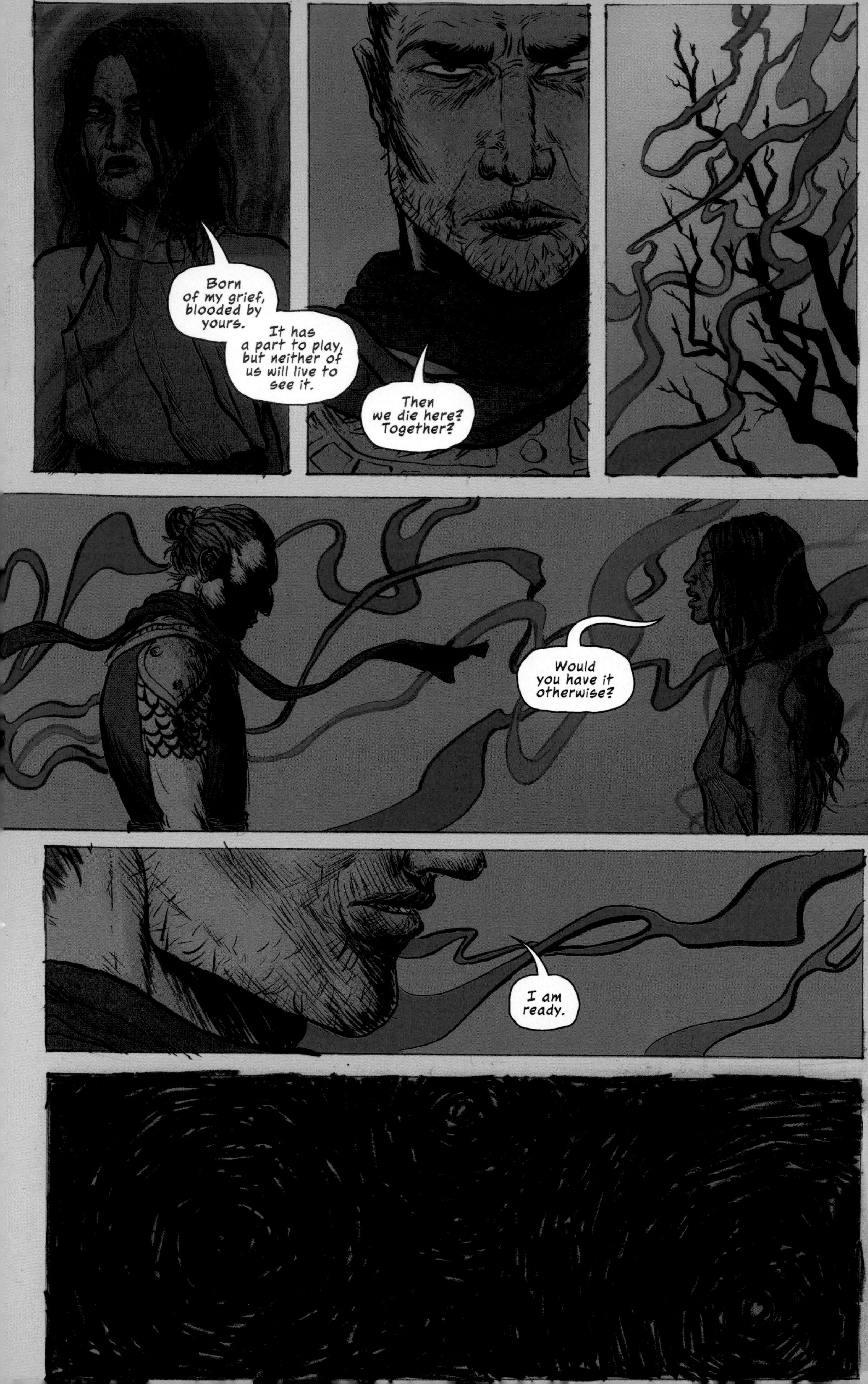
Born of my grief, blooded by yours.
It has a part to play, but neither of us will live to see it.
Then we die here? Together?
Would you have it otherwise?
I am ready.

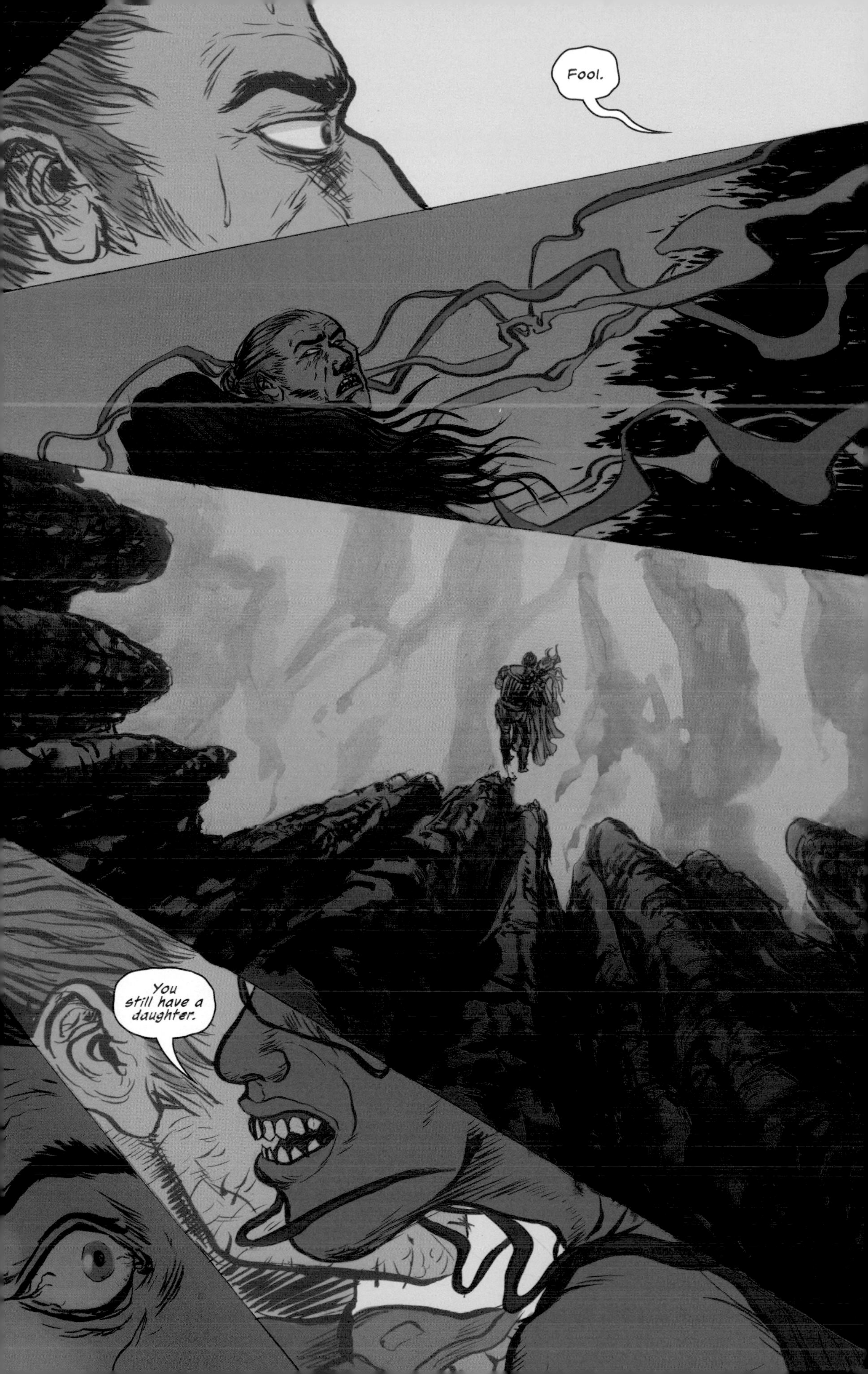
Fool.
You still have a daughter.

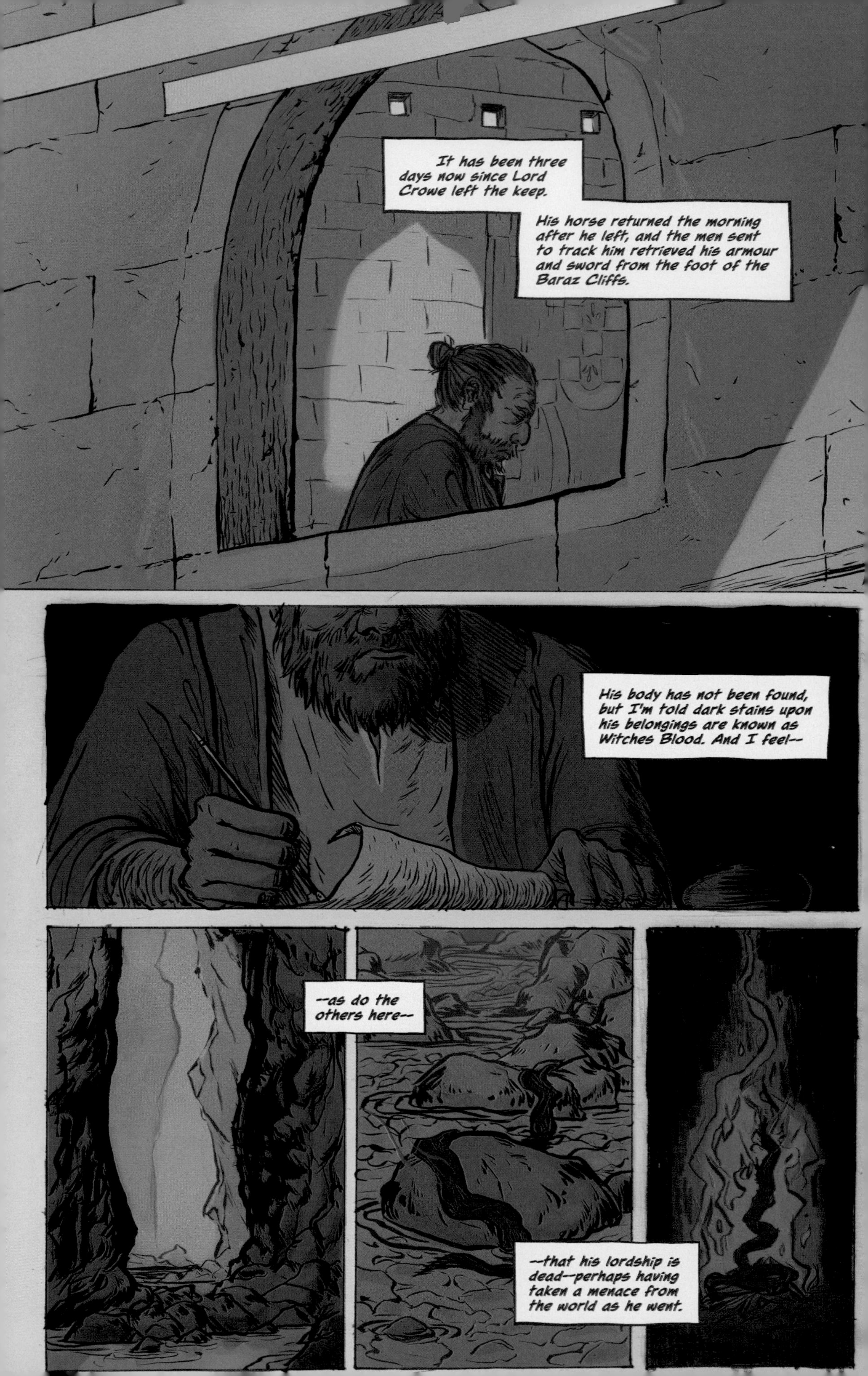
It has been three days now since Lord Crowe left the keep.
His horse returned the morning after he left, and the men sent to track him retrieved his armour and sword from the foot of the Baraz Cliffs.
His body has not been found, but I'm told dark stains upon his belongings are known as Witches Blood. And I feel--
--as do the others here--
--that his lordship is dead--perhaps having taken a menace from the world as he went.

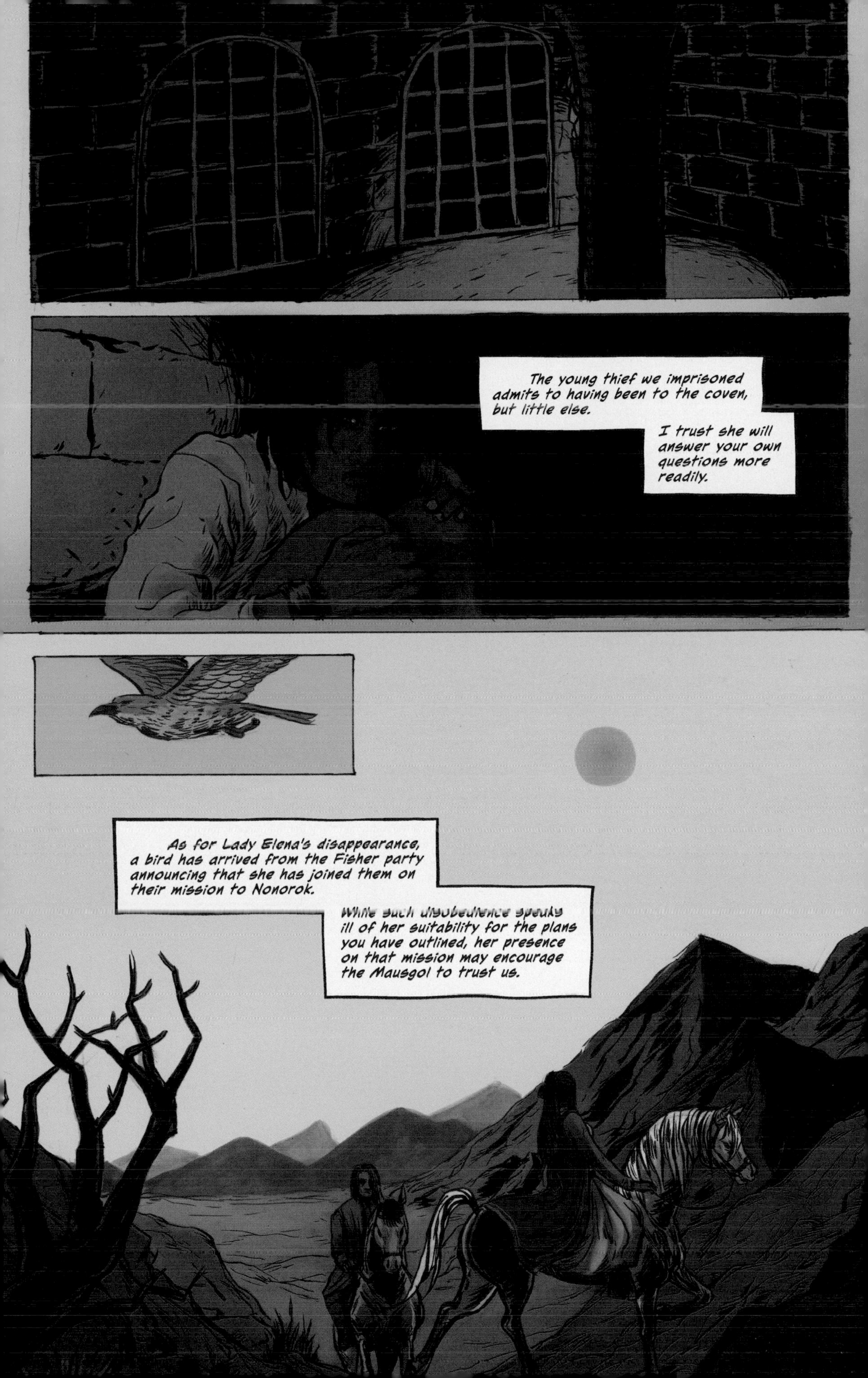
The young thief we imprisoned admits to having been to the coven, but little else.
I trust she will answer your own questions more readily.
As for Lady Elena's disappearance, a bird has arrived from the Fisher party announcing that she has joined them on their mission to Nonorok.
While such disobedience speaks ill of her suitability for the plans you have outlined, her presence on that mission may encourage the Mausgol to trust us.

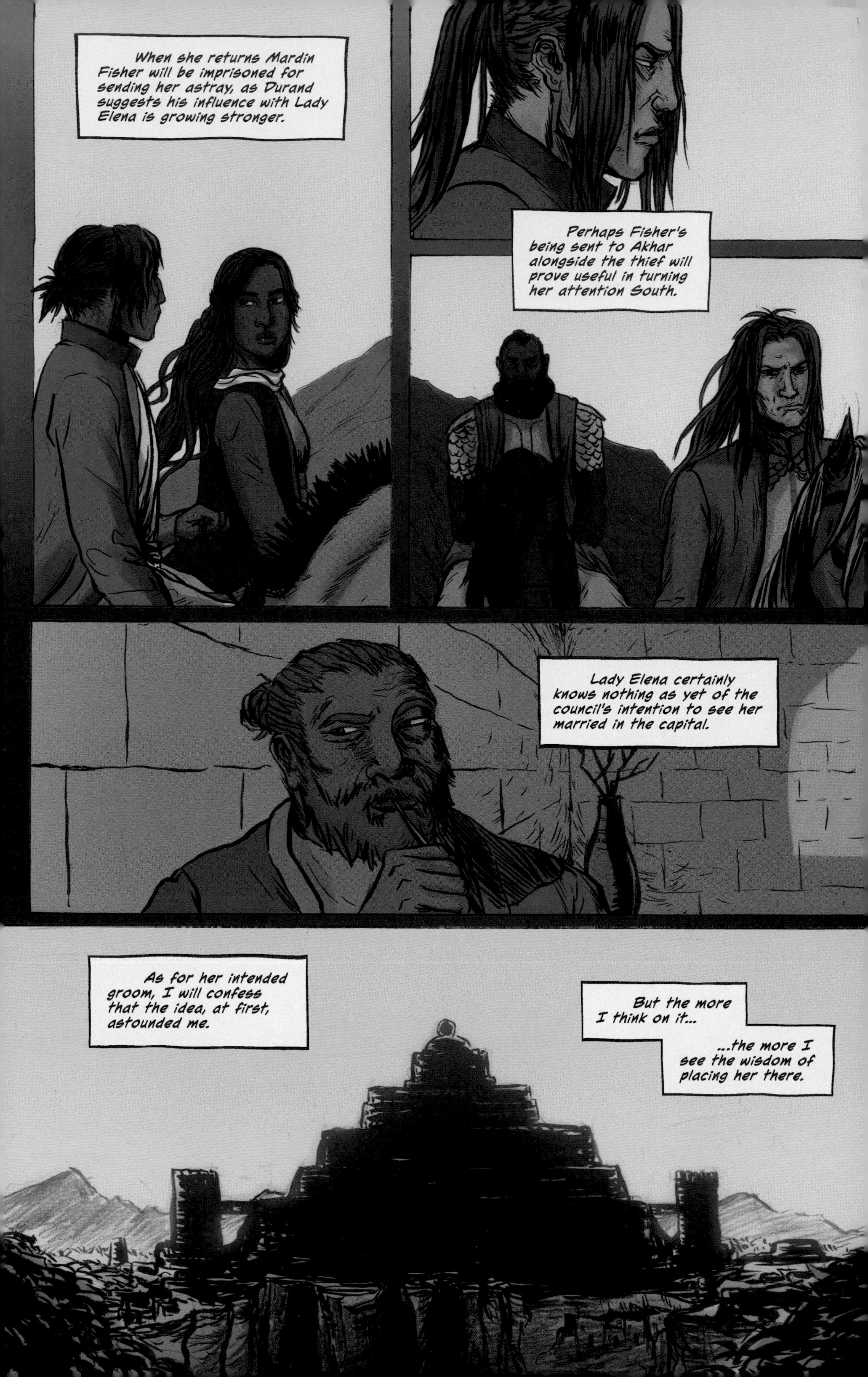
When she returns Mardin Fisher will be imprisoned for sending her astray, as Durand suggests his influence with Lady Elena is growing stronger.
Perhaps Fisher's being sent to Akhar alongside the thief will prove useful in turning her attention South.
Lady Elena certainly knows nothing as yet of the council's intention to see her married in the capital.
As for her intended groom, I will confess that the idea, at first, astounded me.
But the more I think on it...
...the more I see the wisdom of placing her there.

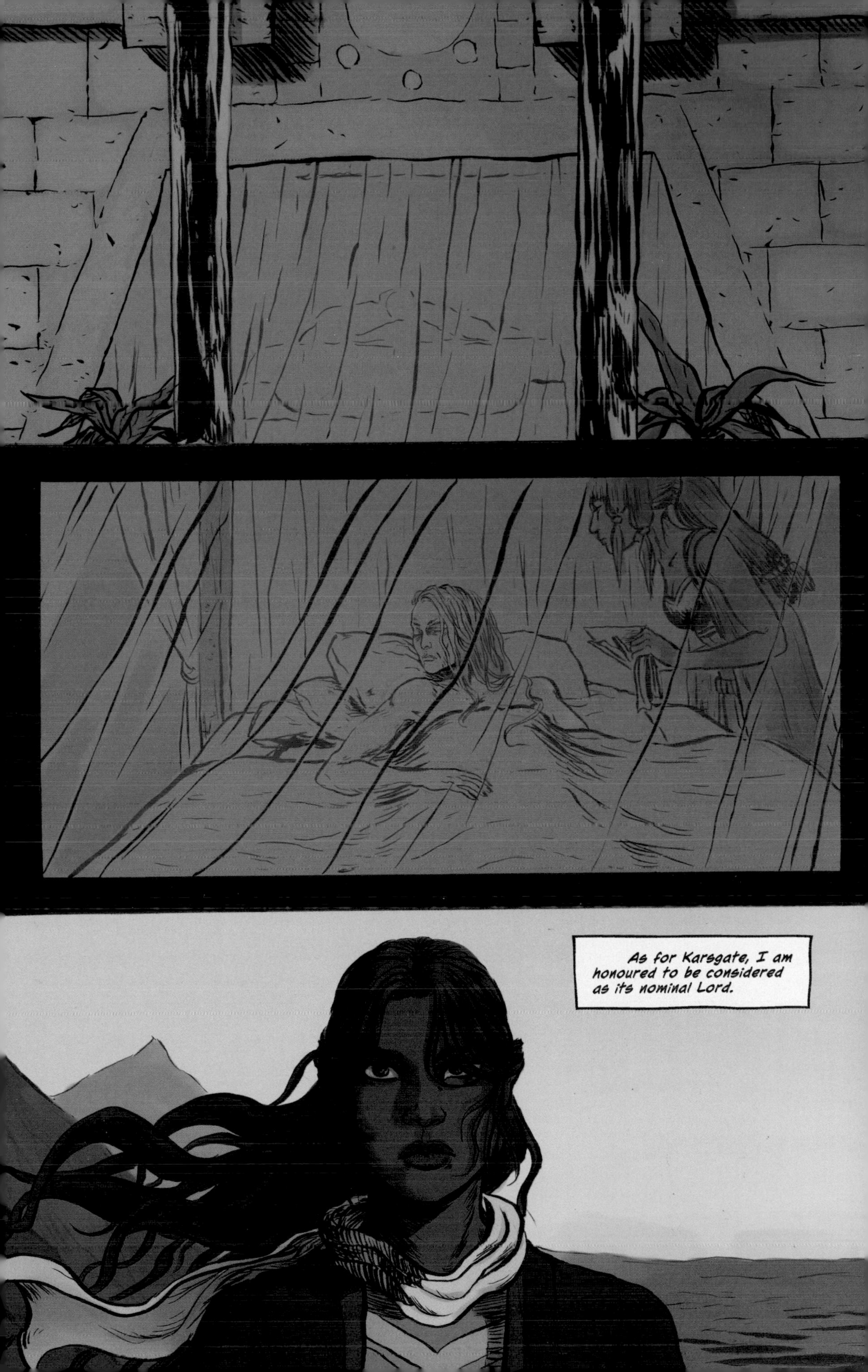
As for Karsgate, I am honoured to be considered as its nominal Lord.

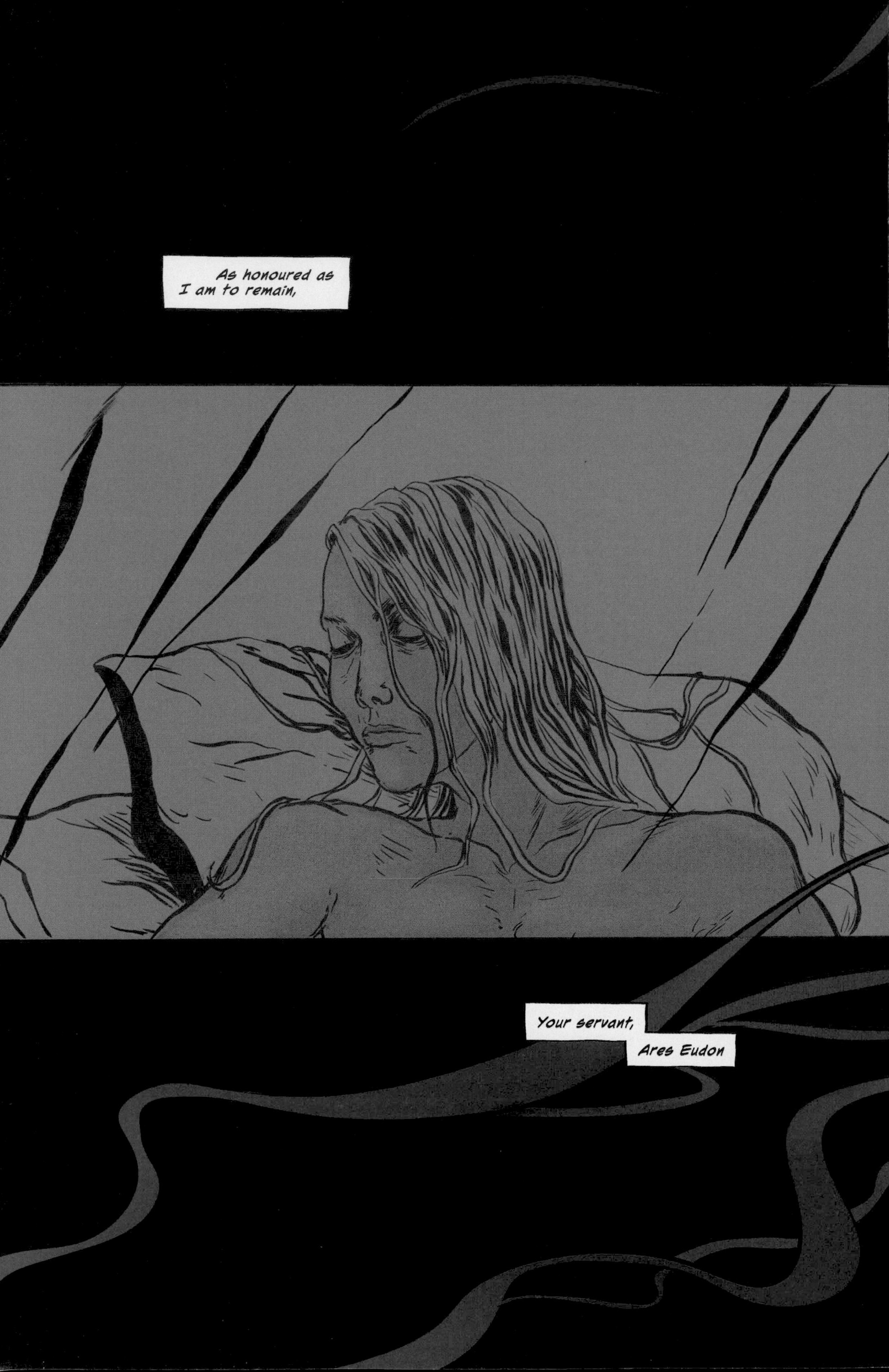
As honoured as I am to remain,
Your servant,
Ares Eudon

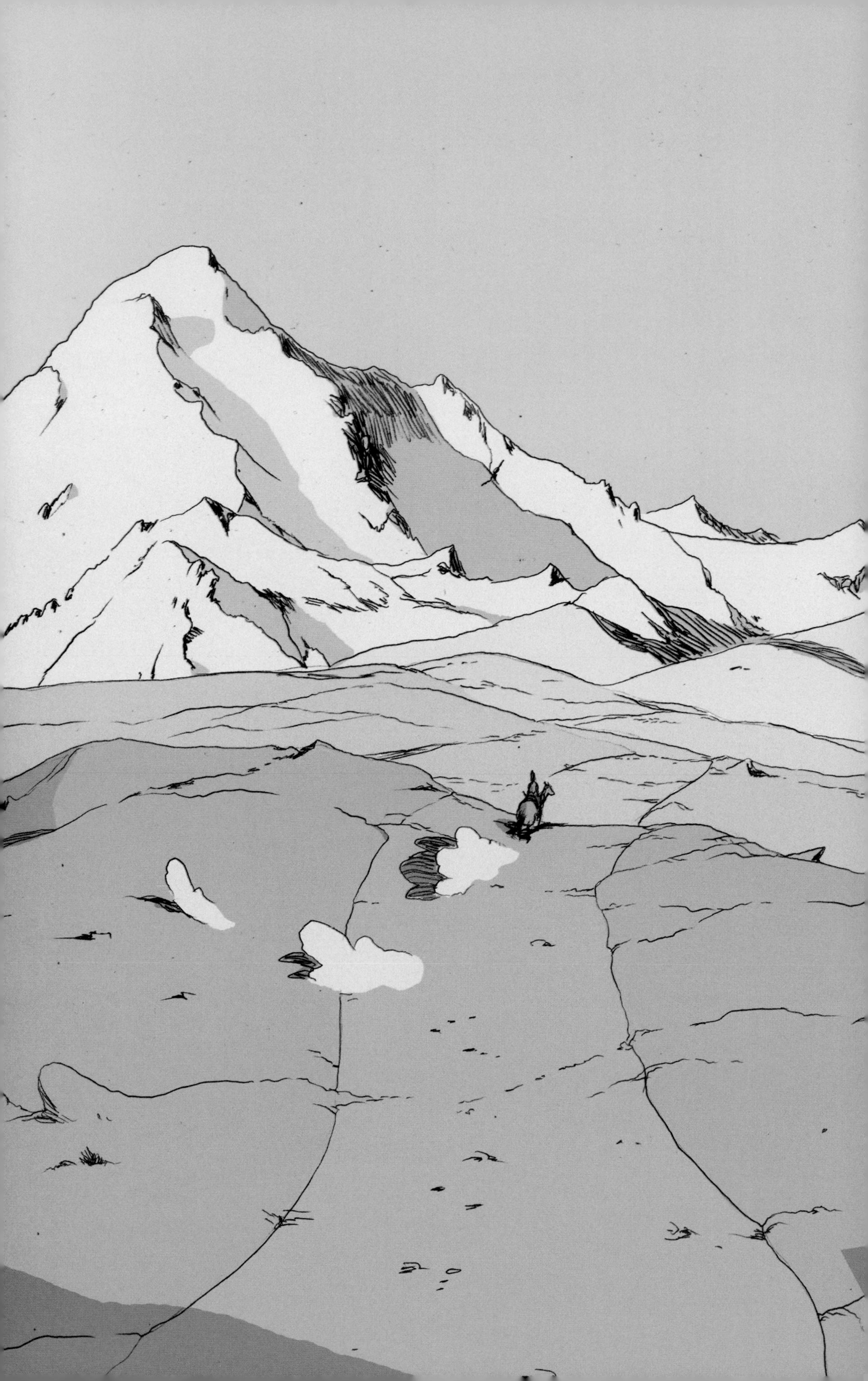

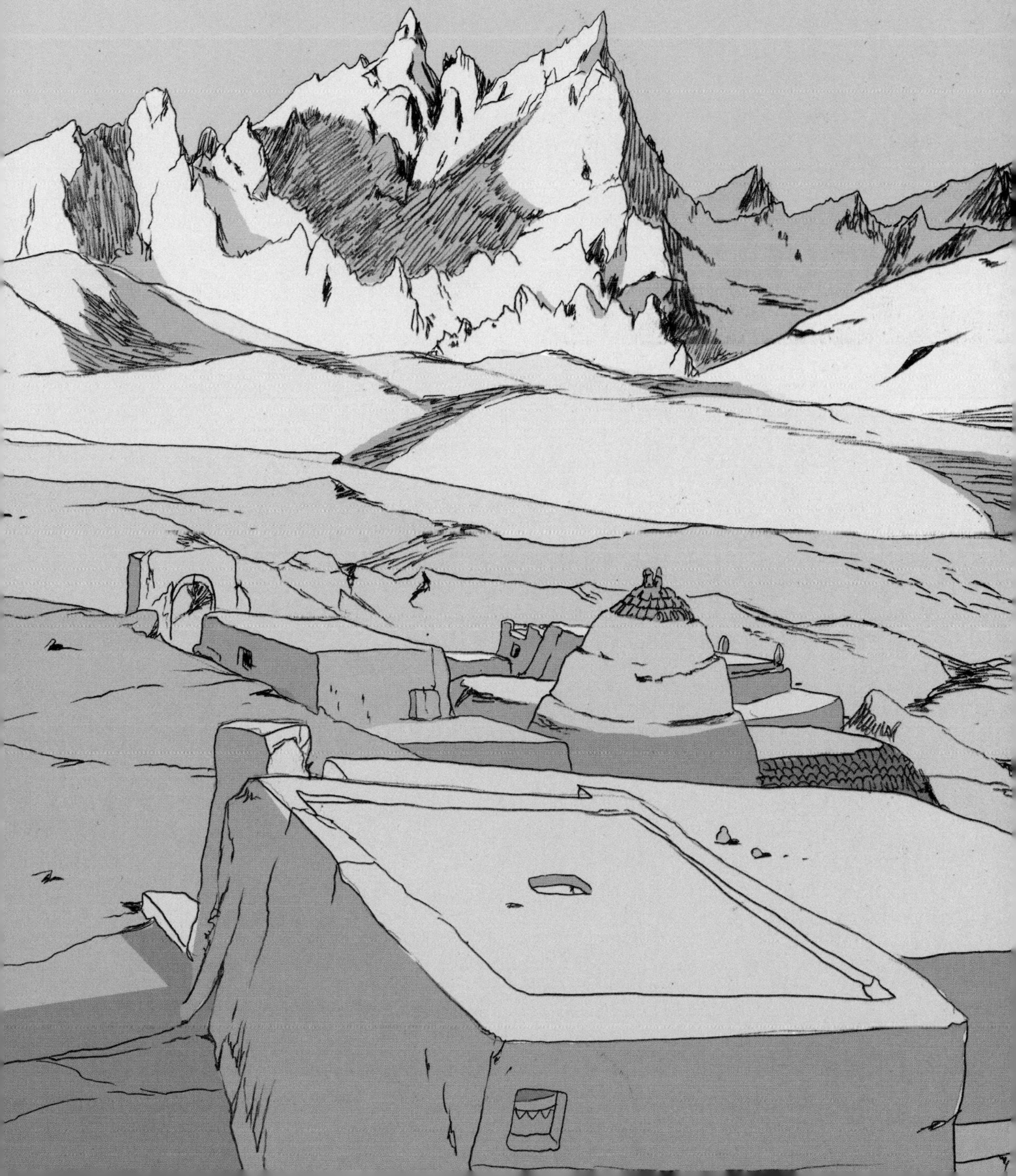

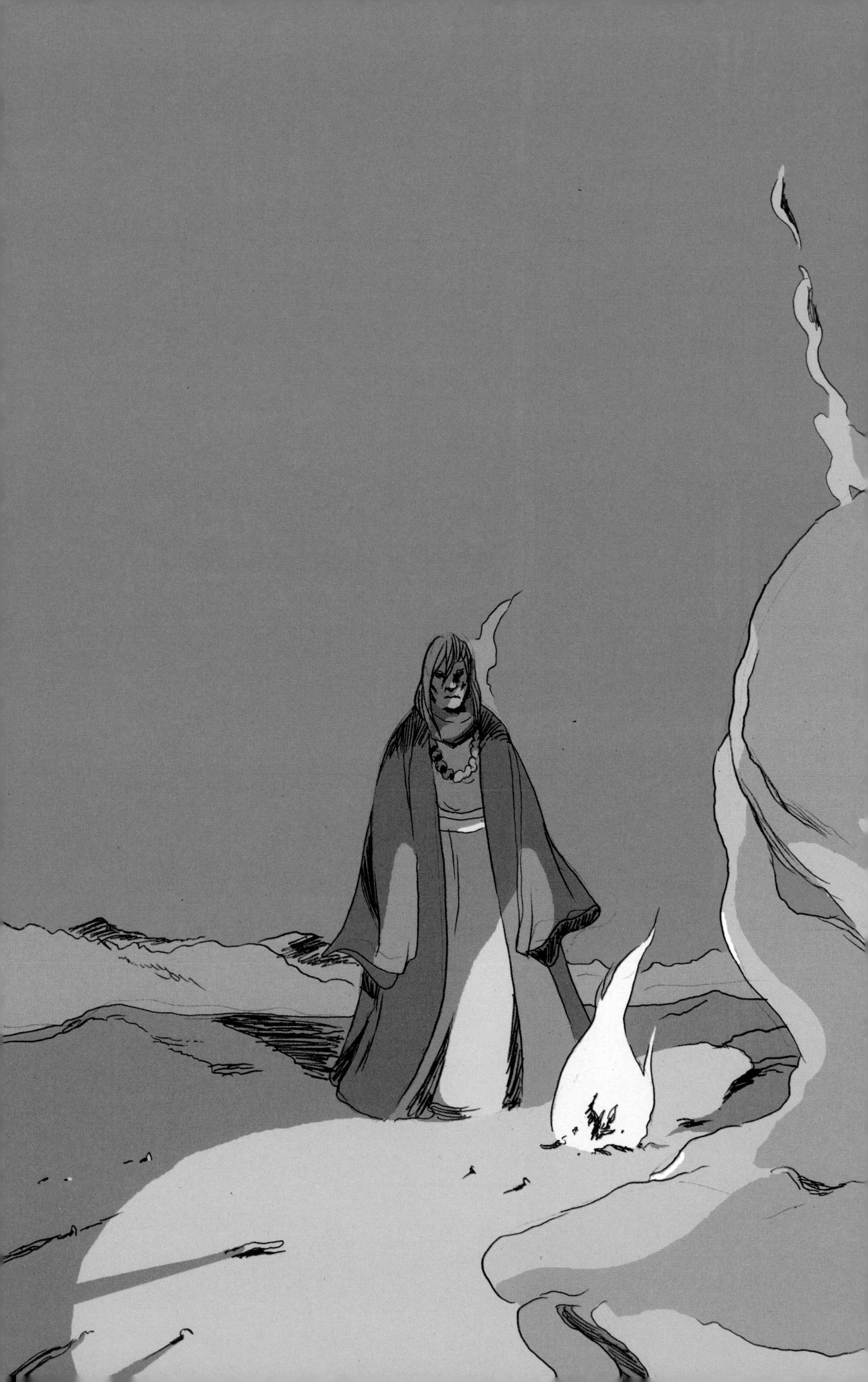

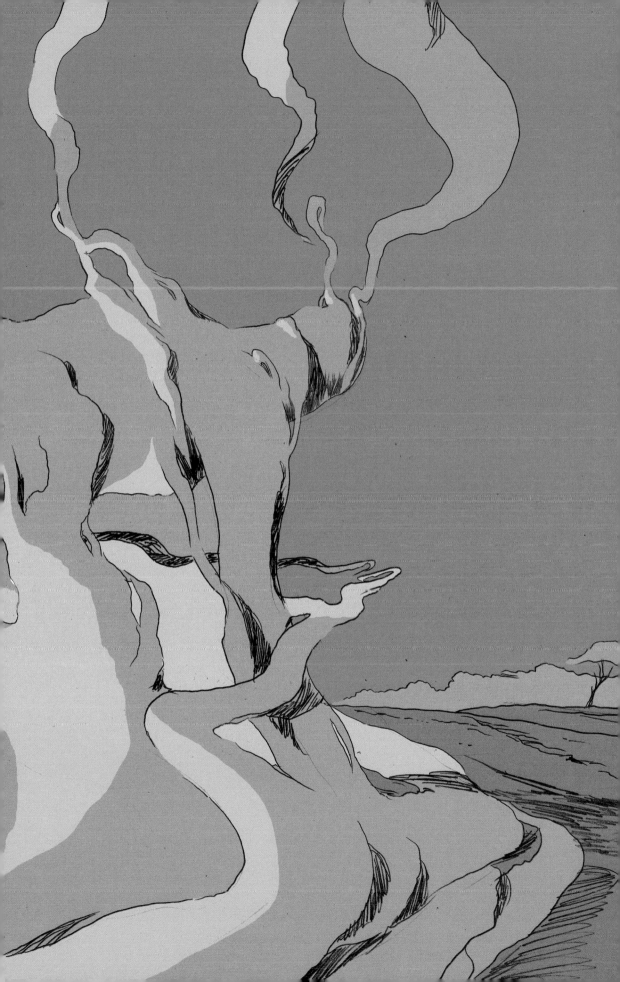

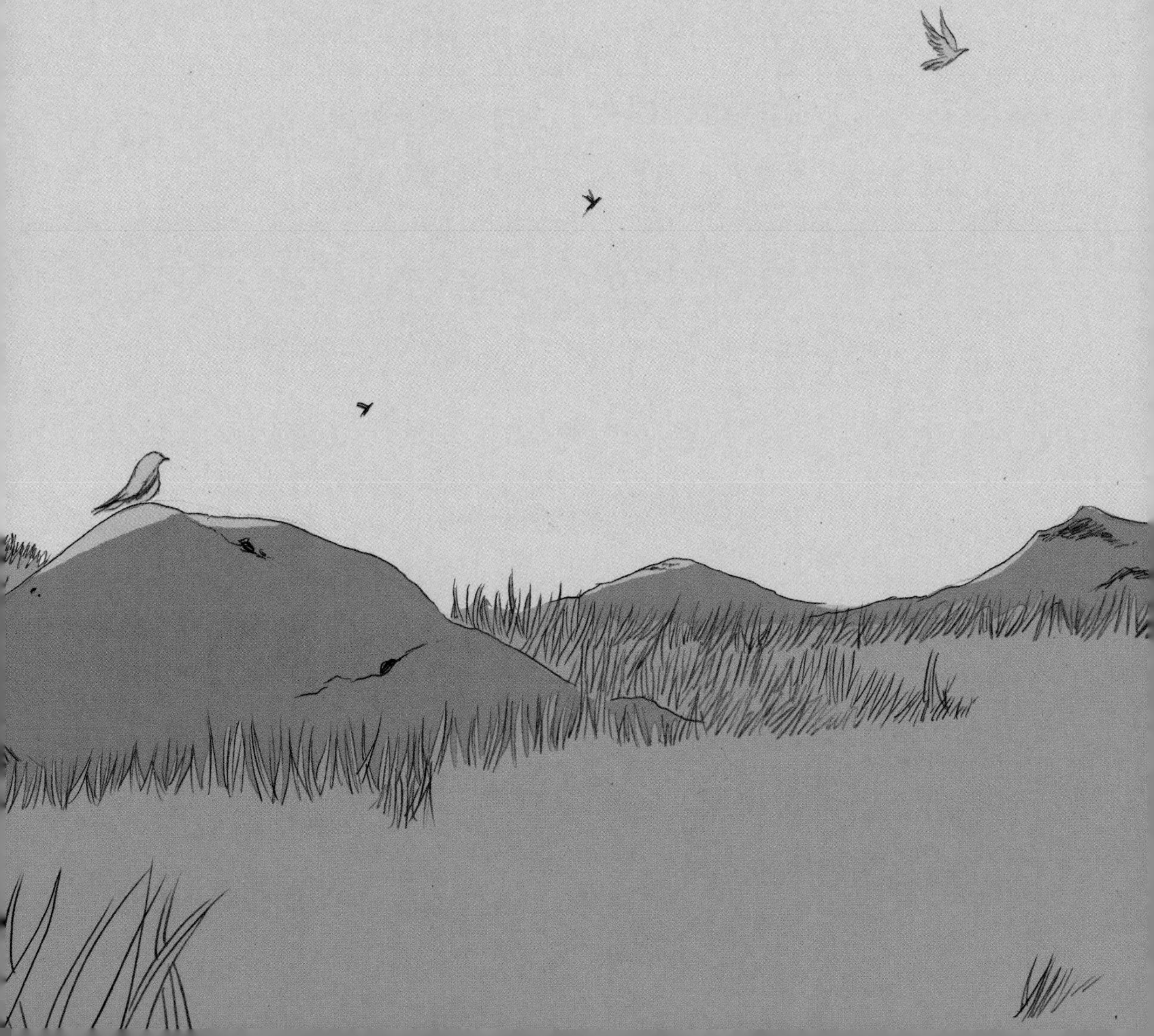

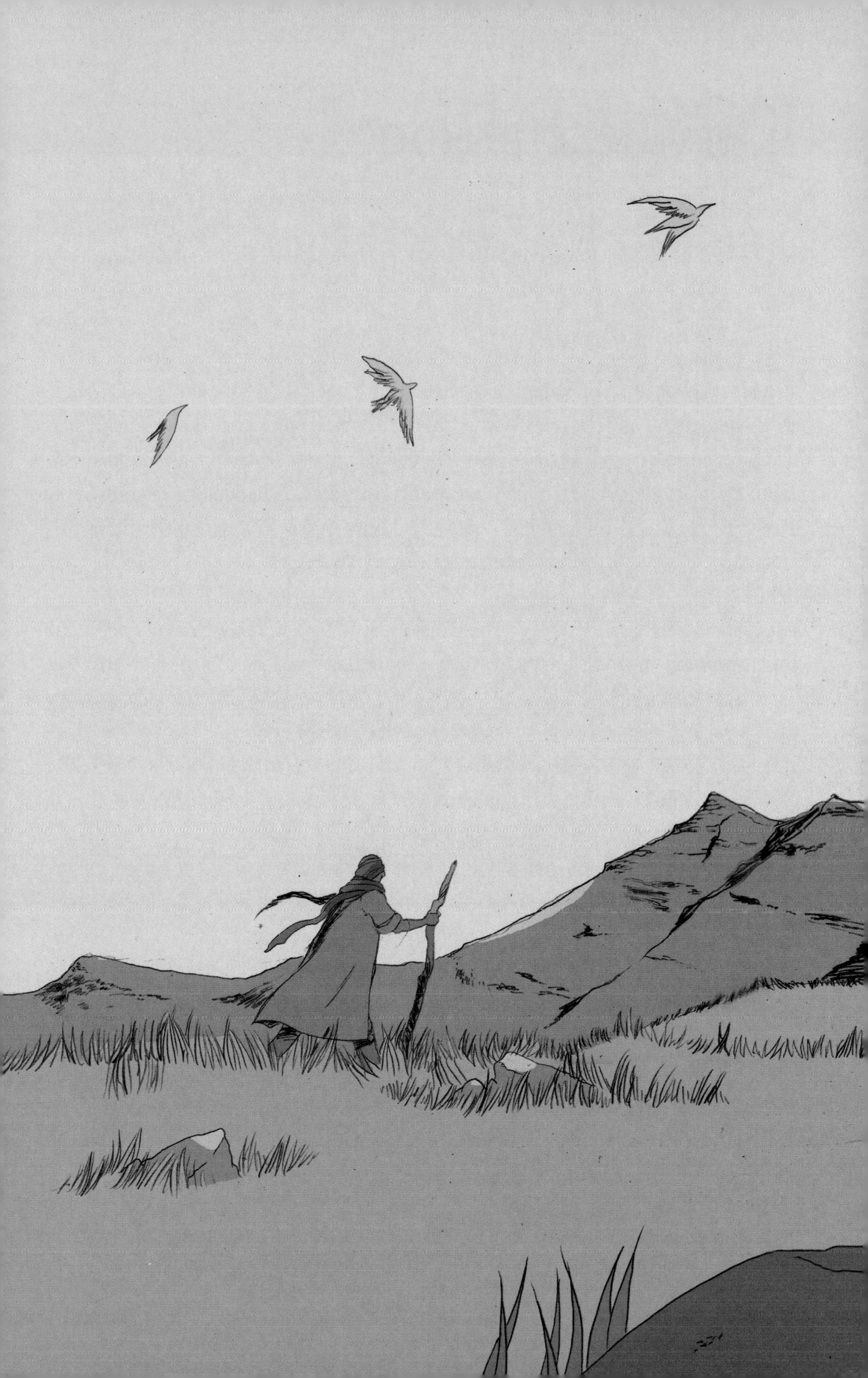

Karvale Passage

The Long War was fought along the ridge of mountains that form a natural border between two nations: Vol and Akhara.

Were it not for the vast desert plains and towering mountains that lie between them, the greater population of Vol might have absorbed coastal Akhara long ago. Though Volan fighters travel with relative ease over the expanse of Kamat-Val where their army has never, (or so it is said), been beaten, the mountains have never welcomed them. Even so, the Vol began the Long War by invading Akhara along the only route they understood. While the greater part of the Long War was fought among these mountain defenses, Vol's real focus was the Karvale Passage.

The Karvale Passage, thought by some historians to be older than both nations, could not have been constructed without at least the collusion of the Mausgol, though why the reclusive Mausgol would want such a thing - and why the architecture differs so from their own distinctive style - remains unclear. At the start of the Long War, Karvale Passage had been sealed for nearly three hundred years at either end. The road itself was riddled with crevasses and prone to falling rock. Nonetheless as soon as the Volan army managed to break into the passage, it became once again the fastest route through the mountains. Fortunately for Akhara its scouts sent word of the breach in time, and Akharan troops managed to reopen the passage on their end and meet the advancing Volan army midway through the subterranean ruin.

Goblins understand mountains; how they are made; how and why they move. While they are rumored to detest any action that alters the structure of their territory, as any brave miner who has attempted to remove stone from that region will attest, the Mausgol must have dreaded a victorious army – on either side - reclaiming the passage. So as the opposing armies funneled in and clashed beneath the earth, the goblins did not join the fighting or flee from it. They only watched, and waited.

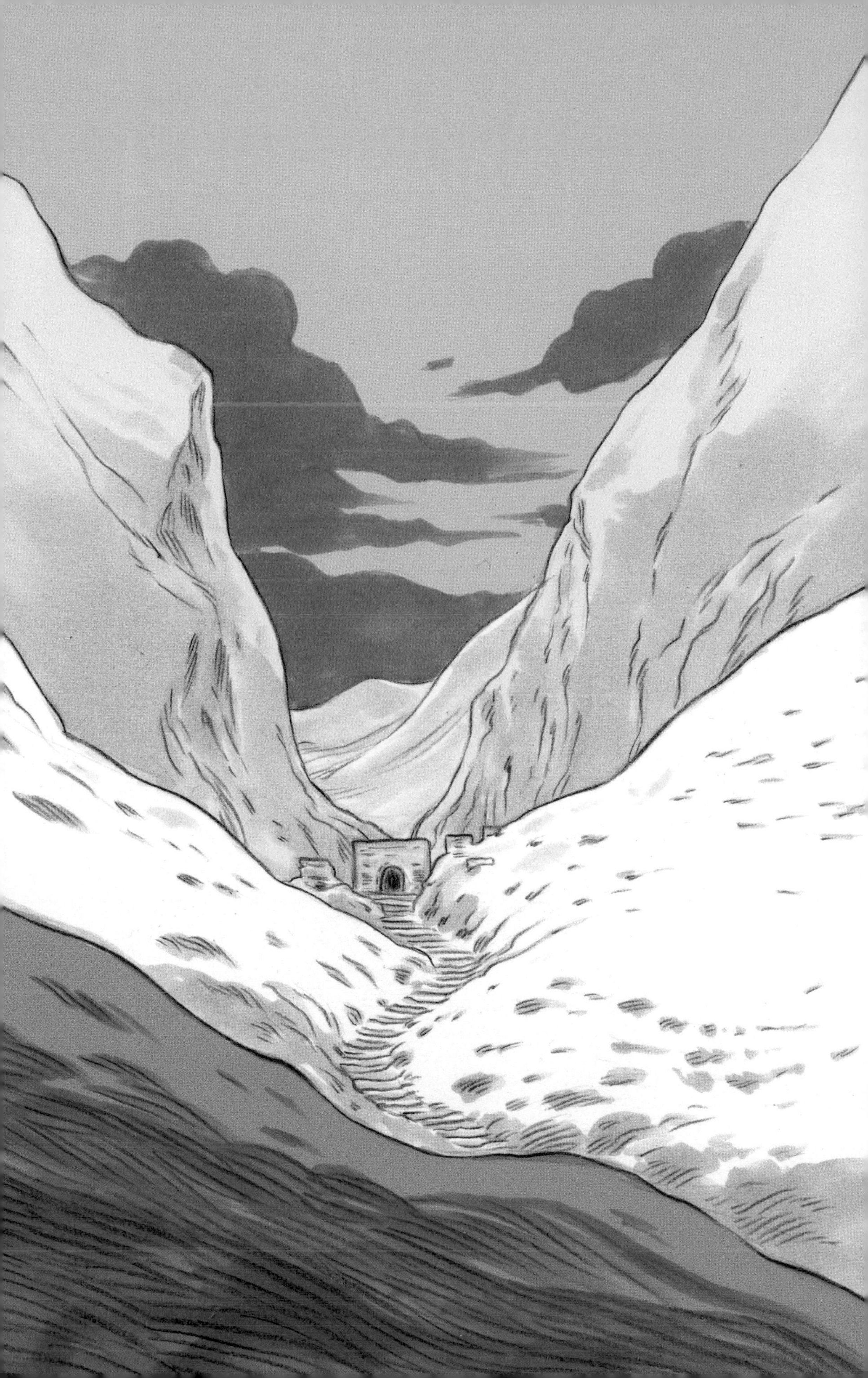

The Eight Gods of Akhara

Rhyd is the patron of lords, soldiers and powerful men. In his stories, he is the active power: a creator and a destroyer, and though Rhyd is the first of the gods and nearest to perfection, his anger is his driving flaw.

Iosa is the matron and the host, the god of hearth and home. Her stories describe her tending house and managing visitors. The classic tale of Iosa features a stranger who appears on her doorstep, to be welcomed or punished according to his actions or his underlying worth. Though her setting is domestic, Iosa is acknowledged as the judge and the gatekeeper of the gods.

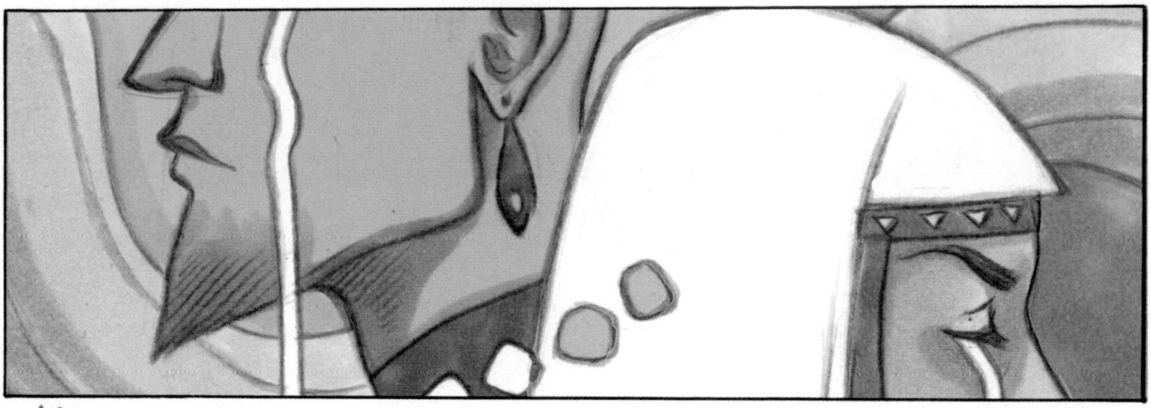

Attar & Nanira are the lovers. Their many stories combine to form a lengthy, tragic romance in which Attar believes that Nanira has betrayed him for another man. In truth she is streadfast, but he acts on his assumptions and discovers too late that he was foolishly mistaken.
Though the story ends in tragedy, its telling is cyclical, as if the gods replay their fate over and over, always with a new chance of altering its course.

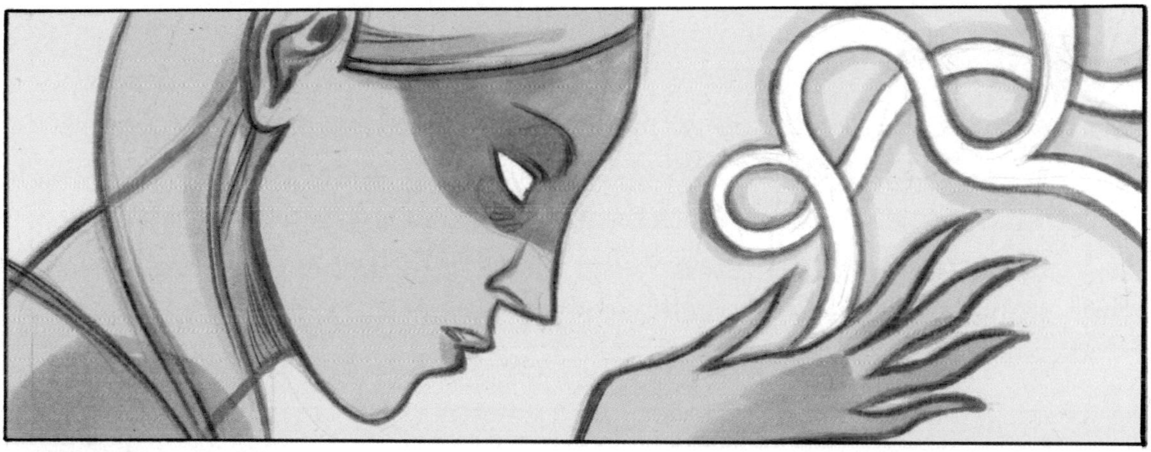

Onil is the youngest god - the innocent - a patron of healers and peacekeepers. Her stories often promote non-violent resistance, or gentleness as an antidote for aggression. Another common theme sees Onil retrieving rare herbs, always just in time to save a sick patient.

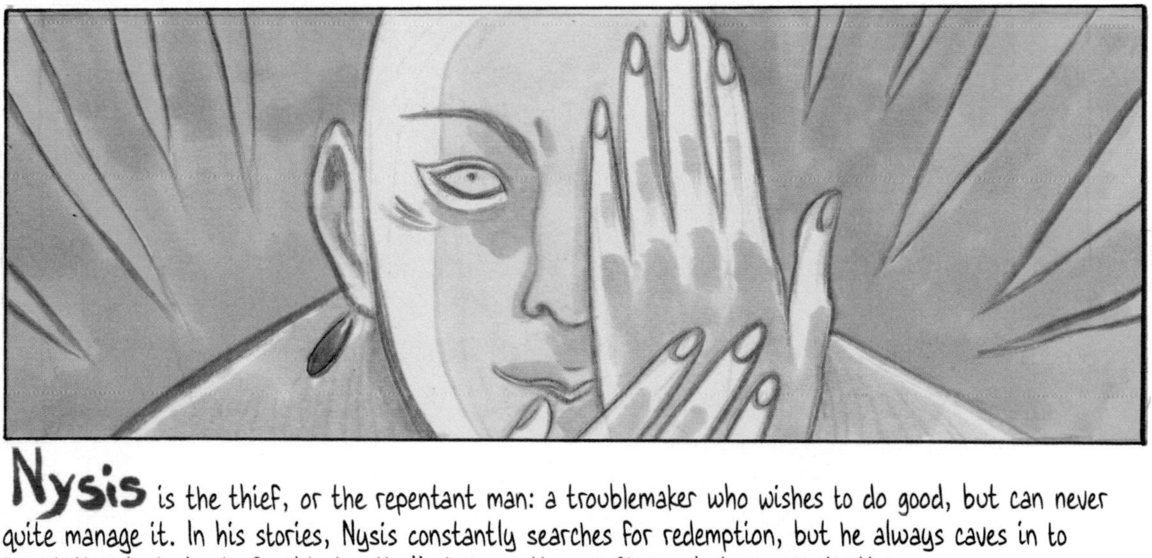

Nysis is the thief, or the repentant man: a troublemaker who wishes to do good, but can never quite manage it. In his stories, Nysis constantly searches for redemption, but he always caves in to temptation just short of achieving it. He is a cautionary figure, but a sympathetic one.

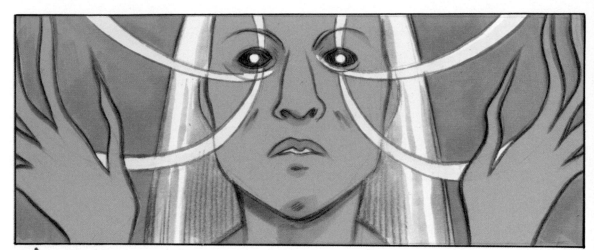

Hanhara is the shunned woman: the unrepentant evil. She turns away from the forces of good in order to purchase power, and her stories describe her resultant descent. Like Nysis, Hanhara is a cautionary figure, but far less sympathetic. People associate her with witches (though witches themselves seldom show any interest in formal religion), and she's often cited as an example of why women should not be placed in positions of authority.

Vekha is the wanderer, a wise and mysterious old man. He has few stories of his own, but he shows up in other tales, often in the guise of a hermit, and always arriving to tip the balance at some crucial moment.

Early Costume Designs

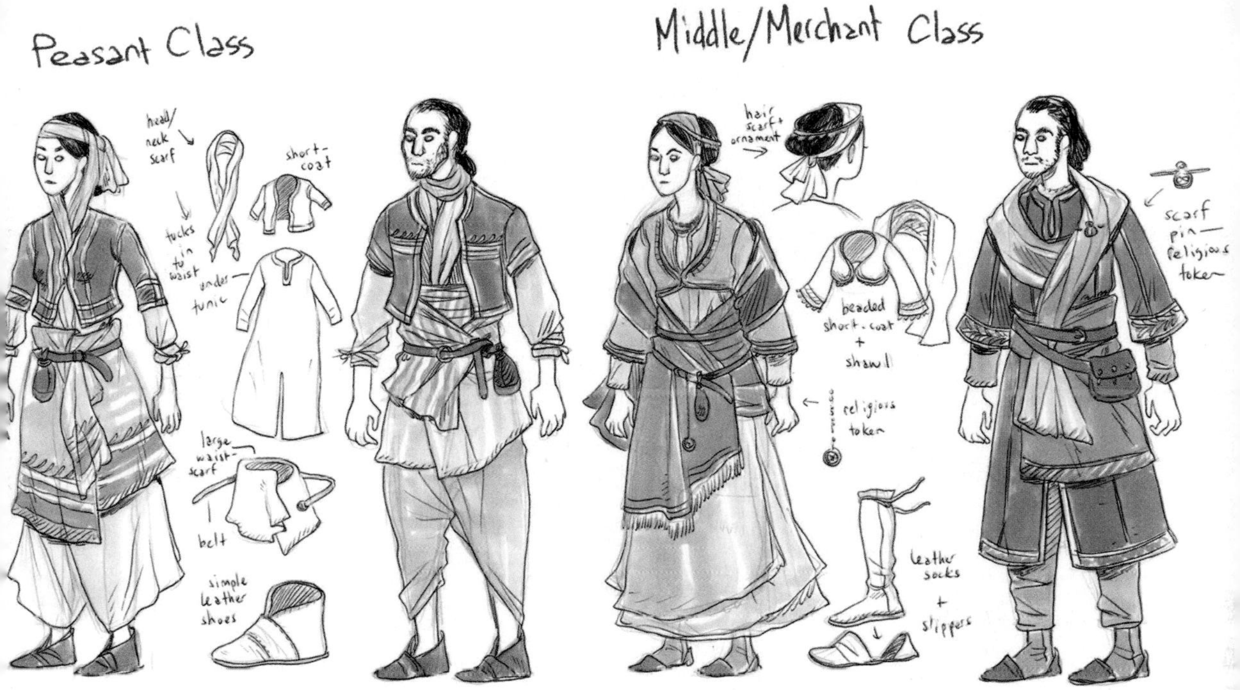

Peasant Class
Middle/Merchant Class
head/neck scarf
short-coat
tucks in to waist
under-tunic
large waist-scarf
belt
simple leather shoes
hair scarf + ornament
beaded short-coat + shawl
religious token
leather socks + slippers
scarf pin — religious token

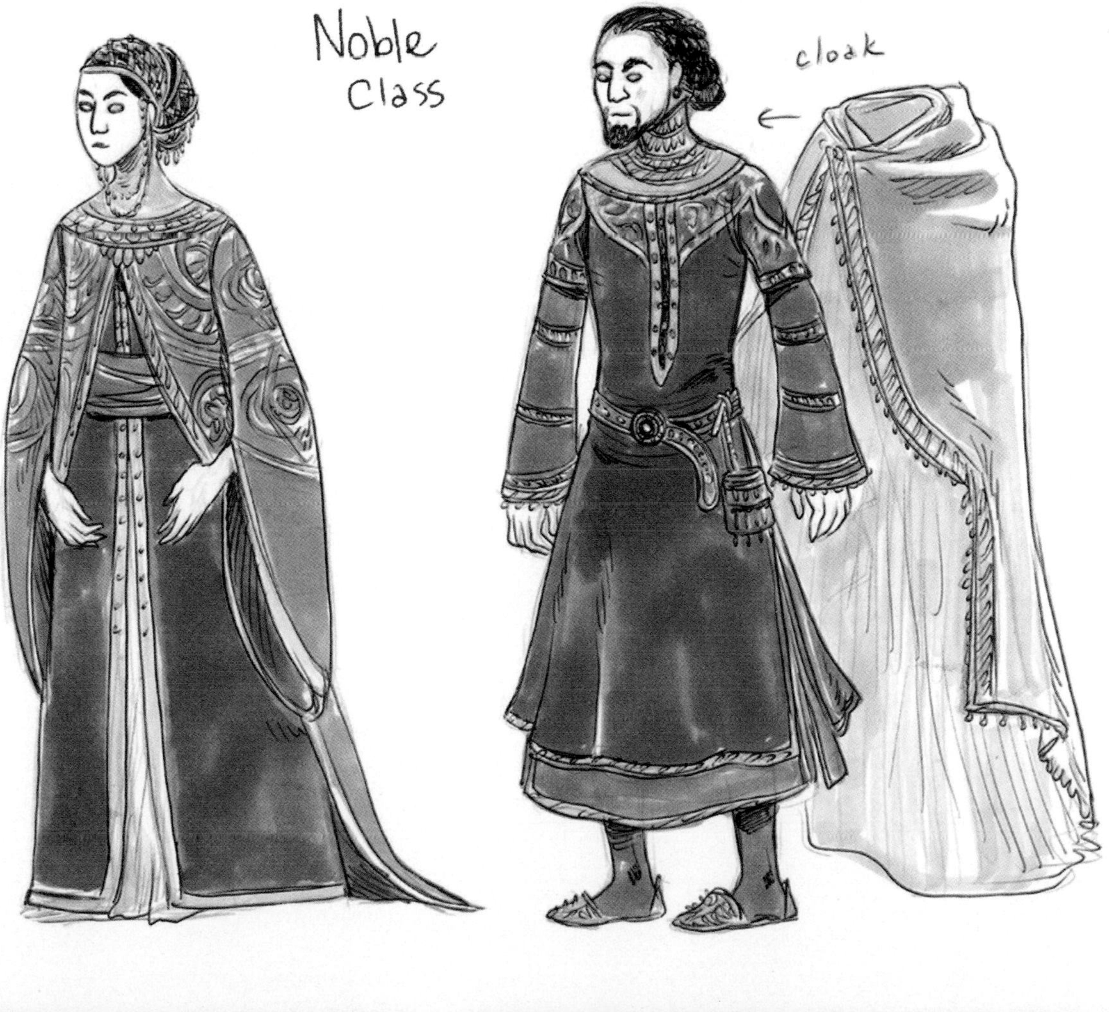

Noble Class
cloak

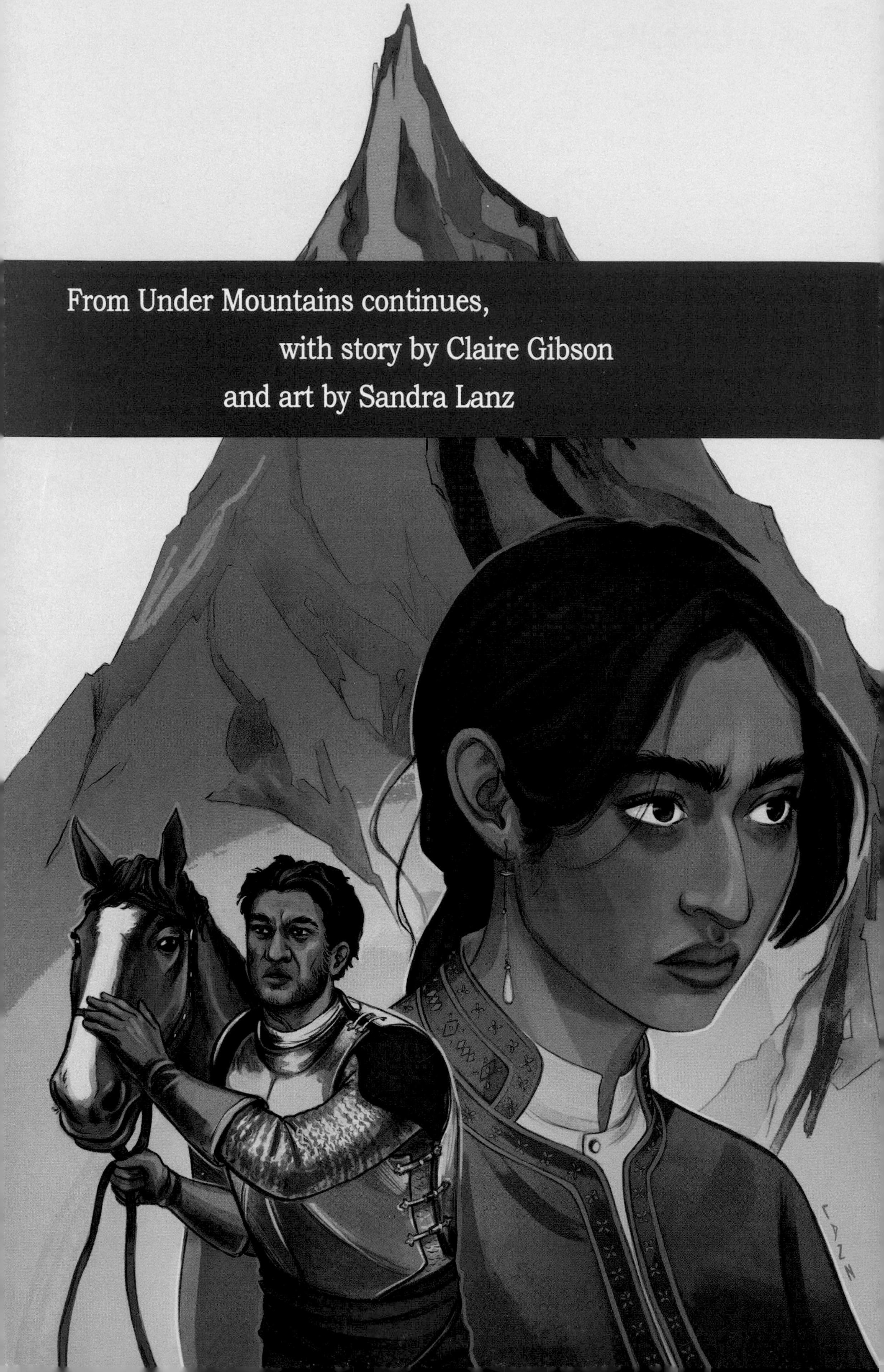
From Under Mountains continues,
with story by Claire Gibson
and art by Sandra Lanz